July

By the same author

The Flower Boy

JULY

KAREN ROBERTS

Weidenfeld & Nicolson

LONDON

First published in Great Britain in 2001
by Weidenfeld & Nicolson

A CIP catalogue record for this book
is available from the British Library.

ISBN 0 297 64643 5

Typeset by Deltatype Ltd, Birkenhead, Merseyside

Set in Garamond

Printed in Great Britain by
Clays Ltd, St Ives plc

Weidenfeld & Nicolson

The Orion Publishing Group Ltd
Orion House
5 Upper Saint Martin's Lane
London, WC2H 9EA

This book is dedicated to my mother Maureen, who I'm sure guides me from up there, my father Tony from whom I have undoubtedly inherited whatever talent I have, my beloved brother Jeremy and my sisters Nikki, Jacquie and Francine whom I adore, my other Michael who has brought so much love and gentleness into my life, and all our children – Fabianne, Tashelle, Destiny, Jay, Michael, Miriam, Puki Bear and Eman, who will one day know and love our land as much as we do.

ONE

On the twenty-third of July 1983, the world went mad. In the throes of insanity, it killed a few thousand people, destroyed the lives of a few thousand more, and changed Priyanthi's life for ever.

In the space of a few hours, benign shopkeepers, friendly neighbours, cheery newspaper boys and devoted lovers turned into vicious killers, bent on slaking their sudden blood-lust. Hands that had only held shopping bags, school books, fish and other hands wielded knives, crowbars, machetes and Molotov cocktails. Mouths that had only uttered greetings and niceties spewed venom and chants for blood. Streets that on other days smelled of araliya in bloom, rotting garbage and home cooking smelled acridly of fire and fear.

Skies that were usually blue and cloudless were obliterated by dense black smoke.

For ever afterwards, smoke would remind people of the day the world indulged in its sudden furious orgy of madness. The day that people allowed the howling maniac who sullenly dwells in all of us waiting for a whiff of opportunity and a moment of weakness to escape.

It wasn't really the world that went mad, just Colombo and a few other parts of Sri Lanka, but it was all Priyanthi knew, and although it was only her world and not the *whole* world, to her it felt as if the entire human race had temporarily lost its senses. Some people lost their senses not temporarily, but for ever.

Priyanthi was not one of those lucky ones.

Niranjan was. Niranjan with his thin intense face and sudden smile. Niranjan who went to Ampitiya to become a man of God and discovered that he was just a man.

In the days that followed, Priyanthi and thousands of others wondered what had happened. How it had happened. What they might have done to avert it. What they might have done differently throughout it. But these were the futile meanderings of mummified minds.

How was anyone to know that neighbourhoods could turn into battlefields in a matter of hours? That it took only a few minutes to turn little old ladies into frenzied looters who would go home triumphantly bearing their stolen strings of shampoo sachets like garlands for a rabid god?

No one could have guessed that inside his father, or inside her lover, or inside his laundry man lurked that lethal mixture of violence and remorselessness found in serial killers. No one could have guessed that such usually gentle people were capable of such unusual rage.

No one claimed responsibility for the murder and the mayhem or for the calculated destruction of Priyanthi's life. Once it was all over, no one cared to remember except Priyanthi and a few thousand people whose lives had also been tossed into the inferno with such careless abandon. Priyanthi cared. But only for herself.

Along with the grief and incomprehension had come selfishness. Each torn soul took care of its own wounds and bruises and left the others to take care of theirs.

At funerals, people wept alone.

Bit by bit, the country raised itself out of its stupefaction and began cleaning up. Houses were rebuilt. Some houses were re-let or sold, for the owners had left for other parts or for their higher abodes, depending on what fate they had suffered.

Shops were painstakingly cleaned up of broken glass, fallen beams and the charred remains of shelves, and then rebuilt, rewired and restocked. The usual arguments took place between the insured and the insurers. Guilt was apportioned, blame was laid and excuses were made. None were good enough for Priyanthi. In her opinion, no one had lost quite as much as she had.

Through the haze of incredulity and suffering, only one thing was clear. What had been broken could not be replaced and repaired. Not really.

How could one pick up shattered shards of trust, put them back together again and expect things to be exactly the way they used to be? Nothing would ever be the same again. Especially not Araliya Gardens.

Two

❧

Priyanthi had lived at Araliya Gardens all her life. In fact, she had very nearly been born there, because Herath's old Morris Minor taxi had refused to start when it was time for her mother Enid to go to the hospital.

When the labour pains started at three in the afternoon, her father Stanley wanted to go immediately for Herath. Enid laughed and told him to wait, that it would be hours yet before anything happened. So he paced the living room, smoking cigarette after cigarette, while she calmly hemmed yet another cotton baby dress.

In spite of the cool breeze blowing through the open door, his brow was damp. The sweat under his arms turned the light blue of his cotton bush shirt to a patchy dark blue. Like bad batik.

Priyanthi's brother Hemantha was three at the time, and didn't understand what was happening, except that there was going to be a baby arriving soon. When he was bundled off to a neighbour's house to play, he went willingly. Like most children, he was happier at other people's houses and the neighbours had two children of their own.

Nearly three hours later, Enid looked up from her yellow chain-stitch flowers. 'You'd better go and get Herath now,' she said calmly. Stanley was out of the house before she finished speaking.

He found Herath leaning on his ancient taxi, reflectively smoking a beedi and waiting for his summons. Unknown to Enid, Stanley had already alerted Herath by means of a message sent through Banda the servant boy. 'Let's go!' Stanley gasped.

Herath got into the taxi and Stanley squeezed himself into the front seat. Herath turned the key in the ignition and nothing happened. Stanley started cursing but Herath assured him that the car would start any minute now. 'Like a woman,' he said. 'Always takes a while.'

Fifteen minutes later, Herath admitted defeat and got out of the taxi. Stanley alighted too, wondering what to do. He jingled the change in his pockets, a sure sign that he was beginning to panic.

'I'll run to the junction and see if Padmasiri's taxi is there,' Herath offered, but Stanley was already gone, running back down the road.

By the time he arrived at Bala's house, his shirt was more dark blue than light. He rang the doorbell, praying someone was at home. There was no way of telling because the car, if it was there, was parked in the garage at the back. Bala himself answered the door, hastily knotting his sarong and combing his hair back with his fingers.

'Stan, what's the matter?' he asked, surprised to see his neighbour in such a state. Stanley was usually the quieter of the two. Even after they had had a few drinks together, Bala was the one who sang old songs and danced the baila, while Stanley drummed on the kitchen table with two wooden spoons.

'Enid!' Stanley gasped. 'She's in labour and that old bastard Herath's taxi won't start!'

Bala didn't hesitate for a moment. 'Go and get Enid ready. I'll get the car and come next door,' he said.

Stanley didn't stop to thank him. There would be time enough for all that later. He rushed off.

Enid was standing at the front door, her overnight bag in her hand. She looked out at the road. 'Where's Herath?' she asked, gasping as another contraction started its upward spiral.

'Don't ask. Thank God Bala was at home. He's taking us to the hospital.' He grabbed the bag from her just as Bala's Plymouth stopped outside with a screech of brakes. Fifteen minutes and five contractions later, Enid was wheeled into the delivery room and Stanley was summarily dismissed by the grim-lipped, starched-capped ward sister.

Bala led the way to the hospital cafeteria, which was empty except for a pimply girl behind the counter. They ordered two teas and Bala asked where he could find a phone. 'Forgot to tell Violet where I was off to in all the excitement,' he explained.

When he came back, Stanley started to thank him, but he just smiled. 'Don't worry about it, Stan. What's the use of having neighbours if we cant help one another in an emergency?'

They sipped their tea and smoked a Gold Leaf each, ignoring the pimply girl, who was staring meaningfully at the No Smoking sign on the wall. Flies got a free ride on the blades of a ceiling fan that turned slowly. A few got dizzy and clung on to the plastic-painted, once-white walls. Others slid to the floor and lay supine amid the crumbs and cigarette ends.

'What's taking her so long?' Stanley said, jingling the change in his pockets and looking at the door.

Bala laughed. 'Calm down, calm down,' he said. 'Can't rush these things, you know.' Then another thought struck him. 'Where's Hemantha?'

'Left him at Dierdre's place.'

Bala laughed. 'He'll be force-fed her terrible cooking. You should have left him at our house. Niranjan was at home.'

'I looked over the wall, but I didn't see anyone. I'll bring him round for the night if that's okay with Violet.'

'No problem. You know Violet – loves kids. In fact, she's been hinting recently about having another. One's expensive enough.' He glumly blew a stream of smoke towards the ceiling and watched as it got entangled with the fly-infested fan blades and then disappeared.

Stanley looked sympathetic. 'Ask me. Don't know where this one came from. When I saw Hemantha's Montessori fees, I told Enid two's the limit and that's that.' He looked again at the big clock on the cafeteria wall. 'Do you think that thing's slow?'

Bala laughed. 'Why don't you go and see if anything's happened? I'll stay here and have a staring match with Miss Friendly over there.'

Stanley was on his feet in a flash. He had wanted to go a few minutes before, but didn't want his old friend to think him over-anxious and foolish. It wasn't as if this was his first baby.

* * *

Stanley Silva bought the house at No. 9 Araliya Gardens when his father died and left him their ancestral walauwwa down south. Within a week of the funeral, he turned a deaf ear to his mother's pleas and sold off the old place, which was falling apart anyway. Of the hundred and forty thousand he got for it, he put forty in his account at the Bank of Ceylon and bought the Araliya Gardens house with the remaining hundred.

Enid and he had been married just four months at the time and the charming three-bedroom house was everything a young couple could have hoped for. They moved in the old mahogany furniture from the old house, renovated the kitchen and put in parquet flooring. Enid went to work on the gardens and by the end of the next year, the avocado and mango trees were doing well and so were the orchids and araliya trees that lined the boundary walls.

Once a year, they gave the exterior walls a whitewash and the gates a new coat of rust-proof red paint. It was a beautiful house, one of the prettier ones in a street full of pretty houses.

Araliya Gardens is a relatively small road off the main Galle Road, which starts somewhere near the Galle Face Green in downtown Colombo, and ends in Galle, which is at the southern end of the island. The Galle Road hugs the coastline, but leaves enough room for roads leading from it down to the railway tracks which border the southern parts of the island.

On the other side of Galle Road, on what is called the land side, the network of large roads leading inland begins. The Galle Road is the main road through Colombo, taking two lanes of traffic either way, three if you count the cars that cruise on the pavement during rush hour. Huge petrol tankers, construction vehicles, container trucks, buses, cars, three-wheel taxis, motorbikes, bicycles and bullock carts shove each other aside for space. Occasionally, to add to the confusion, there are

7

even a few elephants on their way to some temple ceremony, and sometimes one of them runs amok and destroys a few cars and a mahout or two.

During rush hour, traffic slows to a crawl, sometimes to a standstill. Horns blare, abuse is yelled and accidents happen every few yards. Drivers squeeze their cars through impossibly tight spaces just to get one car ahead. To prove a point. Motorcycle riders weave crazily through the stationary cars, their sari-clad pillion riders sitting side-saddle and hanging on to handbags and sari potas.

Traffic policemen wisely stay in their police stations during rush hour.

But once you turn down one of the roads that lead to the beach, it starts to quieten down. The further down you go, the more muted the Galle Road sounds become, and once your ears adjust to the quiet, you hear other sounds. Residential sounds. Radios, people, dishes, running water, doors, babies. Nice, normal, middle-class sounds.

Unlike on the Galle Road where only people and vendors and confusion grew, down the side roads there were bougainvillaea, araliya, mango and of course kottan trees, under which one always found a flat stone and a rock for cracking kottans open. There were manicured hedges, flower beds ringed with upside-down, half-buried beer bottles and night-blooming jasmine creeping up people's gates. In the spirit of friendly competition, each house strove to look slightly better than the other.

Further down these sea-side roads, you could hear the dull booming of the sea over the other sounds. People who lived towards the end of these roads said they couldn't sleep anywhere else, so used had they become to the bass-toned lullaby of the ocean. But they also complained that salt spray ruined their irons and televisions, and clouded up their windows.

Right at the end were the railway tracks. One going into the city and one going out.

For some reason, suicidally inclined people loved the railway tracks. They placed their necks carefully on the iron lines and waited for the Matara express or the Fort express (depending on the time) to thunder over them, then watched with open eyes their headless, twitching bodies. They loved the drama of decapitation. The grief (and guilt) it gave their loved ones to pick up not just a body, but also a head from the mortuary.

Some people were run over without meaning to be. They walked on the railway tracks because they didn't want to get sand in their shoes, and were caught unawares by an express train. Either way, a lot of people died on the railway tracks. And a few old, half-blind cats and dogs.

Beyond the railway tracks and before the sandy beach began, there was a line of huts that ran the length of most of the island, like the railway tracks did.

The walls of the huts were built from an odd assortment of woven coconut leaves, coconut barks, tar, plastic sheeting and mud. The roofs were made from sheets of corrugated tin held in place with old car batteries, old tyres and anything else heavy enough to withstand the frequent storms that battered the coastline.

The fishermen lived here with their families. They were hard-working, tough-talking people who kept to themselves and looked at strangers with suspicion in their eyes. Each night their boats went out to sea and returned at dawn. Then the beach rang with chants of *hodi helley helley-a!* as every able-bodied person pulled in the nets full of flipping and flopping fish. Their hands pulled in unison, their muscles bulged in unison and their voices sang in unison.

It looked like a strange primitive opera.

Fish mudalalis, shop owners, restaurateurs and others swarmed down the beach to attend the early-morning fish auctions, like the flies that swarmed on the fish itself. They haggled for many minutes and at the end of it all, the fish was borne away to restaurants and five-star hotels and the fishermen went home to bed.

It wasn't only fish you could buy on the beach, especially in the tourist-frequented areas. Imported cigarettes, straw hats, fresh pineapples on their stalks (for extra authenticity), batiks, beads, illicit liquor and marijuana (in tiny plastic packets or ready-rolled) were available from smiling, over-friendly touts who worked the beach looking for gullible visitors. Sex and babies were also up for sale on the beach.

In some areas, the huts faded away and huge black rocks took over. In the evenings, they were dotted by umbrella lovers, young couples who met illicitly at the beach and whispered and kissed behind their umbrella shields. Fathers cast disapproving looks and hurried their wives and children past and perverts crept up to expose themselves to the lovers or to masturbate furtively behind spread-out sarongs.

But since Araliya Gardens was a dead end which didn't lead to the beach and its legitimate and illegitimate attractions, its residents didn't have to worry about these things. People like Enid and Violet didn't even know they existed.

* * *

When Stanley and Enid bought their house at Araliya Gardens, No. 11 next door was empty. The previous burgher owners had migrated to Australia and their broker occasionally brought prospective buyers to look the place over. Every time his car stopped outside the gates, Stanley and Enid twitched back their lace curtains and peeped to see what kind of people he was bringing.

When a raucous burgher family came to view the place with their loud teenage children, Stanley and Enid held their breaths, but thankfully, they didn't like it. That could have been because Stanley put his baila music on full volume until they left, or because Mr Munasinghe from across the road decided to stand immediately outside the gate and stare unblinkingly at them in his odd, unnerving way. Or it could have been the huge piece of plaster which broke away from the damp ceiling and landed painfully on the burgher gentleman's foot.

By the time Bala and Violet came, the broker was getting

desperate and the by-now Australian owners were short of cash. The asking price for the house had dropped dramatically and although the ceiling needed to be repaired, Bala knew a bargain when he saw one.

When Stanley and Enid, who were at their usual post behind the curtains, heard the visitors speaking to the broker, they grimaced. Tamils! Of all the neighbours they could have had!

They felt a little better when Bala and Violet actually moved in, because the first thing they carried into the house was a statue of the Virgin Mary. Christian Tamils were not so bad as Hindu Tamils, they decided. At least there wouldn't be strange incense smells and odd rituals to contend with.

Stanley and Enid were Sinhalese Buddhists of the educated class, which meant they both spoke classical Sinhalese and perfect English, hers learned from the Irish nuns at St Anne's and his from attending a prestigious college in England.

Theirs had been a love marriage, quite rare in their society, but their parents couldn't have done better if they'd made the match themselves. Enid was fair-skinned and pretty and came from good Kandyan stock. Stanley was not quite so fair, but he made up for it with his perfect manners and excellent job. Enid's parents were even willing to forgive him for being from the south.

When they met, Stanley was Deputy Chief Accountant at Ceylon Foods, no small achievement in an establishment overrun with British managers and burgher middle managers. The Managing Director liked Stanley Silva because he had been educated in England and because he wore navy blazers to work despite the stifling Colombo heat.

Enid was learning social graces from her mother, who was one of Kandy's prominent hostesses. She was educated, unemployed and ready for marriage. They met at a dinner party in the Kandy home of a mutual friend and by the end of the evening had fallen in love.

* * *

Dierdre and Ed Jobsz were one of the first families to build a house down Araliya Gardens and had lived at No. 7 for almost ten years before the Silvas arrived. They were Dutch burghers, the products of various intermarriages between the Ceylonese and the Dutch invaders, and had pale skin and blue eyes, unlike the Portuguese burghers, who were more swarthy and therefore looked-down-upon.

Ed had been a high-up in the railway but now ran a successful trucking company, which accounted for their money. They had a beautiful house, a nice car and a friendly word for everyone.

Dierdre was the undisputed doyenne of the neighbourhood and cheerfully adopted all the younger wives down Araliya Gardens. Although they talked behind her back about her atrocious cooking, they liked her. She kept a spotless house and could always be counted on in an emergency.

Within months of the Silvas moving in, Dierdre took Enid firmly under her wing. She taught Enid how to arrange flowers and colour-co-ordinate her cushions with her curtains. Enid reciprocated by often sending Dierdre a dish of her excellent chicken curry, which Ed eagerly looked forward to.

When Bala and Violet came, Dierdre and Ed had been a little dubious about them too, but when they went over to inspect the new arrivals and discovered that Bala was an English teacher at St Mark's and Violet wore dresses, they pronounced them fit for friendship.

Violet was a shy, quiet woman who had a soft spot for children, and when she found out that Dierdre had two, she offered to baby-sit as often as needed, an offer Dierdre took up with alacrity because Emmy, her old servant woman, was not up to keeping track of two active boys. Matthew and Mark were generally well behaved; although their habit of ringing door bells and running away irritated the residents of Araliya Gardens, no one had yet complained to Dierdre.

* * *

Araliya Gardens had been named for the abundance of araliya trees which grew in almost every garden. It was a charming name for a nice upper-middle-class neighbourhood. Because it was a dead end, it was quiet, and the only cars that drove down were driven by people visiting someone living there. Occasionally, someone got lost and came looking for directions, but strangers generally weren't welcome. If an unknown car or bicycle made its way down the road, Mr Munasinghe, who was retired and therefore had nothing else to do, or Dierdre's servant Emmy would go up to them and ask them to state their business. This direct approach usually intimidated people and made them turn their cars around and drive off in a hurry. There was no fear of offending anyone. With just sixteen houses in all, everyone knew everyone else's visitors by car. Or by face. Sometimes, even by name.

It didn't take long for Stanley's family and Bala's to become good friends. They made it a point to have a few drinks at least once a month, usually joined by Ed Jobsz, who was as garrulous as his wife. On these occasions, Enid, Violet and Dierdre sat together, boasted about their husbands' recent accomplishments and giggled when the men got tipsy and started their singing sessions.

However, the families also took great care not to impose on one another, not to ask favours, and although a cup of sugar was occasionally borrowed, it was always returned.

Even though Stanley sometimes accepted a lift from Bala, he had never asked him to drive him anywhere until now. And even now, despite the fact that it was an emergency, Stanley felt bad. Although if he had to ask someone, better Bala than anyone else.

* * *

Bala was born in a less than affluent suburb of Colombo called Mutwal, to middle-class parents, but from the moment he started going to school, it was obvious to everyone that he had upper-class dreams. Initially, his father was extremely proud when Bala came home with the highest grades in his class. He beamed with pleasure when Bala was made president of the English Literature Society, the Science Society and the Drama Society. When Bala won the Senior Oratorical Trophy for an impassioned delivery of a speech to do with freedom and justice, his father sat in the front row and applauded enthusiastically, but a little frown of worry marred his brow. Bala had been very good. Almost too good. As if he really believed what he was saying.

After his final Advanced Level examination, Bala was awarded a special prize by the school for having scored the highest aggregate score at the A Levels. His father took the family to Pilawoos to celebrate and spent most of the evening clapping his son on the shoulder and telling him how proud he was.

The trouble started when Bala announced that he wanted to go to university in England.

'England,' his father said in shock. 'How the hell are we going to be able to send you to England? We barely have the bus fare to send you to school every day!'

'The universities here are very good, son,' his mother said gently.

But Bala remained adamant. 'I have to go. It's the only way I'll be able to get us out of this,' he said, looking around their small gloomy one-bedroom home with its mean little windows and cracked, ant-infested floors.

'What's wrong with this?' his father demanded angrily. 'I worked hard my entire life to be able to put this roof above your head, and now you complain?'

Bala stared at him. 'That's just it. You worked hard all your life – I know that. I saw you struggling day after day. And this is as far as you got. I want better. Is that wrong?'

'That's perfectly okay with me as long as you figure out how to pay for this fancy English education of yours. I have nothing in the bank. Everything I possess went to pay your private school fees, your private tuition, your fine English books.' He slammed his cup down on the table and left the house, banging the door behind him.

'Son,' his mother said, laying her hand on his head, 'how much will this cost, this England school?'

'I don't know,' he said.

'More than ten thousand rupees?' she asked a little fearfully.

Bala didn't know whether to laugh or weep. He did neither. 'I think so. I'll find a way.'

Eventually, he got the money. He went to his father's brother's home, the one who lived in Nugegoda and was a gold merchant. The one who never came to their home, who never missed an opportunity to shower scorn on his brother for being such a failure. The one Bala wanted to kill every time he saw him. He explained the situation, asked for the money and swore to repay it as soon as he got a job and started working. His uncle gave him the money, but not before making him grovel for it. He made him sign a paper swearing to return the money. He called in his wife and told her what Bala wanted, saying 'You see, when these people want something, they come to me!'

Bala lowered his head and waited.

Bala was accepted at Oxford and left for England soon afterwards, vowing that his education would be his liberation.

On one of his trips home, he went to Jaffna to visit relatives there and saw Violet, fresh and innocent in her Chundikuli Girls' School uniform, a few jasmines tucked into her long braid. He vowed to marry her, and four years later he did.

It took Bala more than eight years to repay his uncle. He soon found out that his expensive education had only made him even more restless. At Oxford, he spent animated evenings discussing Ceylon and her politics. Sitting in his comfortable rooms, sipping warm cider and chatting with other young people, Ceylon seemed like some unfamiliar but interesting place. Not like home. It was easy to be impartial from a distance. To see both sides. From Mutwal, Ceylon was bleaker. Darker. More introverted. More sinister. Less possible to live happily in.

* * *

Bala looked up as the cafeteria door opened and saw from Stanley's anxious face that there was no news. He held out the packet of Gold Leaf and lit Stanley's cigarette for him. The pimply girl banged a cup on the counter but they ignored her. She pursed her lips and started rearranging her stale sandwiches in their grimy glass case. A few flies flew into it before she shut it again.

'Bloody trauma, this waiting,' Stanley sighed. 'I swear this is the last time. I'm too old for this.'

'Bear up, old friend. When this is over, we'll have a nice drink together. And since this is a celebration, we'll even ask that burgher bugger to join us.'

They laughed, because in reality they both liked Ed Jobsz tremendously.

'How's work?' Bala said, hoping to take Stanley's mind off the matter at hand.

'Not bad. Good fellows at CF,' Stanley said. 'How's the teaching going?'

Bala laughed. 'You know, I look at each new student and wonder if this will be the one. The one who'll become President, the one who'll write a book or become a poet, the one who'll be in the Oxford Union.' He himself had been part of the Union, something his mother was still intensely proud of and boasted about endlessly, although she had no idea what it actually involved.

'And?'

'And they're all bloody hopeless idiots.'

They both laughed. Bala continued, 'You can see them looking at their expensive wristwatches and waiting for the bell to ring. To leave Eliot and Shakespeare to old bastards like me.' He sighed. 'At this age, what do you expect? All they have on their minds is girls.'

Stanley smiled. 'Surely it can't be as bad as all that?'

Bala moved his chair and stretched his legs out. 'No. I'm exaggerating as usual. There are a few bright chaps. Young Ludowyke, for instance. He'll go far if he applies himself.'

'Luddie's son?'

'Yes. He's got his father's brains.' Desmond Ludowyke was a prominent lawyer whom they both knew.

A nurse popped her head around the cafeteria door. 'Mr Silva?'

They both got to their feet so quickly they overturned a chair. The pimply girl scowled.

Stanley rushed to the door. 'Yes? I'm Stanley Silva.'

The nurse smiled. 'Your wife just delivered. You can see her in a few minutes. Room seven.' Her head disappeared.

'Boy or girl?' Bala shouted.

'Girl,' came the reply.

Bala grabbed Stanley's hand and pumped it enthusiastically. 'Congratulations, Stanley! Congratulations! Lucky man – one of each. Now you can relax.'

Stanley just grinned.

A few minutes later, he stood looking down at his new daughter. She was red and wrinkled and had a quiff of black hair that stood straight up like a cock's comb. 'What shall we call her?' Enid asked softly.

'A good Sinhalese name like we did with Hemantha. No more Anglophiles in my family.'

'How about Priyanthi?' she asked sleepily. 'It's got such a pretty ring to it.'

'Okay,' Stanley said, not taking his eyes off the baby. At that moment, he would have agreed to almost anything.

It was the ninth of September 1963.

* * *

Three days later, Priyanthi was brought home.

'She's got your eyes,' Violet said.

'Thank God she doesn't have Stanley's nose,' Dierdre said. 'Would have had a dance finding her a husband with that honker on her.'

'Dierdre!' Violet said. 'I think Stanley's nose is very nice.'

'On him maybe.'

Enid listened to the exchange with amusement. 'Hemantha has my nose,' she said.

Dierdre snorted. 'More's the pity.'

Violet and Enid exchanged exasperated looks but wisely kept quiet. When Dierdre got going, she was as hard to stop as the Fort express on a Monday morning.

Mrs Munasinghe came to visit bearing a feeding bottle. She peered into Priyanthi's sleeping face, and made clucking, spitting noises at her until the baby woke up and started to bawl. Mrs Munasinghe finally wheezed out of the house leaving Enid to cope with the results of her little visit.

When Enid opened the gift, Dierdre was indignant. 'A feeding bottle! Bloody cheek if you ask me. That's like saying you don't have enough milk to feed the mite yourself.'

Enid sighed. 'Too much. I can hardly walk, they're so full.'

Dierdre was instantly full of concern. 'Poor thing! Why didn't you say so? Violet, go and soak that towel in some hot water.' Within minutes, she had organised everything and Enid was full of gratitude as the aching in her over-full breasts eased a little.

* * *

Two weeks after Priyanthi came home, the Silvas had a party to celebrate. It was a lunch party held on a Sunday when everyone was off work. All the neighbours were invited and Enid's parents came down from Kandy for the occasion. They left Kandy just after dawn so they would arrive early enough to spend some time with their daughter and her family before the other guests arrived. After the greeting, exclamations and gifts of gold, mother and daughter went to the kitchen to cook lunch, assisted by Banda the servant boy. It was to be a traditional Sinhalese meal – yellow rice, brinjal pahi, ala thel dala, pickle and of course Enid's famous chicken curry. For dessert, there was buffalo curd and kitul honey.

Just after ten, Violet and Dierdre came over to help and the spacious kitchen rang with the bang of pots and pans, and the spicy tang of gossip. Banda peeled onions and garlic, ground chillies and mustard seed, and listened avidly, storing all the juicy titbits of information to share with the other servants down the road.

'Amma, how are you doing these days?' Enid asked.

'Not bad, child. Your father is getting crotchety in his old age. Can you imagine he refused an invitation to have dinner with the Senanayakes, saying he couldn't be bothered to get involved in their petty politics?'

Dierdre laughed. 'Good for him,' she said, but Enid looked shocked. Everyone knew how important the Senanayakes were. She wondered if her parents would be invited there again.

Only Violet looked puzzled. 'Who are the Senanayakes?'

Three pairs of eyes turned to look at her. '*Who* are the Senanayakes?' Enid's mother's voice rose in disbelief. Then her face cleared. 'Of course you wouldn't know. They're Govigama people from Kandy.' She didn't mean to sound condescending, but she did anyway.

Violet looked uncomfortable.

'Go and get some karapincha from the garden,' Enid said sharply to Banda, who was hanging on every word. He went off sulkily.

'You're too lenient with him,' her mother said severely.

Dierdre sighed and blew into the deep neckline of her magenta dress. 'My Emmy is such a disaster too, but servants are so hard to get these days. Good ones, I mean. Not like that prostitute the Pereras had.'

'Dierdre!' Violet and Enid gasped. Enid's mother looked horrified.

Dierdre looked unconcerned. 'It's true. Ed saw her when he was walking home one night, standing with her back to the bokku wall with one of those ruffians from the junction.'

'That doesn't make her a prostitute!' Enid said.

'No, but going into the Perlyn with a middle-aged mudalali does,' Dierdre declared triumphantly.

'Did you see her?' Violet asked, by now intensely curious. Araliya Gardens was usually so quiet.

'Mrs Perera did. But then, maybe she was also giving it to Mr Perera,' Dierdre said reflectively.

'Dierdre, you mustn't say things like that! What if Mrs Perera heard you?' Enid's mother sounded faint.

'Auntie, she lives five houses away on the other side of the road. If she heard me it would be a bloody miracle.'

Enid's mother said nothing, but pursed her lips and privately thought a burgher was a burgher and all the money in the world couldn't change that. She made up her mind to talk to Enid later on, to advise her not to fraternise too much with Dierdre. What if baby Priyanthi started talking like that with all those bloody words? She shuddered and hurried to the tap to wash her hands as if that would somehow wipe away the possibility.

Violet decided it was high time the subject was changed. 'Bread has gone up again,' she commented.

'Yes, and coconuts too. At this rate only millionaires will be able to afford food on the table,' Enid said, grateful for the diversion.

Enid's mother sniffed. 'Stop talking as if you're married to a pauper, child. Stanley is well off.'

'Not for long, if prices continue to go up like this,' her daughter said.

Dierdre fried the sliced brinjal and wondered why Enid's mother was such an unbearable snob. Thank God she lived in Kandy in her bloody ancestral mansion and not here at Araliya Gardens. They had no room for high-society snobs in their cosy little community.

* * *

Soon after noon, the neighbours started trickling in.

Mrs Fernando, the widow from No. 1, came with her teenage daughter Sonali, the Soysas came with Angeli, their precocious five-year-old who kept telling people to 'shaddup', Mr and Mrs Munasinghe supposedly brought their ancient servant woman to help but everyone knew it was so they wouldn't have to cook for her, the Handunges from No. 16 came minus their three children, which was a blessing since they were atrociously behaved, the Senaratnes brought Nihal and Nilanthi with them, and the Pauls, who were the only other Tamils at Araliya Gardens and lived at No. 2 further up the road, brought Radhika, their pretty six-year-old. Mr and Mrs Perera couldn't come because they had just fired their servant girl (she *had* been at the Perlyn) and had no one to look after their two-year-old.

The rest of the neighbours, the Fonsekas from No. 3, the Karunanayakes from No. 4, the Wijesinghes from No. 10 and the Gunasekeras from No. 12, sent their apologies, but also gifts, which was all right.

After everyone looked at Priyanthi, who was bedecked in frilly yellow cotton for her first public appearance, and laid their offerings on the table conveniently placed near by, they settled down. The men sat in one corner of the living room, the women formed a gossip circle in the other, and the children ran outside to play.

The men all settled for cold Lion Lagers, with the exception of Mr Munasinghe, who determinedly ignored his wife's glares and asked for a 'small arrack', knowing very well that Stanley's small arracks were enough to knock off a horse. The ladies all asked for passion fruit juice, with the exception of Dierdre, who determinedly ignored Enid's mother's glares and helped herself to a cold Lion Lager.

Hemantha and Niranjan had organised a game of hide-and-seek and both of them fought to be 'it'. Hemantha won as usual, but Niranjan didn't mind because he got to hide with Radhika Paul behind the huge pile of bricks at the corner of the garden. He shot adoring sideways glances at her and wondered why Hemantha's new sister was so ugly.

Hemantha and Niranjan had been friends all their lives. All three years of their lives. They played together every evening after school, while Violet and Enid stood in the shade and chatted. The boys fought occasionally, but always made up.

After a while, the game got boring and the children drifted off in different directions, some indoors to find a drink, and others to the back garden to lift stones and look for insects. Niranjan and Hemantha sat under the araliya tree, tired out from the heat and the excitement.

'I got a sister,' Hemantha said importantly.

'I saw,' Niranjan said. 'Will she play with me also?'

Hemantha considered this. Then he shook his head. 'No. This is my baby. If you want one, ask your Ammi to bring you a sister from the hospital.'

Niranjan looked upset. 'But *I* always share my toys with you.'

Hemantha thought about this and had to acknowledge that it was true. 'Maybe I'll let you play with her later. After I finish.'

THREE

Enid was pleased that Hemantha and Priyanthi got on so well together. Hemantha didn't display any jealousy, and although he hardly played with his sister, he was still enormously protective. Priyanthi grew up in the watchful shadow of her brother, who looked threateningly at anyone who he felt was not being nice to his sister. Once, he overheard Mrs Perera telling someone that little Priyanthi was 'a bit on the fat side' and threw a stone at her which broke one of her front teeth. Stanley offered to pay for her to get it capped and ended up paying to have all her cavities filled and her wisdom tooth pulled out, although he didn't know.

Hemantha was nine and Priyanthi was six. She went to St Mary's and he went to St Mark's where Bala taught English to tenth-graders. Both Hemantha and Priyanthi studied in the Sinhalese language, not because Stanley wanted it that way, but because Sinhalese was the official language of the country, and that included education. Tamil was an optional language, but not English. English could only be chosen as a second language.

It was particularly difficult for children who spoke only English at home, especially the burghers, who struggled to cope with botany and geography terms in Sinhalese. When they got low marks, the teachers sniggered among themselves and said that stupidity was a result of cross-breeding with foreigners.

Niranjan also went to St Mark's and was in the same grade as Hemantha, but he was in the Tamil class. They went to school together and came home together.

Violet and Enid took it in turns to walk the children up the lane to catch the school bus each morning. It never stopped at the bus halt, but a few feet away. As if the driver got some kind of perverse pleasure from making sleepy children run. Violet or Enid (depending on whose turn it was) walked home slowly, waving greetings to the Pauls or the Senaratnes or whoever was out at that time.

After they had given their respective servants instructions about lunch, the two of them wandered over to the wall that separated their properties, to chat.

These were daily chats that the men knew nothing about, not because either of the women went to any particular lengths to conceal them, but because it never occurred to them to tell the men. This was woman talk.

* * *

Enid, freshly showered and wearing a cotton shift in her favourite lilac colour, rested her elbows on the wall and looked into the other garden, but there was no sign of Violet. Which probably meant that Bala had left late again. She decided to take a walk around her own garden, enjoying as she always did the sight of the tiny white pigeon orchids growing in their coconut husk cradles. Everyone complained about how difficult they were to grow, but Enid had a gift for growing things. The mango tree was full of flowers and would be heavy with fruit in a few months. Even the grass was a special blue-green variety she had grown from seeds. Her garden was the envy of Araliya Gardens, and people often popped over to ask for a cutting of some plant she had successfully grown. She always obliged although they never grew anywhere else.

'Enid? Enid!'

She went over to the wall. Violet was peering over, her long hair spread out like a fan around her shoulders.

'My goodness, look at you!' Enid said mischievously. 'No wonder Bala gets late for work!'

Violet blushed. 'Nothing like that,' she said. 'I washed my hair early morning and it still hasn't dried. I thought I'd leave it for a bit. I don't want to catch a cold.'

Enid grinned. 'Nice story.' Then she sobered. 'Hemantha's report card came in yesterday.'

Violet nodded. 'Niranjan's too. Bala was so angry. Imagine, after all these years of coming first, he suddenly comes only fourth. Only twenty children in the class, also.'

'Fourth and you're complaining. My one didn't even pass in Geography. Came thirteenth.'

Violet looked sympathetic. 'What did Stanley say?'

Enid grimaced. 'He came home so late last evening and was so tired, I didn't have the heart to tell him.' She frowned. 'I don't know what Hemantha's problem is. The teachers can't be bad because Niranjan is doing so well. Just think – I send him for private tuition too. Two hours a day, but it hasn't helped at all.' She flapped her hand at a bee that was buzzing around her face. The araliyas attracted them at this time of year. 'He's so – uninterested. The teacher said he never concentrates on anything and just fools around in the class.'

'Enid, have you considered sending him to boarding school? Maybe that would help.'

Enid looked depressed. 'I've thought about it, but how to, child? He's my only boy, no? Stanley also said something about it to me the other night but I pretended not to hear.'

'How about Priyanthi? How's she faring?'

Enid brightened up. 'Violet, I've been blessed with that child. She is so good. And she loves school.'

Violet reached out and patted Enid's hand. 'You see?' she said gently. 'There's always a good side to everything.'

Enid laughed. 'You're such an optimistic soul, Violet.'

They both saw Dierdre at the same time, walking purposefully towards them.

'Don't say anything about Hemantha in front of her,' Enid hissed urgently.

Violet looked affronted. 'As if.'

Dierdre huffed over. 'You two! Always gossiping over the garden wall like a pair of lovers. So? What do you think?' she demanded.

They both looked blankly at her.

'My dress,' she said impatiently. 'Beatrice Kulatunge made it for me. Got the pattern from a magazine Elmo sent from Australia.'

'Who's Beatrice Kulatunge?' Violet asked.

Dierdre shook her head. 'Violet, Violet, what am I going to do with you? Beatrice Kulatunge is only the most famous dressmaker in Colombo!'

They looked at the dress. It was a crimson polyester that did nothing for Dierdre's ruddy complexion and light brown hair, and the swathed skirt made her already substantial hips look enormous. The tight, low-cut bodice squashed her ample breasts together, making them look like embracing lovers. Her gold chain completely disappeared between them.

She saw their expressions and sighed. 'Oh, you may as well be the ones to tell me how bad it is. Ed just rolls his eyes.'

'It's not ugly or anything,' Violet said hastily.

'No, no, it's not ugly,' Enid added. 'It's just—'

'Awful! I knew it,' Dierdre said glumly. 'My fault though – she advised me to find a simpler style but this one looked so beautiful on Twiggy in that magazine. Ten rupees for nothing!'

They stared. 'Ten rupees!' Violet said finally. 'Dierdre, the tailor up the road charges less than five for a dress.'

'But look at what he sews!' she retorted.

Two pairs of eyes looked down at their cotton dresses. Then they looked at each other and sighed. Dierdre didn't mean to be insulting. It was just the way she was. And at forty-five, no one really expected her to change. She was such a good friend in so many important ways.

'So what were you two gossiping about?' she demanded.

'Nothing,' they said simultaneously.

'Oho. Must have been report cards then.' Dierdre had an uncanny ability to make correct guesses. 'So who flunked and who did well, or do I need to ask? If it's any consolation, my two gave Ed a heart attack yesterday. He asked me how on earth Matthew was going to get into boarding school in England if he continued like this. As if I know!'

'Matthew's going to boarding school?' Enid asked curiously. 'Won't you die when he leaves?'

Dierdre laughed and her breasts shook alarmingly. 'My dear, I'll die if he stays. Mark is becoming quite a handful as it is, and if Matthew stays, I'm afraid he'll get into trouble.'

'What trouble?' Violet asked.

'You know, hanging around with undesirables, smoking, drinking, women, those things.'

Enid looked horrified. 'But Dierdre,' she said, 'you're such a good mother and Ed is so strict with them. What makes you think he will do those things?'

'Inevitable, dear,' Dierdre said wisely. 'Boys, you know. And unfortunately, the stricter we are with them, the more they rebel. You'll learn soon enough.' She looked at the slim watch on her fat wrist. 'My goodness, I'd better go, otherwise that idiot Emmy will burn everything. Cheerio, girls.' She hurried back to her home, completely oblivious of the turmoil she had thrown them into.

For the rest of the day they both worried about their sons. When Bala and Stanley came home after work, they both noticed how preoccupied their wives were.

When Enid was putting Priyanthi and Hemantha to bed, she prayed to the devas to protect her children from the evil of the world, although she didn't really believe that evil existed. There was certainly no sign of it down Araliya Gardens. She watched Hemantha's lids droop and told herself that no son of hers would get up to awful things like smoking and drinking.

Next door, Violet was talking to Niranjan. 'Son, you must be a good boy and study hard so you can take care of your father and me when we get old.'

'Okay,' Niranjan said, standing at the mirror and turning his eyelids inside out.

She turned to leave. 'Amma?'

'Yes?'

'When can I have a sister like Priyanthi?'

She smiled. 'Soon. Pray hard to Baby Jesus.'

Niranjan wondered how hard Hemantha had prayed to Baby Jesus. He made a mental note to ask him, although he didn't know what Baby Jesus had to do with babies. Unless He was the designated baby-provider to the world. Which would explain why He was called Baby Jesus.

Niranjan got into bed, clasped his hands together and earnestly implored Baby Jesus to send him a baby. Preferably a girl. Preferably tomorrow.

Violet repeated the conversation to Bala at dinner. He laughed. 'Once he has a sister, he'll want to get rid of her.' He finished eating, drank some water and used the rest of it to wash his hands in his plate. 'Anything sweet to eat?'

Later, they sat on the lawn, enjoying the fragrance of the araliyas which mingled with the sweet-spicy scent of jasmines which Violet grew everywhere. Up the walls, up trees, up the door posts, even on the gates. The tiny white flowers looked like little stars in the dark. Violet plucked a few every morning, tucking a couple into her braid and placing the rest reverently at the feet of her plaster-of-Paris Virgin Mary who sat on a special shelf with a blue altar lamp and a rosary blessed by the Pope.

'Violet,' Bala said thoughtfully, 'do you think we should consider moving?'

Violet looked puzzled. 'Moving? Why? I love Araliya Gardens!'

Bala looked contemplative. 'Not to another house. I meant to another country. Like Australia or England.'

Violet stared at him. 'Why? What's wrong with living here?' Then a thought struck her. 'Are you having problems at work? Is that why?'

'No, no. My God, you women love to jump to conclusions.' He sat forward in his chair and took her hand. 'I am not having any problems. In fact, I think I might get a promotion soon. No, I am wondering about this place, you know. How wise is it for us to stay? Look at what's happening – people are being edged out every day. We're Tamils and soon it will be our turn. Minorities and all that.'

'But what about the burghers?' Violet demanded with a tremor in her voice. 'They're a minority too, people like Ed and Dierdre. *They're* not leaving.'

'They're still here, but for how long? So many burghers and Tamils have already left. The government is squeezing us out, with all this language nonsense. Soon we won't be able to even get decent jobs.'

'But you've already got a decent job,' she said faintly, wondering if this was a bad dream or just some kind of a phase that Bala was going through.

'Yes. But it's the principle of the thing. Many people don't. Educated people, university graduates, are driving CTB buses and working as labourers. It can't go on without something erupting.' He looked grave. She said nothing.

He saw the fear, worry and sudden insecurity washing over her face like an unhappy wave and made an effort to smile. She was such a good, simple person and he hated to see her upset. 'Anyway, let's leave all that for now and go to bed.' He stood up and pulled her up as well. 'I remember you saying something about Niranjan wanting a sister. We'd better work on it.'

She smiled and followed him inside, but worry clouded her eyes and for once her heart was not in their lovemaking.

* * *

Bala didn't bring the subject up again for another year, a year which passed happily and relatively peacefully for the residents of Araliya Gardens. There had only been one unpleasant row between Mr Munasinghe and Mr Paul. Mr Munasinghe, for some curious reason, insisted on depositing his garbage outside Mr Paul's house. Usually Mr Paul laughed it off, because everyone knew Mr Munasinghe was not quite right in the head, but this time he had stood outside Mr Munasinghe's house and shouted that the next time he would call the police. Mr Munasinghe didn't comment because he was too deaf to hear.

Bala and Violet had other things on their minds – little Nirmala had been born just a month ago, and even though

Violet had worried about having a child ten years after Niranjan, the birth had been an easy one. Violet's family lived in Jaffna, in the far north of the island, and although her mother had planned to come to Colombo to be with Violet for the birth, Nirmala decided to arrive two weeks early. So it was Enid who held Violet's hand and murmured encouraging words to her, who wiped the sweat from her face, who cried with Violet when Nirmala emerged, wrinkled and bawling. It was Dierdre who stayed with Violet in the hospital on the first night and gently carried a hungry Nirmala over to her mother to be fed. Dierdre's servant Emmy cooked kiri kos for Violet so that her milk would come quickly, and Enid's servant boy Banda mowed Violet's lawn while she took care of her new baby.

Niranjan was overjoyed. After seven years of secretly envying Hemantha, now he had his own sister, and newer than Hemantha's too, but he still secretly envied Hemantha because Hemantha's sister could talk, while his only made funny noises.

Although Priyanthi was hardly ever included in their games because she was not only a girl, but also younger than they were, Niranjan found her fascinating. Her gentleness, her dimples and dresses made her so utterly un-boylike. She never pestered them or demanded to be allowed into their games, preferring to play quietly with her dolls while Hemantha and Niranjan wrestled or went around the garden trying to trap spiders and birds.

Sometimes when Hemantha disappeared inside for a drink or to go to the bathroom, Niranjan crept up to where she sat and watched her change her dolls and talk to them in the same crooning voice that his mother used when she spoke to baby Nirmala. He didn't dare do that when Hemantha was around, because Hemantha was very possessive about his sister. Even though he ignored her most of the time, he couldn't bear it if anyone else showed her any attention. Especially not his friend.

Once, Niranjan had heard her crying, and leaving the game of tigers that he and Hemantha were playing, he went off to investigate. He discovered her heartbroken because one of her dolls' arms had somehow come off. She cradled the armless doll and sobbed as though her heart would break. He gently took it from her, worked the plastic arm back into its hole and went red with embarrassment when she threw her chubby arms around his neck and kissed him fervently. He didn't know Hemantha had been watching until a clod of grass hit him on the head.

'Ouch!' he cried, turning around. 'What did you do that for?'

Hemantha glowered. 'Are you a sissy or what? You want to play with my nangi's dolls now?'

Niranjan stood up rubbing his head. 'I wasn't playing. I was repairing it. I'm going home,' he declared, and went home.

By the next day, the friendship was back to usual, although at school one of the boys in Hemantha's class said, 'Someone likes to play with girls' toys,' in a sly way when he passed Niranjan in the playground.

* * *

At ten, Niranjan was a model son, studious but as mischievous as any other child his age. His report cards from school always said the same thing. *Excellent student but too playful. Must pay more attention.* But since he always was at the top of his class, his parents didn't see any cause for concern. He was a good boy.

Hemantha was his closest friend. They sat next to each other on the school bus, ate each other's sandwiches during the lunch break and waited for each other after school so they could go home on the same bus. Even when Hemantha was punished and had to stay late writing lines, Niranjan waited with him. The teachers shook their heads and wondered how two such different children were such good friends.

After doing their homework, they both rushed through their baths and went out to play. Sometimes they played at Hemantha's, sometimes at Niranjan's, and sometimes they played cricket on the road with the other boys. They rarely fought because Niranjan usually let Hemantha have his way, but it was clear to everyone that Hemantha had the makings of a bully.

He always pushed and shoved while playing, once causing Niranjan to fall and cut his head quite badly on a stone.

Violet always told her son to pray for Hemantha to become a good boy, to 'be bigger than him'. So Niranjan tried to be bigger but since Hemantha was at least six inches taller and had the belligerence of a bull, it was difficult.

Hemantha was an enigma even to his own parents. He could be unbelievably sweet and an unbearable bully at the same time. 'It's as if he is two different people,' Enid moaned to Stanley. He was protective of Priyanthi but also occasionally yanked at her hair and laughed gleefully when she burst into tears. She was slightly afraid of him.

He tormented Violet's servant girl, and one day she complained to Enid's servant boy Banda that Hemantha was a val kolla, a perverted boy, because he was always asking to see her breasts. When she refused, he'd aim a painful kick at her ankles and shoot off back home before she could complain. Banda, who was not overly fond of Hemantha, told Enid. When she questioned Hemantha, he looked mutinously at her and said he'd only asked once. Enid lectured him long and hard about good behaviour, and decided that Stanley didn't really need to know about the incident. No point worrying him needlessly, she told herself.

Enid unconsciously shielded Hemantha in a number of situations simply because he was her son. Her only son. Sons were prized and boasted about at family reunions and applauded at sports meets. Daughters were nice but needed dowries, big girl ceremonies and careful watching.

* * *

Dierdre often asked Hemantha and Niranjan over to her house. They loved going, because although she cooked terrible food, she let them run around and laughed when they played pirates on her sofa, using her cushions for shields. Their own mothers didn't let them do those things. She also gave them a few cents here and there to buy sweets and generally gently spoiled them.

Her own children had gone away to school and Hemantha and Niranjan filled a vacant spot in her heart. She had a big heart. They were easy to love most of the time, so the fit was comfortable if not perfect. But sometimes, she looked at them and felt afraid. They were so different and Hemantha had a temper that could erupt without warning. She saw how he spoke to Niranjan, the kicks he aimed at Niranjan's shins when he thought no one was looking. There was a streak of viciousness in him that worried her.

When she spoke to Hemantha and told him to be a good boy and not to hurt his friend, Hemantha listened meekly but his eyes were always bland. Sometimes an odd smile would play about his mouth which made Dierdre want to slap him.

* * *

The two boys' families had grown closer in recent years, and on Sundays they often went to the beach together to spend the day lazing under the shady coconut trees, paddling and playing. The Mount Lavinia beach was their usual spot, because although it was some distance from Araliya Gardens, it wasn't always littered with dog droppings. Or fisher-children droppings.

The two families packed plastic picnic chairs, blankets and towels, and lunch, orange crush and beers in rigifoam boxes, and set off.

The men set up the chairs, stripped down to their shorts and chatted idly over beer, pausing every so often to eye a scantily clad tourist walking past. It was left to the women to organise lunch and see that the children were safe.

Enid and Violet sat in the shade with their hats and sunglasses on, while Priyanthi built sand-castles by herself and Nirmala dozed in her pram, her tiny, transparent eyelid-curtains drawn down against the bright sunlight. They chatted and exclaimed over each other's sandwiches, eagerly pulling out pens and paper from their voluminous handbags to write down recipes.

Despite the heat, they kept all their clothes on, but left their

33

nylon underskirts at home. Occasionally they saw a woman in a string bikini walking by and cast disapproving looks in her direction. The next five minutes were spent piously bemoaning the lax morals of the West.

Chee, child, can even see her bum and all!

No shame!

While the grown-ups did grown-up things and Priyanthi did girl things, Niranjan and Hemantha walked up and down the beach collecting shells, digging holes, trapping unsuspecting crabs and running into the water for a dip when they got too hot. The sand was fine and powdery, the water mostly clean and warm.

Niranjan covertly watched Priyanthi building her lonely sand-castles, and wished he could go and play with her, even just for a bit. She looked so alone. But he was afraid of Hemantha's derision, so he didn't even suggest it. He didn't want to be called a sissy at school.

These days, Hemantha kept company with a group of bigger children who loved to torment the younger ones, grabbing their sandwiches and waylaying them as they made their way back from the tuck shop. Once, a boy complained to a teacher that Hemantha and his friends had stolen his chocolate milk, and got beaten up after school.

'Come on, Nira!' Hemantha called. 'Let's go look in the rabbit's ears. We may find some lizards.'

Niranjan obediently followed. No one knew the real name for rabbit's ears, the shrub that grew wild along the island's sea shores. It had been nicknamed rabbit's ears because of the funny shape of its leaves. While Hemantha poked and prodded underneath, hoping to send a crab scuttling into the open, Niranjan gathered a bunch of the purple flowers that looked like miniature trumpets. He divided them into two and ran over to give a bunch each to his mother and Hemantha's.

'Oh, isn't he a sweet child!' Enid exclaimed with pleasure. She grimaced. 'You'll never find my one doing things like that.'

Violet smiled. 'Children are different,' she said, secretly glad that Niranjan was so little like Hemantha. She loved Hemantha as if he were her own, but that didn't blind her to his faults. She knew he picked on Niranjan but she didn't say anything. Anyway, what *could* she say? Enid, your son's a bully? No, that would hurt Enid, and little boys' squabbles were no reason to upset her neighbour, who was almost like a sister to her.

When Niranjan went back, Hemantha cast a derisive look in his direction. 'Sucking up to the mothers again, Nira?'

Niranjan opened his mouth to say something and shut it again.

What was the point?

FOUR

❧❧

In 1970, the government changed and the Sri Lanka Freedom Party came into power. Opinions were rife as to whether this Prime Minister was more capable of handling such a cultural and religious hotbed, and battling unemployment and inflation, which had risen to ridiculous levels, but most people reserved their judgement. Let's wait and see, they said.

Some with optimism. Some with derision. Some with weariness in their voices.

The situation worsened. Educated young people found themselves with no jobs, or jobs far beneath their qualifications. Resentment bubbled underneath their resigned attitude and soon surfaced in the form of the Janatha Vimukthi Peramuna, or JVP, a group of ultra-left youths driven by two powerful motivators – poverty and idealism.

In mid-1971, a JVP attempt to overthrow the government was brutally squashed. Thousands died and hundreds more were arrested, although naturally, the official figures were far lower. It was a tense time because the army with its unlimited powers was as feared as the JVP.

Curfews were declared, schools were closed and basic supplies became even more scarce.

During the days of the insurrection, the people at Araliya Gardens grew closer, drawn together by fear and worry. Little knots of men gathered at gates to discuss the situation. Wives willingly shared whatever few provisions they had. Children armed with papaya stalks played Army–JVP.

Occasionally, dusty green army jeeps zoomed down the

road, soldiers hanging out of them with loaded guns and narrow-eyed, suspicious looks. The little Araliya Gardens knots would speedily untie themselves and disperse, children would be pulled inside, gates would be locked and doors shut quietly. Lights were put off. Curtains twitched. Prayers were muttered.

The adults found the situation nerve-racking, the children found it exciting. They were too young to understand the enormity of what was happening. To count the deaths. To mourn a lost generation.

After the JVP ringleaders were incarcerated and things settled down somewhat, the rumour mill began its insidious circle. The army had gone crazy, people said, arresting innocent men, going on shooting sprees and raping village virgins. Even a former beauty queen. The protectors of the people were suddenly looked upon with the same suspicion and fear as the insurrectors had been.

No one said anything, though. Fear was an effective gag.

But people like Corporal Fernando, who lived down the next road and had been a sort of hero until that time, were no longer met at the market with mock salutes and cheery hellos. Instead, people cast their eyes downwards and hurried off in the opposite direction.

The government continued to wield its control with harsh economic and social changes. Plantations previously privately owned were nationalised almost overnight. So were most trade ventures and industries.

In 1972, Ceylon officially became Sri Lanka. The Democratic Socialist Republic of. Not that *that* meant anything. In fact, it only made the minorities feel even more like minorities.

It was such a – *Sinhalese* name.

* * *

At the beginning of each week, Enid, Dierdre, Violet, Mrs Munasinghe and the other female residents of Araliya Gardens joined a long queue at the government co-operative. They left their homes early in the morning so they didn't have to be the last in line, but they still were.

They walked up the road together, minor differences disappearing in a mesh of solidarity. Discussing food and famine. Shaking their heads and wondering where it would all end. In spite of the mesh, the conversation was careful. After all, one word in the wrong ears could mean so many things. If someone became too vociferous in their criticism, the others didn't sympathise. Their faces agreed. *I know, child! My children are also asking why we don't have enough bread at dinner time! They will first starve us, then ask for our vote, and if we don't give it, they will use force to take it from us!* Their mouths remained mute.

At the co-operative, they sighed when they saw the queue. People who owned property stood behind unemployed servant women. In the co-operative queue, everyone was equal and they all had the same possessions. A ration book printed on cheap cardboard for each member of their families, a purse carried in their hands or tucked into their blouses, and an umbrella to ward off the heat, which built up steadily as the morning wore on.

The line could be seen from nearly a mile away, not a line of people but a line of umbrellas. Some with floral patterns on them, some striped, some plain black, some grey that had once been black. Some with little buttons that, when you pressed them, opened up the umbrella in one mechanical motion (from rich relatives in countries that didn't have ration books and co-operative queues). Others that had to be struggled with, that opened backwards before they opened forwards. Some with their spokes demurely covered by umbrella material and others with their spokes protruding into the umbrellas of other people.

The umbrellas shielded them from the sun overhead, but not from the heat, which built up steadily as the day wore on. It emanated in vaporous clouds from the tarred road, fought its way through rubber Bata slippers and up skirts and reddhas, where it became sweat and collected behind knees.

When a person finally reached the top of the queue and finally came face to face with someone (instead of the back of the person in front), they handed over their ration cards for scrutiny. The man behind the counter was in the same situation, but temporarily felt more powerful because, unlike them, he could at least *handle* substantial quantities of food. He enjoyed lengthily studying the ration books, knowing people couldn't afford to protest. He had the authority to send someone to the back of the line if they created a problem. He also had the authority to determine what problems were.

For instance, a heavy gold necklace around someone's sweaty neck was a problem. An impatient drumming of fingers on the floury counter was a problem. A voluptuous woman who didn't respond coyly to his admiring looks or comments was a problem.

Eventually, provisions were handed out. Slowly. Stingily. With a superior attitude and a challenging look.

Two chundus (each a fraction bigger than a tea cup) of rice per person per week, an equally pitiful amount of flour and sugar were borne home with a mixture of triumph and despair.

Each morning, people stood in queues outside bakeries from three a.m. to buy bread, which was also rationed, two loaves per person. Unless one happened to be on good terms with the baker. In which case it was three loaves. Or two loaves and a roast paang, the small flat bread that children loved and adults shunned under normal circumstances. But these weren't normal circumstances.

By six a.m. it was all gone. The people at the back of the queue came home empty-handed and spent the remainder of the day empty-stomached. Farmers toiled in the baking heat, hungry and disillusioned. Blue-collar workers opened their lunch boxes and ate slowly so that the meagre amounts of food lasted a bit longer.

Poor people abandoned their pride and searched rich people's garbage bins for scraps. The rich abandoned their dignity and begged for an extra loaf of bread at bakeries. And humbly accepted humiliation as well as weekly rations from the co-operative man.

There was no money to buy food on the black market. For the few that had money, there was no food available.

Even fabric was rationed – two yards per person. Large people like Dierdre had to rely on the generosity of their relatives in Australia and England. Dresses got shorter, but it had nothing to do with fashion.

People were murdered over loaves of bread.

Malnourished children with bloated stomachs and empty eyes filled the corridors of the government hospitals. Some received treatment. Others died. Parents grieved, cursed the government and then tried to look on the bright side. One less mouth to feed.

Survival had become a way of life.

* * *

The minorities were being squeezed into corners that became smaller every day. Burghers emigrated in their droves to Australia and England to join relatives already there, becoming cinema ushers and cleaning ladies. They spent their evenings drinking cheap whisky and reminiscing about the good times back home, conveniently forgetting the mass dismissals and subsequent struggle for survival. At night, they gave thanks for their new, grim life, which was still infinitely better than the one they had left behind. That had been mere existence at best.

Some Tamils migrated too, but most stayed on.

The origins of the conflict between the Sinhalese and the Tamils are shrouded in the dusty pages of seldom-opened history books. No one had any real desire to know how or when it had all begun. But everyone knew it went far further back than a few years, a few nationalistic governments and a few hurt feelings.

Some people were of the view that it was the fault of the British, who had brought in Tamil labourers from India to work on Ceylon's tea plantations. Others claimed it went all the way back to the Cholas from India, who had invaded the island many centuries ago. Still others, intent on displaying their knowledge of Ceylonese history, said it had begun when Prince Vijaya, an exiled prince from India, landed on Ceylonese shores centuries before the Cholas arrived.

Most agreed that the first real concerns about the different ethnic groups living together harmoniously and being treated fairly were probably voiced during the early 1900s, when the constitution for an independent Ceylon was being drafted. Without the British to act as mediators and moderators, without an outside party to complain to and blame, who would the minorities turn to? Several prominent Tamil intellectuals expressed their doubts about the future. Some said that the only way to avoid racial problems from developing was to give the Tamils, who were, after all, the largest ethnic group after the Sinhalese, a separate state. Their own mini country within a mini country.

Although the Tamils were the largest minority, they only accounted for less than twenty per cent of the total population, which at the time numbered under fourteen million. The island itself is just over 25,000 square miles. The conclusion arrived at was that the island was too small to divide and the Tamils too few to justify such a division.

And so it began.

At first it was a whisper, which soon became a murmur as more people took it up. It was only a matter of time before it became a rousing call to arms, and then a war cry.

The Tamils had always been a diligent race who looked ahead to the future. They worked hard, lived frugally and saved frantically so their children could go to good schools and universities. The children came home armed with hard-earned degrees, and while some secured good jobs and were content with their lot, others wanted more.

They didn't want to be tolerated by the system. They wanted to be part of the system.

So they entered politics, contested elections and did reasonably well. But 'reasonably' wasn't included in the vocabulary taught to them at their expensive universities.

There, far away from the petty politics of a tiny island nation, they had been told they could do anything, be anything. They felt lied to. Cheated.

Everyone knew the actions of the present government, the arbitrary privatisations, the change in official language and of the country's name, were not just a consolidation of their powers, but also a warning to the minorities. It was a warning the Tamils took seriously.

They started to become more defensive, more demanding.

In the process, resignation gave way to resentment.

Educated people like Bala felt like outsiders. And, for all Bala's friendships with his Sinhalese neighbours, he envied them their position. *They* didn't spend sleepless nights trying to foretell a shaky future and worrying about their children and what place there would be for them when they finally grew up. *They* didn't feel insecure every time there was an inspection by the education authorities.

Many of his Tamil friends had excellent jobs – they were doctors, lawyers, accountants, engineers. Well placed. Well respected.

It was the *attitude* that rankled. The *we* and the *our* that excluded them. Sometimes deliberately. And sometimes not.

* * *

Violet and Bala were standing at their gate one evening. A light breeze blowing in from the sea stirred the frilly parasol on Nirmala's pram and made the leaves on the trees start their chain reaction of whispers.

On the road, Niranjan and Hemantha were playing cricket with some of the other boys. Further up, they saw Mr Paul coming home from work and waved to him.

After a while, Enid drifted out with Priyanthi in tow.

'Evening,' Bala called out.

'I don't know what has happened to Stanley,' Enid complained. 'Six o'clock and still no sign.' She looked up the road worriedly.

'He's probably working late,' Bala said.

'They make him work like a dog, child,' she replied fretfully. 'Some days he comes home after the children are in bed.' She called out to Hemantha, 'Putha! Come here!'

Hemantha ran over, annoyed at her for interrupting his batting. 'What?' he demanded.

She was too worried to notice his rudeness. 'Go up the road with Niranjan and see if your father is coming, child.'

He looked impatient. 'Amma, he'll come. What's the point of Niranjan and me going? We can't make him come sooner.'

'Go, child,' she pleaded. 'Something may have happened to him.'

Bala walked over. 'Enid, he's probably trying to get a bus. Wait a few minutes. If he doesn't show up, we'll all take a walk up the road.'

Hemantha didn't wait to hear his mother's response. He ran back to his game.

They heard Dierdre before they saw her. 'Enid! Enid!' she cried shrilly.

'She's like a bell,' Enid muttered.

Dierdre appeared at her gate and brightened up when she saw the three of them. 'Good news!' she hollered, waving an airmail envelope.

Dierdre had many relatives abroad and was always getting parcels of Kraft cheese, Marmite, Cadbury's chocolate and other imported goodies, which she generously shared with them. They assumed this was to do with a package from Uncle Sonny or Auntie Dolly or someone.

'Boys are coming home for a month,' she panted. 'Just got the news! My, won't Ed be thrilled!'

Bala looked around. 'Where is Ed?'

'He phoned a while ago to say there was a big traffic jam in Kollupitiya. Some protest or another.'

Enid looked relieved. 'Stanley's probably caught in it.'

Dierdre leaned against the gate, which creaked protestingly. 'This country! I don't know what's happening to it. Ed was seriously talking about going off to England and joining Dicky and Eileen.'

Bala shot Violet a look, which she chose to ignore.

'You know Dicky and Eileen, Ed's brother and his wife. Can't say I'm too keen on her, but he's a real gem. He's written to us so many times and told us to sell up and come.'

'Why don't you?' Enid asked curiously.

Dierdre looked pensive. 'I don't know, child. It's not easy at our age to just pack up and go. We've lived in Colombo all our lives. And Ed's got his business here.'

'But you're not old. You could start again somewhere. Somewhere more tolerable than here,' Bala said thoughtfully. 'Even retire if you have enough.'

Dierdre grinned. 'Been going through our bank slips again, Bala?'

'I think you should go, Dierdre,' Bala persisted. 'You have relatives and all. It will be easy for you.'

Violet, who had been leaning on the wall listening to the exchange, straightened up. 'I'd better go in and start dinner,' she said, a little distantly.

'What are you cooking? Some of your fabulous thosas?' Dierdre asked, obviously angling for an invitation.

'Why don't you join us when Ed comes home?' Bala suggested. 'You two as well, Enid.'

'We'd love to,' Dierdre shot back almost before he had finished speaking.

Enid smiled at Violet. 'Will there be enough?'

'You always say I cook for an army. Actually, I made extra thosa mix for tomorrow, but I can always make something else. Do come,' Violet said.

'I've got some crème caramel left over from yesterday. I'll bring that,' Dierdre said brightly.

Bala grimaced and then winced as Violet dug him in the ribs.

* * *

A few hours later, the three couples sat in Bala's garden, talking quietly. Around them cicadas chirped and the araliya tree divested itself of yesterday's blossoms. They were slightly limp and darker pink with age, and they made soft plopping sounds as they fell.

The children were in bed because tomorrow was a school day. Although Bala had to wake up early too, he showed no signs of being tired. He enjoyed chatting with Ed and Stanley and didn't have to worry if Violet was having a good time; Enid and Dierdre were her best friends. So they 'put a few shots', as Ed called it, and talked about everything from politics to parenting.

'What was the protest about?' Bala asked.

Ed snorted. 'You know these buggers – always protesting about something or the other. At least it didn't get out of hand this time.'

'Apparently they were protesting about the rice,' Stanley said.

Enid heard. 'I don't blame them. The stuff they give us at the co-op is not fit for dogs.'

'That's probably what they think we are,' Bala said bitterly.

'Bloody traffic jam went on for ever,' Ed complained.

'And you sitting in your fancy car! Poor chap!' Stanley hooted derisively. 'Feel sorry for us, the working class, sweating it out on the buses!'

Ed grinned. 'It's not my fault that you choose to put your millions into the bank and not buy a car like the rest of us.'

'Millions!' That was Enid, all indignant. 'If only!'

'*I* don't wear a diamond the size of an ice cube on *my* finger,' Dierdre said with an arch look.

'That's my engagement ring!' Enid protested. 'Only diamond I have.'

Stanley held up his hands. 'People! You're going to get me into trouble now. I'll be frog-marched down Sea Street before I know it!'

Sea Street was where all the jewellers had their shops.

45

They all laughed. Bala noticed Stanley's glass was empty. 'Come on, man! Why so shy? Let's go inside and get another.'

'Bring me a beer!' Dierdre called out after them. Enid and Violet exchanged a look.

At midnight, Violet stood up. 'I'm going to start the thosas,' she said, and got a round of moans in reply.

'So early?'

'Sit, sit and enjoy the breeze!'

'Trying to chuck us out already. Shame!'

Violet sat and tried to look stern, but failed. Enid and Dierdre were used to the course these evenings took, and although Violet was too, she always tried to stop the drinking before it got to the singing stage. Now they would get drunk and start their songs, and tomorrow she would have to avoid Mrs Munasinghe's accusing looks and Mrs Paul's arch comments.

Sure enough, about two drinks later, Bala broke into song. It started with 'My Bonnie Lies Over the Ocean', but when it got to 'Sweet Violets', the ladies escaped to the kitchen, Dierdre with some reluctance.

They giggled while the thosa pan heated.

'What will the neighbours think!' Violet said.

Enid looked at her. '*We* are your neighbours, Violet.'

Violet blushed. 'I was talking about Mrs Munasinghe and Esme Paul – she always looks funnily at me.'

'That's because you're not fat and ugly like her and because you don't wear huge pottus on your forehead. Mind you, if I was that ugly, I'd do something to hide my face too,' Dierdre said.

'Dierdre!' they said simultaneously, pretending to be shocked, although they were enjoying her comments hugely.

'Jealousy, child, jealousy,' Dierdre proclaimed piously. 'And who can blame them? Look at us!'

They looked. Violet was now thirty-odd and still slim and shapely, her hair as black and long and lustrous as ever. Enid had put on some weight, but she looked after herself with monthly visits to the beauty salon in Nugegoda. Dierdre looked down at herself, her two-hundred-pound figure resplendent in

mauve and black polyester. 'Look at us,' she repeated deso-
lately.

They burst out laughing.

Matthew and Mark Jobsz returned home for their month-long
school holidays with suitcases full of imported things and
imported British accents. Ed was able to use his connections to
get off paying customs duty, which would probably have
amounted to double the value of the things themselves. A
hundred-rupee note slipped here and there took care of the
problem.

When they returned from the airport, almost all the neighbours contrived to be outdoors to catch an early glimpse of the
boys from England, as they were now known. As if the first ten
or so years of their lives had been wiped away by just one year
in England. As they passed Enid's house, they were instructed
to 'wave to Auntie Enid', who just happened to be watering her
plants at the time.

That evening, Dierdre and Ed had a dinner party for their
few relatives still in Sri Lanka, and for their neighbours. The
boys were washed and dressed in their England clothes and put
on show.

'Look, child,' Dierdre exclaimed, her eyes shining with pride.
'Went away looking like two sprats and now see – proper
young men.'

The proper young men cringed and tried to look enthusiastic.
They were both tall and fair, with light brown hair and blue
eyes, inheritances from their ancestral associations with the
Dutch invaders. Some legalised by marriage. And some not.
Violet kissed their cheeks and said hello. Enid chucked
Matthew under the chin and said my how he'd grown, in a
slightly accusing voice. As if he wasn't supposed to. Bala and
Stanley shook hands with them and slyly asked about English
girls. Dierdre stopped talking to hear their responses, but they
only went bright red and looked at the floor.

Niranjan, Hemantha and Priyanthi stood and stared.

Nirmala dozed in her pram, sweating in her yellow nylon net party dress and imitation patent-leather shoes.

Ed's relatives were a jolly bunch and the evening progressed cheerfully and noisily, with drinks refilled in record time and Elvis Presley on the stereo. People sat or stood around in groups and tapped their shiny pointed shoes in time to the music.

'So, studying hard?' Stanley asked the boys, who were still on display.

'Mmmm,' they mumbled.

'Marry two nice English girls! Then you don't ever have to set foot in this godforsaken place again!' advised Cal Jansz, Ed's second cousin.

Dierdre glared at him. 'Why? Ceylonese girls were good enough for you lot.'

The conversation progressed to politics and the boys thankfully escaped to the garden, followed by Niranjan, Hemantha and Priyanthi. The younger boys were full of questions about cars in England and television and things, and were given highly exaggerated accounts which made their eyes wide with wonder.

Priyanthi still said nothing but stared at the two boys. She thought they looked like the handsome princes from her fairy tales. Blond, blue-eyed and with recently acquired English accents.

After Elvis had been listened to a few times over and all the Lion Lager was gone, Dierdre served dinner. Everyone breathed an inaudible sigh of relief when they heard she had ordered it from the Golden Gate, although the men were too drunk to notice the difference.

The crème caramel custard, however, was all hers and the boys washed mouthfuls down with water, wishing they were back in England. School cooking was infinitely better than this.

Enid and Violet refused dessert on the grounds that they had 'eaten like pigs' already. 'Have to watch the weight,' they said, shuddering slightly at the sight of the wobbly crème caramel.

At about two a.m., sleeping children were gathered up and people staggered home with promises of 'next time, our place'.

Ed had passed out, half on the sofa, half off. The boys were already asleep in their room. Dierdre looked in on them, muttered a quick prayer that they would marry good burgher girls and went off to bed.

* * *

The month went by quickly, with Dierdre trying to fatten up her sons, Matthew and Mark escaping to Violet's and Enid's to avoid their mother's cooking, and Hemantha and Niranjan competing for their attention. Niranjan just hung around and gazed worshipfully at them, running errands and obeying orders like a little slave. Hemantha used a different tactic. 'Niranjan plays with my sister's dolls,' he confided to them, when Niranjan wasn't around. Or, 'Niranjan cried when he fell in school.'

When Matthew and Mark asked Niranjan to go and steal one of Bala's cigarettes, he refused. Hemantha pilfered a whole pack of Gold Leaf from his father's cupboard, and even smoked one with the boys down by the bokku.

'Have one,' they said to Niranjan, who shook his head.

Matthew and Mark stayed at the bokku to finish off the rest of the pack, but Hemantha and Niranjan had to go home. They made a detour via Sumanapala's corner shop to buy some minty-smelling Chestos. According to Hemantha, they effectively disguised the smell of cigarettes. Which made Niranjan wonder how many times Hemantha had done this.

They sucked on their sweets and walked home. At Niranjan's gate, they stopped.

'You won't tell, will you?' Hemantha demanded. If his father ever found out, he knew he would get whipped.

'No.'

Hemantha held his hand out. 'Promise?'

Niranjan looked indignant. 'I don't have to promise. I'm your best friend.'

The hand stayed where it was. 'Promise anyway.'

Niranjan stared at Hemantha for a long moment, turned on his heel and went indoors. Hemantha cursed under his breath. He was quite sure Niranjan wouldn't tell, but he wanted to be extra sure. He loitered outside long enough to finish the Chesto, and when he went indoors he went straight to the bathroom to brush his teeth. Just in case.

Hemantha had only been whipped twice by his father. The first time was when he was six and had kicked his mother. And the second time was when he had thrown his plate of food on the floor in a rage. He remembered both times very well.

FIVE

༉

Enid watched her daughter clambering high up into the branches of the araliya tree and sighed. Priyanthi was ten and showed no signs of having realised she was a girl and not a boy. She had given up her dolls a few years ago and didn't seem to be interested in anything remotely feminine any more, preferring to play cricket with the boys (when she was allowed to) or read.

Enid sighed again. She had been so happy when Priyanthi was born, because although she loved Hemantha dearly, you couldn't dress boys up in frilly dresses and tie satin ribbons in their hair. Until Priyanthi was seven, she accepted the fussing and frills and ribbons. After that, she flatly refused them. These days, she seemed to live in Hemantha's old clothes – shorts, T-shirts and trousers.

One day, Enid had found her standing in front of the mirror, laboriously cutting off her hair with the kitchen scissors. Long thick locks littered the floor and Enid wanted to weep. It was too late, though, so she tidied up the haircut as much as she could and told Stanley she had found lice in Priyanthi's hair. Even so, he was furious.

Enid had been ashamed too, because people would automatically assume that either Priyanthi had lice or that her mother couldn't be bothered to take care of her hair. Most Sinhalese girls from good families had long hair.

When the Sinhalese and Tamil New Year drew near, Enid begged Priyanthi to wear a dress, at least for the day. For the sake of peace, Priyanthi agreed. She wore it for a whole hour, and when Enid next looked out of the window, she saw Priyanthi back in her tattered shirt and trousers.

Although the Silvas were quite Western in their outlook, Stanley still insisted on celebrating the Sinhalese and Tamil New Year in the traditional way. Enid complained about the amount of work involved but she actually enjoyed it. So did the neighbours.

Being Catholic Tamils, Violet and Bala didn't celebrate Avurudhu, but that didn't stop them from going next door for the celebrations. Just as Stanley and Enid went over to Violet's for Christmas.

Avurudhu is on the fourteenth of April, but the rituals and ceremonies begin on the thirteenth, which is technically the Old Year. The special Avurudhu almanac with its auspicious times and auspicious colours is published in the newspapers several days before, to give people time to plan their festivities and sew their clothes. On the thirteenth, hearths (or stoves in more modern homes) are extinguished at the auspicious time. From then until the New Year officially dawns, no fires are lit and nothing is cooked. No housework is done.

People troop off to temples to pray for prosperity in the New Year and to give thanks for the Old Year. But for the rest of the day, no one goes out. People stay in to await the New Year and even those who don't celebrate Avurudhu know better than to visit. They wear their new clothes (in that year's auspicious colour), keep their radios on and (depending on the auspicious time) wait for the New Year to be announced. Although no one really needs a radio because the country explodes at the auspicious time with the sound of fire-crackers. Municipality workers grumble and arrive at dawn to sweep the streets of the debris which litters it like confetti, before New Year morning.

Hearths are lit and milk is allowed to boil over in a new clay pot, signifying hopes for prosperity in the New Year. Milk rice is cooked. The table is laid with kavum, kokis, athirasa, aasmi and combs of bananas. The oil lamp is lit. At the various auspicious times, the family eats, pays homage to its elders and exchanges gifts of cash wrapped in betel leaves. Then the first visitor arrives, usually a person of wealth and social standing, who will bring good luck to the family.

Bala had always been the Silvas' first visitor, much to Dierdre's secret disappointment.

The first year they celebrated Avurudhu at Araliya Gardens, Stanley told Enid, 'He's the nicest, most decent person we know and I don't care if he happens to be a Tamil.'

Enid's mother, when she found out, was horrified, insisting that it could only bring bad luck. 'A Tamil, child! What is this Stanley thinking of? You know what they say – a bad face brings bad luck throughout the year,' she declared in her special voice of doom.

Enid felt vaguely uncomfortable about it too but she said nothing. She didn't want Stanley to think her small-minded.

This year was no different.

At the auspicious time, Bala arrived bearing gifts of sweet-meats and five rupees each for Priyanthi and Hemantha. Niranjan didn't like this part because no one gave *him* money. He wasn't a Buddhist. Or even a Hindu. Although he liked being a Catholic, he would have cheerfully converted just for the Avurudhu money.

At the end of the day, he had to watch Hemantha counting his spoils – about twenty rupees given to him by a variety of doting aunts, uncles, grandparents and visitors.

Somehow, Niranjan didn't mind that Priyanthi got an equal amount – she didn't wave it in front of his face and loudly calculate how many kimbula buns and chocolate milks it would buy her from the school tuck shop.

Niranjan followed his parents into Uncle Stanley's house and stopped dead. Priyanthi, who usually ran around in faded old shorts and shirts with her hair escaping its school braid, was wearing a dress. It was bright red, with a long skirt and puffed sleeves, and her hair was caught up on top of her head with a shiny red ribbon. She was even wearing black shoes and white frilly socks. She looked beautiful and acutely uncomfortable.

She stared at Niranjan and finally stuck her tongue out at him. That brought him to his senses and he quickly looked around to see if anyone else had seen him staring. Thankfully Hemantha was too busy waiting for his money, and the adults with greeting each other with the usual 'myee, what a lovely dress' and 'sha! nice slacks', to notice.

He muttered his greetings and tried to slink off to a corner, but was waylaid by Hemantha.

'Ten bucks already and the grandparents haven't arrived yet,' he whispered gleefully.

Niranjan looked envious. 'What are you going to do with it?' he asked.

'Gold Leaf,' Hemantha whispered back.

'Cigarettes make you get cancer and die quickly,' Niranjan said piously.

Hemantha guffawed, but quickly stopped when everyone turned to look at them. 'You don't really believe all that, do you?'

They wandered outdoors.

Niranjan tried again. 'It's not good for you.'

Hemantha scowled, tiring of the advice. 'Listen, no one's forcing you, okay? Just don't say anything to anyone. That's all.'

Inside, Priyanthi was helping her mother to lay kavums and kokis on a paper-doily-covered platter.

'Ammi, can I go and change now?' she pleaded when she had finished.

Enid frowned. 'Wait until your grandparents come. Your grandmother is always telling me to make you nice clothes – if only she knew how many are just hanging in the cupboard.'

Priyanthi started to look sulky. 'Why can't they just let me be? I like what I wear.'

Enid sighed. 'Priyanthi, you're the only girl in the family. They want you to grow up to be a lady, not some tomboy.'

'Just because I don't like dresses, it doesn't mean I'm a tomboy,' she said.

Enid was rapidly losing her temper. 'Why can't you be like Radhika Paul? Look at her. She's always well dressed and so well behaved.'

'That's because she's looking for a boyfriend,' Priyanthi retorted.

'There's nothing wrong with that – she's old enough,' Enid said, slightly shocked that Priyanthi even knew the word 'boyfriend'.

'She'd probably find one if she didn't try so hard. Look at her walking – she shakes her bottom so hard, it wriggles!'

'Priyanthi!'

'It's true,' Priyanthi said with a sulky look.

'What's true?' Violet asked, entering the kitchen. She looked from mother to daughter and wondered what it was this time. She didn't envy Enid. Priyanthi had become quite a handful, and Hemantha – well, everyone knew Hemantha was going to get into trouble one day.

'This child!' Enid said. 'I don't know where she hears these things from. Saying things like that about Radhika!'

'Actually, I heard you and Auntie Dierdre talking,' Priyanthi retorted sweetly, and walked out of the kitchen.

Violet tried hard not to laugh. 'Well, I suppose we'd all better remember that small pitchers have big ears,' she said.

'You laugh,' Enid said crossly. 'Thank your lucky stars your one is still young. Wait until she reaches this age.'

Violet sank on to the small kitchen stool. 'But that's it, Enid, don't you see? It's only this age. She'll grow out of all this soon. Soon you'll be wishing she was still in her old trousers and shirts and only interested in cricket!'

Enid didn't answer. She was looking out of the kitchen window. Outside, Priyanthi was settling down under the araliya tree. The red dress had been replaced by a pair of faded blue cotton trousers and a crushed white shirt. The socks and shoes and her ribbon were gone.

Enid opened the kitchen window and leaned out. 'Priyanthi!'

If she heard, Priyanthi gave no sign, settling herself comfortably into the gnarled crook of the tree. Enid closed the kitchen window and sighed. 'The fireworks will start when the grandparents arrive.'

'They're your children,' Violet said quietly.

'Try telling that to my mother,' Enid retorted. Enid's parents arrived moments before Dierdre and Ed. Hemantha materialised like magic to collect his Avurudhu money and then disappeared again. Enid's mother looked around. 'Where's Priyanthi?'

'Out playing,' Enid said hastily. 'Let her be. Sit down and have something to drink. You must be tired.'

When Enid went into the kitchen to get the drinks, her mother followed her. 'Did you have to have those people as your first visitors again?' she whispered loudly, adjusting the emerald brooch which clasped the fall of her crimson sari.

Enid glanced at the closed door. 'Yes, Amma, and his name is Bala,' she said shortly.

'But Tamils, child? Are there no decent Sinhalese people in the world? Talk to Stanley and tell him to use his head. What am I going to tell people in Kandy when they ask me who you had?'

'Whatever you told them last year, Amma,' Enid said, picking up a tray. At the door, she paused. 'By the way, apparently Bala's about to be made Headmaster.'

Her mother's mouth fell open. Enid smiled sunnily and slipped out of the kitchen.

Behind the door, her mother still stood there, oblivious of a fly buzzing around her ear. A Tamil Headmaster at St Mark's! What was the world coming to? But it did put a different complexion on things. One couldn't ignore a Headmaster, even if he was a Tamil. Why, her grandfather had taught for forty years at Peradeniya and he had only been a deputy. She shook her head. This country was heading for disaster, she told herself darkly.

A few minutes later, Dierdre and Violet looked at each other in amazement as Enid's mother seated herself next to Bala and began an animated conversation with him about higher education and the improvements that needed to be made to the system. Even Bala looked mystified, although he answered politely enough. Enid's mother was too well bred to be openly rude, but she always treated him as if he had some kind of contagious disease.

Stanley looked over at Enid and raised an eyebrow in question. She simply smiled.

After lunch, Enid's mother rose. 'Come, let's take a walk around the garden. I'm dying to see how your orchids are doing. Mine are not very healthy these days.' She waggled her fingers at Bala and started for the door.

Enid hung back. 'It's too hot, Amma,' she said.

'Nonsense! What are you, a foreigner? Come, come.' She sailed out, fanning herself with the end of her sari.

Enid followed reluctantly. Dierdre and Violet followed Enid, in answer to her pleading looks.

'She should stand up to that old battleaxe,' Dierdre muttered to Violet.

'Shhh!' Violet said. 'She'll hear.'

'All the better. And I used to think *my* mother was bad! She was a bloody saint in comparison to that one. Now what?' as the two in front suddenly stopped.

Enid's mother turned to look accusingly at her daughter. 'Enid. *What* is that child wearing?'

Enid looked uncomfortable. 'Amma, what can I do? I can't force her into dresses. She hates them.'

'Yes, but at least for the New Year? Think of the bad luck.' Her mouth was a thin line. 'She looks like a street child.'

Enid tried to contain her temper. 'Amma, let her be. She'll grow out of it.'

'When? When she's an old maid of thirty and no one wants to marry her?' her mother replied acidly.

Dierdre stepped forward. 'Nothing wrong with not being married. Not with the hooligans around these days,' she said cheerfully, trying to defuse the situation. She succeeded in doing exactly the opposite.

Enid's mother drew herself up to her full height. 'That may be okay for people from *some* communities, but not for Sinhalese Govigama people like us.' She turned and stalked back to the house.

Enid glared at Dierdre. 'Why did you have to interfere?' she demanded, almost in tears. She hurried in after her mother.

Dierdre and Violet stood looking after them.

'Me and my big mouth,' Dierdre said at last.

Violet sighed. 'Not to worry. She'll be gone soon and Enid will be back to normal. You know how tense she gets when her mother comes to visit.'

They walked over to where Priyanthi sat. She lifted her eyes from her book. 'Hello, Auntie Violet, Auntie Dierdre,' she said. 'What happened to Amma and the Kandyan dragon?'

'One breathed fire and toasted the other,' Dierdre said, grinning.

Priyanthi grimaced. 'Was it my fault?'

Dierdre nodded. 'I'm afraid so.'

Priyanthi looked guilty. 'I should have kept that damn dress on until she left. It's just that the damn skirt was tickling my knees and the sleeves scratched.'

'Don't say those words,' Violet scolded gently.

Dierdre laughed. 'Not to worry,' she said practically, 'if it hadn't been your clothes, it would have been the kavum.'

Priyanthi laughed too, her face lighting up with amusement. Even at ten, it was quite obvious that she was going to be a beauty some day. Her skin was a beautiful golden brown with a hint of olive. Her hair and eyebrows were jet black but her eyes were dark brown and full of secrets. She had a Kandyan nose, straight and just a bit too big, and a wide mouth that seemed to be always twisted in a sulk.

Hemantha took after his father, dark, swarthy and heavily built.

Priyanthi was one of those strange children who seemed to have been born grown-up. She didn't gurgle and coo when she was a baby, but stared around her with intense interest. Enid had initially been worried that her daughter was a bit slow and had wanted to take her to a child specialist, but Dierdre had robustly told her not to worry. 'This one is an observer. Let her be.'

The only observer Enid knew was the Sunday one that was delivered to her doorstep, but if Dierdre said it was okay, then it probably was.

When Priyanthi started toddling, she didn't grab things or pull at tablecloths like other children. Instead, she walked over to whatever caught her attention and just stood there staring. Her intensity unnerved Enid.

She was also a loner. She didn't play much with other children unless it was a game of cricket, preferring to read under the araliya tree. She spent all her pocket money on books. Not the comics that Hemantha read, but proper books. Often Enid would find her reading under her bedclothes, by the light of the torch. She didn't speak unless she was spoken to. But she listened a lot. As a result, she knew more about people than people knew about her.

Six

❧

It was hot, even for August. The mango tree was heavy with fruit. Fruit flies and bees buzzed around the ripe golden globes, feasting on rotting, half-eaten fruit. The banana tree leaned tiredly against the wall in the corner of the garden, sagging under the weight of a huge bunch of still-ripening bananas. Its shiny leaves browned and curled at the edges.

Clusters of araliya flowers and jasmines filled the garden with their heavy, heady fragrance, their petals shielding sleeping, satiated bees from the afternoon heat. Enid's special blue-green grass was overgrown, but she didn't have the heart to tell Banda to mow it. Among its long blades, a tiny wildlife preserve flourished, undisturbed and unthreatened.

Enid had Banda build little wooden frames over her pigeon orchids and covered them with muslin, but the orchids drooped anyway. Every morning, she carefully moved her roses into the shade. Every night, she moved them out again.

Beyond the gate, the tarred road softened in the heat, and its surface grew cracked and tracked.

Inside the house, the fans turned valiantly, but offered little comfort. During the day, Enid fanned herself with a newspaper and the children went around in cotton shorts and shirts. At night, they threw off their thin blankets and opened the windows. They slept and dreamed about Eskimos and icebergs. The price of king coconuts shot up, but Violet still kept a supply at home for Bala and the children to drink. She worried about dehydration. For most of the day, Dierdre lay on the sofa with ice-packs on her forehead. Emmy grumbled as she re-filled ice trays, but stood for longer than necessary in front of the open fridge. It was too hot even to go to the beach.

Mrs Munasinghe went to Nuwara Eliya to visit her sister. Mr Munasinghe decided to surprise her by spring-cleaning the house in her absence. He moved all their belongings out on to the street while he polished the floors and painted the windows in lily-white lacquer. By the time he had finished, the purple flowers on the sofa cushions had faded to a dusty lilac and the tropical fish in their ornamental tank had boiled and now floated belly-up among the plastic weeds and reeds. Mr Munasinghe fortified himself with several arracks before going to the station to fetch his wife.

Dierdre, Violet and Enid stood talking on the road. Occasionally, a little breeze blew in from the sea and they lifted their faces to catch it. Wishing they could pocket it. Bottle it. Dierdre's face was flushed and red. Shiny lines of sweat collected in her neck wrinkles. 'My God, if this keeps up, I'll die,' she declared, wiping her face with a cold, eau-de-cologned towel. 'I had three baths yesterday.'

Violet looked alarmed. 'You mustn't,' she said. 'It's not good for the skin.'

Dierdre laughed. 'I couldn't care less about my skin, child. I'd rather live with bloody ugly skin than die from this heat.'

Enid blew down into the neck of her dress where sweat had pooled between her breasts.

'I feel like taking off all my clothes,' she muttered.

'Better wait for Mr Paul to go inside then,' Dierdre said. Then she looked around. 'What happened to Violet?'

'Don't know. Must have gone inside to see to Nirmala.' She was too hot to care.

Violet appeared with three glasses on a tray. 'Here,' she said.

'Violet, if there was an award for the most thoughtful soul in the whole world, you'd win it,' Dierdre declared, gulping down the cold king coconut water and sighing with pleasure.

Enid drank hers more slowly, savouring the feel of it slipping down her parched throat. She saw Stanley walking down the road and saved half the king coconut water for him. 'Here, you look like you need this.'

Stanley drained the glass, wiped his neck with a sweat-soaked handkerchief, murmured thanks and the two of them went off to their house.

Dierdre looked at her watch. 'Better go and see what that old witch Emmy is up to. Must have cremated the steaks by now. Thanks for the thambili, darling. Real life-saver.' She walked slowly home, ineffectively flapping her handkerchief around her face, trying to generate a breeze, but actually generating nothing more than an aching wrist.

Violet stood at the gate alone. Bala had gone to the market, and although she usually went with him, her head had been aching all day.

She looked up the road and saw a flash of white near the bokku. Must be the children playing. She frowned. Hemantha was going from bad to worse. Yesterday, when she was talking to him, she could have sworn she smelled cigarettes on his breath. She wanted to tell Enid, but didn't know how. She wondered if she should tell Dierdre and let Dierdre tell Enid. But if Enid got to know that she had told Dierdre, she would be upset and no wonder. Dierdre was a kind soul but hadn't earned the nickname Reuter for nothing.

She had carefully sniffed at Niranjan's clothes after he'd gone to bed but thankfully, all they smelled of was grass and armpits. Normal boy smells. Not grown-up cigarette smells.

She had also seen Hemantha looking in a funny way at Radhika Paul, but she told herself she must have been mistaken. The boy was only thirteen, too young to be interested in girls.

She peered towards the bokku. 'Niranjan! Niranjan! Come in, son. Time for dinner.' There was no answer, so she started walking down the road. It was well lit and after all, this was Araliya Gardens. She reached the bokku and looked into the bushes that lined it. 'Boys? Where are you? Time to come in.'

A figure detached itself from the darkness but it wasn't either of the children. It was a man. In the evening gloom she couldn't make out if he was young or old, fat or thin. All she saw was the startled whites of his eyes, and then he was gone, running off in the opposite direction. She heard laughter, looked back down the road and saw the boys coming out of the Senaratnes' house. 'Boys!' she called. 'Where were you? I was looking for you.'

They stopped and waited for her. 'We were looking at Uncle Sena's animal books,' Niranjan said.

She looked closely at him and he looked back at her, his dark eyes wide and innocent. She relaxed. 'Come, let's go. Your father will be back any minute and he'll be angry if he sees you out at this time.'

'*My* father doesn't get angry,' Hemantha said cockily.

She ignored him and frog-marched Niranjan home. Bala came home about half an hour later, his basket bulging. He looked tired and angry.

'Sit down. I'll get you something to drink,' Violet said, feeling guilty that she hadn't gone with him. As if that would have made a difference, although shopping didn't seem quite so tedious when they went together.

'Bloody thieves,' Bala muttered.

Violet moved to stand behind him and started massaging his temples. 'What happened?' she asked quietly.

'Usual thing. Trying to charge the earth for small things. They get away with it too.'

'Any onions?'

'Not one. That woman must be eating the lot herself.'

'Dhal?'

'Only that vile stuff they call dhal. None of the red mysore.'

'Even if they had it, we probably wouldn't be able to afford it,' she said philosophically.

Bala leaned his head right back so he was looking up at her. 'Violet, let's write to Chella and see if he can help us to get to England,' he said suddenly.

Her hands stilled. Her eyes clouded over instantly. 'It'll get better. I'm sure it will,' she said, her voice slightly distant.

He shook his head. 'No. It's only getting worse. There's no

place for us here. I know it and you know it too. I know you're afraid of the move, but it can't be worse than this.' His eyes were gentle but his voice was urgent.

She tried to move away, but he reached for her hand and pulled her round to his lap. 'Bala, Niranjan is still awake,' she protested.

'So what? You're my wife.' She struggled to get up but he refused to let her. 'At least think about it,' he pleaded. 'Think of the children.'

She framed his face in her hands and looked into his eyes, which were red with tiredness and dark with worry. 'I am, I *am* thinking of the children. Of their friends, of their school, of everything they've ever known. That's why I don't want to go. But if you want, I'll think about it.'

* * *

Sometime in the night, Bala suddenly sat up in bed.

Violet woke up too. 'What's wrong?' she murmured.

'I don't know. I thought I heard something. Is the window in the children's room open?'

She sat up. 'No, I closed it. But go and check anyway.'

He came back a few minutes later. 'Nothing. Maybe just an owl or something.'

She looked at him. 'There are no owls here. Maybe you're just fretting, thinking about all these problems. Try and sleep. You have to wake up early.'

They settled down once more, his arm comfortably heavy over her waist. Then they both heard it. A creaking noise that wouldn't have woken them up, had they been asleep.

Bala jumped out of bed and grabbed the torch from the table. 'Come and lock the door behind me. I'm going to see who it is. Don't put on the light.'

'Be careful,' she pleaded and locked the front door. She moved the curtain aside and watched.

She saw the yellow torch beam sweep across their house and over Enid's. Then she heard a shout. 'Ado! Mokada karanné?' Hey, what are you doing?

She opened the window a crack and peered out, trying to see through the darkness. She heard a scuffle and then Bala's voice calling out for Stanley. Within seconds, lights came on in most of the houses around and men spilled out on to the road. Ed, Stanley, Mr Paul, Mr Senaratne, even Mr Munasinghe.

Ignoring Bala's instructions, Violet pulled her housecoat on over her nightie and stepped out. Everyone was talking at the same time.

She saw Bala, gesticulating wildly, his voice loud with anger. 'What happened?' she called out.

'Hora! Hora!' Mr Munasinghe said loudly.

'A thief?' Her hands went up to her cheeks. There had been no robberies down Araliya Gardens since they had moved there. She remembered the man she had seen near the bokku, earlier in the evening.

'Bastard got away,' Bala said grimly.

'Who? Did you see him?' She wrapped her housecoat more securely around her and went to the gate. Now Dierdre and a few other women were emerging.

Bala came over to where she stood. 'Young fellow skulking near Stanley's place.'

There was a loud cry from Enid's house. Enid's voice. 'Oh my God! Oh my God!'

They all rushed in and found her in the spare bedroom, the one her parents slept in when they came to stay. Enid stood frozen in the middle of the room. The vertical iron bars across the window had been bent, probably with a crowbar, making an aperture large enough for a small man to slip through. The tall antique almirah was wide open. An assortment of velvet jewellery boxes lay strewn around the floor, all of them gaping open and empty.

Stanley went white and leaned heavily against the wall. 'Bloody bastard,' he muttered.

Violet hurried over and put her arm around Enid's shoulders. The children had woken up and stood wide-eyed and open-mouthed; Dierdre shepherded them out. 'I'll take them and your two over to my place,' she murmured to Bala. Priyanthi and Hemantha were annoyed at missing all the excitement, but they went. Going anywhere at this time of the night was an adventure. Dierdre hurried back a few minutes later hoping she hadn't missed anything important. Emmy had been told to look after the children.

Stanley still looked dazed. 'I'd better call the police.' He went to the living room to phone. Enid was sobbing softly.

Twenty minutes later, a police jeep screeched to a halt outside No. 9 and two sleepy-looking policemen emerged, tucking rumpled khaki shirts into rumpled shorts. They walked around the outside of the house, exchanged meaningful looks and then came inside to where the little group stood. One of them pulled out a notebook. 'What has been taken?'

'Jewellery,' Enid said in a low voice.

'List?'

Enid gave it. Four gold chains, sixteen bangles, of which four were plain and the rest machine-cut, seven pairs of earrings (four studs, three hoops), one ruby necklace with a matching bracelet, one sapphire choker, three diamond rings.

Dierdre's eyes grew larger with each item. She had had no idea that Enid possessed so much jewellery, that the pretty parquet-floored house had been a treasure trove for so much. That Enid in her poplin dresses and Bata slippers had rubies and sapphires and diamonds. She felt slightly peeved, as if Enid should have told her exactly what she had, item by item.

'Who saw the man?' the policeman asked sternly.

Bala stepped forward. 'I did.'

'Name?'

'T. Balasingham.'

Two heads shot up simultaneously. 'Tamil?'

Bala couldn't stop a challenging note from creeping into his voice. 'Yes. Why?'

The older one stared. 'No reason. Just asking. What were you doing up at this time?'

'I heard something,' Bala replied.

'What?'

'A noise.'

'What kind of a noise?'

'A creaking.'

'And the man was—?'

'A man.'

'Wearing what?'

'A pale shirt, sarong hitched up, he was about twenty-five, dark-skinned, moustache, I think.'

'Tamil?'

Bala stared at the policeman. 'I don't know. He didn't stay to have a conversation.'

'He ran away?'

'No, he came in and had a coffee! Of course he ran away!' Bala wasn't bothering to hide his sarcasm now. Violet wanted to tell him not to lose his temper but she was too afraid to speak. They were acting as if Bala was the criminal.

Stanley stepped in impatiently. 'Officer, don't you want to take fingerprints or something?'

The policeman laughed a little derisively. 'At this time? No, no, fingerprints tomorrow morning. Don't touch anything. Tomorrow morning, we will come back.' He turned to look at Bala. 'Tonight, we will need a statement. At the station.'

Violet looked frightened. 'Now? Can't they come tomorrow morning?'

The policeman shook his head. 'Now.'

Bala shrugged resignedly. 'I'll go and put something on and get the car.'

Ed offered to go with them but Stanley shook his head. 'Thanks, but there's no point in us all going. I'll go and dress and we'll be on our way.'

After the two policemen had left with Bala and Stanley following in Bala's car, Violet, Dierdre and Enid sat talking in Enid's living room. Dierdre went to check on the children and returned with the news that they were fast asleep. Violet sat next to Enid and held her hand. 'Was everything insured?'

Enid nodded. 'I think so.' Her eyes filled with tears. 'Violet, he even took Priyanthi's jewellery, all the things she got when she was born!' She started sobbing again.

Dierdre got up and went to the kitchen to make some cocoa. 'Better not to drink coffee in this state, child. Might never go to sleep.'

They sat and sipped cocoa and talked quietly until they heard the car.

The two men came in looking tired.

'What happened?' Violet asked anxiously.

'Nothing much,' Bala said. 'They took my statement and swore they would get everything back. Officious bastards.'

Stanley and he moved the heavy cupboard across the window so no other nocturnal visitors could get into the house, and then they all went to bed.

Bala fell asleep almost immediately, exhausted by what had happened. Violet stayed awake thinking of what had happened. Wondering if Bala was right after all. She wondered if these things happened in England and Australia, if policemen looked suspiciously at innocent people just because they were Tamils. But the thought of leaving everything familiar to her was frightening too. She sighed, wishing she was brave like Dierdre.

For the next few days, everyone was extra nice to Enid. Dierdre baked one of her infamous crème caramels and brought it over. Violet sent a bunch of king coconuts and some thosas and chutney. Mrs Paul came to chat and commiserate and brought a plate of devilled beef. Everyone was openly sympathetic and covertly envious; news of Enid's extensive jewellery collection had spread.

'See, child, can never tell looking at someone's face, no?' Mrs Senaratne murmured enviously to Mrs Munasinghe.

'Millions of rupees' worth. Never wears anything, though,' Mrs Perera said breathlessly to Mrs Paul.

'Dark horse, our Enid,' Dierdre said to Violet, who smiled and said nothing.

Hemantha had become quite a hero in school. His account of the robbery was far different to what had actually happened. In his version, *he* had seen the thief, grappled with him, and only let go when the thief threatened him with a huge knife, 'this big', extending his arms to their full width. Niranjan marvelled at his friend's ability to so embellish the truth, but didn't contradict his story.

A week after the robbery, Stanley had a call from the police informing him that the thief had been caught and requesting him to bring 'that Tamil chap' to identify him.

The OIC swaggered over to meet them. He was impressed because they lived at Araliya Gardens but wondered if Stanley was mad to put up with a Tamil living next door. Although, admittedly, this one looked educated and spoke well. 'Told you we would catch the scoundrel,' he boasted.

They nodded impatiently.

'Wait here. I'll get him,' the OIC said.

'Better be ready for this,' Stanley warned Bala. 'You know how brutal these police types can be.'

Bala nodded but nothing prepared them for what they saw. The man was kicked in, cringing every time the OIC's boot connected with his back or legs or shoulders. His eye was crusted with dried blood and swollen shut. Both hands were swollen, some of the fingers obviously broken. His bottom lip was neatly split down the middle and the blood which dripped from the cut was fresh. He had a long gash on the back of his head. When he saw them, he prostrated himself at their feet, weeping. 'Sirs, spare me, please. I have given everything to the police. I only took it because my family was starving. Please don't leave me here – they'll kill me!'

There was a sickening crunch as the OIC's boot connected with the man's ribs. 'Kill you? That's too good for vermin like you!' the OIC roared, turning to smile proudly at Stanley and Bala. As if he expected to get a handshake for his handiwork. Or a pat on the back at the very least. After all, no one could brutalise a suspect like he could.

Stanley, who had been staring in horror, finally stepped

forward. 'That's enough,' he said sharply. 'My God! That's enough!'

The OIC stared at him indignantly. 'You think we should treat them like heroes or what? This is the only way to get confessions out of these lying dogs. Anyway, what do you care? You're getting your things back.'

He strode off to his drawer and opened it. In a dirty cloth lay the Silva jewels. He took them out and placed them triumphantly on the table. 'Can't give them to you yet,' he said. 'Must file a case and all. Get him at least ten years.' He turned to Bala. 'Just identify him and we'll do the rest.'

Bala looked at him, his lip curling in disgust. He shot Stanley a look and said, 'I can't.'

The OIC looked up sharply. 'What?'

'I can't identify him,' Bala said clearly. 'Look at his face! Even his mother couldn't identify him.'

'How to file the case then?' the OIC demanded, looking like a sulky child who had just been told he couldn't have any sweets.

'Well, you should have thought of that before you went to work on him,' Bala replied calmly, although his eyes were black with rage.

Stanley had never felt so proud of his friend. He walked over to the table. 'Well, maybe someone else stole these and gave them to this man to sell or something. In any case, without a proper identification you can't file anything, so I'll just take these and go home.'

The OIC sank back in his chair, took off his sweat-stained cap and threw it on the table. 'It's because of people like you that we can't keep law and order in this country,' he said angrily. 'First you come crying to us, then you want to be like Gandhi. Just take the lot and that piece of shit over there and get out.'

Stanley started to say something, but Bala caught his eye and nodded towards the door. No point in getting into an argument with this scum, he was saying. Stanley started gathering up the jewellery. Suddenly he stopped. 'The ring.'

The man on the floor looked up fearfully. 'Sir, it's all there. I swear it on my children's heads!'

The OIC looked shifty. 'Ring? There are two rings there.'

Stanley walked over and placed his hands on the table. 'There were three. Three diamond rings. My wife's engagement ring is missing. I want it back,' he softly.

The OIC jumped up. 'You see? He kept the ring,' he said triumphantly. 'Told us that this was everything, but obviously he was lying. What do you expect from dog shit like this!'

'I don't think so,' Stanley said, still speaking very softly, 'but if you insist, we can take this matter up with DIG Gunathillake, who is a *very* good friend of mine.'

The OIC looked hunted. A sudden sheen of sweat appeared on his forehead. He went back to his table and started rummaging around. 'Let's see – if he brought it in, then it must be with the other things. Unless it somehow fell out of the cloth.'

Bala and Stanley waited. They saw the OIC's hand sliding into his open drawer, then emerging. He pretended to pick up something from the table. 'Here it is! Must have fallen out,' he said with a forced smile.

Stanley took it from him and walked out. He paused by the man on the floor. 'Get a job. Or beg. It's better than this,' he said.

They stood outside, breathing in the fresh air gratefully. 'I'd kill for a stiff drink right now but we'd better get this stuff home,' Stanley said.

Bala nodded.

Enid was ecstatic about getting her jewellery back. Neither Stanley nor Bala told anyone about what had happened at the police station. Not even Ed. What was the point?

That evening, they sat on Stanley's lawn and drank steadily until late. But even the alcohol couldn't erase the memory of what they had seen that afternoon.

SEVEN

❦

Bala got his promotion. He was now Head of the English Department at St Mark's. Whatever that meant. The three-hundred-rupee pay rise that accompanied the promotion had disappointed him bitterly, but when he had brought it up with the Headmaster, all he got was a vague reply about pay scales and inflation.

'It's a disappointment,' Bala said.

'It's a good salary,' the Headmaster countered. For a Tamil. He didn't say it, but Bala heard it anyway. He left the room, his jaw clenched. He had waited three years for this promotion. Now it felt like a slap in the face. He was almost tempted to refuse it, but the three hundred rupees took precedence over pride.

Prices were going up almost daily. Going to the market was like a nightmare, one the entire country went through every day. Bargaining had become a means of saving a few cents, not the good-natured sport it had once been. These days, shop-keepers and stall owners got angry if a customer tried to bring a price down. If it's too expensive, don't buy it, they said with surly attitudes.

Violet was also disappointed about Bala's rise, but didn't say anything for fear Bala would bring up the subject of emigrating again. Although even she had to admit that it was tough. School fees, clothes for the children, food and electricity bills ate up all her housekeeping money. It had been months since they had gone out to eat. Even a hot dog at Fountain Café was a luxury they couldn't afford. Now she was thinking of letting her servant go, because her thirty-rupee salary could be put to better use.

It pained her that she couldn't afford to give Niranjan money for an occasional trip to the cinema with his friends. Although he never asked. It didn't help that Hemantha came over and flaunted his pocket money in Niranjan's face. 'Look, Nira, my grandmother sent me ten bucks! I'm going to see a film. Get some money and let's go!'

Niranjan would make some excuse, but Violet saw him looking longingly at the money.

Niranjan was sixteen and at an age when he had started noticing girls. All his friends had girlfriends, although all that meant was having long conversations on the telephone, going once in a while to see a film and meeting at bus stands after tuition classes. All of which cost money – not a lot, but when you had a girlfriend, you had to buy her a bottle of cold Portello on a hot day. At least.

Since Niranjan didn't have any money of his own, he was forced to defer the girlfriend situation temporarily, but it still rankled. Hemantha kept teasing him and saying that maybe he didn't like girls and liked boys instead, but Hemantha didn't have Niranjan's financial problems. Hemantha's parents doled out money to him whenever he wanted it, although Auntie Enid obviously knew about the smoking and all.

What she didn't know was that recently, Hemantha had started going in the evenings to the Perlyn for a beer with his junction friends. On those days, he told his parents he was going to stay over at a friend's house so they didn't smell the alcohol on his breath when he came home. Niranjan had been invited to go along, but he didn't like the junction boys. They were rough types who got into brawls and walked behind girls making vulgar comments.

* * *

Niranjan was tall and thin. His mother kept telling people he would fill out soon, even though no one asked, and fed him copious quantities of curd and milk to speed up the process. He was a handsome boy with dark eyes and a shock of dark curly hair. His smile was his best feature. It came suddenly like the sun from behind a cloud, and made his quiet face come to life. Unlike Hemantha, who wore denim bell bottoms so long that they raised clouds of dust when he walked, Niranjan dressed neatly. Shirt, slacks and his slightly worn leather shoes. Violet liked him to look 'decent and presentable' and he hadn't really minded until the day he heard Kamini telling someone that she thought boys in bell bottoms were cute.

That put quite a different complexion on things.

Kamini Saverimuttu went to St Mary's and was what the boys called 'a bomb bit'. She had long curly hair, dancing brown eyes and a huge smile. She also had the largest breasts Niranjan had seen on a fifteen-year-old. If he had a choice in girlfriends, he would have chosen her instantly. But not as things were. To be Kamini's boyfriend, one had to have money for weekly cinema trips, cold Portellos every other day and even a taxi ride or two when she finished tuition classes late and missed her bus.

The Saverimuttus lived in a huge house down Bullers Road and had a bevy of servants and pedigree dogs. Kamini's parents were quite liberal and allowed their daughter to go out with her friends as long as she was home by eight p.m. She was allowed to bring them home, both boys and girls, and as long as they didn't drink or swear, they could swim in the pool or watch films on their projector.

At Kamini's, Hemantha behaved in an exemplary manner, not only because his father knew Jay Saverimuttu slightly but also because he was trying to win favour with Kamini. So were all the other boys who fought to carry her books, buy her Portellos and earn a smile from her. Niranjan didn't even attempt to get into the running, but worshipped Kamini from afar. Occasionally she teased him for being so quiet and he blushed. When she tossed her hair or walked close to him, he could smell the delicate perfume she wore. It made him faint with longing.

He wasn't the only one. At tuition class, Mr Mendis would stop in mid-sentence when she swayed in late, give her a weak smile and wonder if he could persuade her to come to his house for some extra lessons. Hemantha's approach was more direct. 'Looking bomb today,' he would say, his eyes unashamedly roving over her curves. She'd give him a coy look and say, 'Chee, Hemantha! Don't say things like that aney!' in a voice that really said 'Don't stop saying things like that.' When Hemantha slipped his arm about her waist and stroked her hips, she slipped away saying, 'Don't do that, Hema! I'll get angry with you.' She pouted her full glistening lips and teased him with her eyes.

Despite her adult figure, grown-up clothes and liberal parents, Kamini didn't really follow through with all the promises she made with her eyes. Although she allowed her current boyfriend, whoever it was, to hold her hand, kiss her and feel her back while slow-dancing, she didn't permit more. While she loved her obvious power over the opposite sex and the frissons of excitement she felt when one of them kissed her long and lingeringly, Kamini was from a good family, which meant that she was expected to maintain a reasonably good reputation so her parents could find her a good match when the time came. She was also expected to be a virgin on her wedding night, which was a lot to expect from an eager fifteen-year-old with the body of a goddess, but that was the way things were. Nice girls didn't get deflowered before their wedding nights, and even then were expected to hate the experience. Everyone knew that.

So while Niranjan didn't get to realise his Kamini fantasies, he was pretty sure no one else realised theirs either. There was some comfort to be gained from knowing that.

* * *

One evening in July, Stanley rushed in after work, dumped his briefcase, pulled off his tie, dropped his navy blue blazer on a chair and hurried out again. Enid followed him, wondering

75

what all the fuss was about. Stanley leaned over the wall. 'Bala! Bala!'

Enid came to stand next to him. 'What on earth are you yelling for? You'll disturb the whole road.'

Bala appeared at his front door. 'Where's the fire?' he said, grinning. 'Or is Enid having another baby that we didn't know about?'

'Superb news, man!' Stanley said excitedly. 'Remember I was telling you about the Ceylon Foods bungalow down in Bentota? The place all the top executives stay at?'

Bala nodded.

'Well, I was just having a chat with Mr McGregor about how expensive it was to take a holiday these days and he offered to let me use it for a week next month! I didn't even have to ask!'

Bala beamed. 'That's excellent news, Stan,' he said. 'You certainly deserve a break. Enid and the kids too.'

Stanley grinned broadly. 'I think you deserve a break too – you and Violet and *your* kids.'

Bala stared. 'What do you mean?'

'There are four bedrooms and a cook to do all the work – more than enough for both our families. You can get a week off, can't you?'

Violet, who had drifted out, could scarcely contain her excitement. 'Do you mean it? We can go with you?'

'Of course. I checked and they said it was no problem!'

Violet turned to look at Bala, her eyes shining. 'Can you get a week off? You're due so much leave. We didn't even take a vacation last year.'

Bala nodded. 'I'll get it. One way or another.'

Stanley reached out over the wall, grabbed Bala's hand and shook it enthusiastically. 'Good man. We'll have a great time together. Imagine ... swim all day and drink toddy all night!'

The women moved away a little to talk.

'I hope Priyanthi can still get into her swimsuit,' Enid said worriedly. 'She's suddenly started filling out.'

'We'd better do a trip down to Cargills or Millers before we go. Get some nice food to take with us,' said Violet.

Enid stared. 'Cargills or Millers? Violet, it costs the earth to shop there. Only the diplomats go there!'

Violet smiled. 'I was saving for train tickets to Jaffna – I thought we could at least go and see my family. But now, since we're going with you, I can afford to spend some of it.'

When the children were told about the proposed trip, their reactions varied. Priyanthi was pleased because she saw a whole week of sitting on the beach and reading. Hemantha was less than enthusiastic. At sixteen, a family holiday wasn't his idea of fun. Besides, imagine a whole week of not seeing Kamini! What if she decided to find a boyfriend while he was away? Niranjan was a little more enthusiastic, although he too wondered how he would survive a week without Kamini. Nirmala was thrilled. She loved going to the beach and the prospect of spending a whole week there was exciting. Although she didn't exactly know how long a week was.

When Dierdre got to know about the trip, she was happy for them, but crestfallen that she wasn't going.

'The busy season has started. Ed will never be able to go,' she said sadly, ignoring the fact that no one had actually invited them.

Unlike Stanley's and Bala's families, they often went on trips with their friends. Every April, they went up to Nuwara Eliya for the season and came back full of gossip, stories and strawberries. Every July, they went down south for a week, usually staying at one of the posh tourist hotels that lined the coast. They brought back mangosteens, brooms, mats and sunburn.

* * *

Two days before they were to leave for their holiday, Enid and Violet took the bus into the Fort, Colombo's main shopping district. They left at about 9.30 a.m. to avoid the office rush, but the buses were still crowded. They pushed their way through the jam of passengers and strap-hung until Bambalapitiya, when two seats became vacant at the very front of the bus. They sank down gratefully and talked about what they were going to buy.

At Kollupitiya, more people boarded the bus. The two women were still going over their shopping list when they heard a cough near them. A saffron-robed Buddhist priest stood by the seat, his begging bowl concealed under his robes. Although he was looking away, his black umbrella tapped impatiently on the floor of the bus. The small sign beside the seat said *Reserved for Clergy*.

'Oh bother,' Enid muttered. 'Why did he have to get into this bus?'

They both stood up and moved back into the throng of sweaty people. The bikkhu took their seat without thanks. With an air of ownership. Violet couldn't help the shaft of anger that shot through her. *Reserved for Clergy* meant reserved for Buddhist clergy. No one gave Catholic priests the same privileges. Or Hindu priests, for that matter.

The bus finally stopped at Fort and they alighted. The streets were crowded with office workers and shoppers, and lined with stalls selling everything from toys to clothes. Here, he who shouted loudest sold. People argued and haggled, cars and buses honked impatiently, and loud music blared out from street-side restaurants. The noise was deafening. It was like a mad, colourful Tower of Babel.

They took a while to find Cargills' discreet entrance, literally fighting their way through the covered walkways, trying not to step on the cheap wristwatches and plastic toys that were displayed on mats. Something brushed roughly against Violet's bottom and she swung round in time to see a well-dressed middle-aged man rushing past, eyeing her furtively. She almost told Enid and then decided not to. She felt guilty all day. As if *she* had invited the man to touch her.

Cargills was like a pocket of quietness in a sea of complete confusion. Music played quietly, gentle remakes of popular hits, quietly efficient shop assistants hid in corners and materialised magically at the slightest hint of confusion on a customer's face, imported goods sent out their quietly expensive smells, luring unsuspecting people into their exorbitantly priced, discreetly packaged traps.

Enid and Violet padded through the store, trying not to look too intimidated by their surroundings or too shocked at the price tags on the cheese, chocolates, Nescafé and imported alcohol. The quiet shop assistants flicked their eyes over them, expertly (and inaccurately) summed them up instantly as window-shoppers not real shoppers, and dismissed them. Quiet questions raising quiet brows. Quiet scorn on quiet faces. Quietly concealed looks and unkind smiles. Not quiet enough.

'Let's go to Millers,' Violet suggested weakly, slightly desperately. Enid agreed with alacrity. At Millers, it was the same. But now that they were here, they decided to brave out the quietness and get on with what they had come to do. They conferred in whispers and finally went to the cash register carrying their treasures, trying not to look worried, trying to look blasé. As if it was normal for them to shop here. As if they did it all the time. As if they were surprised that they were not remembered.

The cashier looked a little pitying as he rang up their purchases: one large packet of Kraft cheese looking smug and imported in its blue cardboard box, one small bottle of Nescafé and a bottle of Black & White whisky for the men. This last cost more than Violet spent on groceries for the whole month, but the thought of the men's surprise and pleasure made her pick it up decisively.

They made their way through the foot traffic and went to the Pagoda for lunch, wincing at what a few Chinese rolls cost, but determined to make the most of this rare trip into town. Ordinarily, they shopped at Dehiwala junction, venturing to the Wellawatte market area for special things like Christmas cake ingredients.

It took forty-five minutes for the bus to arrive, and when it came eventually, it was already full. This time, they had to stand all the way back to Dehiwala, turning their faces away from sour-smelling armpits and suggestive looks. A bald man in a sarong came to stand behind Violet and threw himself against her every time the bus lurched a little. Why me? she wondered despairingly. She moved away and he followed her. Enid saw and came to stand between them, staring angrily at the man until he dropped his eyes and moved off.

'Perverts,' she muttered.

'Yes, child, what to do. Always rubbing and trying to touch,' said a woman in a sari standing next to them.

Enid looked away. No use in getting into bus conversations with strange people. She tightened her grip on her handbag. Colombo was full of pickpockets, sometimes operating in pairs. One person struck up a conversation, and while the victim's attention was held, the other slid his hand into her handbag, relieving her of her purse.

At Wellawatte a thin little beggar boy boarded the bus. He had a little rabana, a drum, which he started playing with his knuckles while singing a sad song about his father who had walked out on the family, his mother who had TB and his seven brothers and sisters who were starving and too weak to walk. After the song, he turned his drum over into a makeshift hat and walked slowly through to the front of the bus, collecting a few cents here and a few insults there. When he reached Enid and Violet, he summed them up in a second, ignored Enid and turned his sad, empty-eyed gaze on Violet. She started fumbling in her purse.

Enid looked incredulously at her. 'You don't really believe his sob story, do you? He's probably being paid by someone to do this!'

Violet pulled out fifty cents. 'I don't care. He's so sweet.'

Enid sighed. Violet looked so trusting, she was an automatic target for every con man. The little beggar boy reached the front of the bus just as it stopped near the Roxy Cinema in Wellawatte. At the top of the steps, he paused and looked back at the passengers. His face lit up in a mischievous grin. 'My father is at home, my mother's fine and my sisters and brothers ate so much today that they were sick!' he sang out, and hopped off smartly as the bus pulled away.

Most of the passengers dissolved into laughter, although some of them cursed loudly and wished all kinds of terrible fates on him. Enid looked grim, but Violet just smiled and shrugged. 'My intentions were good.'

* * *

They planned to leave no later than 7.30 a.m. on Saturday morning. Rather than take an assortment of small bags, Enid and Violet decided to take a large suitcase each with all the family's clothes in it. For once, Priyanthi was allowed to pack what she wanted, although Enid insisted that she take at least one dress, just in case.

'Just in case what?' Priyanthi demanded mutinously, and got a quelling look back. She scowled and subsided.

They also packed sheets, towels and pillow cases because, as Enid said, 'God knows who slept on them before us. Maybe even English people.'

Violet shuddered and slipped a bottle of Dettol into her suitcase for sterilising things.

Hemantha was angry. This was his last night at Kamini's. At least for a whole week. And he had been ordered home at eight. His father curtly told him that if he didn't come home then, the doors would be locked, and since they were leaving early in the morning, he would have to find somewhere to stay for the time they were away. And although Hemantha had a lot of acquaintances, he had no real friends who would put him up, or put up with him, for more than a night at most. So he came home at eight and went straight to bed.

Niranjan didn't go to Kamini's that evening. When Violet asked why he was not going out, he murmured something about being tired. The truth was he had wanted to go, but didn't want to get into a goodbye competition with Hemantha, although Kamini would probably have forgotten to say goodbye to him anyway. She hardly noticed him and he didn't really mind. In fact, he welcomed her indifference, because it was easier to respond to. The few times she did speak to him, he was so consumed with shyness that he mumbled inanities and got laughed at by her and the others.

He was restless. He imagined Hemantha and Kamini kissing and saying their goodbyes and scowled. He went outdoors, leaned on the gate trying to think of other things, but he kept coming stubbornly back to Kamini. He listened to the evening noises. Muted traffic in one ear, faint bass ocean sounds in the other, making up a weird stereophonic overture to evening that the mosquitoes and cicadas embellished with their own violins and horns. What was it like, he wondered, never to be still?

'It's beautiful, isn't it?'

He looked around startled, and saw Priyanthi standing at her gate, her face a study of light and dark. The evening gloom and the intrusive neon of the street light.

'What?' he said blankly.

'The sky. Look at those colours.'

He looked up. It was quite beautiful, pastel pinks and blues suddenly streaked with violent gold or red. As if it couldn't quite decide what colour to be. Like a huge painted ceiling to the world. A gigantic Sistine Chapel that required no Michelangelo.

'I love this time of evening,' she said reflectively. 'It's as if the whole world gets quiet before night falls.'

• He smiled. 'That's quite poetic, Priyanthi,' he said.

She stared at him through the indistinct light of evening. 'Are you making fun of me?'

'No,' he protested. 'I really meant it.'

She turned. 'Anyway, I have to go. See you tomorrow.'

'Priyanthi.'

She turned back. 'What?' Her tone was not encouraging.

'Nothing,' he muttered, feeling stupid. Why had he called her back like that? As if he had something important to tell her? Now she'd *really* think he was odd.

He had heard her once speaking to Auntie Dierdre, who was

asking her why she spent so much time alone. 'I know your brother is never home, but why not play with Niranjan, dear?'

Priyanthi had twisted her mouth in that way that irritated her grandmother so much. 'I don't know. He's a bit odd,' she'd said.

Niranjan had been crouching on the other side of the wall, weeding the border. He stayed down until he heard them walking back to the house, surprised at how hurt he felt. He didn't think *she* was odd. She was just – young. She was three years younger than he was, which made her only thirteen. Still a child. He liked her but he hardly noticed her. Not with voluptuous fifteen-year-old Kamini taking up most of his time and thoughts.

He didn't think he was odd either. The next evening when he was at Kamini's house with the rest of their friends, he had wanted to ask her if *she* thought he was odd. She would probably have said yes. And Hemantha wouldn't have given him any peace after that. So he worried about his oddness, but quietly.

Priyanthi walked into the house, trying not to feel as if she had revealed something private about herself. She wondered why she had even got into a conversation with Niranjan. He was nice enough but he was her brother's friend. Not hers. He didn't come right out of the blue and tell her how beautiful the sky was. They didn't have that kind of closeness. So why had she? She mentally kicked herself for opening her mouth. Loneliness did strange things. Loosened tongues, let down guards.

Priyanthi read voraciously and had the gift of being able to appreciate the beauty around that most people took for granted. Hemantha had once found her gazing with awe at a sliver of sunlight that had somehow found its way inside the house and slashed a path of light on the dark mahogany sideboard. He asked her what she was doing. Three times. She shushed him. As if his voice would frighten the sunbeam away.

Her thoughts, too, were deep and layered. Usually she kept

them to herself. Hemantha wasn't exactly the kind of person who could silently appreciate a sunset. Or a moonrise. Her mother was always busy and so was her father, although she had once heard him sigh with pleasure at the sight of a particularly twilight sky. She thought it was a sigh of pleasure, but it could equally have been a sigh of tiredness. He worked hard.

She longed to talk to someone about a book she was reading, or a thought she was thinking, or a dream she was dreaming. But there was no one. Only Auntie Dierdre seemed to understand, but once she started talking, she wouldn't shut up. She'd go from the sky to aeroplanes, to England, to the cost of living, and Priyanthi would end up wondering, bewildered, what they had been talking about in the first place.

EIGHT

❦

They left at 8.30, much later than planned, because a whole hour was spent trying to fit their things into the boot of Bala's car.

'What do they have in here? The bloody kitchen sink?' Bala demanded, his arms straining to hold up a bulging suitcase.

'No, the whole bloody kitchen,' Stanley replied, wiping sweat off his upper lip with his already damp shirt sleeve. 'Look at the state of us – we haven't gone anywhere and we're already exhausted.'

Ed walked over to say goodbye and grinned when he saw the luggage. 'Moving to Bentota for good, I see.'

'Easy for you to laugh,' Stanley said sourly. 'Give us a hand, if you want to be useful.'

Ed obligingly lifted a suitcase and promptly put it down again. 'My God! Have they got the kitchen sink in here?'

'Two,' Bala said succinctly, while Stanley tried unsuccessfully to shut the boot. Every time he thought he had, it flew up and stayed open, like a huge laughing mouth.

Bala's second-hand Plymouth was built to take four people comfortably, five if they didn't mind getting squeezed a bit. After parties, he had even managed six and a child. Eight was a record. He drove. Stanley sat in the front seat with Nirmala on his lap. Hemantha and Niranjan had commandeered the two window seats at the back, and between them, Violet, Enid and Priyanthi sat packed like sardines in a too-small can. Priyanthi was in the middle, right in between the two front seats. She had to sit forward so they all had space. Her feet rested uncomfortably on the raised ridge on the floor of the car and her knees were almost touching her chin. Bala drove safely but fast and every time he hit the brakes she had to clutch at the backs of the two seats to stop herself from catapulting into the front, and out through the windscreen. The area between her shoulder blades ached punishingly and the back of her neck was already going stiff.

This many people in one car wasn't unusual in a country where only a tiny percentage of the population could afford any means of private transport. In fact, the same thing happened in rural areas, only on bullock carts, which could take up to fifteen, especially if they were going to a musical show or a play. A tractor (minus trailer) could take six. A bicycle could take four or five people on it if they were relatively small. People hung and clung and struggled to stay on, and although it was technically against the law, the police usually looked the other way, unless there was an accident or someone did fall off. After all, they were in the same boat too, carrying their wives and children on their official bicycles when they were off-duty. Wealthy motorists in their luxury cars screamed abuse at the overcrowded vehicles or snorted derisively as they thundered by.

But this was the Galle Road, the highway leading south. Here there were no bullock carts and tractors, just a raggedy mélange of Morris Minors, Volkswagens, Plymouths and Datsuns, most of them completely unroadworthy. The trees on the side of the road were coated with a grey layer of dust and smog.

Priyanthi sighed and wished she could have sat by one of the windows. They were in Ratmalana now and she was intensely curious to see what they were passing, but her view was limited to a narrow gap between two beefy shoulders and Nirmala's hair, which was tied on top of her head with a red satin ribbon which further obstructed Priyanthi's view.

There were fewer houses in this area than in Dehiwala, but more coconut trees. People hurried about their Saturday business wearing colourful reddhas and harried expressions.

They drove past a pola where vegetable and fruit vendors, people selling clay cooking pots and coconut shell spoons, peanut and sweet vendors, shoe-makers, knife sharpeners and self-proclaimed spiritual healers fought a vocal battle to drown each other out.

The spoils of war were a sale.

They drove into Moratuwa where another pola was in progress. Same noise. Same war. In the front of the car, Nirmala tucked her head in Stanley's armpit and went to sleep. It was an armpit she knew, for it was one she had fallen asleep in many times before. The smell of Stanley's Old Spice aftershave mingled with a faint odour of perspiration and her little nostrils twitched in response. Her eyelashes fluttered gently like soft dark moths.

Stanley and Bala talked quietly about Bentota and the south. Their conversation was vivacious and slightly urgent. Like tourists taking crash courses in culture, history and politics so as not to offend the locals.

In the back seat, Hemantha looked out at the coconut trees and wished he was back in Colombo at Kamini's place. Today was Saturday, and after tuition, they usually spent a few hours sitting on her boundary wall and chatting idly. But this was August, so there was no school and no tuition. Still, that didn't stop Kamini's little bevy of admirers from coming to visit her every evening.

Niranjan looked at the coconut trees on his side of the road and wondered what Priyanthi was thinking. She had given him a funny look and muttered a greeting when they had met that morning. Beyond that, she hadn't spoken. To anyone. He didn't know why it bothered him so much. So suddenly. It must have been due to yesterday and the ambiguous note on which they had parted. He had noticed her this morning like he never usually did. The cotton printed shorts and matching top had registered, as had the sock-less tennis shoes. He had also realised that she had hair that looked slightly red in the sunlight. He grimaced. No wonder she thought he was odd.

* * *

87

Violet and Enid were quiet. They had woken up before Mr Munasinghe's insomniac cockerel and had gone to bed late the night before. Now they tried to stay awake, remembering things to do, things to get, things to check, things to remember. Despite the lullaby of the car engine, the murmur of the men's voices and the gentle motion of the car, the housewife part of them stayed determinedly awake. Grimly alert. As if going to sleep would lose them housewife points.

Priyanthi wondered what they were thinking. Probably going over their things-to-do-today-and-for-the-rest-of-the-week lists, she guessed accurately.

She looked over at Hemantha. He was squinting out of the window, looking at countless coconut trees he wasn't counting. Or even seeing. Must be thinking about Kamini, she thought. Although personally, she didn't understand why. Kamini had always been nice to her, probably because she was Hemantha's little sister, she thought cynically, but she was so – *obvious*. She reminded Priyanthi of Radhika Paul. Pretty girls didn't need to flaunt what they had, but it was almost only pretty girls that did. The plainer ones, the ones who should have been swaying their less obvious backsides and making-up their less interesting faces, didn't. Odd.

She didn't have to look at Niranjan to wonder what he was thinking. He'd been brooding because she had hardly said a word to him since they started off. She didn't see why she should. It wasn't as if they spent hours talking or anything. It was optimistic of him to expect a conversation today, on the basis of a non-conversation yesterday. Especially after what he'd implied. That she was a thinker or something.

* * *

Bala turned round to look at his back-seat passengers. 'Well? Aren't you lot going to get out?'

They looked around. The car was stopped in front of a street-side café. Hotel de Paris in the middle of the Panadura junction. They got out looking crushed and crumpled. Stretching like newborns.

Inside the café, it looked even less like Paris. Six tables, all completely different from each other, and an assortment of chairs, ranging from what looked like a genuine antique to a stained white plastic garden chair. A large sign on the wall proudly proclaimed the menu:

Cutless
Bred
Stringhoppers and sambol
Hoppers and sambol
Egg Hoppers and Curry
Cheese Omlett
Fish Omlett
Egg Omlett
Bisteak
Soups: Onion, Peas, Beas
Fresh Tea
Fresh Coffee
Ice Coffee
Lenom Juce, Lime Juce

Priyanthi read it and grinned. The Egg Omlett made her laugh out loud. She looked over and saw Niranjan reading the menu too, a similar grin on his face. Hemantha glanced at it as he walked by but didn't seem to see anything wrong with it.

The place smelled of fresh bread and the thick, slightly bitter aroma of Harischandra coffee. The mudalali beamed. Colombo folk, he told himself, mentally rubbing his hands together and adding a Colombo tax to his Panadura prices. 'Ah, Mahattaya, what can we get you this morning?'

Stanley beamed back, quite willing to play the Colombo gentleman in exchange for some preferential treatment. He looked around the little group. 'What shall we have?'

Enid was busy checking to see if there were any flies. There weren't. In spite of its humble decor, the place was spotlessly clean. 'You order.'

Stanley looked at Bala, who nodded. 'Go ahead.'

'We'll have some coffee, some fresh bread and – what cutlets do you have?'

'Fish. Just fried. By my wife,' the mudalali said. As if that meant anything to them. His wife could very well have been a rotten cook. Like Dierdre.

'Right. Bring us a plate. And some kimbula buns for the children.'

Priyanthi grimaced. She hated kimbula buns with their crocodile look and sugary surface which melted into a sticky mess in no time at all.

They sat at the largest table, which was covered with newspaper. Enid examined her chair before she sat down, but other than an ancient tomato sauce stain sunk deep into the wood, it looked clean enough. Five minutes later, the coffee arrived in a dented aluminium pitcher, with six chipped cups. It was strong, milky and sweet. The bread, when it came, was crusty on the outside, cotton soft on the inside, and the cutlets were steaming and peppery. It was one of the best meals they had had. Even the kimbula buns were fresh and still crunchy, not limp and soggy like the ones the roll man brought round in his bicycle box every evening. They wiped their hands on the carefully torn squares of newspaper which served as napkins, just like the hundreds of labourers and office clerks did after they had their hot bread, cutlet and coffee breakfasts.

The men lit up a Gold Leaf each while Hemantha gazed longingly at the packet. He had a packet in his bag, but he didn't dare sneak off and smoke. In the close confines of the car, someone was sure to smell the tobacco on his breath.

While the men smoked and the mothers talked, Priyanthi pulled out her book and started reading. Niranjan could see the cover from where he sat. It was called *Jalna* by Mazo de la Roche, obviously old and much-read. Who the hell was Mazo de la Roche and what was Jalna? It sounded vaguely Indian. He wished he read more.

Hemantha wandered off and struck up a conversation with the mudalali, who wanted to know where they were from, what his father did, where he went to school, whose car it was and everything else. Hemantha told him that they were from Colombo 7, the car belonged to his father, who was the top man at Ceylon Foods, and that he was starting university in England soon.

'Ceylon Foods?' the mudalali repeated, impressed. 'We order sausages and bacon from there.' He mentally added a further wealth tax to their total.

When they called for the bill, Stanley was surprised. 'Just shows,' he said, 'inflation even in these parts.'

Bala snorted. 'What inflation! This bugger obviously saw the car and saw "suckers" written all over us.'

Even so, it was still cheap in comparison to what they would have spent in Colombo, although they wouldn't have thought to stop at a wayside café in the city. Middle- and upper-class people didn't eat at wayside cafés and restaurants in the city. Unless, of course, it was after an evening out at one of Colombo's fancy nightclubs, when slightly tipsy men needed something to soak up the alcohol before they went home and the women craved a kadé koththu after the dancing and Babycham. But even then, they went to certain cafés, places declared suitable for occasional slumming. They sat outside in their cars, listened to pop music, and ate koththu roti with forks.

* * *

They reached Kalutara and stopped at the Kalutara Temple to put a few coins into the pin katé, the alms box, which apparently would ensure that the rest of their journey continued safely. The temple's huge white stupa gleamed softly in the morning sun, and the bo tree near by rustled in that peculiar way bo trees do – each heart-shaped leaf on its slim, long stem rustling individually as the breeze blew through. The thousands of rustling leaves created a tinkling sound, like music. It was a peaceful place, with its floral offerings, flickering oil lamps and bare-footed, saffron-robed monks. Somewhere along the way, the Kalutara Temple had been adopted by Christians and

Hindus, who also stopped to pray and deposit money in its alms box.

'Put this in the box and say a prayer for all of us,' Enid instructed Hemantha, giving him two rupee coins.

He jumped out, and when he was out of their sight, pocketed one of the coins, shoved the other into the box, muttered a prayer for Kamini to miss him fiercely and ran back.

'Did you say a prayer for our safety?' Enid demanded.

He scowled. 'No, only for mine,' he retorted, which wasn't far off the truth. He worked his way into a comfortable position, ignoring the annoyed look Priyanthi was giving him.

'Will you stop wriggling?' she finally cried in exasperation. 'I'll be on the floor soon.'

'Sorry,' he said unrepentantly.

'I want to read in peace,' she said.

'You'd better stop reading,' her brother said, grinning. 'You might turn into one of those mad genius types.'

'I'm not mad!' she said hotly.

'I didn't say you were mad. I said you might *become* mad,' he said.

'Children!' Enid flapped a hand weakly. 'It's too crowded in here to quarrel.'

'We're talking, Amma,' Hemantha said. 'There's a difference.'

'I was talking. You were spoiling for a fight,' Priyanthi retorted.

'Enough, you two,' Stanley snapped suddenly from the front seat.

They both subsided, Hemantha still grinning and Priyanthi scowling.

Niranjan, who had watched the argument with interest, turned back to his window. He thought Hemantha was a bully, even with his sister, but it was none of his business. Priyanthi was Hemantha's sister. If he wanted to bully her, it was between them. Still, he couldn't stop the slow anger that simmered somewhere in him.

The road ran alongside the rail tracks now, the same rail tracks which ran past Araliya Gardens. Beyond the rail tracks were coconut trees. Beyond the coconut trees were huge black rocks placed there to stop erosion. A futile effort really, because it still happened. Beyond the rocks was sand, pale gold and inviting from this distance, probably littered with shit from closer up. Dog shit from the dozens of stray dogs which roamed the beaches, and human shit from the fisher children, who didn't have toilets and who came to the beach each morning, squatted unconcernedly and relieved themselves, then pranced straight into the water to play, swim and wash up. Sometimes.

At this early hour, the fishing boats were lined up on the shore, their rust-coloured sails billowing gently like ball gowns. Beyond the sand was the sea. Calm and pale, silvery blue, with scarcely a ripple marring its smooth surface. It hid its treachery well. Here and there, a few fishermen repaired nets and sat in groups to talk. About the price of fish? About the sea? About their boats? Who knew. The other fishermen lay sleeping inside their mud huts, the sea breezes blowing pleasantly over their sunburned, aching limbs.

Stalls broke the monotony of the roadside. Baskets, mats and brooms. Mangosteens. Hats. Pots. Clusters of king coconuts like orange orbs.

They whizzed past, Enid and Violet gazing longingly at the displays, exchanging meaningful looks, tacit promises to stop on the way home.

A coconut tree bent over the road like a ballerina doing a particularly difficult arabesque. Another tree had bark which looked like a corkscrew, spiralling straight upwards. Niranjan even spotted twins. Two coconut trees growing out of a single base. It looked grotesque. An aberration of nature which should have been cut down long ago, but had been kept because of its use as a landmark.

'Go past the pointed rock and keep walking until you see the two-headed coconut tree.'

Niranjan stuck his head out and twisted his neck to see the tops of the trees. There were so many of them, they formed a kind of canopy overhead. The coconuts sat in green and gold bunches under the leaves, some with pale gold flowers that sprouted out like fireworks. Then he saw something else. Ropes. Connecting the coconut trees. For what?

He wanted to ask but he didn't. His father or Uncle Stanley would have probably answered him and even been pleased at his interest, but Hemantha would only laugh. And Priyanthi would think he was odd. So he said nothing, but shaded his eyes with his hand and stared upwards intently. Ropes. For what?

* * *

'It's here somewhere,' Stanley was saying. 'On the right.'

Bala glanced at him. 'Stan, the beach is on the right. If we're going to a beach house, it must be on the right, right?'

'Right!' chorused the back seat, dissolving into laughter.

'Okay, this is the Bentota station. Now let's see ... here! Here! Turn right here!'

Bala swung the car sharply to the right, causing the back-seat passengers to pile up on one another. They drove down a sandy track for a few yards and then came to a stop in a clearing. They got out, stretching stiff limbs. Priyanthi stared around her. 'It's fantastic!' she exclaimed. Niranjan, who was a few feet away, heard her.

'Yes, it is,' he said.

The house was old and spread out comfortably across the clearing. It had a wide veranda with no doors and faded green trelliswork which hung over the edge of its dull red roof like a fringe. The same trelliswork bordered the big windows, which were thrown open to catch the sea breezes and sunlight. Five carved wooden pillars supported the roof of the veranda. The floor was a warm grey. Shiny and cool.

Priyanthi thought it looked like a smiling person. She saw houses as people. Even cars. Their headlights were their eyes and their radiator grills were their mouths. Some smiled. Some bared their teeth in evil grins. Some looked small and afraid. She looked around the garden, which had no grass or orchids like at home, but sand, coconut trees and another kind of tree with droopy bunches of leaves and strange big fruit, which looked vaguely like pineapples. She found out later that they were called mangroves.

In a corner was a small cement square and a tall, ancient shower, its head encrusted with a thin film of salt. Behind them was the track which led to the road. In front was the sand and the Indian Ocean. To the left, they could just see the gleaming white roof of some tourist hotel. To the right were more trees.

The front door burst open and an old man hurried out wiping his hands on his colourful checked sarong. He was bare-bodied, his dark brown skin making his teeth look startlingly white. His scraggly chest hair was also white.

'Sirs, madams, childrens!' he called out. 'I is Siri. I cook.' He spoke in English.

'Hello, Siri,' Stanley answered in Sinhalese. 'I am Stanley Silva and as you can see, we speak Sinhalese.'

Siri looked disappointed. 'Must speak with white gentleman English,' he continued in English. 'Otherwise not understanding anything even.'

'Well,' Stanley said, smiling, 'you can speak Sinhalese, because we understand.'

He nodded. 'Okay,' he said in English.

Enid and Violet exchanged a look. Priyanthi, Niranjan and Hemantha grinned. Siri was going to be fun.

He led the way inside. The large living room was cool and airy, with its huge windows that looked out over the beach. There was an upholstered antique couch called a kavichchiya in these parts, four large rattan chairs with white rope seats and a low antique table.

A pale circular straw mat covered most of the floor.

White raw cotton curtains blew inwards, nudged by the breeze.

It was a beautiful room.

'Sit, sit. I bring drink,' Siri said.

The children giggled. Enid and Violet looked reprovingly at them.

'Can we see the rest of the house first?' Stanley asked in Sinhalese.

'Of course, yes,' Siri said expansively. In English.

The dining room opened off the living room, with a large eight-seater table and chairs in light wood which matched the sideboard against the far wall. There was a wide corridor leading from the dining room with four bedrooms, all decorated in exactly the same way. A large double bed covered with a raw cotton spread, wicker dressing table, clothes rail, small rectangular upholstered stool and straw mats on the floor.

Big windows with white raw cotton curtains opened out to the coconut trees and sea.

At the end of the corridor were two bathrooms with mirrored cabinets, shower curtains and tiled floors covered with straw mats. Enid sighed with pleasure.

'Want see kitchen also?'

They turned. 'Oh yes,' Enid and Violet said together. The men exchanged a smile and the children rolled their eyes. They trooped into the kitchen and stopped, gasping with delight.

The kitchen was like any other but with one difference: the entire back wall had been removed, or perhaps never built, and so one side of it was open to the garden. Large shallow steps as wide as the kitchen itself led outside to the sand. It had been cunningly designed so that the cooking area, which was a traditional wood fire hearth, was shielded from the wind.

'It's beautiful,' Enid said softly. 'I wish my kitchen at home was like this.'

'Not beautiful when rain,' Siri said sadly. 'Or when childrens brings sand in shoes.'

Priyanthi went to the steps. 'Look at the thambili trees!' she exclaimed. 'They're full!'

'I bring?' Siri enquired hopefully.

'What, from the tree?' Priyanthi asked incredulously, looking at his frail frame.

'No, no, from frigerator,' Siri said. 'You go sit saloon. I bring.'

But they were already settling down comfortably on the

steps. Siri sighed. These were definitely not white people. White people knew where to sit and how to be served. These were sitting in the same place where he, Siri, sat in the evenings with his tot of toddy! And he could swear that the distinguished-looking man who had driven the car spoke with a distinct Tamil accent. Shame, but better than having no one, he thought. In English.

* * *

Priyanthi walked out to the beach, revelling in the emptiness which stretched endlessly on either side of the house. To the left, the coastline curved sharply, concealing the private beach of the tourist hotel whose expensive roof they had glimpsed earlier. The sand was white and powdery. She felt that if she knelt down and sniffed at it, it would smell like the Pears Baby Powder Auntie Violet put on Nirmala. Her toes curled confidingly into it. Here and there, she saw shells and pinkish-white corals washed up by surging tides. The pale blue water lapped silently at the shore. Coconut trees moved slowly, like lethargic ladies on a hot day. She closed her eyes and imagined that the beach was a mysterious road that led to strange wonders. But which way to go? With her eyes still closed, she slowly turned around a few times and then stopped. She opened her eyes. She was facing the direction of the hotel.

She started walking quickly and rounded the bend, curious to see the tourists, but then stopped in shock. Three people, two women and a man, were walking towards her, chattering and laughing, their heads thrown back to the sun and the breeze. They were white, red actually. The two women only wore skimpy bikini bottoms. Their breasts swung unconcernedly as they walked and talked. Priyanthi stared at the man and blushed as she realised that he was wearing a tiny pair of swimming trunks which barely covered his genitals. In fact, the sides of it were mere pieces of string.

They came closer and smiled as they saw her. She tried to smile back but her face was frozen. She looked down at the sand and pushed her toes savagely into it. She wished she could push her entire body in and disappear. Even so, she couldn't prevent herself from looking at them as they passed, chattering in some foreign language. One of the women was quite young and the other was quite old. The young one had round, bouncy breasts and the old one had long, hanging breasts. Like a dachshund's ears. The backs of their swimsuits were like the amudés that farmers wore when working in the fields, a waistband with a strip of cloth which disappeared into the buttocks. The man too.

Priyanthi stayed where she was. She didn't want to go any further. She didn't want to see any more bare breasts and bums. But she didn't want to walk behind any either. She sat down and waited. She felt acutely embarrassed. She had never seen anyone's breasts before, even her mother's. Enid was careful to change in the bathroom. She herself had breasts, but small ones which she was quite ashamed of. She couldn't imagine walking on the beach with them uncovered. She couldn't understand how anyone could. She hoped no one else from the house was out on the beach. Seeing what she had by herself was bad enough. To know someone else had, and to know that they knew that she had seen as well, was enough to make anyone die from embarrassment.

After a while, she heard them coming back, their feet thudding softly on the sand as they ran. She lay back hastily and closed her eyes. She stayed still until she heard them running past, imagining their breasts jiggling and bobbing and red from too much sun. When she was sure they had gone, she jumped up and ran back to the house without a backward glance. The wind streamed into her hair, through it and out again. Her foot landed on a crab's little hole, causing a huge avalanche of sand to swamp his tiny home and bury his babies alive. Another crab scuttled out of the way of the running giantess.

Priyanthi saw none of it. She turned into the compound and cannoned into Niranjan, causing them both to topple to the sand in a heap of arms and legs. She extricated herself from the tangle, spat sand out of her mouth and gaped at him. 'What are you doing?' she asked.

He brushed sand out of his hair and from his face. 'What am *I* doing? I'm not the one running around like a demon's after me!'

She reddened. 'I'm sorry,' she said, offering no explanation.

He stood up and dusted his shorts and T-shirt. 'See you later,' he said sarcastically and began to walk out of the compound.

She jumped up and grabbed his arm. 'Where are you going?'

Now he started to look distinctly annoyed. 'For a walk. Do you mind?' looking pointedly at her hand on his arm.

'Yes,' she said. 'I mean, no. Don't go. Stay and talk to me. There's nothing to see anyway.' She knew she probably sounded insane, but she couldn't let him go that way and see them. The Shameless Three. It sounded like a bad Enid Blyton book, she thought hysterically.

He removed her hand. 'Bye,' he said.

She ran after him. 'No! Please don't go that way! Please!' Her voice sounded high and desperate.

He stopped. 'Why?'

She looked down. 'Because,' she muttered.

'Because what?'

She looked up at him beseechingly. 'I'll tell you later, okay? But don't go now. Go the other way.'

He shook his head. 'The sun,' he said pityingly. 'You must wear a hat, you know. It does strange things to certain people.' He walked off, but not towards the hotel. She followed. Just to make sure he didn't suddenly change his mind. He looked back and grimaced slightly when he saw her walking behind him.

* * *

The trees were thick, about four deep, and staggered in height like the seats in a football stadium. Tall coconut trees at the very back, mangroves in the next row, some tall shrubs and finally shabby scrub with thorny branches and dry leaves.

The surface of the sand was smooth and untouched except for a few faint crab trails, and Priyanthi felt better for knowing the Shameless Three hadn't been this far down the beach, that these trees and sand and crabs and waves hadn't been forced to witness their nakedness. She blushed again at the thought of them.

Just ahead, Niranjan had stopped, but since she was walking with her head down, she didn't see until she bumped into him. She stepped back, cursing silently and steeling herself for another verbal onslaught, but he didn't seem to have even noticed. He was staring ahead, at the shore side. She looked too. A river, the Bentara Ganga, she found out later, curved gently in a little lagoon just a few feet away. Clear water licked delicately at a small sandy shore. Far away, she could see a bridge and a few boats, but here there was just the river and them. She looked back. Not twenty yards away was the sea, separated from the river by a broad strip of sand.

'What is this place?' she whispered.

'I don't know,' Niranjan replied, frowning. 'This should be where the river meets the sea, only it doesn't.'

Priyanthi walked down to where the warm water lapped around her ankles. She waded in until she was knee deep and sat down on the sandy bottom. Niranjan still stood on the shore. She felt a tickling sensation on her feet and wriggled them, wondering if it was a curious crab. A shoal of tiny silvery fish flickered away. She laughed in delight.

'Niranjan! Come in! You've got to see this!' she called, still laughing.

He hesitated for a moment, then pulled off his T-shirt and waded in to sit next to her.

'Sit perfectly still,' she said in a soft voice.

In a few minutes the fish swam up, circling their feet cautiously. Having decided that it was safe, they got to work, nibbling on the soles. Niranjan looked startled but managed not to jerk his feet away. A grin spread across his face.

'A free, all-natural pedicure,' he pronounced.

'It's so peaceful. Like a private paradise,' she said.

Far away, traffic sounds tried to penetrate the serenity, and succeeded only partially. The sound of the waves behind them was louder. Occasionally, they heard a motor boat, but didn't see it.

'So what did you see that you didn't want me to see?'

Priyanthi started and the fish darted off in alarm. 'What?'

'Why didn't you want me to go the other way?' he repeated.

'Just,' she said lamely.

'Just?' He looked at her, wondering how she could sound like an adult one moment and a child the next. 'What did you see?'

'People,' she muttered, staring out into the distance where the colourful speck of a distant wind-surfer broke the blue monotony.

'People? People sent you running off like that?' He sounded incredulous.

'Not just people,' she said, half angrily.

'People with—?' He was having to draw this out of her like pulling a tooth. Painfully.

She blushed and looked down. 'People without.'

He looked uncomprehending for a moment, and then it dawned. 'Naked people?'

'Sort of.'

'Oh. How many?' He sounded as embarrassed as she was.

'Three.'

'Men?'

'Two women and a man. Without tops. In tiny panties. Even him.' She dug her toes deep into the sand and the fish swam away. 'Why do they do that?'

'Suntan,' he said simply. She looked unconvinced, so he tried to explain further. 'They live in countries where it's always snowing and raining and stuff, so when they come to places like this, they want to feel the sun on every possible inch of them.'

She looked at him. 'Maybe they just want people to know they've been somewhere sunny.'

He laughed. 'That too.' Then he looked at her curiously. 'Why did it upset you so much?'

'I don't know. I didn't think there was anyone on the beach, and when I saw them like that, I was shocked. They didn't even try to cover up. What if I was a fisherman?'

'I don't think you would have minded so much,' he said, grinning.

'I saw some of Hemantha's books,' she said suddenly.

'What books?' he said.

'They were actually magazines. Not books. One was called *Playboy.*'

Niranjan went red. Priyanthi didn't notice.

'They had really awful pictures in them,' she continued, tugging absently at her hair. It was shoulder-length now, thanks to Enid's repeated entreaties. 'Girls. Wearing nothing. Showing everything.'

He didn't say anything. He felt a little guilty because when Hemantha had brought the magazines home, he had invited Niranjan to come over and look at them. And Niranjan had looked. At each page in every magazine. He had fantasised about Kamini. So had Hemantha.

'Have you seen them?' she asked suddenly.

He looked away.

'Have you?' she demanded.

Now he was forced to look at her. Her brown eyes were clear and steady as she gazed at him. She seemed to be pleading with him to say he hadn't, but he couldn't lie. Not to those honest eyes. He nodded.

She stood up silently and waded out back to the shore.

'Priyanthi, wait. I want to tell you something.' He didn't want her to leave. Not like this. 'Wait.'

She walked off in the direction of the house, without appearing to have heard him.

He groaned and let himself sink back into the water until it covered his whole body, face and all. He stayed under as long as he could, and then sat up gasping for air. He felt like a worm. No, lower than a worm. He wished with all his heart that he could have said 'no'. He remembered the look in her eyes, which had clouded over with disappointment before she turned away. And in that moment, he realised that he didn't want her to feel disappointed with him. Unreasonable as it seemed.

He sat there, oblivious of the fish slipping in and out of his toes. Slowly, anger replaced the guilt. What was wrong with him? he asked himself. He was behaving as if she was Kamini and he'd let her down badly. This was Priyanthi. She was only thirteen and his best friend's sister, not some potential girlfriend or something. So what did it matter what she thought? Who cared if she was disappointed?

She was only a kid, not old enough to start passing judgement on people. She didn't seem to have minded that Hemantha looked at those magazines. So why not him? It wasn't as if he was a priest or a saint or her boyfriend. He laughed angrily. Boyfriend! Hemantha would kill her if he even thought she had one!

He wondered if she did. People did at thirteen. Especially girls. Kamini said she'd had her first boyfriend when she was twelve. He tried to imagine Priyanthi being someone's girlfriend and couldn't. The thought was too ridiculous. And yet, why not? She was attractive. He had noticed that recently. She was tall, and although she was still thin, she had definitely started to fill out. Why, in her swimsuit, she even had some curves. He had noticed the small breasts that pushed against the thin nylon, the curves of her bottom that the too-small swimsuit couldn't conceal. Her face was not pretty, but she was far from uninteresting with her wide, laughing mouth and snapping eyes which missed nothing. Stop it! he told himself fiercely. One day without seeing Kamini and he was starting to think his skinny neighbour was a raving beauty! He kicked at the fish, which swam away laughing, stood up and strode back to the house. He would ignore her, he decided. The coconut trees nodded, agreeing with him. Mocking him.

* * *

The house was empty. Everyone had gone to the market to buy meat and vegetables and other things for their week's stay. Even Hemantha had gone, hoping to slip away and get enough cigarettes to last the week. Siri had been suitably impressed with the Nescafé and whisky, and had labelled them high-class Sinhalese, which was almost as good as white people. Although not quite. He couldn't get the kitchen step scene out of his head.

Niranjan went to the outdoor shower and stood under it, the icy water feeling good against his heated skin. He pulled at the waistband of his shorts and allowed the water to run inside, noticing that the skin underneath was visibly lighter. That made him think of the sunbathers and he grimaced. He looked around the garden, wavy and edge-less through his watery vision, and wondered where Priyanthi had got to. Hopefully she was sulking in some corner.

He dried himself and went in to change. Later, he examined the contents of the huge refrigerator, and found a large pitcher of king coconut water. He poured himself a glass and sat on the kitchen step to enjoy its sweet, slightly tart taste. Siri seemed to have disappeared.

He felt her before he saw her. Her indecision and tension washed over him in waves. He didn't turn or look sideways when she came to sit next to him. Far away, a few gulls screamed and a few waves crept up the shore. A dog barked somewhere.

'I'm sorry,' she said.

'For what?'

'For being so – whatever,' she said quietly.

'Fine.' Out of the corner of his eye, he glanced at her. She had also showered, and had changed into a red sleeveless top and shorts. The colour cast a rosy glow on her skin.

'I don't know why I got so upset. I mean, Hemantha looks at that stuff. I just didn't think—' She broke off.

'I only looked because he showed them to me. I don't think I'd go and buy stuff like that. And I thought it was quite disgusting.' He didn't know why he was explaining himself to her. It was just important that he did.

'So why did you look?'

'You know what Hemantha's like.'

She nodded silently.

They both heard a noise and turned, but it was only a stray cat looking for scraps. A tiny, scrawny creature with huge, hungry eyes that reminded Niranjan of the girl sitting next to him.

'Do you like me?' she said.

The suddenness of the question caught him unawares. 'What?'

'Do you like me?'

He felt uncomfortable, wondering what she was getting at. 'Yes, I suppose so. I don't really know you,' he said, shooting her a wary look.

She looked impatient. 'Not like a girl or anything. Like a friend.'

He relaxed. 'Yes. But I still don't know you too well.'

'Do you want to?'

He thought about it. Did he want to be friends with her? This funny, uncomfortably direct person who was three years younger than him, but more years older than him sometimes? Did he want to be friends with her honest stare and odd morality? Did he want to risk Hemantha's derision, his sarcastic comments and jealousy just for her?

'Yes,' he said, surprised at how sure he was.

The tension left her in an audible whoosh and she smiled. She slid closer to him, linked her arm through his and leaned her head against his arm. He was shocked at how comforted the gesture made him feel, at how much he wanted to protect her from naked people and porn magazines.

They both heard the car at the same time and sprang up. Everything was too new to share. So new it was still dangerously destructible. One word or look could shatter it to pieces too small to ever put together again.

She ran off through the house, her feet making no sound on the rush matting which covered most of the floor, a smile trembling on her mouth. She wanted to run out to the beach and twirl endlessly on the sand until she got dizzy and flopped down into its warm embrace. *They'll think I'm mad!* She composed herself as best she could and went reluctantly to greet the others.

Niranjan walked round the garden to the front of the house and tried not to look guilty. *I haven't done anything bad! It's not as if I agreed to be her boyfriend or something.* Still, he avoided Hemantha's eyes.

* * *

The next hour was spent putting away the groceries and exchanging Bentota town stories.

'You should have seen the foreign girls, man!' Hemantha whispered to Niranjan. 'Tiny bikinis, bobs all over the place.'

Niranjan didn't reply, wondering what Hemantha would say if he knew that Priyanthi had prevented him from seeing two half-naked foreign women. Enid and Violet were talking about the shops. Apparently, they were quite impressed with the selection of things available, the imported food, shampoos, razor blades and things. 'Because of the foreigners,' Enid said wisely.

'They're the only ones with money to buy at those prices,' Violet said, still faintly shocked not just at the prices, but at the way the foreigners dressed.

She had seen one woman in shorts so short that the lower half of her bum was clearly visible beneath them. Reddish-pink half-moons. Her bra-less state was accentuated by her white cotton halter top. Violet had blushed for her. She had never been down south before, and since the tourists in Colombo dressed a little more modestly, this was her first real encounter with the sun-worshippers. Enid was a little more blasé, but the shorts and halter top had shocked even her.

'Might as well have nothing on,' she had commented acidly, and glared at Stanley as he replied, 'Yes, that would be much better!' In front of Hemantha too, who was also ogling the woman shamelessly. She sniffed loudly as they passed the woman.

They invaded Siri's kitchen and were putting away the vegetables, soft drinks, arrack (in case the whisky ran out, which Bala and Stanley fully intended to make sure happened), butter, milk and bread, when Siri reappeared carrying a bunch of young coconuts.

He dropped them on the sand and ran in. 'No, no, madams! Siri put things. Not madams!'

The 'madams' gave in. They enquired about lunch and were told he would have it ready 'now now'. When they asked if they could help, Siri looked horrified, so they went to relax in the cool living room where the fan was on. Stanley and Bala opened the precious bottle of whisky and tried to persuade Enid and Violet to 'have a shot', but they refused.

'Come, come, one shot won't kill you!' Bala boomed.

'Ladies don't drink alcohol,' Enid said primly.

Hemantha looked scornful. Kamini drank Babycham at her parents' parties and her mother drank imported sherry and smoked long cigarettes in a black tortoiseshell holder. Hemantha imagined his mother smoking and nearly laughed aloud. He looked longingly at the bottle, wondering if he would be able to sneak some later. Bala was swirling his drink and the whisky made golden shadows among the diamond-like ice cubes. Hemantha stood up abruptly. 'Nira, let's go for a walk,' he said, jerking his head meaningfully in the direction of the hotel.

'Too hot,' Niranjan said, and closed his eyes.

Priyanthi smiled to herself. Her world was a translucent red behind her closed lids.

Hemantha grabbed Niranjan by the hand and tried to pull him up. 'Come on! I want to take a walk.' He tapped the packet of cigarettes in his shirt pocket.

Niranjan sighed and stood up. 'Okay, okay. Let's go. But just to the back,' he said in a low voice.

As they walked off, Hemantha looked at Niranjan. 'What's the matter with you? We could go down to the hotel and see the chicks. Maybe even get a couple.'

Niranjan sighed. 'Hemantha, it's too hot. Why don't you go?'

Hemantha threw him an angry glare and strode off.

Priyanthi was looking for sea shells around the compound. Apparently, previous visitors had had the same idea, because all she found were some broken bits of coral and a few crab holes. She examined them. There was a tiny dead crab at the mouth of one of the holes, his white, salt-encrusted body lying belly up, his legs pointing up to the cloudless sky. She touched one with the tip of her little finger and it crumbled. The sand sparkled in the sunlight as if there was silver dust mixed in with it. She picked up a handful and let it run through her fingers. After it was all gone, a thin film of dust clouded her knuckles. She tried to dig a crab grave but sand kept sliding into it. Finally, she let him just be there, exposed and dead.

She wondered how many cigarettes Hemantha was smoking and how long it would take him to die. She would feel sad, but not too much, she thought. She loved him and she knew he loved her, but his love was a possessive love, a conditional love, a be-a-good-girl-and-don't-get-in-my-way love. Did that qualify as love?

She thought of Niranjan. Was he was smoking too? Somehow, she didn't think so. That must infuriate Hemantha, because he was aware that Niranjan's good behaviour only showed up his own bad behaviour. But oddly enough, Hemantha still wanted Niranjan as a friend. As if Niranjan was a link with a better world. The family and Araliya Gardens world which Hemantha seemed to hate so much these days. She knew he spent most of his time with a bunch of rowdies from the junction. She had heard her father discussing it with Uncle Bala, who seemed to think it was a phase he would grow out of. Her father had yelled at her mother one night because it was past midnight and Hemantha wasn't home yet. As if it was her fault. And later that night, she had seen her mother standing by the windows in the darkened living room. She had heard the muffled sobs. All because of Hemantha.

Priyanthi knew about Kamini too. She had seen a letter that Hemantha had written, one of the scores of letters he wrote that he would never post. It had been so soppily romantic and so full of atrocious spellings that she had collapsed with laughter. He had declared himself in love with every inch of Kamini's anatomy and had gone on to describe each part in glorious detail. When she got to the bit about 'your gogoues uncles', she immediately had a vision of a bevy of uncles all be-rouged and lipsticked, wearing wigs and evening gowns, and thought she would die laughing.

She wondered if Niranjan was in love with Kamini too. If he wrote her letters he would never post. If he spent his nights dreaming of her gogoues uncles. Not that she could blame him. Kamini *was* quite beautiful, although her reputation wasn't really spotless. The girls said she was available and sniggered jealously. The teachers frowned disapprovingly at her shorter-than-short school uniforms, but said nothing because her father was a generous benefactor and frequently gave the school fat cheques. When they thanked him, he grinned and said, 'Keep Kamini happy. That's all I want.' So Kamini was kept happy.

Everyone knew why, and Priyanthi, who could never understand the morality of the whole thing, wondered if the nuns went to chapel and asked for forgiveness for being so greedy. For being so willing to sacrifice their Christian morals for the sake of a few rupees. A few hundred rupees. A few thousand rupees. How many inches of skirt could be removed with a thousand rupees?

NINE

❦

A slightly chilly sea breeze crept inland and rippled softly through the coconut trees, making their fronds whisper against the windows. Priyanthi sat up and squinted sleepily, wondering what had woken her. Tired of playing with the window, the breeze slid in and coiled around her bare shoulders, leaving a rash of goose bumps in its wake. She hastily pulled the blanket around her and looked at the next bed, where Nirmala was sleeping. She lay down again and closed her eyes, but sleep had woken up. She draped the blanket around her, slid off the bed and padded over to the window.

It was just before dawn, because the stars were fading and the sky was that peculiar silvery grey. The crescent moon hung stubbornly in the sky like a mocking smile, refusing to give way to the sun. Beneath it, the sea lay silent and unmoving.

Priyanthi quietly went into the bathroom and brushed her teeth, taking care not to open the tap too much. She quickly put on a pair of trousers, a shirt and a jacket of Hemantha's which was dumped on a chair in the living room. She slid into her rubber Bata slippers and pulled her hair into a hasty ponytail.

The front door was locked and the bolts were stiff and unresponsive, so she went to the kitchen. There was no sign of Siri. Maybe he went home to sleep. The kitchen door was more co-operative and swung open when she pushed it.

The wind blowing through the open kitchen was sharp and she drew the jacket closely around her as she made her way down to the beach. The water was moving, but so gently that it made only a thin line of ripples at its very edge. A sheet of silver gossamer with a fine lacy border. It shyly tasted the early-morning sand, then tiptoed backwards.

Priyanthi sat down on the sand and waited. Presently, the sky started to lighten, the silver pushed aside by rough streaks of pink and gold. The surface of the sea became a moving reflection of the sky. A few gulls swooped down looking for breakfast. Crabs went home to their holes. Fish fled to deeper waters. The colours became more intense as the sun rose higher all the way over on the other side of the island. Birds rose and went in search of early worms. Sleeping dogs stirred. Coconut trees stretched.

On the shore, Priyanthi hugged her knees and wept. She didn't know why she was crying. Was she weeping for the unbearably beautiful dawn unfolding in front of her, or for herself? Was she weeping because she was happy or because she was sad? She didn't know. It just felt right to weep. And since there was no one there to watch, no impatient brothers or indecent tourists, she wept in peace. When at last she finished, she felt drained but also fulfilled. Empty but curiously replete.

She wiped her face on the sleeve of Hemantha's jacket and started back to the house. She turned the corner and almost bumped into Siri, who let out a little yelp of fright. 'Child, what doing this time?'

'I couldn't sleep,' she replied.

'Bed not good?'

'Bed very good,' she hastened to reassure him, wondering if her English would become as fractured as his if she stayed here a month.

'Want coffee? Imported Nescafé?'

Her mouth watered. 'Oh, yes please.'

Siri beamed and led the way into the kitchen, then frowned as she sat on the step. 'Child, why sit on step like servant? Chair not good?'

She laughed. 'Chair good. Step better.'

Siri sighed and busied himself with the coffee. 'Yes, yes. Bentota good, no?'

She nodded, then realised that his back was turned. 'Yes.'

A mug was placed in her hand. 'Thank you,' she said, burying her nose in it. The coffee was heavenly, hot, milky and sweet.

She sipped it, thinking about her crying jag on the beach.

Wondering what had brought it on. Worrying if she was unhappy even though she didn't feel unhappy. She frowned.

'Morning.'

She looked in amazement at Niranjan. 'What are you doing up this early?'

He smiled. 'That's odd coming from you.'

'I couldn't sleep,' she said a little defensively.

'Maybe the smell of coffee woke me up,' he said, taking the cup Siri handed him. 'I looked out of my window and everything looked so beautiful and peaceful that I had to come outside.'

She was apprehensive. 'What did you see?'

'The sea, the sand, the sunrise . . .'

'And?'

He looked at her. 'And that's it. Why? Did I miss something?'

She heaved a silent sigh of relief. 'No. What time is it?'

'I don't know. About six, I think.'

'It'll be hours before anyone wakes up. Especially after last night. Do you want to go for a walk?'

Niranjan stood up, took her hand and pulled her to her feet. 'Let's go.'

They walked to the edge of the compound and then paused.

She looked at Niranjan. 'Shall we go towards the hotel? There won't be anyone out at this time and I really want to see what's beyond it.'

They started walking. The wind was keen and Priyanthi shivered in spite of her jacket. The tiny hairs on her arms rose in protest.

Niranjan looked concerned. 'Are you cold?'

'A little.'

'You should eat more,' he said, looking at her critically. 'You're just skin and bone.'

'You sound just like my mother,' she said crossly. Then she brightened up. 'Weren't they funny last night, your mother and mine? I thought they would die when my father gave Siri the whisky.'

Niranjan laughed. 'I think it's our fathers who will die when they realise they did.'

* * *

The previous night, they had had a barbecue. The younger ones were given the task of digging a pit. They filled it with coals, got the fire going, and laid a piece of oiled wire mesh over the top. The fish and huge prawns they had bought earlier from the market had been sitting in a lime juice, salt and chilli powder marinade for over three hours and came off the mesh succulent on the inside and crisp on the outside.

From sundown, the two men had been sipping steadily from the bottle of whisky. At dinner time, when Siri came out with plates, he was persuaded to have a drink as well, much to Violet and Enid's horror. But the men were insistent, generous drunks, and Siri needed very little persuasion.

One drink led to another, and the end of the evening saw Siri with his sarong raised high above his knobbly knees, dancing the baila while trying to balance a plate on his head. Hemantha, Priyanthi and Niranjan egged him on with catcalls and applause. Nirmala retired into Violet's lap and peeped out with apprehensive eyes.

Afterwards, the men staggered inside, fell upon their beds and passed out. Violet and Enid were left with the task of cleaning up since Siri had also vanished, presumably to pass out on his own bed.

Hemantha disappeared with Niranjan, probably on a cigarette walk.

Priyanthi sank to the sand and lay there watching the millions of stars that pierced the inky blackness of the sky. Most of the house lights had been switched off, so the stars shone without competition. Unlike in Colombo, where harsh fluorescent street lights, yellow house lights and white head-lights doused their brilliance with their electrical superiority. A shooting star streaked across the sky and she desperately tried to make a wish before it disappeared, but none came to mind. Not that she really believed in all that.

In the distance, she could hear music from the hotel, where half-naked, sun-burned tourists were having a similar dinner of barbecued fish and prawns at tourist prices, where waiters smiled with extra servility hoping for bigger tips and a group of straw-hatted, saronged musicians played country and western music on their box guitars and bongo drums.

* * *

'Come on! We'll take all day at this rate.'

She quickened her pace. 'This is supposed to be a walk, not an exercise run,' she said acidly.

'Okay, okay. Stop sounding so irritated,' he said, slowing down so she could keep up.

They rounded the bend and came upon the hotel. It was a huge C-shaped building which stretched its expansive arms out to the Indian Ocean. In its white concrete embrace were manicured gardens with carefully trimmed coconut and frangi-pani trees. In the centre, a kidney-shaped pool full of impossi-bly blue water, with sun beds, deckchairs and blue-and-white umbrellas arranged around it.

This stretch of beach was loudly labelled private. A profes-sionally painted sign said 'HOTEL GUESTS ONLY' and two strategically placed red flags at either end were supposed to warn tourists of rough seas, but were in reality to dissuade them from venturing further to the areas where locals swam, fished, defecated, gawked at half-naked white people and hawked plastic-packeted marijuana, see-through sarongs and their voluptuous sisters. Sometimes even themselves.

There were sun beds here too, but minus mattresses, which would be brought out later when the tourists awoke and came out in their bikinis (or parts of their bikinis) to lie down in supplication to the sun. Now, the sun beds looked naked too.

Niranjan and Priyanthi took their time walking past, stopping to stare at the imposing white building, to sit giggling on the deckchairs, to write 'wear some clothes' on the sand. When they got past the second red flag, which marked the end of the hotel property, the scenery became wild and untamed and wind-blown once more. The coconut trees were thicker here, and they walked between them, on an uneven carpet of thick grass which Priyanthi decided she far preferred to her mother's special blue grass.

Niranjan suddenly stopped. 'There,' he said.

'What?'

'See the bark of this tree? It's got ropes tied to it. As if someone climbs up regularly.'

At about two-foot intervals, strong coir rope made footholds right up to the top of the tree. Their eyes followed the rope steps and Priyanthi suddenly gave a cry. 'Look! There's a pot tied up there!'

Niranjan kicked off his shoes. 'It's toddy. That's a toddy tapper's tree. I heard my father talking about it. I'm going to climb up.'

Priyanthi flung away her own slippers. 'Me too,' she said.

Niranjan turned around. 'We can't both climb at the same time. Let me go first, and if it's not too difficult, then you can come.'

He climbed up, his muscles aching with the effort. 'I don't think you'll be able to,' he called down.

'Then tell me what's up there,' she yelled.

'Only a pot under this bunch of coconut flowers. Wait! There something's dripping into it.'

'What?'

'Sap.'

'What?' she shouted louder.

'Can't you be quiet?' he said, looking down at her. 'You'll wake up the whole town.'

She bit her lip and stood there, hopping from one foot to the other, impatient to know.

She heard an exclamation. 'What?' she shouted.

'Shut up!' he hissed loudly, climbing down.

He sank down to the grass and leaned against the tree. She sat cross-legged next to him. 'What did you see up there?' she demanded in a fever of impatience.

'Ropes,' he said.

She looked puzzled. 'Ropes? Just dangling ropes?'

'No, ropes from this tree to the next one and from that one to the next one and on and on. Connecting about twenty trees maybe.'

'But what would anyone put ropes there for?'

He squinted up, trying to see through the tops of the trees. 'They're for walking on.'

She looked even more confused. 'How could anyone walk on ropes? I know they do it in the circus, but up there?'

'They're for toddy tappers,' he said slowly. 'You know, men who climb coconut trees to collect the sap from the flowers to make toddy. But I thought they climbed each tree separately.'

Slowly comprehension dawned. 'You mean it's like a whole lot of rope roads up there?'

He nodded. 'It's so clever. Instead of going up and down every tree, they just climb one, then walk the rope to the next and the next until they've finished them all, and climb down the last.'

She shivered. 'How could they walk on ropes? It's so high and windy. If they fall, they'll surely die. What kind of work is that?'

Niranjan nudged her. She heard someone whistling tunelessly and peered over Niranjan's shoulder trying to see who it was. The man walking towards them was not old, but not young either. His skin was burned almost black by the sun and stretched strongly and shinily over his frame. Muscles bulged in his upper arms and lower legs, but his torso was lean, almost skinny. Priyanthi could clearly see the lines of his ribs and his collarbone, which lay around his throat like a necklace. He had a cloth wound around his head to keep off the heat and all he wore was a sarong, bunched up, pulled back between his legs and tucked into the waist. It looked like an untidy pair of knickers, and was worn commonly by those who worked in the fields and needed freedom of movement. A coil of rope was looped and slung over one shoulder and a sharp curved knife with a cloth-covered handle was tucked into his waistband. He saw them and stopped. And stopped whistling.

He stood there for a moment, seeming to sum up their unexpected presence, then sauntered over. 'Oho, what's this? Two young lovebirds?'

'We're not lovebirds! We're friends!' Priyanthi said indignantly, ignoring Niranjan's furious nudge.

The man nodded slowly. 'Friends. That's good. Better than lovebirds.' He sat down on his haunches near them and pulled out a small plastic bag from his sarong. He opened it slowly and extracted a betel leaf, a piece of areca nut and a daub of chunam. He popped the areca nut into his mouth and chewed it thoroughly, contemplatively. Then he placed the chunam and the betel leaf in his mouth and chewed those too, pausing every few seconds to roll the mixture together in his mouth. He carefully folded the empty plastic bag and tucked it back into his sarong. All the while, he looked at them. Not threateningly or angrily, but as if he was trying to read them. Or understand what they were doing here at this time of the morning.

He had coal-black eyes.

They looked back at him defensively. Like two people looking in through someone's window and finding someone looking back at them.

'So, what are two friends doing here?' he finally asked. 'It's very early. Even for friends.'

'We were just going for a walk and we stopped to rest,' Niranjan said.

The man rocked back on his heels and looked appraisingly at Niranjan. 'Ah, Tamil boy. With a Sinhalese friend.'

Niranjan felt slightly uncomfortable. 'Yes. Why?'

The man looked at him. 'No reason. Just an observation.' There was the merest hint of a smile in his voice.

'Where are you going?' Priyanthi said, anxious to re-route the conversation.

'Well,' he said slowly, 'I was going to work, but that will have to wait for the time being.'

'Why?' she asked curiously.

'My path is being blocked by two friends. One Sinhalese and one Tamil.'

'There's plenty of room,' Priyanthi said. 'Where do you work anyway?'

He pointed up.

Niranjan leaned forward. 'Up the coconut tree?'

The man nodded. He didn't smile but he didn't look unfriendly either.

'You're the toddy tapper?' Priyanthi asked.

'Yes.'

'Aren't you afraid?' she said.

He thought for a minute, then nodded solemnly.

'You are?' Niranjan said, looking slightly disappointed.

'As long as I am afraid, I am alive,' the man said obliquely. He spat out a stream of betel juice, which streaked the sand like a splatter of blood. He covered it with some sand and then looked at them. 'So what are you doing here? You're obviously Colombo people.'

Niranjan waved in the direction of the house. 'We're staying at a house near the hotel. Just for a week.'

The man nodded. 'I know it. White people stay there usually. Nice kitchen.'

Priyanthi looked at him suspiciously. 'How do you know what it looks like?'

He looked back at her, his expression slightly mocking. 'Siri is my brother-in-law. My sister's husband.'

Priyanthi frowned. 'She must be old. Your sister, I mean.'

'Yes.' He stood up. 'I must start before the sun gets too high.'

They stood up too and moved away from the tree. He pulled the knife from his waist, held it between his teeth, and without saying another word started climbing the coconut tree.

There was something in his perfect co-ordination which reminded Priyanthi of a ballet dancer. He leapt softly from rope step to rope step, his feet barely touching anything. Only his arms strained from the effort of pulling his body. Different muscles rose and rippled, apparent even from where they stood. He finally reached the top of the tree and crouched in its branches. Presently, he straightened up again and disappeared into the umbrella-like tops of the coconut trees.

Priyanthi started running, her eyes fixed upwards, trying to follow his progress. Most of the coconut trees grew quite close together, but some were further apart, and between these, she could see the two long ropes stretching to the next tree. One for feet, one for upstretched arms. She gazed upwards, willing him to show himself, and as if he had heard her, he suddenly appeared, feet twisted sideways to grip the rope beneath them, eyes fixed straight ahead, sunlight glinting off the knife between his teeth. She watched with bated breath until he disappeared once again, and when he did, her shoulders slumped with relief. She felt oddly responsible for him, which was stupid since she had only known him for all of five minutes. Maybe ten. And she didn't really know him at all. She felt that he had found out more about them than they had about him.

'Priyanthi, come on. Let's go back,' Niranjan called.

'Let's stay a bit more, just until he comes down,' she pleaded.

'The sun is coming up and the tourists will be out,' he warned. 'And the others will be waking up too.'

Much as she wanted to see the toddy tapper again, she didn't want to risk seeing any naked people, especially not with Niranjan. Neither did she want any searching questions or snide comments from Hemantha, so she went, but reluctantly.

The hotel beach was still empty. They spotted a few figures near the pool, but it was too far to see if they were dressed or half-dressed.

* * *

'Oh shit,' Niranjan muttered.

Priyanthi looked shocked. 'You mustn't use words like that,' she scolded, and then stopped when she saw Hemantha standing at the entrance to the compound. She stole a look at Niranjan. He looked hunted. With good reason, she knew, because Hemantha would first demand to know what Niranjan was doing with her, where they had been. Then he would torment Niranjan, tease him for being soft, call him a sissy. And all because of her. She had to do something.

So she turned to Niranjan and smiled widely. 'Thanks for coming with me, Niranjan. It was stupid of me to get so scared of some man with a knife.'

Hemantha stared. 'A knife? What's this about?' His voice was gravelly from sleep. Dried drool left white powdery marks around his mouth and on his chin.

Niranjan opened his mouth, but before he could speak, Priyanthi continued quickly. 'Yes, I woke up early and was walking along the beach when I saw this man walking towards me and he had a knife and I got so scared that I ran back here. Niranjan was awake and when I told him what happened, he told me to take him to where the man was, so that's where we've just been.'

'And was the man still there?' Hemantha asked, looking a little dazed. Niranjan didn't fit his image of the brave knight rescuing the damsel in distress. Priyanthi didn't usually behave like a damsel in distress either.

'No,' Priyanthi said triumphantly. 'He must have seen Niranjan and run away.'

Hemantha looked doubtfully at Niranjan. Although they were the same height, Niranjan was as thin as a rail whereas Hemantha was built like a boxer. 'Did you see him, Nira?'

Niranjan just stood there, torn between saving himself and being honest.

'Well, did you?' Hemantha was starting to look suspicious now, his narrowed eyes skidding from Priyanthi to Niranjan.

'Of course he did,' Priyanthi said hastily. 'He was just a toddy tapper.'

'A toddy tapper?' Hemantha said, his frown disappearing. 'Of course. That's why he had a knife.' He ruffled Priyanthi's hair, prepared to be affectionate now that everything had been explained clearly to him. 'You goose. What did you think? That he was going to murder you and leave your dead body on the beach so that the gulls could pick your eyes out?'

Priyanthi flushed. 'Do you have to be so disgusting? I am your sister, you know.' She walked off to the house.

Hemantha stared after her. 'What's the matter with her? I was only making a joke.'

Niranjan sighed. 'Sometimes your jokes aren't very funny, Hemantha,' he said wearily, and walked off behind Priyanthi.

Hemantha threw him a hard look as he went past. 'Careful, Nira,' he said, 'or I might think you prefer my sister's company to mine.'

'I think right now I'd prefer anyone's company to yours,' Niranjan retorted, not caring any more.

Damn Hemantha and his talent for twisting everything. For making him lie like a child over a perfectly acceptable, innocent episode. Although in a way, he was glad Hemantha didn't know the real story about the toddy tapper.

* * *

Priyanthi ran indoors, murmured good morning to her father, who was sitting on the veranda drinking coffee and trying not to look hung-over, and went inside to change into her swimsuit.

'Are you going for a swim, dear?' Enid enquired.

Lord! Where else would she be going in her swimsuit? 'Yes, Amma,' she replied briefly.

'Wait a bit and we'll all go,' Enid suggested brightly.

Stanley groaned. 'You lot go. Bala and I are just going to relax for a while.' He groped for his sunglasses, which were on the small table near by, and put them on. His head pounded in a way not befitting an imported whisky hangover and his tongue felt like an expensive pile carpet. He wanted to go and brush his teeth but he was afraid he would throw up. Bala's eyes were bloodshot and he was quieter than usual, but he was in better shape than Stanley was.

'If you had had dinner when we told you, you wouldn't be in this state,' Enid commented.

Stanley lowered his sunglasses to roll his eyes at Bala.

Violet looked uncomfortable. She wasn't as outspoken as Enid and didn't criticise or question her husband. Especially not when there were other people present.

Enid hadn't finished. 'I hope you know the whisky is almost finished,' she said triumphantly.

'Thank God,' Stanley muttered, massaging his temples.

'If you insist on pouring it down the servant's throat, it obviously won't last very long,' she continued acidly.

Bala burst out laughing. 'He probably appreciated it more than we did. Anyway, it was worth it, just to see him dance.'

Even Stanley managed a smile.

At that moment, Siri made an entrance, carrying a tray with a few glasses and a pitcher of thambili. He set it down on the table.

'With glucose. Very good for bad head,' he pronounced.

'Did you have some?' Bala enquired, his eyes still closed.

'Yes, headache all gone,' Siri said triumphantly.

'Good, then maybe we can have some breakfast,' Enid said sarcastically.

'Ready,' Siri said, shooting her a hurt look. These Sinhalese people. Not like the white people at all. No style. No trust. Why, even if he was dying, he'd still make breakfast! Even if they did sit on kitchen steps like servants.

'Leave him alone, Enid,' Stanley said wearily. 'Poor bugger didn't ask for it.'

Enid snorted and went inside to see if breakfast was edible.

Violet sat quietly and wondered why Enid was making such a fuss. They were on holiday after all, and if the men wanted to have a few drinks and get rowdy, what was the harm? Even giving Siri a tot of whisky wasn't a crime. Violet couldn't understand why Enid was so angry about that. After all, it had been her, not Enid, who had paid out the small fortune for the whisky. She spotted Niranjan walking around the house and out to the beach with his towel slung on his shoulder, and frowned. He had been so quiet since they had got here. She wondered if he was having a good time, if he was bored, if he was missing his Colombo friends, especially that pretty girl Kamini.

Violet knew about Kamini because she had seen a photograph taken at a party. In the photograph, Niranjan wasn't looking at the camera, but at a pretty girl standing next to Hemantha. She had casually asked who the girl was, and didn't miss his blush when he said, 'Just Kamini.' The Saverimuttus were well-known society people, far more respectable than Hemantha's junction lot. But it still worried Violet a little; they weren't in the same income bracket as the Saverimuttus and the last thing she wanted was for her only son to fall in love with some rich, unattainable girl. But at least he kept out of trouble and away from Hemantha's friends.

Violet had gone to the market some weeks ago and come upon Hemantha standing with a bunch of rough-looking boys when he should have been at school. They were all smoking and making comments at passing girls. She hurriedly crossed the road, wishing she was more like Enid, who if she had seen Niranjan in a similar situation would have walked straight up and demanded to know why he wasn't at school. But I'm not like Enid, she told herself, a little sadly. She hadn't even had the courage to tell Enid what she'd seen, although she had told Bala, who said Hemantha deserved a good hiding. Stanley would have definitely agreed, only Stanley didn't know. Every time Hemantha got into trouble, Enid made sure Stanley didn't know. She told Violet he had work to worry about and didn't need to know the 'little troubles' the children got into. The fact was, Hemantha was her only son, and she knew her husband and was doing everything she could to avoid the confrontation which would surely come one day.

Violet hadn't missed the fact that Niranjan had been spending some time with Priyanthi in the last two days. She thought it was nice of him. Priyanthi was a strange child. A loner, who seemed to be more grown-up than her age. In Violet's opinion, that wasn't healthy. Children needed a childhood. Priyanthi seemed to have skipped hers. Maybe Niranjan would draw her out a bit, make her have some fun.

But Niranjan was so serious too. Not that that was bad, but sometimes Violet wished she heard his laughter ringing through the house, his music playing loudly in his room, his friends having fun in the garden.

Like a normal boy.

TEN

❧

That week passed in a haze of sunshine, laughter and secrets. Every day, everyone went down to the beach, even Enid and Violet, although they stayed under the huge golf umbrella Stanley had brought along. They went swimming, even Enid and Violet, who refused to wear swimsuits and instead ventured into the water in their cotton dresses which, when wet, were far more revealing than the brief bikinis the tourists wore.

Stanley and Bala looked at their wives with renewed admiration and the two couples took long afternoon siestas, emerging flushed and exchanging secretive looks.

The two families built a huge sand dagoba, a replica of the Kalutara one, and even found a small bo plant growing near the house, which they uprooted and solemnly stuck near their Bodhiya. Enid was horrified, declaring that they would all get into trouble if anyone saw. 'Who knows, even that old man might say something to someone,' she said, referring to Siri, with whom she had been on icy terms since the night he had got drunk.

Lord Buddha had attained enlightenment under a bo tree in Bodhigaya in India, which was why every temple or shrine had one planted near by. No one was definitely sure, but it was said to be a criminal offence to uproot a bo tree. When the little shoots sprouted out of cracks in walls, people surreptitiously pulled them out, looking over their shoulders to make sure they were not being observed.

Enid's concerns were slightly unfounded, because although the police occasionally patrolled stretches of beach, they didn't venture into private areas like this. They were usually on the look-out for people smoking marijuana or indulging in indecent behaviour deep in the mangroves. Local couples feverishly kissing and caressing or rich middle-aged tourists having sex with poor teenage beach boys who were given an appreciative slap on the buttocks and a fat wad of rupee notes which was next to nothing in their own currencies.

Homosexual prostitution was big business on the southern beaches. It was a quick way to earn money, and young boys were lured into it by unscrupulous fathers, uncles or friends. Once they got over the initial horror and shame of it and realised that they made more from one encounter in the bushes than their parents did from months of hard work, they remained prostitutes. To them, it was far less hazardous than sailing all night on a treacherous sea or teetering on treetop ropes.

In the evenings, the two families went for walks in the town, played charades or split into twos and wandered off in different directions, Enid and Violet into the living room to talk, Bala and Stanley out to the veranda to drink (they had moved on to arrack and toddy now that the whisky was all gone), Hemantha and Niranjan to the beach so Hemantha could smoke. Nirmala usually went to bed early and so Priyanthi was left to her own devices. She spent her time reading, thinking and waiting for morning.

* * *

Unknown to the rest of the family, Priyanthi and Niranjan woke up early every morning, sometimes before dawn, and stole off to the little clearing past the hotel. Only Siri saw them go but he said nothing. He knew where they went and who they went to see.

The day after they first met the toddy tapper, Priyanthi woke up before dawn and dressed quietly. She went silently through the kitchen and down the steps.

Niranjan's long, lean shadow separated itself from the other shadows outside. 'What took you so long?' he whispered.

She just smiled, immeasurably glad to see him. They hurried

out and walked quickly along the beach, not seeing the gulls skimming the silent surface of the water, not hearing the frantic fish slipping away from their unerring beaks.

When they got there, the small coconut tree grove was empty and they wondered if the toddy tapper was already up in his trees. Then Niranjan shook his head. 'Too early. He is probably on his way.'

They settled themselves under the tree and waited. In the distance, the sky lightened and the now familiar colours streaked their way across it, dimming stars, chasing the moon away.

In the staff quarters of the hotel, waiters rose and sleepily buttoned up their smart uniforms in preparation for another day of tourists and tips. They emptied quantities of pink, pepperminty Dantamukta tooth powder directly on to their tongues and rubbed it across their teeth with their nicotine-stained forefingers. Nicotine from Capstan filterless cigarettes and imported Benson & Hedges graciously given to them by benevolent benefactors. At home, their wives had imported soaps and their children wrote with imported ball-point pens. Perks of the job.

Elsewhere, farmers tied their loin cloths, hoisted mammoties on sunburned shoulders and made their way to the fields. Bus drivers let their engines warm while they sipped plain tea. Bakers stoked huge oven fires and pulled out batches of fragrant bread. Vegetable vendors set up their rickety stalls and sprinkled yesterday's vegetables with water so they looked less tired. Weary fishermen pulled their boats to higher ground and went home to sleep and dream of bursting nets and real houses.

They heard his whistle before they saw him and sat forward in anticipation. He strode into the clearing and stopped. 'Oho. It's the friends.'

They smiled.

He walked up and sat on his haunches a few feet away from them. He pulled out his little plastic packet and went through his betel chew ritual while they watched and waited. Patiently. Curiously.

'Why did you come?'

The question took them by surprise.

Niranjan looked a little affronted. 'If we're in your way, we'll go.'

The toddy tapper shook his head, not looking at them. 'You're not in my way. I simply asked why you came.'

'To see you,' Priyanthi said.

He looked up. 'Oh yes?'

They nodded.

'Why?'

'No reason,' Priyanthi said.

He nodded again. As if he knew the reason. 'You have names?'

'I'm Priyanthi.'

'I'm Niranjan.'

'Priyanthi. That's a good Sinhalese name,' he commented.

Niranjan looked a little dejected. Then he continued, 'And Niranjan. That sounds like a name for a king. Will you be a king one day, I wonder?'

Niranjan looked uncertainly at him, wondering if he was joking, but there was no smile on his face. 'I don't know if I want to be a king.'

'Why not?'

'Imagine being responsible for so many people ... for an entire country ... it must be awfully hard.'

The man nodded. 'Yes. But perhaps not that kind of king.'

Priyanthi frowned. 'What other kind is there?'

The man cocked his head and thought for a while. 'The world is full of kings and queens,' he said eventually.

Niranjan looked sceptical. 'What do you mean?'

The man smiled. It was the first time they had seen him smile. He put his fingers to his mouth, expertly spat out a stream of red betel juice and covered it with some sand. 'It's like this. You know kings and queens? Like we used to have long ago? Parakrama, Dutugemunu, Kasyappa, Vihara Maha Devi?'

They both nodded.

'They're one kind. Then you get the other kind. The farmer who is king of his field, the fisherman who is king of his boat, the son who is king of his home, the toddy tapper who is king of his trees.'

'But they're not real kings,' Priyanthi said, frowning.

'Of course they are. And sometimes they're better kings than the real kings. Maybe because their kingdoms are smaller, their subjects poorer and therefore less demanding, their duties less. My kingdom only has these trees in it, so I can look after every one of them properly.'

'Are they yours?'

He laughed. 'No, child. They're not mine. I only work for the owner.'

'So the owner is the real king, isn't he?' Niranjan said somewhat challengingly.

He turned to stare at Niranjan. 'It is not necessarily he who owns a kingdom who is king, but he who cares for it.'

Niranjan fell silent, digesting this new thought. The man started folding up his plastic bag, a sign that he was about to leave them. He tucked it into his waist and stood up.

'Wait,' Priyanthi said.

He looked enquiringly at her.

'What's *your* name?' she asked.

'I am the King of the Coconut Trees,' he said grandly, and lithely began climbing up the tree.

* * *

'What do you think of him?' Priyanthi asked Niranjan.

'I can't make up my mind,' he said, dragging a coconut leaf along the sand, making long ridges that later in the day a tourist would come across and photograph carefully with his expensive Nikon camera, convinced he had discovered the tracks of a strange jungle animal. The man at the Quick Photo developing place in Bentota town would look at the prints, scratch his head and think to himself that these tourists got crazier by the day.

'What do you think he meant about kings and everything?'

'I don't know. I think he was trying to teach us something.'
'You don't know?'
'Not really. He's a strange one.'
'I like him,' Priyanthi said.
'So do I. I think,' Niranjan said.

They reached the house. Thankfully, Hemantha was nowhere in sight. He was still sleeping, having bribed Siri the previous night to bring him a bowl of toddy from the town.

'I don't know why this child is still sleeping,' Enid said. 'Niranjan, go and wake him up, will you?'

Niranjan went. He bent over Hemantha, who was snoring loudly with his mouth open, and then reeled back from the stench of stale alcohol. He wrinkled his nose in disgust, and shook Hemantha's foot hard. Hemantha stirred and made tasting noises with his tongue.

'Wake up, you slob,' Niranjan hissed, shaking his foot. 'Wake up!'

Hemantha stirred, then opened one bloodshot eye. 'Go away,' he mumbled. 'I want to sleep.'

'I don't want you to get up. Your mother does, and unless you wake up right now, she's going to come and wake you herself and I don't think she's going to be too pleased with your toddy breath,' Niranjan said, and left the room.

The next morning, they waited for their friend under his coconut tree. Today, the sky was overcast and there were no colours in it. Just fat black-grey clouds that looked like lowered brows. The rest of the sky was a sulky silver. It was decidedly chilly and Priyanthi was wearing a flannel shirt under Hemantha's jacket. Even so, she shivered when the wind brushed her bare neck and ankles. The coconut trees stirred fretfully as gale-force gusts tore through them, and even the short shrubs on the beach bent this way and that like squat dwarves in a grotesque ballet. The beach was used to sunshine and gentle breezes. This kind of sullenness was hard to respond to.

Niranjan and Priyanthi were quiet. She had wondered if he would want to go in this weather, but all he said when he emerged from the house was 'Let's go.' It was hard to tell what time it was because there was no sun to rise, no light in the sky. It felt late, and they both silently wondered if he would come at all. Did toddy tappers tap toddy in these hostile conditions? Even if they were kings of coconut trees? Then they heard his whistle and they looked at one another and smiled.

Today, he wore a banian, the sleeveless vest people usually wore under their shirts. Niranjan looked at it and wondered if he had worn it because it looked like rain, and if so, what sort of protection it would afford. He looked slightly sad and preoccupied.

As usual, he stopped at the edge of the clearing and looked at them. They looked back at him. Then Priyanthi jumped to her feet and raced across the clearing to him. 'You came!' she exclaimed, grabbing his hand.

He looked down at her hand in his and smiled. 'Yes. I have to work, no?'

He let her hand lie in his as they walked to where Niranjan was.

'The Tamil friend,' he said in greeting.

'Yes,' Niranjan said, smiling. The qualification didn't sound bad any more. It was like a title of sorts, he thought.

The toddy tapper nodded approvingly. 'You understand,' he said. 'It took you a while, but I knew you would eventually.'

Niranjan wondered if he could read minds. Like Priyanthi could sometimes.

The toddy tapper squatted and pulled out his plastic bag, and they waited quietly until he had his betel chew firmly lodged in his cheek.

'Why do you chew betel?' Priyanthi asked.

He didn't look up. 'Why do you come here every morning?'

She looked puzzled. 'To see you.'

'Why?'

'Because I like you.'

He nodded. 'That's good.'

She lapsed into silence, trying to figure that one out.

'Is that why you're wearing a banian today?' Niranjan asked, smilingly.

He laughed. 'No. That's not why.'

Niranjan looked at him.

He spat out some betel juice. Then, after he had covered it with sand, he spoke. 'I got hurt here,' pointing to his chest.

'So you wore it to protect your wound?'

He seemed to hesitate, then he shook his head. 'No.'

'Then why?' Niranjan persisted. Priyanthi was starting to feel uncomfortable. It was obvious that he didn't want to tell them, so why was Niranjan pushing him?

The man rocked back on his heels, the smile now gone. 'I didn't want you to see it,' he finally said.

'Can we see it?' Priyanthi asked immediately.

He shook his head.

'No?' Priyanthi was disappointed. Her eyes dulled and her mouth drooped at the corners.

He sighed and lifted his banian. Under the ribs on his left side was an ugly gash about six inches long. It was covered with a thin film of yellow ointment. Some herbal medicine probably. The wound wasn't deep but the skin looked as if it had been scraped off. Violently.

Priyanthi shuddered and covered her eyes with her hands. Niranjan just stared, horrified at the sight.

The toddy tapper started to pull it down again, but stopped as Priyanthi said, 'Wait.'

She crawled forward and looked at it. Then she gently traced its outline with her fingers and looked up at his face, her eyes swimming with tears. 'What happened? Did someone hurt you?'

He had gone very still, his eyes dark with some unreadable thought. He took her hand, bowed his head and placed it on his forehead. After a moment, he gently laid it back in her lap. He pulled his banian down to cover the bruise.

'Did someone hurt you?' she repeated.

'Yes.'

'Why?'

'It's a long story,' he said, looking through them and the trees and the oppressive sky. Seeing something else altogether.

'Will you tell us?' she persisted.

'Why not.' He sat back on the sand, crossed his legs lotus-style and looked at them. They inched closer and watched him with intent faces. Priyanthi's eyes kept going back to the now concealed gash.

'I have a family,' he began. 'A wife and two children. They live over on the other side of the road beyond that coconut grove you can just see from here. My wife is a good woman, beautiful, hard-working and uncomplaining. Every morning, she cooks for us, washes and dresses the children and sends them off to school. Then she cleans the house and goes to work. She stands by the side of the road selling toddy.'

'The toddy that you collect?' Niranjan asked.

He nodded. 'It doesn't belong to me, though. She sells it for the owner and is paid twenty-five cents for every bowl she sells. She stands from late morning until lunchtime in the scorching heat, smiling and waiting for people like your parents to stop and buy toddy. Just after noontime, she returns to our hut and feeds us, and after the children lie down for their afternoon nap, she goes out again and stands there until late at night. Some days, she makes five rupees, some days more, some days less. Some days, she comes home with nothing. Those are bad days.'

He paused to spit out some red betel juice which slowly sank into the sand like blood. Then he gazed towards the road where his home was, where his wife was getting ready to go out and stand by the side of the road.

Traffic was just starting. They could hear the dull whooshing sounds of cars and buses and lorries full of coconuts driving past. On the other side of them, huge grey foaming waves crashed on the sand, leaving faint rims of foam as a testimony to their anger.

Niranjan and Priyanthi waited.

'Yesterday, she sold nothing. I don't know what the reason was. Maybe people didn't feel like drinking toddy and getting drunk. Maybe only poor people with no toddy money went by yesterday, but how could that be? If people have cars, then they must have toddy money. Maybe the gods were just angry with us yesterday. Whatever the reason, she didn't sell a single bowl. In the evening, the owner, Mr Fernando from the big yellow house in the town, sent his man to collect the day's toddy takings. When my wife told him she hadn't sold anything, he didn't believe her. He accused her of hiding the money, of stealing from his employer. I was sleeping inside, but when I heard him shouting, I went outside. I explained to him that my wife would never lie, much less steal. I told him that he was wrong to insult her and to bring dishonour on her by saying these things. He is an influential man, more educated than I am. I am only a labourer. I spoke reasonably and without raising my voice. He had a bicycle chain in his hand. He usually carries it around with him in case of trouble. He hit me.'

Niranjan was shocked. He wasn't so shielded by his parents that he didn't know things like this happened. But it was the first time that it had happened to someone he knew. As much as he could claim to know the toddy tapper. 'What did you do?'

The man smiled bitterly. 'Nothing.'

Now Niranjan was really shocked. 'Nothing? But he hit you. For no real reason.'

'Yes. But what could I do, Tamil friend? He works for the man I work for. He is powerful, feared, hated. People like me don't hit people like him.' His voice was flat. Somewhere deep beneath it, anger and frustration wrestled to rise to the surface.

Niranjan shook his head in disbelief. 'What would he have done if you had hit him?' he demanded.

The toddy tapper's face was expressionless. 'He would have probably swung the chain at me one more time, maybe across my face, and left.'

'So why didn't—'

'Then he would have come back late at night. Not alone this time, but with others. They would have dragged us out of our beds, beaten me so that I would have been still conscious but unable to move. Maybe they would have raped my wife in front of my eyes, slapped my children a few times and left. And of course, I would have lost my job.' The account was delivered in a monotone, more credible because of its singular lack of drama or animation.

The two of them just sat there, trying to understand all of it and failing. They had seen people get angry with one another and shout, Niranjan had seen two men get into an argument which had led to a fist fight. But those incidents were the kind that flared up suddenly in the heat of anger. Not this carefully calculated, precisely planned violence.

While he was talking, Priyanthi felt a peculiar weakness slowly flow through her body, leaving her hands limp and her heart sluggish. Niranjan felt as if he had just taken a downward ride in a really fast elevator. His stomach felt hollow. He wondered if it was wiser for them to leave. Priyanthi was his responsibility and maybe they could become involved in all this just by talking to the toddy tapper. Who knew who was watching?

They sat there, the three of them, staring at each other intently as if trying to read each other's minds, when in reality they were trying to read their own. Eventually Priyanthi moved to sit next to the toddy tapper. She laid her head on his knee and looked up at him. 'I don't understand how people can be like that. I am not yet grown up. But I am so very sorry that this happened to you,' she said softly.

He stroked her hair with his hard, callused hands. 'I pray that you will never know that kind of violence, but I am afraid you will. I don't think many people live and die without experiencing it at least once.'

She looked up, frightened. 'You think so?'

'I know so.' Then he straightened up. 'What am I doing?' It was a question that didn't require an answer. 'I must be mad, sitting here and telling you my troubles, frightening you with my silly predictions. And look at how late it is! I won't have a job tomorrow if I don't hurry up today.' He jumped to his feet.

Niranjan looked anxious. 'Will you be okay climbing in this weather?'

He smiled. 'Thank you for your concern. My wife too

worries on days like this. She says it's a bad omen, but I know it is just the gods testing my courage.'

'Why do you do it? Can't you get any other work?' Niranjan said.

'I could. I love doing this. I feel like a hero when I am up there, brave and invincible.'

He started climbing. Halfway up, he stopped and looked down at them. 'Tomorrow, I will take you to my home,' he said.

The hotel pool area was empty. Inside, the manager wrung his hands and cursed the gods for taking the sunshine away. If it rained, the tourists would grumble and lounge around the hotel and look accusingly at him. As if he was personally responsible for the weather. He decided to send a message to the local dance troupe and schedule a low-country dance performance for the evening. At least there would be plenty of photo opportunities.

Priyanthi wondered what sun-worshippers did on gloomy days.

Just before they reached the house, it started to rain. Big, painful drops that turned into a downpour in seconds. As if the sky had been waiting for a signal from somewhere. They stopped and looked at each other, struck by the same thought. Would the toddy tapper be safe?

The distinct line of the horizon had disappeared so the endless expanse of restless water merged unhindered with the grey sky. The coconut trees and mangroves writhed and swayed and occasionally a large mangrove fruit dropped to the sand with a dull thud. Blue-white lightning flickered through the sky and thunder crashed immediately afterwards, distant now, but getting closer by the minute. When Niranjan was a child, he had asked his mother what thunder was; she had told him it was the angels playing cricket in heaven.

This was a particularly rough game.

* * *

The two families stayed indoors all day. Priyanthi leaned

against one of the wooden posts on the veranda, an open book in her hand and worry in her eyes. She stared out over the beach where the rain still sheeted down and wondered if he was all right. If he had made it safely from tree to swaying tree and down again. She wondered if his wound hurt when it got wet, for it surely would have.

She had always loved the rain.

Until now.

Eleven

❧

Colombo was usually warm and humid even during the south-west monsoon when it rained steadily for two months. In Colombo, the monsoon meant that office workers walked through huge puddles to work, leaping to avoid being splashed by careless three-wheelers, cars crept along trying to avoid pot-holes concealed by mud, drains overflowed and carried rotting vegetables from the market areas. Buses ploughed past bus halts reluctant to stop for dripping hordes of people with their streaming umbrellas, and taxis did brisk business.

During the rains, the days were warm and wet. The nights, however, were cool and slightly crisp. The air was redolent with the fragrance of flowers borne on damp monsoon breezes. Gardens smelled of wet earth and fresh grass.

In homes, diligent housewives cleaned up mud tracks with tiring repetition. Grated coconut, after its milk had been extracted for cooking, was carefully stored in plastic bags. When floors became dull from the wet, it was strewn around, rubbed by hand on every inch and then swept up and thrown away. The tiny quantities of oil still left in the coconut made floors shine better than any commercial polish could.

Pans were placed under leaks in roofs and housewives flew around shutting windows against the wind and rain. In spite of all this, their houses looked muddy and smelled damp. Children wore plastic rain coats to school and stepped daintily around puddles so their white canvas shoes didn't get dirty. They still did.

Rain fell in the night, crept in through gaps and leaky

shutters and lay on classroom floors, sometimes an inch high. Classrooms had to be swept and mopped before lessons could begin. Chairs had to be wiped with old newspapers but the damp seeped into the cheap jak wood. Children wore damp patches on the backs of their school clothes like special monsoon badges.

The rate of student absence was high due to rain-related illnesses. After school, children deliberately stood outside bus shelters so they got wet. They played in puddles, sailed paper boats down swollen drains and got coughs and colds. The pungent smell of boiling koththamalli herbal tea drifted out of kitchen windows.

Priyanthi didn't play in the rain, but she did lean out of her bedroom window at night to breathe in the rain smells. It was like the smell of sunshine on fresh washed sheets which had been dried outdoors on clothes lines or flat on the springy grass. Just different.

* * *

She returned her attention to her book, but found she couldn't concentrate. She laid it down and went to the kitchen. The steps were wet so she couldn't sit. Siri had strung a clothes line between two coconut trees and a few dusters flapped wetly on it. He must have forgotten to take them in and now it was too late. Another gust of wind blew in from the sea and the line rocked wildly, the dusters looking like frightened children on a dangerous swing. She thought of her new friend being blown about on his flimsy rope roads and shuddered.

Siri came in carrying some coconuts. He was wearing a plastic bag on his head, and although it had kept his hair dry, the rest of him streamed water over the steps. He shook himself off like a dog and entered the kitchen.

'Siri,' Priyanthi said tentatively.

'Yes, child. Want hot cocoa? Siri make soon soon.'

'No. I don't want any.' She hesitated.

'Yes?' Siri said encouragingly.

'You know the toddy tapper, don't you?'

'Toddy tapper?'

'The man who climbs coconut trees and taps toddy?'

Siri smiled proudly. 'Oh! Yes. I know. He sister, my wife.'

'Where does he live?'

Siri waved vaguely in the direction of the road. 'Near there.'

'Are you going to see him today?'

'Not now. Maybe later,' Siri said, looking keenly at her.

'Could you—?' She broke off, not knowing how to ask.

'Yes?'

She took a deep breath. 'Could you go now and see if he's okay?'

Siri smiled gently. 'Toddy tapper okay, child.'

Priyanthi was still worried. 'Yes, but it's so windy and he went up this morning. And he's hurt. I thought, maybe you could make some cocoa and take it to his family. There's no need to tell anyone else,' she said, trying to sound casual.

'Okay,' he said equably. 'You want to come?'

She longed to go, but she didn't dare. Not today while everyone was in the house. She would be missed and she knew her mother would have twenty fits if she knew Priyanthi had gone out with Siri. She shook her head. 'I can't. But you go.'

Siri nodded. 'Ten minutes, I go.'

She smiled her thanks and flew into the house. The two sets of parents and Nirmala were sitting in the living room reading and talking. Niranjan and Hemantha were locked up inside their room, where Hemantha was hanging out of the window and smoking while Niranjan read.

Priyanthi tiptoed into her parents' room and rummaged through their suitcase until she found what she was looking for. A tube of Savlon cream. Then she saw a Kandos chocolate at the bottom of the suitcase and took that too. The toddy tapper's children needed it more than they did, she decided.

She ran back to the kitchen and handed them to Siri. 'Take these and give them to him.'

Siri nodded, but began to look a little worried.

She understood. 'If anyone asks, I'll say I took them,' she reassured him. He looked relieved. She watched as he poured the steaming cocoa from the huge ceramic pot into an old arrack bottle and twisted the cap on. Then he poured some into a mug and handed it to her.

'If madams ask, you tell Siri went to bring firewood,' he instructed.

She nodded and watched as he put on his plastic bag hat and disappeared into the veil of rain.

When he came back about half an hour later, carrying a load of dry wood, she was waiting for him in the kitchen. He grinned at her.

'Sepalika say thank you.'

'Sepalika?'

'Wife of toddy tapper.'

'Oh.' She hadn't expected this. 'What did he say?'

'He not home.'

'What? Where is he?'

'Gone to see Fernando mahattaya.' Siri didn't seem too concerned, considering the fact that he obviously knew what Fernando mahattaya's henchman had done.

Priyanthi felt the anxiety mounting. 'Is there a problem?'

'Don't know.' He turned away and started stoking the fire, adding more wood, blowing gustily to get the embers glowing. He coughed violently as smoke billowed out into the kitchen. 'You go, child. Get cough.'

She went.

* * *

All through that day, Priyanthi sat on the veranda, fretting. A dozen different scenarios passed through her mind: his body lying broken at the bottom of a coconut tree, his wife and children bloody and beaten and him dead, the henchman dead and the toddy tapper in jail awaiting trial ... not once did she imagine him sitting at home with his wife and children, sipping a cup of hot cocoa and enjoying his family. Not after what he'd told her this morning.

'What are you doing here, Priyanthi? Come and play charades with us,' said Auntie Violet, looking a little worried.

She appreciated Auntie Violet's concern, but just wanted to be left alone. 'No thanks. I'm not in the mood.'

Violet sighed and went away. That child was never in the mood.

A little while later, Stanley drifted out. 'What's my favourite girl doing out here all by herself?' he boomed heartily.

'Just thinking,' she replied briefly, thinking of what he would say if she told him she was worried sick about a toddy tapper she had met on the beach a few days ago, who had got into an argument with his employer and got beaten for defending his wife's honour.

'Well, come along. Everyone's playing charades in the living room.'

'I don't want to,' she said loudly. Why didn't they just let her be?

'Okay, okay,' Stanley said, wondering which genes from which side had produced this strange intense child who wasn't like either Enid or himself. Not even like her brother. Priyanthi was very much her own person.

She waited until he went off back to the loud laughter in the living room and then sneaked off to her bedroom. Nirmala was with the others, so it was empty. She felt lonely and wished she had someone to talk to. Niranjan didn't seem to want to risk an argument with Hemantha by talking to her during the day, and while part of her could understand that, another part of her hated him for being so weak, so willing to be intimidated by her brother.

She made up her mind to keep a diary when she went back to Colombo. Although it wasn't the same as talking to a person, at least she could safely share her thoughts and imaginings and dreams with something, if not someone.

By seven in the evening, the storm hadn't abated at all. In fact, it seemed to have gathered fury and momentum during the day and now sounded like a whole hell of tortured souls screaming for salvation. Stanley and Bala had brought out their bottle of arrack, procured on an earlier trip into Bentota town. This evening, even the ladies had been persuaded to have a tot in their coffee.

'Good for keeping colds away,' Bala said solemnly, winking at Stanley.

'In that case . . .' Enid allowed herself to be persuaded and then persuaded Violet, who was chilly enough to give in without too much trouble. Nirmala was curled up on the sofa listening to the adults talk and Hemantha had fallen asleep in one of the armchairs.

Niranjan stood at the window and hoped the rain would stop by tomorrow morning. The thought of another day indoors filled him with dismay. He didn't understand why it had become so important for Priyanthi and himself to see the toddy tapper every day. He just knew it was.

He hadn't missed the fact that Priyanthi had been absent from the family fold all day. He knew she was sitting out on the veranda worrying but he was powerless to do anything. Hemantha was waiting for an opportunity to start baiting him again. He was bored because the rain had put paid to his plans to wander over to the hotel, have a beer and watch the foreign girls in their string bikinis and even try to pick one up for some fun in the mangroves.

Niranjan was worried about the toddy tapper too, but less than Priyanthi was. His logic told him the man could look after himself. He was more worried about Priyanthi's worry. Once, he had peeped out to the veranda on his way to the toilet and seen her sitting there with a faraway look in her eyes and a frown between her brows. He had been about to step out and speak to her but Hemantha's voice, impatiently asking him to hurry up, had made him step away from the doorway.

Hemantha's domineering attitude was getting intolerable, but Niranjan sensed that a collapse of the friendship was imminent. They had nothing in common and the only reason Niranjan still spoke to Hemantha was because they had grown up together and had been friends for so long.

The previous day, Hemantha had gone to Bentota town to phone Kamini and invited Niranjan along, generously offering to let him say hello to her. When Bala and Stanley did their arrack run, the boys went with them. And while Bala and Stanley were deciding on whether to buy gal or pol, the boys slipped away to the grocery shop next door and paid a small fortune to phone Kamini. Shop owners didn't like people using their telephones even when the calls were paid for. This man pocketed the money and growled, 'Make it quick.'

Niranjan waited patiently while Hemantha spoke to her, overhearing the conversation in the close confines of the shop.

'So how are you? Missing me and all?' Hemantha was trying to sound cocky but sounded anxious instead.

'Party? What party? You went to a party?'

Niranjan tried to conceal a grin. Hemantha had obviously thought Kamini would stay home and pine for him while he walked the Bentota beach looking for white girls to play with.

'Who did you dance with?' Now Hemantha sounded desperate.

Niranjan tuned the conversation out until the phone was shoved into his face. 'Here, say hello, but quickly. The shop man is looking at us.'

Unwillingly, Niranjan took the phone and murmured hello. Kamini sounded pleased to hear his voice and asked if they were having fun. Niranjan mumbled something and hung up.

Hemantha was lost in thought on the way home, his eyes cloudy and his mouth vulnerable. Niranjan couldn't summon anything more than fleeting pity for him.

* * *

The rain pounded down, leaving coin-sized depressions in the sand and lowering the branches of coconut trees and mangroves. Niranjan wondered where Priyanthi was and decided to go and find her. He missed her chatter and inquisitive mind. Other than a mangy cat who had taken shelter from the rain, there was no one on the veranda. He went to Priyanthi's bedroom, but the door was wide open and he could see it was empty too. He made his way to the kitchen. There she stood, silently cooking rotis on a flat griddle over the roaring fire, while Siri shaped balls of dough into flat circles. He was talking to her about the other guests who had stayed at the bungalow, but she didn't appear to hear him.

'Hi,' Niranjan said.

She didn't reply, just flipped the roti over with the flat spatula and viciously prodded its faintly crusty surface.

It was warm in the kitchen and the smell of the roasting coconut and flour mixture filled the air.

'Aren't you going to speak to me?' he asked, laughter in his voice.

She expertly flipped the cooked roti on to a plate which stood beside her and reached for another ball of dough, which she started to flatten between her palms.

Niranjan picked a crusty bit off the roti and she slapped his hand away. 'Come on, Priyanthi. What have I done?'

She turned to him furiously. 'You knew I was worried and you didn't even come. Not once!' She blew hard into the fire, sending a shower of sparks into the air, making the wood crackle. He saw her eyes were full of tears.

He thought of Hemantha. 'I couldn't,' he said.

'You could have! You were too scared!' Two tears escaped and rolled down her cheeks, sparkling like jewels in the firelight. They reached her jaw, trembled for a moment and fell off. He almost heard them tinkle as they hit the hearth.

'Fine. I was scared. Does that make you happy?' He knew he sounded childish, but he had to say something.

Her expression was scornful. 'You sound stupid. Didn't you hear anything he said to us?'

'Are you worried about him?'

She turned to look at Niranjan and his heart contracted at the look on her face. 'Yes,' she said baldly.

'Do you want to go and see him?' The minute the words were out, he wished he could have taken them back, but it was too late. They hung there hopefully, waiting for a hand to reach out and scoop them up. Her face brightened and she scrubbed her tears away with her hands, leaving soot streaks on her cheeks. 'Could we? Aren't you scared?'

He squared his shoulders. 'No. But we'll have to wait until they're having dinner. We'll eat quickly and go. They'll sit at the table after they've finished and talk for ages.' He didn't dare think of Hemantha.

She nodded, smiling tremulously. 'Oh, Niranjan, I've been so worried. Siri went to see him and said he'd gone to see Fernando mahattaya.'

'He's fine,' he said, hoping it was true. He had so much to tell them still. There was so much yet to learn from him.

He wondered how to get away without arousing too much suspicion.

* * *

In the end it was easy. They bolted down their dinner, Priyanthi studiously ignoring the surprised looks she was getting from Enid and Violet. Earlier in the evening, the two of them had been discussing her mood that day, and Enid had wondered if she would appear for dinner. Now here she was, bright and cheerful and eating as if she hadn't had a decent meal in days.

Enid buttered a piece of roti and dipped it into Siri's excellent beef curry. 'So what are you children planning for tomorrow?'

Priyanthi's mouth was full. Niranjan murmured something about the beach. Hemantha merely grunted.

'There's a cultural show at the hotel tomorrow afternoon and we were wondering if you lot would like to go. That's if the tickets aren't too expensive,' Bala said.

Priyanthi choked on her roti and had to be thumped on the back by Hemantha, who was sitting next to her. She shook her head violently.

Violet looked curious. 'Why not? It'll be nice. Kandyan dancing and all.'

The roti finally slipped down her throat and she was able to speak again. 'It'll just be tourist rubbish,' she sniffed.

'Well, I'd like to go,' Hemantha declared, his eyes already gleaming at the thought of seeing some of those pretty white girls.

'Just want to see the girls, huh?' Bala said.

Hemantha grinned. Enid scowled.

Priyanthi shook her head stubbornly. 'I don't want to go.'

'Well, what will you do while we're there?' Enid asked, wishing her children would agree on something for once.

'I'll stay here. Or go for a walk.'

'These rotis are delicious,' Stanley said, reaching for another one. 'And Siri's beef curry is fabulous. I wish we could take him back with us.'

Enid scowled some more. 'What's wrong with my beef curry?' she demanded.

Stanley back-tracked quickly. 'Nothing. Nothing.' He reminded himself to watch his tongue. That was the trouble with arrack. Hit too hard, too quickly, unlike whisky, which spread through the system slowly, leaving a golden glow in its wake.

Hemantha suddenly stood up. 'I'm going to sleep. I've got a headache,' he announced, and slouched out of the room.

Niranjan and Priyanthi exchanged a look. This was too good to be true. Niranjan suspected that Hemantha was thinking about Kamini and her parties and making himself sick with jealousy.

Priyanthi stood up as well. 'I'm going for a walk.'

'Don't go too far,' Stanley said. 'You don't want to get lost in the dark.'

Niranjan stood up too. 'Don't worry, Uncle Stanley,' he said, 'I'll go with her.'

Stanley looked relieved. 'Good boy. Don't take too long, though.'

They ran out to the veranda. Then Niranjan stopped. 'What are we doing? We don't even know where he lives.'

'Let's ask Siri,' Priyanthi suggested, running out into the rain, which had slowed into a heavy drizzle. She made her way to the kitchen with Niranjan trailing after her.

'Wait, Priyanthi, wait!'

She turned impatiently. 'What?'

'Siri might tell.'

She shook her head. 'No he won't. I'm sure.'

Siri was sitting on the kitchen floor, eating his own dinner. He put his plate down and stared at the two of them. 'What matter, childrens?'

'Siri, where does your brother-in-law live?' Priyanthi asked, trying to appear casual. 'We have to go and see him.'

Siri nodded, not looking surprised at all. 'Go to main road, cross to other side, then after small petti kadé, go down small lane. Only one house after kumbura. His house.'

Priyanthi was about to dash out again when she suddenly stopped. She rushed into the kitchen, grabbed a heap of rotis from the plate where they sat, added a huge dollop of onion sambol on top of the pile, shoved it into a plastic bag and put it under her jacket. 'For him,' she explained to Siri, who nodded imperturbably and kept eating.

The main road was lit, but empty. People were in their warm homes, discussing the unseasonal rain over hot dinners. Occasionally a bus or a car whizzed by, throwing up sprays of rain water, which they leaped to the side of the road to avoid. They hurried along and almost missed the small shop Siri had described because it was boarded up, shut for the night.

'There it is.' Priyanthi's eyes were sharp. 'We have to cross here.'

They dashed across the empty road and turned down the small lane which was more like a mini river of mud. They sloshed their way slowly. Only the distant glow of the street lights from the main road provided any illumination.

Niranjan looked about him worriedly. 'We should have brought a torch. We'll probably get lost and wander around in the dark until morning.'

Suddenly they heard a long, mournful cry and stopped. Priyanthi clutched Niranjan's arm. 'Niranjan, I'm scared,' she whispered.

So am I, Niranjan thought. 'It's probably just a cow,' he said.

They heard something moving around in the undergrowth on the side of the road and stood stock still. The cry came again, loud and plaintive. Niranjan laughed. 'What did I tell you! It's only a cow.'

They walked on, holding hands, their feet feeling the way in the darkness. Then they saw a tiny glow a few yards away. 'There it is,' Priyanthi said softly. 'That must be his house.'

They were suddenly shy, wondering what he would think of their coming here at this hour. They could see the hut now, a small hump of a structure with a thatched roof. The door was suddenly pushed open and a figure stood there silhouetted against the lamplight.

'Who is it?' the figure called out in a loud voice.

They stopped.

'Is this the toddy tapper's house?' Niranjan asked, angry to discover that his voice was shaking.

The figure peered out into the light rain. Then there was an exclamation. 'My God! It's the friends! What are you doing here?'

Priyanthi pulled her hand free from Niranjan's hand and flew to him. 'Oh! You're all right!' she exclaimed, her voice breaking with relief. 'I was so worried about you!'

He looked down at her with amazement. Then he looked beyond them. 'Did you come alone?'

Niranjan stepped forward. 'Yes. Siri gave us directions.'

The toddy tapper looked bemused. 'I see. Well, you'd better come inside.' He led the way inside through the low doorway. The darkness smelled faintly of kerosene and damp mud.

Niranjan and Priyanthi were both thinking that he didn't seem too pleased to see them. Should they have waited for tomorrow? Suddenly all the worry seemed childish and foolish.

The dim light they had seen turned out to be a bottle lamp which had been placed on the floor in a corner. In its flickering glow they saw the mud walls which had been roped to keep them in place. At the four corners were sturdy coconut log supports. The roof was made from thatched coconut leaves, and whoever had made it had taken the trouble to neatly trim the ends straight.

The toddy tapper stood in the middle of the small bare room

and finally smiled at them. 'Welcome to my palace,' he said, spreading his arms wide to encompass the room. He seemed very big in it.

They grinned back in relief. He wasn't angry. They looked around the room. There was a long bench against one wall, made from three squat coconut logs with a large, beautifully planed and polished slab of wood nailed over it. A stack of books was arranged neatly on the floor in one corner of the room and there was an assortment of clothes hanging from a few large hooks nailed into the wall. A pile of folded bedding sat in another corner, a few lumpy pillows placed on top. That was all. Straight ahead was another small doorway. Doorless. Beyond it was darkness.

Out of the darkness appeared a tall, slim woman carrying another bottle lamp, with two small round-eyed children clinging to her reddha. The lamp cast mysterious shadows on her face, making her seem ghostly.

Niranjan and Priyanthi smiled awkwardly at her. She looked at them, her eyes dark and unfathomable.

'This is my wife Sepalika,' said the toddy tapper. His eyes softened as he looked at the woman. 'And these are my children Rama and Sita.'

'From the Ramayana!' Priyanthi exclaimed in surprise.

The woman smiled faintly and nodded. 'Yes. It was always one of my favourite stories.' Her voice was low and undoubtedly cultured. Her Sinhalese was not like her husband's.

Now she was in the light of two bottle lamps. Priyanthi and Niranjan stared at her. She had an aristocratic face with long, dark eyes, arched eyebrows and a thin, straight nose, but her reddha was torn and her blouse was threadbare and pinned together between her breasts with a safety pin. It just didn't go together, the face and voice, and the clothes, house and husband. They tried not to stare.

The woman smiled. 'Please sit down,' she said graciously. More graciously than even Priyanthi's grandmother. 'I'll bring some tea. You must be tired after your walk.'

'Tea?' her husband said with some disappointment. 'I was

going to bring them here for some kiribath tomorrow morning, and now all we're going to give them is tea?'

She smiled at him, and then turned to look at them. 'Would you like to share our dinner? It's not very much, I'm afraid.'

Before they could protest, before they could tell her they had already eaten, he cut in. 'Nonsense!' he declared loyally. 'You are the best cook in the world. Whatever you have, it must taste wonderful and we must let these poor travellers have some.' He turned to look anxiously at them. 'You will have some, won't you?'

'We've already—' Niranjan broke off with a wince as Priyanthi's elbow found its mark in his ribs.

'We'd love to,' she smiled.

Sepalika nodded. 'I'll be only a few minutes,' she promised, and went through the door.

The toddy tapper sat on the floor and waved them to the bench. 'Sit there. Or here on the floor if you prefer,' he said. His children stood against the wall and watched silently.

Priyanthi sat on the floor, as close to him as she could. Niranjan sat on the bench.

'I'm sorry we just came like this,' Niranjan said. 'We were worried about you.'

He raised an eyebrow. 'Worried? Why?'

'The storm, and then Siri told me that you went to see Fernando mahattaya, and after what happened yesterday—' Priyanthi broke off with a shudder.

He sighed. 'I knew I shouldn't have told you. I have climbed those trees for the last ten years. I know every bit of them, every sway in them. I treat them well and they treat me well. And as for Fernando mahattaya, I only went to tell him what happened.'

'What did he say?' Niranjan asked.

'Nothing much. But at least he knows. It's better that he does. Now, if something happens to me, at least people know whom to blame.' He didn't sound concerned. He looked down at Priyanthi. 'So you were worried,' he said.

'We both were,' she said, shooting Niranjan a look.

'Were you?' he asked Niranjan.

Niranjan nodded. 'Not as much as she was, though.'

His eyes grew soft. He absently stroked Priyanthi's hair. 'You're a good child,' he said. 'But too much worrying will make you grow old quickly.'

'Tell me about Sepalika,' Priyanthi said.

Above her head, the toddy tapper smiled to himself. Niranjan saw that smile and something in him ached slightly.

'Do you know what sepalika is?' the toddy tapper said. 'It's the name of a flower. A small white flower like a star, with a bright orange stem. Some people call it Queen of the Night. It has the most beautiful smell at night. People say that if you have a sepalika tree in your garden, you are fortunate, blessed by the gods. I have my flower all day and all night. I am blessed by the gods and more fortunate than any man alive.'

Rama and Sita crept closer to listen. He laughed softly. 'They have heard this story so many times but they still love to hear it.'

'Go on,' Priyanthi said impatiently.

'I met Sepalika when I was twenty. I was a brash young man with more muscles than brain. She was two years younger and so beautiful. Like a freshly bloomed flower. I was a penniless labourer. She was the daughter of a rich man. I lived in a hut like this one with my mother and father and my four sisters, working hard so we could collect enough money for dowries for them when the time came. She was the only child of doting parents. Upper-class landowners. I stopped going to school when I was thirteen so I could help my father in the fields. She was about to go to university.' He stopped and became lost in thought. Outside, the wind picked up and blew in through the open doorway. It made the smoke-tipped orange flame of the bottle lamp flicker wildly, casting long shadows of unseen strangers on the uneven mud walls.

They waited.

'I worked in her father's paddy fields during the harvesting season. One day, they said there was to be a big party at the big house. It was his only child's eighteenth birthday. They wanted everyone to come and help that evening. I wore the only sarong I had and my only decent shirt. It was just after six in the evening and the house looked like a page from a child's storybook – strung with coloured lights, flowers everywhere, music playing inside, white-coated caterers running to and fro setting up huge tables with white cloths for the food. There were about seven of us from the village. We were assigned various jobs. Mine was to arrange the chairs in the garden. In circles of ten, the mistress of the house told me, and while I was arranging them, carefully counting because I get easily confused with numbers, she came out. She was dressed in blue. Pale blue sari, hair braided with blue flowers and ribbons. She looked like a mermaid. My heart was pounding so hard, I thought I would faint.' He smiled wryly at the memory. They smiled with him.

'Then she came and spoke to me. I cannot remember what she said. I didn't speak – I couldn't because my tongue clove to the roof of my mouth, I was so nervous. I just looked at her and I couldn't look away. We stood like that for a long time. Then people came and she had to go. For the rest of the evening, my eyes followed her, memorising her, storing away every detail of her for later.'

'Just a few minutes more,' Sepalika called from the kitchen. No one answered.

'The next day, she came to the fields where I was working. We spoke under the old jambu tree which still stands by the small pond. We exchanged words of love and promises, and all the while I wondered if this was not pure foolishness, but it was already too late. My heart was given. From that day onwards, we met every day. For two years nobody knew because we were very careful not to be seen. We talked of love but never of the future, for what future could a labourer have with a landowner's daughter? But one day, she came to me with the news that her father had arranged a marriage for her with a rich man from Galle. That same day, we ran away. We went to Hambantota further down the coast and got married.'

He paused to pop a chew of betel into his mouth.

'And?' Priyanthi prompted.

'We came back and told her parents. They went mad. They locked her up in a room for weeks. Her father set his thugs on me and they beat me up to within an inch of my life. But we had already planned what we were going to do because we knew all this would happen.'

'Then why did you do it?' Priyanthi demanded. 'If you knew you would be beaten and all?'

The toddy tapper smiled. 'I loved her,' he said simply. 'It was worth every blow. But anyway, we carried out our plan. We stopped eating. She refused to eat anything and I sat outside her father's house and did the same. Her parents tried everything. They offered me huge amounts of money to leave the area, they threatened me, they set fire to my parents' house.'

Priyanthi gasped, but he smiled. 'My father and mother are okay. They moved to Aluthgama and they're fine. So finally, her family allowed us to be together. But they cut her off. Not just financially, but from the family. They said that from that moment on, their daughter was dead to them.'

Niranjan shook his head in disbelief. 'Do you still see them? Are they from Bentota?'

The toddy tapper nodded. 'Oh yes.'

'And they don't ever ask about her? They don't want to see her?' Priyanthi sounded incredulous too. Parents didn't do that to children, no matter what children did to them.

'No.'

'But have you tried to talk to them? If they see her perhaps they'll forgive her,' she persisted.

'They see her. Every day, when she stands by the road selling toddy, when she takes the children to the beach, when she walks down to the well to draw water, they see her. Her father is Fernando mahattaya,' he finished flatly.

They stared.

'She could have been a university-educated woman with a rich husband and a beautiful home. Instead, she chose this hut and me. We have everything and nothing. More of everything, though.' He rose and went to the door to spit out his betel. He turned around, and they saw pride in his face. 'Now you understand what I meant about kings and queens. What man wouldn't be a king if he was married to a woman like that?'

Priyanthi found her eyes were full of tears and dashed them away self-consciously. 'You *are* lucky,' she said, her voice wobbling slightly.

He smiled. 'I told you I was.'

An hour later, they hurried through the darkness with him, hoping no one had missed them back at the house. They didn't really care. They had eaten their second dinner of the evening and it had been much better than the first. Red, unpolished country rice with dry fish gravy and coconut sambol. Poor people's food which tasted like heaven when eaten from the earthenware lids of cooking pots. Sepalika didn't have enough plates for all of them. Actually they had only two, for the two children, and Priyanthi and Niranjan had insisted on eating from the lids. Sepalika and her husband ate from two extra earthenware pots.

They had eaten and talked and now they went home reluctantly with promises to return whenever they could. The toddy tapper led the way through the windy darkness. 'Come on! Come on!' he called. They stumbled on, too replete to be walking this quickly.

'Don't say where we went,' Niranjan instructed Priyanthi. 'Just say we got lost.'

'You think I'm stupid?' she retorted indignantly.

They hurried on.

When they reached the house, the toddy tapper melted away into the darkness with a smile and a wave and they ran up to the kitchen. Siri was sitting there, looking anxiously into the distance. He looked relieved to see them. 'Okay, okay. No problem,' he whispered.

'Madams sleeping. I tell sirs you go on beach look for crabs. I tell you safe and you okay.'

'They're not angry?' Priyanthi whispered.

'They drunk,' he informed them.

They grinned with relief and sneaked off to bed.

TWELVE

For the rest of that week, they saw him every morning. They waited until he finished his trips down the rope roads and then went with him to his house to play with Rama and Sita and to feast on Sepalika's cooking.

She viewed them with a mixture of affection and amusement. Sometimes exasperation. They were like two small shadows following her husband everywhere he went. As if there were things to be learned simply by being in his presence.

Which there were.

In everything he told them, there was some kind of a moral, a reason for it being told. Initially, it was a game for them to guess. After a while, it became important. As if the day could not continue without some of his off-beat wisdom.

Sepalika was wise too, but in a different way. An educated way. She had been a prolific reader when she lived with her parents and had books bought for her. And although it had been many years since she had read a book, she still remembered her favourite tales.

Mythology had been a particular favourite of hers. Now, she shared her stories with Priyanthi and Niranjan and her own two children, who settled themselves deep in her reddha and listened with wide eyes. She told them about Narcissus and his vanity, about Jason and his argonauts and about Ravana and his kingdom which had been right here in Lanka; about Rama, who lost Sita to Ravana.

For Priyanthi and Niranjan, the little hut was like a retreat from real life, an ashram where world-weary people went to rediscover the meaning of life and to re-partake of its more simple pleasures.

Araliya Gardens and Dierdre and Kamini's Colombo 7 house seemed like something out of a film they had seen a long time ago. Another life altogether.

Even going back to the spacious beach house, designed and furnished for wealthy foreigners, aroused feelings of discontent, of guilt. They had so much space and so many luxuries while the toddy tapper and his tiny family seemed to be constantly teetering on the brink of starvation. And still willing to share what little food and wisdom they had.

Priyanthi sometimes wheedled some food from Siri and took it to Sepalika, but although she accepted it with gracious thanks, there was always a hint of humiliation in her face and voice.

* * *

On their last day in Bentota, Priyanthi and Niranjan walked quietly to the clearing and greeted the toddy tapper with muted pleasure. They waited until he came down the last tree, which they knew well by now, and walked to the little hut. Neither of them said much, but their thoughts were as deep as the ocean.

He glanced at them occasionally, thought of telling them a funny story to cheer them up and then decided not to. They were entitled to their feelings of sadness. Who was he to take that very necessary sadness away from them?

They chatted quietly with Sepalika, helped her to toss the rice in her winnowing fan to disperse whatever tiny husks remained in it, and later sat quietly watching her cook kiribath, milk rice.

'Today, you leave us,' she said.

They didn't reply. Both their hearts nodded heavily.

'You won't forget us.' It was a statement. 'And one day, you will come back to see us. I can feel it here,' she said, touching her chest.

Still they said nothing. Priyanthi swallowed hard to dislodge the uncomfortable lump in her throat. Her eyes felt hot and gritty. Niranjan gazed out into the green endlessness beyond the open kitchen door. Trees and grass and shrubs which ran into each other, pushed aside one another, fighting for space to grow.

The time to leave always arrives too swiftly. To Priyanthi, it felt as if all the clocks had been put on fast forward.

They stood awkwardly at the doorway.

'Say goodbye,' the toddy tapper instructed his two giggling children, who hid behind their mother.

Priyanthi squeezed her eyes shut for a moment and opened them to find Sepalika regarding her with tenderness.

'It's okay. Remember what I said. You will return,' she said.

Priyanthi nodded. She turned to the toddy tapper, who took her hands in his.

'This is your home. We are your family. Never forget that. Both of you. Stay together. As long as you are together, you will remember us,' he said. His voice was soft with regret.

They nodded solemnly. For some reason, Niranjan remembered his First Holy Communion, remembered how he had squeezed his eyes shut and how his hands had held the long ribbon-decorated candle as if his life depended on it. How he had sucked softly on the Host because his friend had told him that if he bit it, it would bleed.

'Go now,' the toddy tapper said, and watched them walk away. He felt strangely bereft, then he felt Sepalika's hand on his shoulder.

'They will be fine,' she said. 'They are survivors like us. You can see it, even at this age.'

'I hope so,' he replied. 'I hope so.'

Thirteen

In the following year, many things happened.

Dierdre and Ed went to England for a holiday.

Enid became pregnant and had to have an illegal abortion, although no one but her husband and Violet knew.

Priyanthi, after months of secretly wondering if she would ever 'grow up', which was what menstruating was known as around here, and grow breasts, finally did the first and waited impatiently for the second to happen.

Hemantha was arrested by the police for standing outside Kamini's house and shouting threats, after she decided that he wasn't as attentive or intelligent as Prakash Rajasingham.

Niranjan, who had been quieter of late, and pensive, decided that he wanted to enter the priesthood and went off to a seminary in Ampitiya to learn the ways of God.

And after a wave of economy-crippling strikes (if indeed it could still be called an economy), the United National Party swept into power on a landslide victory that decisively demonstrated what the people thought of queues and hunger.

* * *

Dierdre and Ed were away for a whole month, and when they returned, they were bombarded with questions about England.

Was it true that the Queen had garden parties all the time and anyone could go? Was it true that everyone, without exception, had roast beef and Yorkshire pudding for Sunday lunch? What exactly *was* Yorkshire pudding? Was it true that there were supermarkets bigger than even the parliament building, where every imaginable kind of food sat on shelves and waited for people to pick them up and take them home? Was it true that people could furnish entire houses after one visit to the city garbage dump? That rich people threw away perfectly good sofas and tables and refrigerators to make room for better ones? Was it true that cats and dogs ate pork and rabbit and tuna from tins? Was it true that strawberries grew everywhere and that anyone could pick them and take them home? That trains ran under the city?

Dierdre snorted. 'There's no place like home, child.'

Ed just grunted.

They too had wondered about all these things. The reality had appalled them. Their so-called rich relatives lived in tiny bedsits, went off wearily to jobs as hospital cleaners, hotel room maids and cleaning ladies and struggled to find a place in a society that didn't much care for poor people, even though it was full of them.

Dierdre, who had gone to inspect what she had thought would be her new home, ended up by entreating her relatives to come back to Sri Lanka. Their substantial rupees had converted into a few paltry pounds, which were spent on the relatives living there.

They thankfully boarded their plane back to Sri Lanka and its limited luxuries.

While Dierdre was away, Enid started to feel a little under the weather. Which was exactly what she initially blamed it on: the searing, relentless heat. But when she missed a period and started to feel ill at the sight of fried eggs, she went off by herself to see Dr Abeysundera at the Dehiwala junction.

She came back feeling even more ill.

For a week, she fretted and wondered what to do. Finally, one evening after Stanley returned home from work, she broke the news to him.

'My God' he said weakly. 'Now what the hell to do.' Although they still had an active and enjoyable sex life, he was stunned. They didn't use formal birth control and usually stayed away from sex during the 'bad time'.

'When did it happen? We were so careful,' he said dully.

She said nothing. She knew exactly when, like most women do. It had been one night after one of Stanley's drinking sessions with Bala. He usually became quite amorous after a few drinks but normally passed out before he could do anything about it. This particular evening, he had fallen on Enid and when she had protested that it was a bad time, he had promised to pull out before anything happened. He hadn't and she had worried about it for a while but then forgotten all about it.

'You'll have to have it,' he said now, reaching for the arrack in the cabinet. This called for a very stiff drink.

'I can't,' Enid said, horrified. 'The children are grown up. What will the neighbours think? What shame!' she said, a moan in her voice.

'What shame!' Stanley declared more robustly, now the arrack was starting to take effect. 'They also do it, no?'

'I don't care about them. I am not bringing shame on my children by having a baby at my age,' Enid said firmly, and then wondered what to do next. She thought briefly of phoning her mother and asking for advice but the thought of her reaction was enough to make her quickly put it out of her mind.

Dierdre? She would have known what to do for sure but it would be weeks before she got back and Enid knew she couldn't wait much longer.

Stanley, once he realised that Enid was definitely not having this baby, heaved a sigh of relief and completely dissociated himself from the whole issue. He justified it by telling himself he had to work to keep them clothed and fed and that this was women's business anyway.

Enid felt alone and bitter about what she saw as Stanley's indifference to a problem that he had caused in the first place.

She fretted for another two days and finally took herself back to Dr Abeysundera and delicately broached the question of a termination.

'At this age, Doctor . . . children are all grown up and all . . .' She phrased her half-sentences carefully.

Dr Abeysundera nodded gravely, steepled his podgy fingers and rested his chins on them. 'It is illegal, you understand,' he said sententiously.

She fidgeted and looked down at the cracked linoleum on the floor.

'So it's not cheap, you understand.'

She nodded.

'Maybe almost a thousand.'

She gasped and looked up. 'That much?'

'You can always have the baby, Mrs Silva. You're a strong, healthy woman. You should have no problem,' he said maliciously.

She shuddered. 'No, no. Give me the name and address.'

He named a prominent gynaecologist and a reputable nursing home and she looked shocked.

'Him? There?'

Dr Abeysundera nodded, not looking the slightest bit uncomfortable. 'I'll have to call him, of course.'

Three days later, Enid broke the news to Violet, who was secretly horrified at the step her friend was about to take, although she was equally horrified at the thought of someone Enid's age having a baby.

'Will you come with me?' Enid pleaded.

Violet nodded and immediately resolved not to tell Bala. This was women's business, she told herself, unconsciously echoing Stanley's words.

So the following day they went to the nursing home, and four hours later Enid went home crampy, drowsy and unpregnant.

That evening, when Stanley came home, everything was ready for him as usual. Dinner was laid on the table, his glass of water and the aanamalu plantain he liked for dessert. After he had eaten, drunk his water and had his plantain, she spoke. 'You remember that thing?' she said, looking meaningfully at her aching stomach.

Stanley looked blank but soon caught on. 'Oh. Oh yes?' He looked worried.

'I took care of it today.'

His face cleared. 'Good. Good. Feeling okay?'

'Yes. Not bad.'

'Good,' he said again.

And that was the end of that.

* * *

Priyanthi was out buying Christmas cards with Niranjan. It was the tenth of December, and although they weren't Christians, Priyanthi still exchanged cards with all her school friends.

They were at Cheap Side, where she was examining the sad assortment available – lurid roses speckled with silver dust that got on everything, a Nativity scene featuring a Mary who looked remarkably like a popular Sinhalese actress, winter snow scenes painted by people who had never seen snow and robins. Priyanthi tried and failed to see the relationship between Christmas and robins.

Niranjan was outside drinking a Necto.

She finally chose ten cards, reluctantly paid for them wondering how they had the nerve to call it Cheap Side when everything was so expensive, and went outside.

It was drizzling and she thought of the toddy tapper, wondering if he was climbing today, how Sepalika was, if he remembered them.

The friends.

It was almost six months since they had seen him and not a day went by when she didn't think of him and his small home. She had written to him but had no reply. She wondered if he could write.

Niranjan said he had dreamed of the toddy tapper once, that he had been talking to them, sitting under the coconut tree. She was envious.

In the last few months, she and Niranjan had hardly even spoken. It was different now that they were home, because everyone seemed to be watching constantly. If she went out into the garden, Enid pushed open the window and asked her where she was going. If she went to Violet's house, Violet came out to chat, to ask her about school, and she always felt embarrassed to ask if Niranjan was home. When they met it was purely by accident, like today, when Niranjan had been at the gate as she was leaving.

He asked her where she was going, and when she told him, he called out to his mother that he was going to the shop with her.

She often wondered if he felt the same vague sense of loss that she did whenever she thought of those few days filled with sunshine and secrets.

'Come on! It's going to pour in a minute and my cards will get soaked,' she called out, quickening her steps.

Niranjan returned the empty Necto bottle to the shopkeeper, got his deposit and followed her.

She was so busy with her thoughts of the toddy tapper that she didn't notice that he had stopped suddenly and was staring at her, his face fiery with embarrassment.

'I love this kind of rain. It's so fine and powdery,' she said, and got no reply. She looked back. 'What are you staring at? Hurry up.'

Niranjan ran up to her, took her hand and steered her down a small road. 'Let's go this way. It's faster.'

She stared at him. 'But it takes twice as long on the side roads.'

'It doesn't matter,' Niranjan said gruffly.

'Of course it matters,' she retorted. 'Why would we take the longer way home?'

'Please, Priyanthi. Just come. I'll explain later.'

She looked around. 'Did you see Hemantha? Is that it?'

He pulled at her hand. 'Damn Hemantha,' he said. 'It's you. Your shorts.'

She stared at him. 'What about my shorts?'

He blushed. 'There's something on the back. We have to get you home to your mother without anyone seeing.'

She twisted around, tugging at the seat of her shorts. When

she saw the red stain, she was first stunned, then jubilant. After all these months of being afraid she was a freak, of watching her friends having their 'growing-up' parties and listening to them discussing cramps and Kotex, she had finally joined the elite ranks of the big girls. According to what she had seen and heard, breasts were next on the agenda.

A huge grin lit up her face. 'Come on. Let's go home!' she commanded, and ran the rest of the way, with him running behind her, begging her to slow down.

As Niranjan's arms and legs obeyed his brain and ran, his thoughts were in a turmoil. Priyanthi was a woman. He knew that this 'growing-up' thing was like a formal introduction to womanhood, but suddenly, she felt different to him.

He looked at her, noticing things he had never noticed before. All the sharp lines and bones in her body seemed to have smoothed out, rounded out. Her arms, her chest, her hips. He tried to think of when it had happened, where he had been, how he hadn't noticed.

He watched her running, her long brown legs lifting high behind her, and wondered with a sense of shock when she had ceased to be a child.

* * *

Luckily for Priyanthi, Enid was too modern to want to do things the traditional way, so she wasn't locked up in a room for seven days. She was, however, ordered not to play cricket or climb the araliya tree. Priyanthi was happy to comply because the uncomfortable Kotex pad between her legs felt like a brick and inhibited even her walking. For the first two days she looked like a duck, waddling around with her legs apart. Gradually, she became used to it.

But it was more than that. She was thrilled at the thought that she was no longer a child, that she was well on her way to womanhood. 'Can I have babies now?' she asked Dierdre, who laughed.

'Babies! You're a baby yourself. What are you wanting babies for?'

'I don't want babies. I just want to know if I *can* have one.'

'Yes,' Dierdre said, sounding a little dazed. What was going through the child's mind? Priyanthi smiled. 'Good.' That made her a real woman.

For the next few days, she walked around the garden, curled up under the araliya tree and read, and did jigsaw puzzles with Nirmala. She seemed to be completely content in her new role.

'I don't know how long it will last,' Enid said darkly, when Violet remarked on how well Priyanthi was adjusting.

After seven days, she was bathed by her mother and grandmother, without the usual audience of arch-eyed female relatives dropping marriage-related hints.

As was the custom, there was a party that evening, and Priyanthi stood at the door in her new pink dress and greeted her guests with a calm graciousness that made her parents beam with pride. Only when Niranjan appeared with his parents did she grin widely and cross her eyes.

During the rest of the party, she behaved with poise. Niranjan watched her and it seemed to him that the old Priyanthi, the one who cried passionately, fought passionately and thought passionately, was gone for ever. He felt bereft.

Priyanthi read Niranjan's thoughts and smiled to herself. He would soon realise she was the same.

She was just so happy that she wasn't a freak any more; she had been the only one in her class who hadn't yet started menstruating and she had seen the looks, heard the whispers.

She wished it wasn't the middle of the school holidays, that she could run in and triumphantly announce her news. Tell them that she knew that Kotex boxes contained pads and not biscuits. That she too had experienced the cramps and the clots.

* * *

Hemantha and Niranjan were seventeen now, still as different as they always had been and still friends. Not the kind of friends who did everything together, shared all their secrets and talked for hours on the phone, but friends by the location of their homes, by the fact that their families were friends.

If they had been given a choice, they wouldn't have chosen one another.

Violet constantly worried about Niranjan falling under Hemantha's influence and becoming a smoker and a drinker, although her maternal instincts told her her son was made of different stuff.

Enid was grateful for the friendship and hoped that Hemantha would become a little more like Niranjan, although her maternal instinct told her it would never happen. Despite his rebelliousness and his waywardness, Hemantha was still her only son and she adored him, going to extraordinary lengths to keep his escapades and bad habits secret from his father. Stanley suspected that Hemantha wasn't all he appeared to be, but whenever he questioned Enid about it, she always allayed his concerns. Just boyish pranks, she said mildly.

Hemantha was going through a particularly bad time. Kamini had been ignoring him lately and when he asked her what was the matter, she laughed and told him not to imagine things. She still went home with him after tuition and he still went to her house almost every day. She still prettily accepted his Portellos and declarations of undying love, but something had changed.

It took him a while to figure out what it was, and when he finally did, he rounded up his Dehiwala junction gang and went to find Prakash Rajasingham. They found him outside his Flower Road home with his group of wealthy friends, standing beside their expensive cars and chatting.

What was to be a man-to-man talk rapidly escalated into a fist fight, and although Hemantha and his friends suffered far fewer injuries, he knew it was just the beginning.

Just before he ran off into his colonial mansion, Prakash delivered his final insult. 'Kamini prefers me to you. She thinks you're just a thug with no brains and no future. Our parents are friends, and one day we'll get married!'

The arrival of a police patrol forestalled Hemantha's answer.

He drove away with his friends and vowed revenge. He also refused to believe that Kamini had ever said anything bad about him, until two days later after tuition class when she refused to be escorted home by him. 'Why, Kamini?' he asked, aware that he sounded pleading and hating himself for it.

She was furious. 'I know what you and your rowdy friends did to Prakash. When will you learn that you can't get everything by fighting?'

'I heard he was bothering you,' Hemantha said, his heart sinking.

'Maybe I like being bothered by him,' she retorted and walked off leaving him standing there. He heard some of the other girls giggling and felt like slapping them. But he decided to go and plead with Kamini once more. Perhaps this was just a fit of pique that a few promises would dispel. He was just in time to see her getting into Prakash Rajasingham's fancy new Mercedes.

* * *

Two days later, he sat at the Perlyn with his junction friends, drinking gal arrack and cursing Kamini and Prakash.

'Tamil bastards deserve each other,' he slurred.

'Kick them all out. Back to bloody India where they came from,' someone said belligerently.

'Right now!' someone else suggested eagerly.

They staggered to their feet fired by the thought of some action, piled into an old station wagon and sped to Prakash's house.

They were disappointed to discover that Prakash and his family were currently holidaying in Nuwara Eliya. 'Won't be back for another week,' the well-dressed servant boy said, turning his nose away from the reek of alcohol.

But there was still Kamini.

'Betraying bitch!' Hemantha shouted drunkenly outside Kamini's gate. The curtains twitched briefly but that was all.

'Tamil whore!' screamed one of the others, pounding the wall with his fists. 'Whore!'

'How much? We want some too!' someone called out, making vulgar gestures with his hand.

Hemantha felt a brief flash of anger, because somewhere in the sober part of his brain he knew Kamini wasn't a whore. But then he remembered her getting into Prakash's car and reason fled in a wave of anger.

'Bitch!' he screamed. 'Bloody Tamil bitch! Come out and see what we'll do to you.' Someone threw an empty Lion Lager bottle towards the house. A window shattered. Someone else threw a large rock, then a brick.

With all the breaking glass and their screams, they didn't even hear the whine of police sirens until the cars stopped a few feet away from them.

This time, Enid couldn't protect Hemantha. Stanley himself had to go and bail him out and plead with Kamini's parents not to press charges.

The shame nearly killed him.

Literally.

After he came back from the police station with his scared but rebellious son in tow, Stanley sat down in the garden to have a quiet drink. He was dazed at the whole incident, shocked that his son could have done such a thing. It stank of thuggery, and although Stanley knew that part of the blame lay with Hemantha's street friends, he still acknowledged with a heavy heart that his son had become a thug.

He blamed himself for being so involved in his work, for believing Enid and not taking an active part in his son's life. For not being around to recognise the signs and do something to change things.

When things could still have been changed.

When he heard Kamini's father's account of what had happened and the words that Hemantha and his friends had shouted, he had paled in shock. Such racism had never had a place in their household. When he looked at his son, silently begging him to deny the terrible accusations, Hemantha had looked down, and his father sighed heavily and paid the thousand-rupee bail. But he also swore that Hemantha would not set foot out of the house again until he changed his ways.

Stanley drained the last of his arrack and rose slowly to go into the house for a refill. The pain that raced through his chest was so intense and so unexpected that it felled him down to the ground. The sound of the glass shattering on the concrete pathway brought Enid running. By the time the ambulance appeared ten minutes later, Stanley was unconscious and all the neighbours were clustered around Enid's front gate.

Stanley survived the heart attack.

Hemantha didn't survive the humiliation. Where once he had loved Kamini, he now hated her and saw her as the cause of all his problems. He vowed to get even. Because he had no access to his junction friends, he looked to Niranjan and only found disgust and disbelief.

Perhaps if Hemantha had been able to explain the incident away, even blame it on alcohol and emotions running high, Niranjan might have understood. As it was, all he saw was an angry, unrepentant stranger. Besides, he knew what had happened – Enid had sobbingly told Violet and Violet had related the incident to her family in stunned tones.

Their first conversation after the incident was strained at best. Soon, Niranjan stopped speaking to Hemantha.

Hemantha couldn't understand it. This was his friend, and in his book, friends stuck together regardless of right and wrong. He didn't particularly cherish Niranjan's friendship, but he was the only one of Hemantha's friends who was welcome in their house. And now *he* had turned.

Naturally Hemantha blamed it on Niranjan's Tamilness. Those bastards always stick together, he thought bitterly, wondering why he had never viewed Niranjan as one of *them* before. But now he knew, he told himself, and savagely added Niranjan's name to his list of people to get even with. He needn't have bothered.

* * *

170

Niranjan was lost in self-discovery these days.

Although he seldom talked about it, the toddy tapper and his simple wisdom had had a powerful effect on him. So had Priyanthi's passage into womanhood, Hemantha's episode with the police and Stanley's subsequent heart attack.

Everyone and everything around him was in such turmoil. He longed for the simplicity of the toddy tapper's tiny home, his stories and advice. Niranjan remembered his last words to them: *As long as you stay together, you will remember.* But how could he stay together with Priyanthi? They were only friends, and now that his friendship with her brother had ended, there was no reason for him to go to their house any more. No excuses to manœuvre casual meetings between the two of them. He didn't dare walk into Priyanthi's home and ask to speak with her; he was still too afraid of Hemantha. He just wasn't brave enough to ignore Hemantha's challenging looks and cutting comments and carry on regardless. But carry on regardless with what? his conscience taunted him. Priyanthi was just fourteen. Far too young for a relationship of any kind, even though she was more mature than most of the adults they both knew. Besides which, she was a Sinhalese girl. No matter how much Auntie Enid and Uncle Stanley loved him and called him 'son', they wouldn't stand for their daughter getting involved with a Tamil boy.

It was pure foolishness to imagine otherwise.

So in his turmoil, he turned to God.

Niranjan had always been a religious boy. He attended Mass every Sunday with his family and said his prayers every night. Now, he prayed for wisdom and courage. He prayed for direction in his life and consolation from his troubles.

* * *

Violet watched her son battle with a myriad unseen ghosts and unnamed emotions and wished with all her heart she could help him. She knew that whatever war he was fighting needed to be fought alone. Yet she was his mother, and one night she tried to talk to him.

171

They were sitting in the garden. Bala was taking a shower after his daily trip to the market, washing away the smell of fish and poverty. Nirmala was already in bed.

A few cicadas chirruped sleepily and a frog croaked in reply. A moth whispered past in search of a light, his wings flapping silently in the darkness.

'Son, you know that whatever you do, whatever you want to do is all right with your father and me,' she said in her gentle voice.

Niranjan didn't reply. At that moment, he thanked God that she was his mother.

'I know there is something bothering you and that you probably have to figure it out by yourself, but perhaps I can help?' she offered tentatively.

He smiled in the darkness. 'You help, Amma, just by being the person you are.' Then he frowned. 'I don't even know what it is. I just feel like I am being pulled in two different directions and I don't know which one to take.'

She sighed. 'When I met your father, I felt the same way. I had to leave everything that was familiar to me, my family, my home, my home town, and come here, to Colombo. I still don't know if it was the right decision.'

'To marry him?'

She laughed. 'No. I knew that was the right thing to do. But to leave Jaffna? He's not happy here. Now you're an adult, you can see it. He's always talking about going abroad and his reasons are good, but me . . . I don't want to uproot myself again.'

'He feels like an outsider.' It wasn't a question.

She nodded. 'He does, but I don't see how. I just don't feel that way. This country is ours as much as anyone else's. We are descendants from a long proud line of Cholas. Kings. Conquerors.'

Now her son sighed. She sounded like a Chundikuli Girls' School textbook. 'Amma, you have to know that it doesn't work that way in real life. We are still outsiders. You said it yourself. The Cholas were conquerors. No one forgives or

172

forgets that kind of humiliation. We represent it. What do you expect them to do?'

She stared at him. 'But that was centuries ago! How can we be blamed for that?'

'Maybe we aren't actually blamed for it. But the fact remains that according to them, we are not rightful owners. We are just squatters.'

'So what's the solution? Just get up and go?'

'What do you want to do? Stay and fight?' her son retorted. Then he sighed. 'I don't know. I honestly don't. I personally don't feel any animosity, except when you hear of incidents like the one involving Hemantha.'

'Are you happy here?' she asked, sitting forward in her chair, the light from the street lamp illuminating the entreating look in her eyes.

'Am I happy here?' he repeated. 'The question is, am I happy at all? Are you? Is Appa? Will Nirmala be happy when she grows up?'

Violet stared at him. 'What are you talking about? Of course I'm happy, and so are you and your sister and your father. It is just the situation.'

'But is the situation going to change? Or will it always be the way it is? And if so, what do we do about it? Don't you understand what Appa's problem is? He cannot take it the way it is. It makes him angry. And because he knows how futile that is, he wants to remove himself from what makes him angry.'

Violet made a noise which was half-laugh, half-sob. 'I want him to be happy. To get rid of these thoughts that haunt him.'

'Tell him,' her son advised gently.

She smiled tremulously and took his hand. 'I have been blessed.'

He smiled back. 'That's what I was thinking a few moments ago.'

The gate creaked open and Priyanthi stood silhouetted against the street light. 'Can I come in?' she asked tentatively, sensing she had stepped into a private moment.

Violet laughed a little shakily. 'What a question! Of course you can come in.'

She bounded in. 'Thank goodness!' she declared. 'My grandparents have just descended and I wanted to get away.'

Violet frowned. Niranjan hid a smile. Priyanthi's disconcerting habit of speaking her mind would get her into trouble some day, he thought. Again he thought of the toddy tapper.

'Priyanthi, maybe you should go home. They've come so far to see you,' Violet said.

'Oh no!' she replied blithely. 'They didn't come to see me. They came to Colombo for some society lunch thing and they're on their way home. They'll be gone in a few minutes,' she said hopefully.

Niranjan grinned. 'You're not supposed to say things like that. Didn't they teach you anything at school?'

She grinned back. 'No. Thank God!' She rolled her eyes theatrically. 'They might have finished me off!'

Violet sat listening to the exchange, wondering when her son and Enid's daughter had become so – comfortable with one another.

'So what have you been up to these days?' Niranjan asked.

Priyanthi squinted up at the stars. 'Do you think it will rain tonight?'

Niranjan caught his mother's smile. 'Yes, potatoes are quite expensive, aren't they?' he said solemnly.

Priyanthi looked at him. 'What?'

Niranjan laughed. 'Caught you. I asked you what you were up to these days and you started talking about rain.'

'So you talked about potatoes?' She sighed. 'Auntie Violet, this child of yours is quite mad. My brother's brain disease must be contagious.'

'Priyanthi!' Violet remonstrated. 'You mustn't say things like that.'

'Why not? My brother *is* sick in the head. Everyone knows that.'

'Yes, but still . . .' Violet said.

Niranjan felt an irrational swell of pride. Priyanthi was not afraid of anything. 'So what *have* you been up to these days?' he repeated for the third time.

She looked pensive. 'Nothing much. Trying to keep up in school.'

'That can't be too difficult,' Niranjan said.

'I don't know,' she said moodily. 'It's as if the older you get, the harder they try to make it for you.'

Violet laughed. 'You two sound like middle-aged politicians discussing the state of the country. I'm going in to start dinner.' She looked at Priyanthi. 'Would you like to eat with us?'

Priyanthi looked regretful. 'I would have loved to, Auntie Violet, but if I don't go home in time for the fond farewell, my grandmother will get mad at my mother and my mother will get mad at me.'

Violet sighed and went indoors.

The comfortableness that had been there followed her inside.

Suddenly, they had nothing to say to each other.

Someone opened a tap inside the house and water gurgled down the pipes, rushing into the drain outside the house, disturbing the mosquitoes, who rose in a softly buzzing cloud. They flew upward to join the moths and flies clustered around the street light.

Priyanthi stood up. 'I'd better go,' she said.

Niranjan stood up too. 'I'll go with you.'

'Home?'

'No, to the gate.'

'Afraid someone will kidnap me?' she said cheekily.

'No one would dare,' he retorted.

At the gate, she stopped. 'Do you think of him?'

Niranjan nodded, knowing who she was talking about.

'I miss him,' she said.

'Me too.'

'Will we see him again?'

'Yes.'

'You're sure?'

'Yes.' He wasn't sure at all.

She smiled widely. 'I believe you.'

He smiled back. 'You should. I'm the only truthful person left in the world.'

After she had disappeared into her garden, his smile died. His lie lingered. It floated upwards to join the swarm of insects intent on incinerating themselves against the hot white bulb.

Niranjan clenched his fists. What do I do? he asked of the darkness.

* * *

About a month later, Niranjan approached his mother as she prepared a chicken curry in the kitchen. 'Amma, can I talk to you?'

'You are talking,' she said, her casually teasing tone belying the sudden clutch of fear that tightened her throat.

'No, seriously,' he said.

She put down her spoon, pulled the kitchen chair by the open doorway where it was cooler and sat down. 'Yes, son. What is it?'

He sat on the floor and stretched out his legs. 'I want to be a priest,' he said steadily.

She felt her legs start to shake uncontrollably and heard a roaring sound in her ears. Somewhere in her conscience, she asked for forgiveness. 'Are you sure?' she managed, weeping a silent farewell to the wonderful wedding, the loving daughter-in-law and all the grandchildren she had dreamed of.

He smiled. 'I think so. I have been so unhappy recently. I've been praying a lot and looking for an answer and I think this is it. Anyway, it's not as if I can become a priest straight away. I have to do some years at a seminary first. That's a good place to find out if the priesthood is really my calling.'

She nodded. That was just like Niranjan.

Always cautious.

Always cautious.

'Niranjan thinks he wants to become a priest,' she told Bala at dinner.

He dropped his fork and turned to stare at his son. 'What?'

'I think I want to become a priest,' Niranjan said quietly.

'Are you sure?' his father asked, trying to gather his skittering thoughts.

'No. There is only one way to be sure,' Niranjan said.

Bala pushed his chair back from the table and leaned back, regarding his son gravely. 'It's a big step, son.'

'I know.'

'Not easy.'

'I know.'

'You know what you'll be giving up?'

Niranjan looked serenely at his father. 'I'm just thinking of what I'll be gaining.'

'Niranjan wants to be a priest,' Violet told Enid.

Enid stared at her. 'A priest? Why?'

'Why do people want to be anything? I don't know.' Violet's voice cracked and tears coursed down her cheeks.

Enid reached over the wall to take Violet's hand. 'What's this? You're acting as if he died or something. Better a priest than a rotter like my one,' she said, trying to keep the bitterness out of her voice.

'At least your rotter is at home with you,' Violet said, wiping her eyes on her sleeve.

'Yes, but for how long?' Enid said. 'Thank your God, Violet. You have a good son.'

Priyanthi sat unmoving under the araliya tree. Her palms were damp. Although she couldn't see her mother and Violet, their voices carried clearly to where she sat. She hadn't misheard anything. She wished she had. An ant crawled up her bare foot and nibbled on her toe, leaving a white bump on the tanned skin. She didn't notice.

She smiled grimly. So much for the promises. So much for seeing the toddy tapper again. She'd never hated anyone as much as she hated Niranjan at that moment.

Niranjan said his goodbyes to Araliya Gardens and drove with his father to the Ampitiya Seminary in Kandy. The seventy-mile distance didn't seem far, but the roads were so bad that it took almost four hours to get there.

Priyanthi stared after the car, wondering why it felt as if there was a stone in her chest.

A hole in her soul.

The anger she had felt initially had been replaced with a stark sorrow. As if someone had died. She functioned normally enough, but her eyes were wounded. She had taken great pains to avoid Niranjan this past month.

When he came to their house to say goodbye, she stayed in her room until her mother called her out. She didn't meet his eyes when he stood before her.

'Bye, Pri,' he said. His voice was hoarse.

'Bye,' she said, and finally looked at him. From his expression, she knew he would miss her. But not enough to stay.

She may have been able to compete with Kamini, but God was too great a rival.

Fourteen

❧

Christmas of 1977 was grim.

Violet struggled to make it a merry one for Nirmala, but it seemed as if every bit of tinsel and every gift conspired to make her miss Niranjan even more. It was strange really, because he had never been a particularly vociferous part of their household. It was his quietness she missed. That slightly unnerving way he had of materialising next to her. His silent company at the gate when she waited for Bala to come home after work. His willingness to run errands.

Bala felt his absence keenly too, but he was far more practical about the whole thing. It was an honour for any good Christian home to have a child in the service of God, and although he was a little disappointed, he was also proud of his son's decision.

When Bala was about Niranjan's age, he too had toyed with the idea of becoming a priest, but his first glimpse of Violet had dispelled any notions of celibacy.

Violet wrote to Niranjan and asked him when he was coming home for a visit and he replied that he would come soon, but he never did.

These days, Bala concentrated on Nirmala, who was seven years old and becoming quite a handful. She was an active child, precocious, outspoken and determined.

She did well in class, but Violet was always being called in to see the principal. Nirmala had brought her history book in to school. Nirmala had pulled the petals off the principal's precious roses. Nirmala had been caught making faces at the nuns. Nirmala had begun a rumour about a ghost in the library and the children were refusing to go in. Nirmala was bribing the school watchman to buy raw mangoes from outside the school gates. Nirmala had pinned Sister Theresa's wimple to a curtain.

When Violet asked her why she was constantly in trouble, Nirmala just grinned unrepentantly and said, 'They deserve it.' Her attitude threw Violet into confusion, for she was used to dealing with Niranjan, who had been so obedient at this age.

So she left it to Bala to discipline Nirmala. Bala adored his daughter, especially now that his son was gone, and beyond a stern 'don't do that again', he let her be. He secretly delighted in her antics because he felt them to be harmless pranks. One day, when she came home with red stripes on her arm from a caning she had got for talking during lessons, he marched into the school like an avenging angel, pointed his finger at the mustachioed Mother Superior and vowed terrible repercussions for anyone who dared lay a finger on his daughter again.

That was the last time Nirmala got caned.

* * *

Priyanthi, who usually haunted their house at this time of year, since her own family didn't celebrate Christmas, seemed to be taking great pains to avoid it. Violet missed her but was also somehow grateful for her absence.

She would only have been another reminder of Niranjan.

Violet went through the motions of sorting through and chopping mounds of raisins, sultanas, pumpkin preserve, crystallised ginger, nuts and candied fruits for her Christmas cake. Dierdre came to help, knowing Violet would return the favour when she started her own cake.

Violet's Christmas cake was legendary. To begin with, it was huge – almost thirty pounds. Her arms ached from folding the batter in with the fruit, but when it was finally mixed together, she poured it into huge oil-paper-lined trays, sometimes four of them, dotted with stiff peaks of egg white to make sure no cake batter was skimmed off the tops of the trays, and sent it to Renown Bakery to bake. The trays were too big to fit into her oven at home. When it came back, golden and smelling wonderful, she cut it into small squares, wrapped each piece in oil paper and served it generously to all her Christmas visitors along with a glass of her home-made damson wine. Long after Christmas, Enid and Dierdre would pop over for a piece of the cake, which seemed to get better with age.

Dierdre, on the other hand, was as sloppy with her cake as she was with the rest of her cooking. She used the best ingredients and baked her cake herself, but it always came out dry and crumbly, not moist and hinting of brandy like Violet's.

'What to do, child?' Dierdre lamented each year. 'Next Christmas, I'm going to order from Perera and Sons.'

They nodded, knowing very well that by the next year, Dierdre would forget her cake fiasco and dive into the process with the same enthusiasm.

Now they chopped cashew nuts in a companiable silence, punctuated by chewing noises which came from Dierdre.

'If you don't stop eating the nuts, there'll be no cake,' Violet said mildly.

'How to stop, child?' Dierdre said, popping another nut into her mouth. 'This is part of making Christmas cake.' She laughed. 'Remember how we used to tell Niranjan to whistle while he cleaned the raisins, to make sure he wasn't eating any?'

Violet's eyes clouded. 'Yes.'

Dierdre put down her knife and came over to hug her friend. 'Not to worry, dear. He'll be fine. I won't be surprised if he doesn't give up all this rubbish and come home soon.'

'What makes you say that?'

'Oh, I don't know,' Dierdre said. 'These old bones of mine talk to me and tell me things.'

'I wish he would, Dierdre. I know that's bad, but every night I pray for him to come home. Do you think I'm a bad person?'

Dierdre laughed, her ample breasts wobbling beneath her lilac polyester dress. 'What nonsense. How can it be wrong for a mother to want her son? Didn't Mary want her child?'

* * *

181

In Ampitiya, Niranjan rose early, went to Mass, attended a variety of classes, did his share of chores and tried not to miss the smell of his mother's cooking. He wondered if she had already baked her Christmas cake.

At night, when he closed his eyes, Priyanthi's face floated into his vision, unbidden and unwelcome. He sighed and looked enviously at the peaceful faces of the other sleeping seminarians.

Father Benito, the jolly Italian priest whom he had been assigned to for religious education class, looked at the dark circles under Niranjan's eyes and felt a pang of pity. Some girl, no doubt.

In his experience, none of the boys stayed awake night after night longing for their mothers, no matter how much they missed home cooking.

He tried to broach the subject with Niranjan. 'Son, this isn't like conscription, you know. You can always leave if you feel this vocation isn't for you.'

His concern was met with blank looks and grim resolution. He sighed, for he knew exactly what was going through the boy's mind. He'd seen it many times before. They came in here and acted as if they had made some private pact with God to stay and endure the seminary life, even though their hearts were not in it. How could Father Benito tell them that God wouldn't mind if they realised the priesthood was not for them and left? That there were more ways than this to show their love for Him?

No, Niranjan was one of the stubborn ones. Father Benito could see that. He only hoped that the boy wouldn't allow himself to be ordained and then spend the rest of his life regretting it.

* * *

At the 1977 elections, not only was the nationalist government defeated, but it was also stripped of the relative respectability of being the opposition. For the first time, Sri Lanka had a Tamil opposition.

Tamils like Bala felt encouraged. Perhaps there was some hope after all. But demands for a separate state, which up to this time had been little more than optimistic requests, escalated. There was even a name for this chosen land – Eelam.

The fact that there was finally a Tamil opposition gave new hope and new fervour to the propagators of the movement.

Some Tamils saw a separate state as the end to all their problems.

Some didn't see the point.

And the Sinhalese, except for a handful who didn't care, were violently opposed to the idea.

'First they'll want a separate state, then they'll be wanting the whole country,' Mrs Senaratne, who lived further up Araliya Gardens, said acidly to her husband. He spotted Bala out walking and shushed her.

Mrs Senaratne refused to be shushed. 'It's true. And I'm sure people like Bala agree with me.'

'Agree with you?' Bala enquired, smiling politely.

'That this separate state thing is a lot of nonsense,' she said, peering to see his expression.

Bala's face remained carefully blank. 'Depends on how you look at it,' he said mildly.

'What do you mean?' Mrs Senaratne demanded. 'How should one look at it?' Six thick black hairs which grew out of a chocolate-coloured mole on her chin quivered agitatedly.

Bala cupped his chin in his hand and pretended to consider the question. 'Well, from a Sinhalese point of view, you're absolutely right. It is a bunch of nonsense.'

Mrs Senaratne turned to look triumphantly at her husband, who was studying the scratches in the paintwork on his gate.

'But,' Bala continued reflectively, 'from a Tamil point of view, it might be a very good idea.'

The six hairs sprang into motion again. 'A good idea! What utter nonsense! How?'

Bala resisted the urge to laugh. Mrs Senaratne sounded like a hostile Red Indian chief at an enforced peace treaty signing.

He cocked his head and regarded her with all the seriousness he could muster under the circumstances. 'Well, let's see. The Sinhalese have Sri Lanka, right? The Tamils have nothing, right again? Give Eelam to the Tamils and everyone has something. Problem solved.'

Mr Senaratne hid a grin. There was no doubt that Bala was having a good laugh at his wife's expense, but it served her right. Time and time again, he had told her not to discuss politics with their neighbours, but she refused to listen. Now she was acting as if Bala was a spokesperson for the entire Tamil population of the country.

All the rolls of fat on Mrs Senaratne's body – the four on her midriff revealed by her low sari, the two on her arms emerging from the too-tight sleeves, and the three under her chin – joined the six mole hairs in one tremendous quiver.

Then she turned sharply on her heel, twisted her slipper on a brick, and when she finally righted herself, waddled away still muttering under her breath.

'Well, I'd better be going,' Bala said, and left, whistling tunelessly under his breath.

When he entered his own gate, his expression changed. His face hardened and his fists clenched until the knuckles showed white under his brown skin. Violet emerged from the kitchen wiping her hands on a cloth and stopped when she saw him.

'What happened?'

'Oh, just the usual evening conversation with Mrs Senaratne,' he said bitterly. 'Eelam! What nonsense!' he mimicked Mrs Senaratne's high, indignant voice.

Violet sighed. 'You know what she's like. It's best not to take any notice of her.'

Bala, who had been walking into the bathroom, swung round. 'I take notice! I cannot ignore everything or pretend it doesn't exist like you can! I didn't marry you because you were a doormat, Violet. You are quiet and I like that about you, but for God's sake, accept that this situation is intolerable, even if you don't want to do anything about it!' His voice had risen with frustration.

Violet stared at him. In all the years they had been married, he had never raised his voice to her. Just the occasional gentle reprimand when she tried to conceal Niranjan's or Nirmala's bad behaviour or when she was too easy on them. The tiny hairs which ran down the curve of her spine prickled with shock and her eyes burned. She turned silently and went back into the kitchen.

Bala stormed into the bathroom and washed his hands violently, as if that would send the entire episode down the drain. He knew Violet was hurt and he felt guilty, but he was shaking with rage.

The next morning, Stanley was standing by the open front door drinking his coffee when he saw Bala reversing out of his own gate.

'Morning!' Stanley called out cheerfully.

Bala muttered something and drove off, leaving Stanley staring after him, perplexed.

'Something's up with Bala,' he informed Enid.

Enid was unconcerned. 'Must have been another run-in with the school people. Violet will probably tell me later.'

But later that morning, when she wandered over to the wall, Violet didn't refer to Bala's strange behaviour. She seemed distracted and Enid noticed her eyes were red and swollen. As if she had been crying. 'Violet, is something wrong?' she said gently. Violet shook her head.

'You must miss Niranjan,' Enid said.

Violet nodded, but her eyes filled with tears. She muttered something about lunch and hurried off. Enid waited for a while, hoping she would come back. Fifteen minutes later, she went back indoors, frowning.

* * *

In the next two years, Sri Lanka blossomed under the new UNP government, opening itself to free-market reforms and foreign investment like an eager virgin.

Free-trade zones were set up and foreign companies returned

to reap the benefits of cheap labour. The private sector rose from the ashes with renewed energy and optimism.

Suddenly, there were jobs everywhere. Company directors needed secretaries. Administrators needed clerks. Factories needed staff. Construction companies needed foremen and labourers. Even middle-class households could afford to employ more than one servant. Those who had cars employed drivers. To take the missus shopping.

Not just jobs everywhere but jobs for everyone.

The same shops whose shelves had been empty a few years before were now bursting at the seams with every imaginable imported item. Bright blue tins of Kraft cheese, which used to be previously pulled out from parcels sent by foreign relatives with a mixture of stinginess and delight, now nestled smugly and snugly next to Marmite, mayonnaise and Lea & Perrins Worcestershire sauce. And, if the prices were prohibitive for most people, at least they were available.

No longer did people have to swelter in queues under the paltry protection of their umbrellas. Ration books were a thing of the past. Now rice, sugar, flour, onions and imported Mysore dhal sat outside shops in reassuringly huge gunny bags. In the store rooms at the back, more unopened gunny bags waited. And there were more on the way piled in the backs of ships and trucks.

Nothing was cheap, admittedly, but thanks to the jobs, most people ate at least one meal a day. Which was a vast improvement on near-starvation.

FIFTEEN

❧

Priyanthi was almost sixteen and everyone's predictions had come true. She had grown into a real beauty. She had finally stopped cutting her hair and it now skimmed her waist. It looked like a shiny black curtain when it was loose, like a sinuous snake when it was braided.

Although she had become a quiet, reflective adult, she wasn't above an occasional game of cricket with the boys of Araliya Gardens. But all in all, she had finally become Enid's idea of the perfect daughter.

Enid taught her to cook and sew. Her beautifully embroidered cushion covers were displayed with pride at either end of the sofa. When Enid's parents came to visit, Priyanthi made the dessert; her chocolate biscuit pudding always came out perfect, not too sweet and not too soggy. She sat demurely in her pretty cotton dresses and answered all her grandmother's probing questions with patience.

At school, she got top grades every year, excelled in athletics and was the head of the English Society.

Everyone marvelled at what a good girl she was.

It was as if Enid had finally been vindicated.

Enid wasn't to know about the maelstrom of emotions that seethed beneath Priyanthi's docile demeanour, about the ocean-like restlessness that surged through her being, about the dreams that begged release and realisation, about the nights when she lay awake wishing for things she couldn't even identify.

Hopelessness slunk through her like a sullen nocturnal

creature, sniffing out the chinks of light and skilfully filling them in with more darkness.

She read *Wuthering Heights* and longed for a Heathcliff to come into her life and sweep her away from the sheer nothingness of it all. When she closed her eyes and tried to imagine him, it was Niranjan's thin, intense face she saw.

She read Shakespeare, Tolstoy, Byron and Keats under the araliya tree, and wept with longing and fear.

Longing for a life which was more than a mere existence.

Fear that she would live and die without ever having it.

Outwardly, no one could tell. She had discovered long ago that people left her alone if she pretended to be what they wanted her to be. And she wanted to be left alone.

Half a day of listening attentively to her grandmother was a small price to pay for another month of peace.

A week of embroidering meaningless scenes on cushion covers was worth a year of being left alone by her mother.

And if a few hours a day of homework meant a glowing report card at the end of the term, she could do it.

Priyanthi had discovered that everything was relative.

Sometimes Dierdre would come upon Priyanthi staring into her own dark distance. The strange opacity in Priyanthi's eyes dimmed even Dierdre's exuberance. The girl felt too much, too hard, Dierdre told herself, looking compassionately at Priyanthi. She wondered angrily why Enid didn't see that her daughter was quietly going mad from life.

Dierdre tried to talk to Priyanthi, but she wouldn't open up. Months and even years of carefully schooling her features into impassivity and editing her answers to polite phrases made it almost impossible for her to open up to real sympathy, or respond to real understanding.

'There's nothing wrong, Auntie Dierdre,' she would say expressionlessly.

After Dierdre sighed heavily and left, Priyanthi's face would crumple up and the tears would come. Traitorous, ready tears that made her throat ache from the effort of shedding them. She pounded the silvery smooth trunk of the araliya tree as if hurting it would lessen her own pain.

She felt as if she had lost herself somehow.

And the darkness made it impossible to see.

* * *

Radhika Paul from up the road was now twenty and working as a secretary in a big Colombo gem-exporting office. Whenever her mother boasted to their friends about Radhika's job, she made it seem as if Radhika personally owned the vast wealth of gems her office dealt with.

After having several harmless flings with a variety of young men, Radhika Paul rested comfortably in the knowledge that when she decided to get married, she could take her pick from Colombo's eligible Tamil bachelors. Radhika had already decided that marriage was still at least two years away, so she let men alone for a while and concentrated on her job and getting to know the neighbours she had hitherto largely ignored.

Who knew?

Perhaps there was an eligible bachelor right on her doorstep.

Since Violet's was the only other Tamil house down Araliya Gardens, her mother often popped over to chat or offer some piece of unwanted advice. Lately, Radhika had started going over as well, and one of the first things she noticed was the young girl next door, who seemed to be always reading under the araliya tree.

She knew Priyanthi vaguely but had hardly ever spoken to her beyond a casual hello. But now that she had put her love life on hold, she found herself curious about Priyanthi and asked Violet about her.

'She's a loner, that one. A bit like my Niranjan.' Violet's eyes grew sad at the mention of her son. He wrote faithfully once a month, but that was like a measly hand-out to a mother who felt as if a vital part of her had been ripped out and offered unconcernedly to God. She wrote back, cheerful letters full of Araliya Gardens news.

Bala had been twice to Ampitiya to visit Niranjan but she

hadn't gone. Seeing him there would only have made it more real, and she preferred to pretend this wasn't happening. She made thosas and coconut chutney and masala vadas and wrapped up a large slab of Christmas cake for him.

'Where's Amma?' Niranjan enquired.

'Oh, she couldn't leave Nirmala,' Bala said.

Niranjan nodded. He understood. In a way, he was glad she hadn't come. His mother was perceptive; she might have seen through the careful wall he had erected, the one he concealed his feelings behind.

One day, Radhika left her mother telling Violet the best way to make thosas and walked to the next gate. 'Hi,' she said, leaning over.

Priyanthi's hand jerked and her book fell on the grass. She blushed, picked it up and dusted it. 'Hello,' she said lamely, wondering why Radhika Paul was bothering to speak to her.

'What are you reading?' Radhika asked.

'Brontë,' Priyanthi said, holding up the book.

'Brontë?' Radhika sounded both surprised and interested. 'I always found them a bit of a bore. Which one?'

'*Wuthering Heights.*'

Radhika laughed. 'Heathcliff, huh? I'm still looking for mine.'

It was Priyanthi's turn to look surprised. Radhika Paul never seemed short of admirers.

Radhika straightened up from the gate. 'Well, I'd better be going. Come over to our house later if you're doing nothing.'

Priyanthi watched her walk away, envying her confident walk. The sensuous sway of Radhika's rounded behind reminded her of that conversation she had had with her mother all those years ago.

A few days later, Radhika stopped by again. Again she found Priyanthi reading under the araliya tree.

'What happened? I thought you were going to come over to my house.'

Priyanthi blinked. 'You wanted me to?'

Radhika looked slightly impatient. 'Yes. I wouldn't have asked otherwise.' She regarded Priyanthi with interest. 'What do you do all day?'

'I go to school.'

'And afterwards?'

'I read mostly.' Priyanthi blushed. What an interesting life, she thought savagely.

'Do you want to come now? I've got some lipstick that someone gave me that would look quite nice on you. It's too light for me.'

Lipstick? Priyanthi looked bemused. Her mother used lipstick when she went out but had never thought of offering to let *her* use any.

Now she did think about it, as Radhika regarded her quizzically. And the more she thought about it, the better it sounded. She stood up and dusted the seat of her trousers. She carefully tucked the book in a crook of the araliya tree.

'I'll come back and read some more,' she explained self-consciously.

Radhika nodded, smiling slightly. She was a strange one, this Priyanthi, but there was a curiously endearing quality about her. An untouched quality that Radhika liked. 'Don't you have to tell someone you're going out?' she asked.

Priyanthi shook her head. 'No one will miss me,' she said. She sounded matter-of-fact but there was something slightly pathetic about the statement.

'Well come on then.' Radhika briskly led the way to her house, which was just a few yards away.

At the door, Priyanthi paused, suddenly shy. There was a row of shoes and slippers just inside. She slipped off her own blue rubber Bata slippers and waited while Radhika stepped elegantly out of her wedge-heeled sandals.

'Come, come. There's no one here. My mother is busy telling Auntie Violet how to run her life,' Radhika said, walking through the living room and into a bedroom.

Priyanthi stood in the doorway looking around her with

wonder. The room looked like one huge pink and white rose. The illusion was created by the pale pink walls, rose-patterned bedspread and matching curtains, pink and white rug and the white-painted furniture. On the walls were several framed pictures of roses – bouquets, single roses, roses in baskets, roses on beds of white net. The white wicker armchair had a rose-patterned seat, and on Radhika's dressing table was a bowl of pink silk roses.

'It's beautiful!' Priyanthi gasped, wondering whether it was the sheer quantity of roses that made her utter the involuntary lie.

'I love roses,' Radhika said proudly. Priyanthi felt hysterical laughter bubble up inside her and coughed to disguise it.

She ventured further into the rose room. There was no other word for it. In all the period novels involving great mansions and stately houses she had read, there were always Rose Rooms and Blue Rooms and Red Rooms. Now, every time I read about a Rose Room, I'm going to remember this! she thought despairingly.

Radhika sat on the rose-silk-covered stool of her dressing table and proceeded to open lipstick tubes. There were several, as well as a variety of other cosmetics and perfumes.

'That's the one!' she declared triumphantly.

Priyanthi moved nearer. Radhika got up from the stool. 'Sit down and I'll show you how to put it on. You haven't used lipstick before, have you?'

Priyanthi shook her head and sat down obediently. If it's pink, I'll howl, she thought.

It wasn't. It was a beautiful beige with just a hint of brown in it. Radhika applied it expertly, instructing Priyanthi to open her mouth, close her mouth, rub her lips together, all of which she did meekly.

Radhika surveyed the results critically. 'You have beautiful eyes,' she pronounced. 'Let's see ...' She looked over the cluttered dressing table and picked up a pencil. 'Open your eyes wide.'

Priyanthi opened her eyes wide. The pencil was deftly drawn across her inner lids.

'Your eyes don't water. Good. You can use eye make-up without a problem,' Radhika said. 'Look.'

Priyanthi looked. The face that looked back at her didn't seem to be her own. The black kohl made her eyes look enormous and mysterious. The beige lipstick drew attention to her wide mouth, the faint shimmer making it look like the mouths she'd seen on film stars.

'Well?' Radhika demanded.

'It's beautiful,' Priyanthi murmured.

Radhika looked satisfied. 'Yes it is, isn't it? But your eyebrows ...'

Priyanthi frowned. 'What's wrong with them?'

'Nothing that can't be remedied with this.' Radhika picked up a pair of tweezers and started plucking at the hairs that grew in between Priyanthi's brows.

'Ouch! That hurts!' she cried, her eyes watering now.

'No pain, no gain,' Radhika said, and continued relentlessly.

At the end, Priyanthi was forced to admit that the pain had been worthwhile. Now that the stray hairs between and beneath her eyebrows had been removed, her eyes looked even more attractive. She looked gratefully at Radhika, feeling better than she had in months.

'Thank you.'

Radhika smiled. 'Not to worry. Come by any time for a free beauty session. Not that you need very much – you *are* quite beautiful, you know.'

'You think so?'

Radhika laughed. 'Look in the mirror.'

Priyanthi went home and settled herself under the araliya tree, wondering what to tell her mother when her new eyebrows were noticed. The lipstick and kohl pencil were in her pocket.

No one noticed.

She sat through dinner waiting for someone to exclaim with admiration or horror, but Stanley ate his boiled vegetables grumpily, Enid was caught up in her usual table frenzy of checking to see if everyone had enough on their plates, and Hemantha scowled down at his plate and shovelled food savagely into his mouth.

Over the last two years, Hemantha had distanced himself so much from his family that he had become a stranger. He lived in the house, but had nothing to do with the rest of them. Although Enid still loved him as only a mother could love her first-born child and only son, and still went to lengths to keep Stanley from knowing what he was up to, she was exhausted by his antagonism and anger. Because she was the one who loved him most, she was also the one at whom he directed most of his insults and anger.

She had to steel herself before she spoke to him, and almost always avoided doing so when Stanley was around.

Stanley had recovered fully from his heart attack and although he had to watch his diet and go to the hospital for frequent check-ups, he was back to his usual routine.

It was his attitude that had changed.

He had been bitterly disappointed by Hemantha's arrest, shocked to learn the reason for it, and had immediately figured out that it was part of an existing pattern of behaviour. Then he had turned his anger on Enid, accusing her of spoiling their son, of encouraging his behaviour, of giving him money to indulge in his filthy drinking habit. He accused her of betraying the trust he had placed in her as wife and mother.

Time had eased the bitterness, but Stanley no longer threw his arm around his son's shoulders or affectionately ruffled his hair. They avoided each other's eyes and the few words they exchanged were stilted.

It broke Enid's heart to see the gap between father and son widen with each passing month, but it was one she was powerless to bridge. When she tried to broach the subject with Stanley, he curtly told her to stay out of it.

It was a private battle.

Hemantha did nothing to ease the situation or lessen the tension. He was covertly belligerent and rude, and openly uninterested in their lives.

Before the incident, he had never been a willing part of the family circle, but now, it seemed as if he only tolerated them because he had nowhere else to go.

He had failed his GCE O Levels, and in spite of Enid's pleadings for him to re-sit them, he had declared that he wanted to go to hotel school, which didn't require O Levels. When Enid asked Stanley to intervene, all he said was 'If he wants my advice, let him ask for it.' Enid left it at that, knowing that Hemantha would never voluntarily speak to Stanley, let alone ask for advice. So now, Hemantha went to the Ceylon Hotel School near the airport. Stanley paid for the course and gave Enid enough money to cover his bus fare and lunch, but no more. Secretly, Enid juggled her housekeeping money and slipped Hemantha a hundred rupees here and there, entreating him not to drink with it. Her reward was a muttered thank you.

When Hemantha came home on those days, she shooed him to bed before his father got home and smelled the arrack on his breath. He rarely spoke to Priyanthi these days, seeming to forget her very existence unless someone drew his attention to her. Some years ago, Priyanthi had moved into the spare room, only sleeping in Hemantha's room when their grandparents came to visit, which wasn't very often.

At those times, she tried to draw him into a bedtime chat, but he answered in monosyllables. Eventually, she gave up. She had only one sibling and she felt as if she had lost him along with Niranjan.

Two years had passed since the incident with Kamini, but Hemantha still smouldered with rage that was surprisingly fresh in its intensity. Although he now chased after a variety of girls from the hotel school and from the free-trade-zone factories around it, he still craved Kamini the way a reformed drunk craves a drink – with self-loathing. He told himself he didn't love her any more, that he hated her, that when he finally got her to himself, he would avenge himself.

In the meantime, he tried to persuade one of the many fresh-faced, lush-bodied factory girls to make a detour down one of the narrow, leafy lanes near by.

Sometimes he succeeded. After the initial kisses and coy protestations, which he overcame without much difficulty, when he had her blouse open and her skirt raised it was Kamini's refined features he saw in the girl's fresh village face. Her ample curves became Kamini's. Her shy smile became Kamini's inviting one.

Then he lost all reason, grabbing and biting and thrusting with borderline violence. Some liked it. Some didn't. Some complained to their friends, and once, Hemantha was set upon by a bunch of burly Katunayake youths and beaten senseless. That slowed him down for a while, but it didn't stop him.

* * *

While Hemantha struggled with his demons, Niranjan struggled with his. Once a week, he went to confession and told the shadowy figure behind the wicker grille that thoughts of a girl were getting in the way of God. But the numbers of young men taking up religious vocations had decreased recently, so rather than try and counsel the distraught boy, they sent him away with stern admonitions and rosaries to say in reparation. He was consumed with despair, for he sternly admonished himself every night and said dozens of rosaries anyway. They just didn't help.

One day, two years after he had entered the seminary, he listened to Father Benito talking about the seven deadly sins. Father Benito was a born teacher, he had the marvellous ability to bring the confusing precepts of Christianity to a level of understanding for ordinary people. Even his sermons at Mass were looked forward to eagerly, not just by the seminarians but also by the Ampitiya residents. Today, he talked about pride. He said a lot but only a few simple statements penetrated the oppressive fog in Niranjan's brain. And even they did not linger there long, just long enough for him to seek out Father Benito after the class and explain that he had finally understood that the ministry was not his real calling, that he wanted to return home to Colombo. Father Benito tried to look disappointed but his heart sang a psalm of relief. He heard his young protégé's confession one last time and sent him off to bed.

That night, Niranjan's last at the seminary, he closed his eyes and slept deeply and dreamlessly.

Father Benito settled down on his own narrow bed and smiled with satisfaction. The lesson on pride had been a gamble but it had worked. One young person fewer to do God's work, but saved from himself.

SIXTEEN

⁓❊⁓

Niranjan returned to Araliya Gardens as quietly as he had left.

The early-morning train from Kandy arrived in Fort station at half past ten in the morning. He alighted and stood there drinking in the babel of noise and the confusion of smells.

On the two previous occasions he had been here at this very station – once when he was three, on his way to visit his grandparents in Kandy, and once when he had come with his father to meet the Kandy train – he had been intimidated by the press of people and had fearfully clutched at his father's hand.

Now, he welcomed the crowds. They were part of a world he had given up for two long years, a world he had missed and longed for with a desperation quite alien to his nature. His parched eyes drank it all in – the madonna-faced lady who openly and unconcernedly breast-fed her baby, the tea-man who sat on the platform with his tea-making paraphernalia and the thirsty throng around him, the harried-looking engine driver who was engaged in a shouting match with the man who hung out of the train and waved the green flag – Niranjan couldn't remember what he was called – the huge Muslim family who hurried by, their women veiled and mysterious, the wealthy-looking man in national costume who shepherded his fat wife and children through the crowd, the old couple who alighted still rubbing sleep from their eyes.

Beyond them was the Fort with its vendors, shoppers, office workers and jay-walkers.

He was pushed and shoved by the mass of humanity that moved as a whole like an army of ants, sometimes with muttered apologies, often without. He didn't notice. Finally, a disembodied voice on the crackling PA system announced the departure of the next train and woke him out of his sensory reverie.

He picked up his small battered bag and walked out of the station, blinking as the sunlight speared his eyes.

The Dehiwala bus came quickly. He sat on the hard seat, the rexine surface of which was cracked by the sun, and by people idly picking at it, and wondered what his mother would think of his unexpected arrival. It pleased him that it would please her, but in a remote sort of way.

The veneer of stoic acceptance that he had worked so hard to build at the seminary would take a lot of real-life living to crack.

He didn't dare think of Priyanthi.

Not even a fleeting whisper of a thought.

Not yet.

He got off the bus at Dehiwala. The daily market was in full swing and the noise was overwhelming.

Ampitiya seemed like something from another life. Which, in a sense, it was. He grimaced at the irony of it. He had given up this life for that, and now given up that life for this. But at least now he knew.

Araliya Gardens was deserted at this time of the morning. All the children were in school and most of the adults were at work. Only Mrs Munasinghe was pottering about in her garden, but through her milky cataracts, all she saw was a tall man striding past.

Priyanthi's garden was empty, for which he was thankful. He didn't feel like facing Enid or Dierdre and the volley of unanswerable questions which would ensue.

He unlatched the gate and went inside, pausing to inhale the scents of the gardens, fragrances which during the chilly Ampitiya nights had stolen in through the open window and assailed his nostrils, invaded his senses. Even though the seminary gardens only had vegetables growing in them and the only flowers were yards away in the silent chapel.

The front door was open as usual. Even after the robbery next door, no one really bothered to lock doors during the day. As if it was a well-known fact that thieves only operated at night. Which in fact they did. If some smart burglar had decided to stage a daylight robbery down Araliya Gardens, he would probably have been able to get away with a fortune.

Violet was in the kitchen. He stood at the door watching her moving between the stove and the table, transferring vegetables into pots with practised ease, comfortable and sure in her surroundings. She was still slim, although there were rings of age in her neck and her back stooped slightly, where before she had held herself proudly erect like a dancer.

'Amma,' he said quietly.

She was sweeping the contents of her chopping board into the pan on the stove. She stopped at the sound of his voice, tilted her head and listened.

'Amma,' he said again.

Still she did not turn, but the plastic chopping board slipped gently from her fingers and fell with a clatter to the floor, scattering little bits of onion everywhere.

She turned, her eyes already full, already prepared to drink in the sight of him.

'My son,' she whispered, and opened her arms.

He walked into them and lowered his head to her shoulder. They stood there for a long while. The servant walked into the kitchen and stopped in shock at the sight of the lady of the house embracing a strange young man. He was new and didn't know Niranjan except from photos.

Niranjan had grown since. He was taller. His hair was shorter. His eyes were older.

They finally drew apart. 'Come,' Violet said. 'You must be thirsty.' She turned to the servant, who was still standing there. 'My son is thirsty. Cut a thambili and bring it to the living room, please.'

They sat on the couch, holding hands, saying nothing. When the thambili arrived, she took the glass from the tray and held it to his lips. As if he was a little boy.

He smiled at the gesture. 'Aren't you going to ask me what happened? Why I am here?'

She shook her head. 'You will tell me when you want to. It's enough that you are here.'

He sighed, leant back and closed his eyes. 'I couldn't do it, Amma. I tried. God knows how I tried, but it was as if I was at war with myself.'

She smoothed back the short black hair from his brow. 'It doesn't matter,' she said, wondering if God would punish her for the joy that was coursing through her veins, making her dizzy with happiness.

Niranjan finally stood up and smiled wryly. 'I'd better have a bath and get ready for all the questions.'

'You don't have to explain anything to anyone. You went of your own free will and now you have returned. You didn't break a promise or let anyone down,' she said steadily.

Just God, he thought.

* * *

Bala wasn't as tactful as Violet. 'What happened?' he demanded, after he had hugged his son. 'Was there a problem?'

'Only with myself,' Niranjan said. 'I couldn't concentrate. Maybe I just don't have what it takes to be a servant of God.'

Bala shrugged philosophically. 'No matter. You tried and that's the important thing. Have you decided what you want to do now?'

Violet intervened. 'Bala, he's just got home. Give him some time.'

'Well, no use sitting around and doing nothing. He must either continue his studies or get a job.'

'I will,' Niranjan said quietly. 'I just need to do some thinking.'

'It's not easy, you know,' his father warned. 'Even with all these foreign companies coming and all that, they still try to cut the Tamils out.'

Niranjan grimaced. Racism didn't penetrate the otherworldly

peace of the seminary. He had forgotten his father's pet subject. 'I'll do something,' he promised quietly.

Nirmala was overjoyed at the return of her brother. 'I'm so glad you came back,' she said. 'How could you have stayed in that stuffy old church for so long?'

He grinned and ruffled her hair, marvelling at how she had grown. When he had left, she had been just a child. Now she was a girl, pretty and petite, with a poise far beyond her years. 'I have no idea,' he said. 'Did you miss me?'

'Oh yes,' she said fervently. 'You're the only one who doesn't lecture me and tell me to be good.' She frowned. 'That's odd actually because you're a priest.'

'Oh no,' he said hastily. 'I wanted to become a priest but then decided not to.'

'Why?'

'Well, it's a bit hard to explain.'

'That's okay. I'm glad you're home.'

He smiled. 'So am I.'

He played with Nirmala for a while and then wandered out to the garden. Night had fallen while they were talking inside, and now a few stars shone dimly in the sky. The air was heavy with night fragrances and a few fruit bats fluttered sleepily near the banana tree in the corner. Involuntarily, his feet found their way to the wall. Against his will, his eyes searched the next-door darkness, but other than a stray cat scurrying through the bushes, it was quiet. The lights were on in the house next door, and he could faintly hear the sound of voices. He went indoors to bed.

He woke up to the sounds of birds chattering on his windowsill and his mother's voice outside the window. He lay there for a while, enjoying the feel of being in his own bed, in his own room, in his own home. The smell of fresh-washed sheets teased his nose; those at the seminary had a slight musty smell to them, an oldish smell which had made him long for this very smell. Eventually he washed, dressed and walked out to the garden.

'Niranjan!' Enid exclaimed. She leant over the wall, took his face in her hands and kissed him fondly on either cheek. The hands that grasped his cheeks smelled faintly of curry. 'I couldn't believe it when Violet told me you had come home. Priyanthi will be so thrilled. And Hemantha too,' she added, her face clouding slightly.

'How is Hemantha?' he enquired politely, ignoring the thudding in his chest. 'Is he working now?'

'Still at hotel school,' Enid said, trying to sound enthusiastic. Niranjan felt pity for her, knowing how much she loved her son and how disappointed she must be in him. 'Priyanthi is still at school. Doing well too,' she said proudly. 'But your mother must have told you all this in her letters?'

'Not really. I asked her not to. It made me too homesick.'

'So are you staying? For good?'

'Or bad,' Niranjan said, laughing. Enid had always been a favourite, closer to him than any of his own aunts, who lived too far.

'You must come to Priyanthi's sixteenth,' Enid was saying. 'We're having a party for her. A grown-up party with music and dinner. About forty people will be coming and we're even having dancing.'

'Oh,' Niranjan said, wondering how Priyanthi could be sixteen.

'Of course he'll come,' his mother declared roundly. 'Time he had some fun, met some nice people.'

Niranjan finally found his voice. 'When is it?'

'This Saturday. Her birthday is actually on Friday but we thought Saturday was better for the party,' Enid said. She eyed Niranjan critically. 'You're all skin and bone. What did they feed you at that place?'

'Food,' he replied automatically, but his thoughts were far away. Saturday was only three days away.

He didn't know if Priyanthi had been told that he had returned. He had walked over to the wall a few times but he didn't see her. Even her usual haunt under the araliya tree remained stubbornly empty. Once, he thought he heard her voice and he rushed outside, but there was no one there.

Stop it! he told himself fiercely. He was half-hoping he would finally see her and realise that all his dreams and longings had only been the product of a homesick and isolated imagination. There had been no contact between them in two years. The last time he had seen her, she had been a newly grown-up fourteen-year-old. Now she was about to turn sixteen.

The thought terrified him.

Violet was nagging him to go over to Enid's and say hello properly. So far he had managed to put her off, but on Friday she frog-marched him over despite his protestations. 'They'll think you're angry with them or something,' she said on a pleading note. 'Uncle Stanley will be hurt if you don't go. Just for a while at least.'

He wiped his sweaty palms down the sides of his trousers, squared his shoulders and followed his mother into Priyanthi's house.

Enid came rushing out to greet him. 'Hemantha! Hemantha, come and see who's here!' she called.

Stanley came out and beamed with pleasure when he saw Niranjan. 'Back again,' he exclaimed, clapping Niranjan on the back. 'Well, I hope you've got all these silly saintly notions out of your head, once and for all!'

'Stanley!' Enid scolded. She turned to Niranjan. 'Take no notice, child. You know your Uncle Stanley – mouth like an express train.'

Niranjan smiled. 'It's good to be back. I missed you, Uncle.'

'We missed you,' Stanley said, still smiling widely.

'Hemantha!' Enid called again.

Stanley scowled. 'If he's deaf, let him be,' he growled. He chatted for a while, telling Niranjan about his bothersome diet, then excused himself and went back into the bedroom where he had been reading.

Niranjan looked around. 'Where's Pri?' he finally asked casually.

'Gone with Radhika Paul to collect her dress for tomorrow,' Enid said, sounding rather worried. 'I haven't seen it yet. I hope it's not too sophisticated.'

Hemantha emerged.

They looked at one other, one with thinly disguised scorn and the other with open apprehension.

Niranjan stepped forward. 'Hi, Hema,' he said, holding out his hand.

Hemantha let him stand there for a few seconds before he reached out and gripped Niranjan's hand. 'Welcome back.'

Both mothers sighed with relief.

'So what happened to the Pope?' Hemantha asked, sauntering over to a chair.

'Still in Rome, I hear,' Niranjan replied innocently.

Hemantha's eyes narrowed slightly. 'Still a funny guy.'

Niranjan looked back serenely. 'Yeah. You too.' Under the cover of their mothers' conversation, they regarded each other warily. Niranjan was shocked at Hemantha's appearance. He had lost weight but had managed to grow a sizeable beer belly. He looked much older than his nineteen years.

'So what's been happening?' Hemantha was obviously making an effort to be polite.

Niranjan smiled. 'Nothing much. They didn't need me at the Vatican, so I came to convert Araliya Gardens instead.'

Hemantha finally grinned. 'You can start with me. According to my mother, I've got a whole army of demons in me.'

Enid turned. 'What was that, son?'

'Nothing,' he said rudely.

Niranjan resisted the urge to slap him. Apparently these two years hadn't helped Hemantha to grow up at all. After a decent interval of time and a glass of heavily sugared Tang, he murmured something about needing to look for jobs in the newspapers and left, ignoring Hemantha's knowing smile.

'We'll see you tomorrow,' Hemantha called out after him.

'Tomorrow?'

'Birthday party for the princess of the house,' Hemantha said mockingly.

Niranjan nodded and kept going.

* * *

Saturday arrived.

Enid's house was in an uproar. Dierdre had arrived early to help, and so had Violet.

'Where's the Sergeant Major?' Dierdre asked, looking around.

'Who?' Enid looked nonplussed.

'Your mother.'

'Dierdre, you mustn't be like that,' Enid said, but she couldn't hide a small grin. The label fitted so perfectly. 'They couldn't come down early because they had to go to lunch with the Senanayakes, but they'll be here in time for the party.'

'Oh good. We can get some work done in peace then,' Dierdre stated with satisfaction.

Violet had opted to make the seeni sambol and Enid was making the devilled beef and chicken curry. The hopper woman would arrive later and start cooking when the guests were ready to eat.

'Are you serving beers and things?' Dierdre asked.

'No! Not for a sixteen-year-old,' Violet exclaimed, shocked.

Enid sighed. 'I didn't want to, but Stanley says it's the done thing these days. Priyanthi even wants us to sit outside so we don't embarrass her friends.'

'Inhibit, you mean,' Dierdre said with an arch look.

'What do you mean?' Enid looked a bit worried.

'Oh come on, dear. You were young once. They'll want to put the lights off and slow-dance and steal a kiss here and there,' Dierdre said carelessly.

Enid's mouth was set. 'I'm not having the lights off,' she declared.

Priyanthi burst into the kitchen with Radhika in tow. 'Amma, you won't mind if we cover some of the bulbs with coloured cellophane, will you? Otherwise it will be too bright for dancing.'

'What's wrong with normal lights?' Enid demanded.

206

'Come on, Auntie Enid! Just some red cellophane for effect. You'll still be able to keep an eye on us,' Radhika said.

Enid looked undecided.

'Let them, child. No harm done,' Dierdre butted in. Priyanthi gave her a dazzling smile, and she couldn't help thinking that there was a vast improvement in the girl since she had been taken under Radhika's unlikely wing.

'Okay, but you'd better not get up to anything,' Enid said darkly.

Priyanthi looked puzzled. 'Like what?'

Now Violet stepped in. 'Nothing, nothing. Your mother's joking. Now go off and cover your light bulbs.' After they had skipped away, she turned to Enid. 'She's an innocent girl, Enid. You should be careful with what you say. You'll only end up putting ideas in her head where there are none.' The rebuke was delivered gently, but was still so unexpected that Enid stared. Violet turned back to her onions and Dierdre launched into another of her scandalous stories.

* * *

Priyanthi slipped the white dress over her head and turned so Radhika could zip it up. 'Do I look like a bride?' she frowned. 'Maybe we should have chosen a different colour.'

'You look beautiful in white. You have the perfect colouring for it. Very virginal,' Radhika said mischievously.

'Virginal?' Priyanthi was only vaguely aware of what that meant.

'Don't you know what a virgin is?' Radhika asked her in amazement.

Priyanthi shook her head. 'Not really.'

Radhika sat on the edge of the bed, careful not to crease her long skirt and tight, shiny shirt. She had dressed at Priyanthi's.

'Don't you know about sex and stuff?'

Priyanthi looked ashamed. 'No.'

'Your mum didn't tell you?'

Priyanthi looked horrified. 'As if she would. Did yours tell you?'

Radhika laughed. 'I probably know more than she does. No, my friends told me.'

'Will you tell me?' Priyanthi asked eagerly.

'Okay. You know a man has a thing—' She broke off as Priyanthi dissolved into peals of laughter, covering her flaming face with her hands. 'I'm not going to tell you if you laugh like that. Your mother will be at the door wanting to know what we're laughing about.'

Priyanthi stifled the rest of the laughter and wiped her eyes with a corner of the bedspread. 'Okay. I won't laugh. I swear.'

'So, the man's thing is put into the woman's bit down there.'

'NO!' Now she was appalled. 'How?'

'I don't know exactly because I haven't done it yet, but it is. Then they go up and down and some stuff comes out of the man and that's how babies happen.'

Priyanthi was laughing helplessly again. 'I'm sorry, Radhika, I really am, but it sounds so funny. Like a see-saw, up and down.'

Radhika started laughing too. 'It's true,' she said. 'I even saw two people doing it once.'

Priyanthi stopped laughing. 'Honestly?'

'Yes. When we went to Kalkudah ages ago. There was a foreign couple doing it on the beach.'

'Naked?' Priyanthi breathed.

Radhika nodded. 'No shame,' she stated. 'It's probably normal for them to do it all over the place. In the house, on the beach, in the kitchen, on the bus—'

There was a loud knocking at the door. 'What's going on?' Enid asked suspiciously.

They dissolved into laughter again. 'Nothing,' Priyanthi gasped out, and ran into the bathroom to wash her face.

She sat quietly as Radhika carefully put on lipstick, outlined her eyes with the dark kohl and brushed her hair vigorously. 'Leave it down. It's gorgeous,' Radhika advised.

When they came out of the bedroom, Enid pounced on Priyanthi. 'What's that on your eyes? Make-up?' She looked accusingly at Radhika.

'It's okay, Auntie Enid,' Radhika said. 'All the girls use it these days. Why, even you've got some lipstick on.'

Enid blushed and looked a little anxious. 'Is it too dark?'

Radhika the make-up expert looked critically. 'A little, but it's fine for the evening,' she finally declared.

Enid examined her daughter's dress doubtfully. 'It's a bit low.' The white dress *was* lower than anything Priyanthi had worn before. It was cut simply - a low, wide neck, cap sleeves and a low waist from which the half-flared skirt fell. The neckline and hem were edged with tiny off-white seed pearls. Not real ones, but good imitations from a shop in the junction.

'Come on, Auntie Enid. It's absolutely decent,' Radhika protested. 'Dress her like a nun and she'll never find a boyfriend.'

Enid couldn't help laughing. 'Well, we've got an ex-priest next door. The last thing we'll need is an ex-nun.'

Radhika looked interested. 'I heard. Is he coming tonight?'

'Of course. God knows, he couldn't have had much fun stuck in that seminary.'

Priyanthi stood there, dimly aware of the conversation continuing. Niranjan was home and she hadn't even known! And he was coming tonight. She felt panic begin to mount inside her. After waiting for so long, hoping beyond hope that he would change his mind and come back, now that it had happened, she felt as if her brain had frozen.

In the last few weeks, her growing friendship with Radhika had taken precedence over her thoughts of him, although they were never far away. They usually came back at night to haunt her, to taunt her.

She hadn't told anyone of her feelings for Niranjan. Not even Radhika. That was her private cross.

Her mother and Radhika were saying something to her. She forced herself to listen. 'Come on! Let's go and see if the balloons are still alive – they always deflate before the people arrive,' Radhika was saying. Priyanthi allowed herself to be dragged away.

* * *

The balloons were still alive. They had been inflated with the help of Hemantha's bicycle pump earlier in the day. Strings of pink and white antignum which grew in wild profusion in neglected plots of land were wound around the bars of the long windows.

The twenty-five chairs borrowed from the neighbours were set against the wall, leaving plenty of space in the centre of the room for dancing. Hemantha had roused himself out of his sullenness long enough to set up the stereo on a small table in one corner. Records and cassettes, some their own and some borrowed from Radhika, were stacked up next to it. The cellophane twisted around the light bulbs made the room dim and red. Like the horror house at a fair.

Outside, there were more chairs arranged in small circles. These were for the parents.

In the kitchen, the huge pans of seeni sambol, chicken curry and devilled beef sat on the stove. The old hopper woman, who had been fetched from her shanty home, was busy setting up her portable stove on the floor. Her small round hopper pans lay like shiny silver moons on the floor next to her. A huge container of hopper mixture sat next to them. When Enid gave the signal, she would begin.

There was hardly anyone in Sri Lanka who didn't like crispy hoppers, with their soft, spongy centres, especially when they came hot on the heels of a few arracks or beers.

At about eight, people started to arrive. Priyanthi stood at the door, greeted them and accepted their gaily wrapped gifts with smiling thanks, but her attention was elsewhere. Her body and her heart waited like a tensely coiled snake. Alert. Alive.

She saw him before he saw her. Walking towards the gate with his head bowed down, his thoughts somewhere else. He's not too excited about coming, she thought with dismay. Then he was in front of her, smiling his crooked smile. She smiled back tremulously, aware of her knees wobbling very slightly beneath her white dress. Of her heart knocking furiously against the wall of her chest, like a bird in a cage. The music, the laughter, the high, excited voices all faded into the distance like out-of-focus backgrounds.

'So. Sixteen,' he said.

'Yes,' she said, surprised at how normal her voice sounded. Her heartbeat slowed down and her knees steadied as if her voice was a signal for them to do so.

'I looked for you.'

'When?' she asked, surprised.

'Since I got back. Two days. You weren't around.' He sounded faintly accusing.

'I've been at Radhika's,' she said, hating Radhika fiercely at that moment. 'She's my friend from—'

'I know who she is,' he said, the smile back in his eyes. 'You've grown up. Very ladylike.'

'What else was there to do?' she replied. Bitterness hovered at the outskirts of her voice.

He chose not to hear it and flicked her cheek with his fingertips. 'Make-up, huh?'

She looked around. 'For goodness' sake shut up. My mother is having a fit about it already,' she hissed.

He grinned. 'That sounds more like the Priyanthi I used to know.'

'Enough, enough!' Bala bawled from behind Niranjan. 'We'd like to kiss the birthday girl too!' He had already had two arracks at home while Violet got ready.

Niranjan leaned forward, placed a quick peck in the little hollow between her eyebrows and moved past her into the room. She hoped no one else would kiss her on the forehead.

After an eternity, she was able to leave her post by the door and go inside. Her eyes sought and found him in the red-lit room, sitting in a corner talking to a girl. Sharmila from school. Pretty, vivacious Sharmila who had only to click her fingers to have a whole plethora of boys come running. Sharmila who had a red pouting mouth and huge breasts which jutted out from under her tight blue blouse.

Priyanthi's heart sank. Then she squared her shoulders and walked over. After two years of waiting, she wasn't going to give up so easily. 'Hi. Did anyone get you a drink?'

His face lit up with pleasure. 'Yes, your mother did. Come and sit.' He patted the chair next to him. Sharmila saw some friends on the other side of the room and went to join them.

'So what do you think of Sharmila?' Priyanthi asked, her voice deliberately casual.

'I wasn't thinking of her,' he replied. 'I was waiting for you.'

Her heart started to gallop.

The rest of the evening passed in a red-cellophane-tinted haze. Priyanthi and Niranjan talked endlessly, only stopping when Enid came over to admonish Priyanthi for ignoring her other guests. 'I know you haven't seen Niranjan in ages, but he'll understand if you go off and talk to the other people, won't you, Niranjan?'

Niranjan smiled and nodded. He couldn't very well protest. Priyanthi went reluctantly, but returned as soon as Enid went outside again. They talked about everything. The seminary, her school, Radhika, Hemantha, her grandparents. Between the words, in tiny pauses, their gazes locked, then skittered away.

The dancing started.

Hemantha surprised everyone by claiming Priyanthi for the first dance. Their friends applauded the brother–sister couple and Enid smiled mistily from her hiding place near the front door. Even Stanley, on his way to the kitchen for a refill, felt a surge of mellow, arrack-induced love for *both* his children.

Priyanthi danced with a few other people, courtesy dances which seemed to last for ever, and then came back to sit with Niranjan.

'Do you want to dance?' she asked suddenly. The BeeGees were asking how deep is your love in falsetto voices.

Niranjan shook his head. 'I'd probably step all over your feet. We didn't have time to practise in the seminary,' he said lightly.

'Oh come on. It's okay. I can't dance very well either,' she said, grabbing his hand to pull him up. He pulled her down.

She sank back with a little laugh. 'You're a spoilsport.'

Their hands remained clasped. Self-consciousness seeped into the conversation. That, and something else. Around them, people swayed and walked and talked and laughed and sang and drank and kissed in the red-dark, dark-red room.

At around eleven, Enid told the hopper woman to start. 'Better get some food down their throats before they start throwing up all over the place,' she said to Violet.

A long table (borrowed from Mrs Paul) was laid out in the garden, little oil lamps were lit and placed around it, both to illuminate, and to deter the mosquitoes, which were out in their droves at this time. Dierdre kept slapping at her bare arms, making them wobble with a life of their own. Enid and Violet giggled.

The mosquitoes feasted on the men, but they were too drunk to notice.

The food was brought out. Enid ignored Dierdre's pleas to 'let the young ones have a little more fun' and marched inside to announce that dinner was ready.

She looked around for Priyanthi and saw her still huddled with Niranjan in the corner. She frowned. That girl needed some manners. Ignoring all the other guests like that! It was true that Niranjan was a bit like the prodigal son, returning after all this time, but this would never do. She saw Hemantha looking at them too, a scowl on his face. He had sneaked off to the kitchen and stolen a few beers for selected people, which made them that much more determined to dance and drink the night away.

'Dinner's served,' Enid announced loudly.

No one responded. Indeed, no one even glanced her way. Finally, she marched over and switched off the music. 'Dinner's ready,' she said again, ignoring the moans and groans from the dancers.

They straggled out and served themselves. Enid hovered over

the table, keeping a watchful eye on her white damask tablecloth and her prized Noritake dishes, which were a wedding present. She had agonised over using them and finally decided to. After all, she didn't want people saying she didn't have decent china.

Priyanthi and Niranjan ate sparingly, mostly to keep their mothers quiet. Neither of them felt very hungry. It was strange, Priyanthi thought, but after hundreds of times of eating with Niranjan, she suddenly felt self-conscious. He didn't seem to feel it, eating as he always had, but she was aware of the crunchy noises she made when chewing on the crispy rim of her hopper.

* * *

The sky was already wearing its pale pink dawn colour when Enid, Violet and Dierdre finally cleared the tables and picked up empty glasses and beer bottles lying in the grass. Their servants sleepily washed the dishes and plates in the kitchen, too tired to discuss the events of the evening.

The last guests had left an hour ago.

Priyanthi found Enid with five empty bottles between the fingers of one hand and a pile of stacked-up glasses in the other. She kissed her mother's cheek. 'Thank you,' she said. Her eyes glowed like twin beacons in the dark.

Enid looked affectionately at her. 'You're only sixteen once,' she said, returning the kiss. 'Go to bed now. You can sleep in as long as you like. There's no school tomorrow.'

'Thank God,' Priyanthi said, yawning widely. She drifted off to bed smiling to herself, a small, secretive smile.

Enid continued to clear up but there was a little niggle of worry she couldn't quite identify. Priyanthi had spent far too much time with Niranjan this evening. Almost as if— She pushed the thought away. Violet was right. She was just dreaming up things that simply didn't exist. She stacked another pile of dishes in the sink, and sharply told Banda, the servant boy, to hurry up with the washing.

In her bedroom, Priyanthi fell asleep instantly, a faint smile still lingering around her mouth. Next door, Niranjan lay awake, trying to shake off a feeling of foreboding that had come over him as soon as he had walked out of Priyanthi's gate.

SEVENTEEN

❧

Priyanthi and Niranjan drifted into love without meaning to.

There was no doubt they had both been affected deeply by something on the night of Priyanthi's sixteenth birthday, but that was an attraction born of separation. That was the longing people have for what they have not, the excitement of homecoming and the shock of discovery that they had both grown up during the time they had been apart. That night, they were still discovering the people they had become, tentatively tasting the newness, wondering at the changes.

Almost a year had passed since that night and their feelings had evolved into something entirely different. During that year, they met almost every day.

There were two kinds of meetings.

One was when their families were around. Then, they smiled casually and spoke a few words to each other while their parents chatted. They went to great lengths to avoid each other's eyes. If their hands touched by accident, on the gate, on the wall, while giving something to the other, they jerked them away and looked around to see if anyone had seen. Flushes rose to tint brown cheeks.

Studying them, their parents might have shaken their heads wryly and commented on how ill-at-ease they seemed with one another. It's this age, you know, they might have said wisely, remembering with amusement when they had experienced the same awkwardness, the same rejection of the opposite sex.

The other kind of meeting was far different and had begun about six months before. These were hours snatched from the everyday routine of their lives. Secret meetings filled with whispered murmurings, impossible-to-keep promises and a strong sense of despair. They took place in a variety of locations, all chosen for their relative isolation.

Sometimes, Priyanthi met Niranjan at a deserted bus stop after school, where they stood under the rough-edged cement structure and spoke softly, always keeping a watchful eye on the arriving buses. If they were discovered, no one would think anything of it. After all, they were neighbours who had grown up together. Their parents were best friends. It was the most normal thing in the world for the two of them to be standing and chatting somewhere. That didn't make them feel any more confident, though. Or they went to the Vihara Maha Devi Park or down to the beach and joined the scores of umbrella lovers dotting the grass or rocks with colourful regularity. There was an unspoken rule that couples didn't spy on each other. That was left to the perverts.

Here, Priyanthi and Niranjan disappeared into a sea of anonymity.

Theirs was just another umbrella shielding another love.

Enid had been pleased when Priyanthi bought herself the purple and green umbrella, assuming that the girl was finally starting to worry about her skin. Fair skins were prized and Priyanthi was already quite brown. Enid herself didn't venture out of the house during the day without an umbrella and plenty of Ponds cream smoothed on her face.

The park was better than the beach, but it was quite a distance away. At least there they sat on a carpet of grass, not on the rough rocks. Not that they really noticed.

Priyanthi vividly remembered the first time. She had stepped down from the bus after school and seen Niranjan waiting at the bus stop. She first thought he was waiting for a bus.

'Where are you off to?' she asked lightly, praying he wouldn't hear her heart thudding painfully against her chest.

'Nowhere,' he said.

The thudding increased. She just looked at him.

'You want to go for an ice cream to Zellers?' he asked.

217

She looked doubtful. 'My mother might get worried.'

'Tell her you got late at school,' he said.

She hesitated for a minute and then nodded.

And so the deception began.

* * *

Just as they had never meant to fall in love, they never intended to deceive their families. It just happened that way. Ordinarily, it would have been a match made in heaven. They were the right age, although Enid might have thought Priyanthi still a little too young for a boyfriend, they were both bright and they both came from respectable middle-class families. However, Priyanthi was a Sinhalese girl and Niranjan was a Tamil boy and that difference was insurmountable. Sometimes, after they had feverishly kissed and caressed each other during their first five minutes under the inconspicuous umbrella cover, they discussed the dilemma they were in. 'We'll have to elope,' Niranjan said glumly.

Priyanthi looked horrified. 'My God! I can't do that to my mother! And imagine my grandmother – she'll have a heart attack.'

Niranjan grimaced. 'You're so dramatic! Anyway, it's not as if the world would lose one of its kindest people if the old lady does kick the bucket.'

'Don't talk like that,' Priyanthi said reprovingly. 'She may be an arrogant old snob but she's my flesh and blood. But it's not her I'm worried about. My mother would never forgive me, Niranjan.'

Niranjan started to get impatient. 'What's the alternative, then?' he demanded.

She was silent. The alternative was far too heart-breaking to put into words.

He reached for her hand. 'Priyanthi, I don't know what to do. We can't go on like this for ever. We'll have to tell them at some time, because if we don't, they'll get to know anyway. This is a small place.'

A woman walked by them, peering under the umbrellas she

passed. They both tensed, then relaxed as she disappeared under a black umbrella.

'Let's go,' Priyanthi said nervously. 'It's late and I don't want my mother to start getting suspicious.'

Niranjan held on to her hand as she made to stand up. 'Five minutes!' he pleaded.

She sighed and leaned against him. He put his head next to hers. She laid her hand on his face. He laid his hand on hers. She closed her eyes against the hot sting of the tears she felt beneath her lids. He swallowed to dislodge the painful lump in his throat.

After five minutes, they stood up and walked towards the road, the umbrella still open although the sun was beginning to set. Their hands which were clasped just moments ago were apart; his pushed deep into his pockets, hers folded defensively across her chest.

Galle Face Green was a haven for lovers during the early hours of the afternoon. It had been many years since the famous Colombo promenade had actually been green; these days it was more dusty brown than anything else, but its vast sweep from the road down to the ocean still acted like a magnet for all kinds of people.

After the sun set and the lovers went their separate ways, the small kiosks began to open. Balloons, kites, peanuts, soft drinks and the occasional neon lights of an ice cream van blaring raucous music, all ready to lure the families who thronged the green after the lovers vacated it.

* * *

Priyanthi walked into the house and straight into her room. Enid glanced at Stanley, but he was reading his newspaper, oblivious of her concern. The girl had been acting strangely these last few months. On the one hand, Enid was pleased that Priyanthi was devoting so much time to her studies; she stayed late after school for extra tuition and had joined a variety of associations and clubs. On the other hand, all too much work and no play might end up making Priyanthi a dull girl, and that would never do.

While Enid wanted Priyanthi to continue her education for as long as she wanted, she also had grand hopes of making a fine match for her. After all, Stanley had diligently saved for her dowry and the sum that resided in a separate bank account was now quite substantial. The thing was that Priyanthi showed no signs of being remotely interested in boys. True, she was not yet seventeen. But Enid was still concerned.

They were often invited to people's houses for lunches and dinners and there were always young people who seemed to like her. Although she readily accepted invitations to their homes and to go to the cinema, she always cried off at the last minute. 'I'm not a great socialiser, Amma' was her only reply when her mother asked her why she never went out.

'But Priyanthi, it isn't normal for you to only go to school and classes and sit in the house for the rest of the time,' Enid would exclaim despairingly.

But nothing she said seemed to make any difference.

This Saturday, they were going to Percy Samaraweera's house for drinks and dinner. Percy was Stanley's colleague and good friend. Enid and Percy's wife Anoja got on well together and were in the same Housewives Society. Once a month, they met at the society gatherings held either at the Mount Lavinia Hotel or at some other nice location. They always managed to spend a few minutes chatting, exchanging news about their respective families.

Anoja had been off visiting friends in Australia and had just returned, hence the dinner.

Priyanthi showed no interest whatsoever when she was told about the party. When Enid asked her what she was going to wear, she shrugged and said she would decide later. Enid sighed. There was also the problem of Hemantha to deal with. The whole family had been invited, but up to now, they had always managed to make some excuse for him. Stanley preferred it that way. This time, Percy had insisted that they bring Hemantha.

'I haven't seen that boy of yours in ages and my Romesh is about the same age. High time they met.'

Enid fretted all week, wondering if Hemantha would behave himself or take the opportunity to try and embarrass Stanley. About a month before, another colleague of Stanley's had come to the house to drop off some papers, and Hemantha had been rude and uncouth, belching loudly and muttering obscenities. Not in Stanley's hearing of course, but enough to horrify the poor man, who declined an invitation to stay for dinner and hurried off.

Enid sighed again, wondering what bad things she had done in her previous life to deserve this kind of stress at her age.

On Saturday evening, she was even more worried. Hemantha had been slouching around all day, refusing to even listen to her when she told him about how important it was for them to create a good impression. Priyanthi hadn't returned yet from her afternoon tuition class. Ordinarily, she was home at five, but it was almost six thirty and there was no sign of her.

Enid went to the gate and looked down the street, but it was empty. She saw Dierdre standing at her gate and wandered over, glad to have someone to share her worry with. 'This child is so late,' she said. 'I reminded her about the dinner tonight and she hasn't even found anything to wear.'

Dierdre looked sympathetic. 'It's the age, child. They've got other things on their minds at this age. Not dinner parties.'

Enid looked confused. 'Other things like what?'

'Boys,' Dierdre said succinctly.

'Boys? Priyanthi's not interested in boys,' she said wistfully. 'I think she'll die an old maid.'

Dierdre laughed. 'Maybe. And maybe not.'

Violet came out. 'What are you two gossiping about?'

'Boys,' said Dierdre.

'Or lack thereof,' Enid added.

Violet didn't even try to figure that one out. Anyway, she had other things on her mind. 'Niranjan is late again,' she said.

'Last Saturday he came home after seven and Bala nearly had a fit.'

'Where's he gone?' Dierdre asked casually.

'Cricket practice.'

'Every Saturday?' Dierdre enquired, looking off into the distance.

'Yes. At the CCC,' Violet answered. Then she looked at Dierdre. 'Why?'

'No reason,' Dierdre said hastily, wondering how two reasonably intelligent women could be so blind.

'Percy's dinner tonight, child,' Enid said. 'I told Priyanthi not to be late. Now she'll come home, run into the bathroom, pull on any old thing and go looking like something the cat dragged in.'

Dierdre laughed. 'Come on, Enid. That daughter of yours could never look anything but beautiful.'

'You think so?' Enid asked curiously.

Dierdre shook her head in exasperation. 'Mothers never notice, do they? Your daughter is a beauty.'

'So why doesn't she have a boyfriend yet?' Enid demanded.

Dierdre opened her mouth to reply and then shut it again. It was better this way. God only knew what trouble there would be when they were finally found out. She shuddered slightly.

'Are you cold?' Violet asked with concern. 'It's so warm today. Maybe you're coming down with something. Mrs Paul was saying there's a stomach fever going around.'

'I don't know about stomach fever, but I'm sure Mrs Paul has brain fever,' Dierdre retorted.

'Dierdre, don't say that,' Violet said, looking around to see if anyone was in earshot. 'Mrs Paul is a very nice lady.'

'Who tells you how to run your home and your family,' Dierdre shot back. 'Honestly, Violet, I don't know how you put up with all her advice!'

'Radhika's quite nice, though,' Enid said. 'There's been a vast improvement in my Priyanthi since they became friends.'

Dierdre snorted. 'If you mean the lipstick and mascara, she doesn't need it.'

'There she is!' Enid suddenly exclaimed. She hurried up the road to meet Priyanthi, who had just turned the corner. Her steps faltered slightly as she saw the three women.

Enid caught up with her. 'What's the matter with you, child? I told you not to be late today. What will Percy think if we arrive after everyone else?'

'I don't really care, Amma,' Priyanthi said clearly, and walked inside.

'Well,' Enid said indignantly, 'what are these children coming to? Ask a simple question and you get rudeness in return.'

'What's wrong with her?' Violet said. 'Maybe she's not feeling well.'

'Oh, I think she's fine,' Dierdre said. 'These young people lose track of time. No harm done anyway. At least I don't think so,' she muttered, as she saw Niranjan approaching them in his cricket whites, his bag slung on his shoulders.

Violet hurried up. 'Son, what happened?' she said anxiously.

'Bus got late,' he muttered, and walked past her into the house.

'You think he's ill too?' Dierdre said innocently. 'I'd better go. I have things to do. Have a nice time at the party,' she said to Enid.

Priyanthi locked the bathroom door behind her and undressed slowly. She stood naked in front of the spotted oval mirror with its rusty hinges and stared at the stranger looking back at her. Her body was long and lithe, full in all the right places. Pity I'll die a virgin, she thought with bitter humour. She wearily brushed her teeth and stepped under the shower, wincing as the cold water hit her shoulders. She showered quickly, ran into her room and closed the door behind her.

She sank on her bed, unmindful of the damp patches her body made on the sheet. She felt tears welling up in her eyes and furiously blinked them away. Red eyes and swollen eyelids would only infuriate her mother further. Priyanthi wished with all her heart that she could stay at home tonight, but she knew from past experience that there wasn't any excuse that would work. She felt exhausted.

Although her mother thought her tuition finished at five, it actually finished at four. At the same time Niranjan's cricket practice ended.

Today, they had gone to a tiny café in Bambalapitiya, aptly named Rendezvous. It catered mostly for couples who wanted to spend some time together away from the baking heat of the afternoon. The tables were sprinkled with the remains of previous assignations – pastry crumbs, doodles of hearts on cheap paper napkins, initials etched into the wood-veneered table surfaces. The cakes were stale and the drinks were flat, but it was discreet and that was what counted. It had been a particularly difficult meeting for Priyanthi, because Niranjan always got upset when he heard she was going out with her parents. He was well aware that Enid was industriously trying to make a match for her daughter.

'She'll spend the entire evening trying to push you and Romesh Samaraweera together,' he predicted.

'I'll put on my brakes,' she laughed.

He didn't laugh back. 'It hurts, Priyanthi. Why can't I be with you? Why am I not good enough? What does Romesh Samaraweera have that I don't?'

Priyanthi leaned forward and took his hands. She turned his palms upward and traced a pattern on them with her fingertips. 'Don't compare yourself with someone you don't even know,' she said gently. 'And please don't do this to us. It's hard for me too.'

He gripped her hands so hard that she winced. 'What are we going to do?' he asked urgently. 'What *can* we do?'

'I don't know.' A tear trickled down her cheek and she withdrew one hand to arrest its downward journey with a fingertip. It stayed on the tip of her finger, round and trembling.

'We'll have to tell them,' he said suddenly.

She started in alarm. 'Not yet!' she whispered. 'We're too young to even get married, Niranjan.'

'Why?' he demanded. 'I'm working now. I can look after you.'

'I'm only seventeen,' she cried softly. 'I don't know how to be a wife!'

His face softened. 'I know. You're still a baby. But we will get married some day, won't we? You won't let them break us up?'

She shook her head vehemently.

'Promise me,' he insisted.

'I don't have to. You know I love you.'

'Promise me anyway,' he said

She looked into his eyes. Brown but not laughing now. They hadn't laughed in a long time, she thought with a pang. 'I promise,' she said.

A pounding penetrated her thoughts. 'You can't stay in there all evening!' Enid yelled. 'We're leaving in five minutes.'

Priyanthi pulled herself up and went to her cupboard. All her good dresses needed ironing. Then her eyes fell on her one sari, an orange chiffon that her grandmother had given her. She pulled on the backless blouse that went with it and draped the sari quickly. She smoothed some orange lipstick on her mouth and deftly lined her eyes with the black pencil Radhika had given her.

On an impulse, she drew a small black dot in the centre of her forehead, slightly above her eyebrows. A pottu, which was traditionally the sign of a married woman. A Tamil married woman. Although these days, lots of girls wore it as a fashion accessory. It gave her an exotic look and somehow changed her face, made it more oriental, more adult.

'What is that?' Enid sounded horrified. Priyanthi's heart sank. So much for the sari.

'What's what?' she said, hating herself for sounding defensive.

'That thing on your forehead,' Enid snapped.

'The pottu?' Priyanthi said innocently, still hoping this wouldn't lead to a full-blown row.

'Yes!' Enid almost screamed the word.

Stanley came out of the bedroom, buttoning his shirt. 'What's going on?' he demanded. 'You want to wake up the whole road?'

'This child will drive me mad one of these days!' Enid announced, sinking to a chair.

'What has she done now?' Stanley asked, looking from one to the other.

Priyanthi glared at her mother. 'Amma doesn't like my pottu obviously, so I'll go and clean it off.' She went into her bedroom.

'Pottu?' Stanley said in a bewildered voice. 'I didn't see any pottu.'

Enid snorted. 'You only see what Hemantha does. Never your beloved daughter! Pottu! Like a Tamil estate worker!'

'What's wrong with wearing a pottu?' Stanley asked, bending down to tie his shoelaces. He missed the hard look she threw him.

'Everything,' she said. 'She's a Sinhalese Govigama girl, not some Tamil woman.'

Stanley looked up now. 'You know, sometimes you sound incredibly racist, Enid,' he said. 'I personally don't see anything wrong with her wearing a pottu. A dot on your forehead doesn't change what you are.'

'I don't want Percy's family to see her with that ridiculous thing,' Enid said stubbornly.

'Percy is my colleague. I should be worried, not you. Now let's hurry up and be on our way without any more histrionics, please.' Stanley stood up and went outside to wait for them.

Enid stared after him angrily. Sometimes Stanley acted like a fool. It was obviously up to her to find a husband for Priyanthi. Stanley would have her be an old maid and live with them for ever if she left it to him.

Priyanthi emerged from her bedroom with a faint smudge where the pottu had been. Enid opened her mouth to tell her to go and clean it off properly and then shut it again. What was the use? 'Your father's waiting outside,' she said, and went in search of Hemantha.

She found him lying on his bed reading and waiting for his summons. At least he was wearing his brown slacks and beige and brown shirt. They were slightly crumpled but it was far better than Enid had hoped for. 'Come on, son,' she said, her voice softening. She loved her son with all her heart, far more than she could ever love Priyanthi, although she would have died before admitting it. For all his faults and the trouble he got himself into, Hemantha was her first-born, the one she had known longer and loved stronger. That was how she defended her love for him.

Hemantha scowled and rolled off the bed. 'Let the show begin,' he said with heavy irony.

'What show, dear?' Enid asked carefully, wishing she could just ignore his remark, but knowing that it would infuriate him if she didn't answer.

'The happy family,' he said, sneering. He smoothed his hair back with his hands and struck a deliberately aggressive pose.

She finally lost her temper. 'We *are* happy, Hemantha,' she snapped. 'Just because you've got a grudge against the whole world, it doesn't mean we have too.'

She walked out of the room, waiting for the explosion, but thankfully none came.

True to the psyche of the bully, Hemantha backed down if someone stood up to him. It didn't stop him hating them, though, and during the taxi ride to Park Road, where Percy Samaraweera lived, he glared at his mother every few minutes. She pretended not to notice. Priyanthi, who was sitting between them, could feel the animosity flowing from her brother and shivered. It felt like a live thing. A cold, clammy snake which slithered across her bare back.

She wondered what Niranjan was doing. She wondered if things would ever get to a point when it could be him and her and her parents sitting in a taxi and going to Percy Samara-weera's house for dinner. She wondered if Niranjan was right. If they should just come clean and tell their parents. She thought of Hemantha's reaction and shivered again.

'Are you cold? You shouldn't have worn that blouse,' Enid said.

'It's okay. Just a ghost walking over my grave,' she replied briefly.

'Must be your Heathcliff,' Hemantha mocked.

She turned to look at him. 'Heathcliff? Oh, Hemantha, you've finally started reading. How wonderful! I did wonder if you were ever going to get your nose out of the bottle and into a book, and it looks like you've finally done it. Congratulations!' Her voice dripped sarcasm.

Hemantha dug her sharply in the side. 'Shut up!' he bellowed. 'Just because you're wearing a sari, don't think I can't give you a tight slap across your bloody face.'

'Cut it out!' Stanley roared from the front seat.

Enid made a muffled sound of distress.

Hemantha folded his hands across his chest and clenched his fists.

Priyanthi just smiled.

* * *

Percy Samaraweera's house looked like something out of a fairy tale. Strings of coloured lights lined the roof and clusters of tiny pahan flickered at the doorway. Huge terracotta bowls of water lined the driveway, the jasmines which floated fragrantly on their surfaces looking like serene ships on calm seas.

Enid patted her hair self-consciously as they walked to the open front door where Percy and Anoja were greeting their guests.

'Welcome! Welcome!' Percy boomed in a beer-tinted bari-tone. 'What a lovely girl you've grown into! And you, young man – I haven't seen you in years. Your father must be proud of you!'

Hemantha mumbled something. Priyanthi smiled. Enid and Stanley swelled with parental pride, all previous arguments forgotten.

Anoja Samaraweera eyed Priyanthi speculatively. 'You *have* grown into quite a looker, dear,' she said, trying to remember how old Stanley's daughter was. Her son Romesh was twenty and giving her headache after headache in the shape of a string of thoroughly unsuitable girls. Anoja had decided to take matters into her own hands and introduce him to some nice girls from good families, hence the party. Her interested gaze travelled from Priyanthi's long hair down to her pink-painted toenails. She nodded to herself.

Enid beamed.

Anoja waved towards the crowded lounge. 'Go inside and get yourselves something to drink. The young people are in the garden.'

They went. The room was full of people, all beautifully dressed, the subdued lighting not quite able to dim the opulent jewellery they wore. White-coated waiters glided in and out of the crowd with trays of drinks and hors d'œuvres. The murmur of conversation rose and fell, occasionally punctuated by a burst of laughter. Almost immediately, Enid and Stanley were hailed by people they knew.

Hemantha spotted a formal bar set up in a corner of the spacious living room and headed for it. Enid watched him go and hoped he wouldn't get blind drunk and disgrace them all. She had seen the look in Anoja's eyes when she had seen Priyanthi and the subsequent approval in her smile. If Priyanthi and Romesh Samaraweera got married, it would be the beginning of a new life for all of them. She wondered how soon she could invite Anoja over for tea. Or maybe dinner.

Priyanthi wandered through the crowd and found herself at a door leading out to a garden. It was a beautiful garden as gardens went, but not to her taste. It was too manicured, too *contrived*, with its ornamental fountain, gnomes, bird baths and carefully trimmed hedges.

There were some people at the far corner, some sitting on a

few wrought-iron chairs, some standing. She gave them a wide berth and walked over to a corner where a rock garden tried to look as Japanese as it could. There were jasmines creeping up specially designed bamboo frames, a profusion of roses in neat beds, and lilies and gladioli nodding gently in the night breeze.

Even the air smells expensive, she thought, longing with all her heart for the salty tang of sea air, for the slightly musty smell of the toddy tapper's hut, for the feel of fish nibbling at her feet, for Sepalika's stories during the rainy evenings.

'Are you a figment of my imagination, or are you real?'

She started in surprise and turned around. A young man stood close by but she couldn't see his face because of the shadows cast by the trees and bushes.

She laughed nervously. 'I'm real.'

'Thank God!' he said theatrically. 'I couldn't have borne it if you'd vanished at the sound of my voice.'

He moved into the light and she caught her breath. He was without doubt one of the most handsome men she had seen. He is almost beautiful, she thought. His eyes were black and slightly almond-shaped, his nose was aquiline and his mouth was sensual yet strong. An errant lock of wavy hair fell across his forehead as he dipped his head towards her. She was tall yet she had to tilt her head to see his face.

He started to look concerned. 'Are you all right? I didn't mean to scare you.'

Still she stared.

'Oh no!' he exclaimed, making her jump again. 'You don't talk. You're a beautiful princess and a wicked witch cast a spell of silence on you that only a kiss from a tall, dark and handsome stranger can break!'

She lifted an eyebrow.

He put his hands out defensively. 'Okay, okay. Tall and dark?'

She laughed. She had to. He was so funny. 'And handsome,' she said.

He leaned forward. 'Do you really think so?'

'Oh come on,' she said, smiling. 'You know you are.'

'I've never wanted to hear it said until now,' he said seriously.

She suddenly realised she was flirting with a complete stranger without sparing Niranjan a thought. She felt immediately guilty. 'I've got to go,' she said, her smile dimming.

'Did I do something?' he asked urgently.

'No, no, it's just that – I have to find my parents.'

'Let's go and find them together,' he suggested.

'No, I'll go by myself,' she said, wondering if she sounded foolish and gauche.

'No, I insist on going with you. This garden is full of strange things. I wouldn't want you to bump into any of them,' he declared in a loud whisper.

She couldn't help grinning. 'I promise I won't scream if I happen to walk into one of those ugly creatures,' she said, gesturing towards the gnomes.

He made a face. 'They're quite awful, aren't they?'

She felt guilty again. What was she doing criticising Anoja Samaraweera's garden to one of her guests? 'It's not bad actually. It's just not the kind of garden I like.'

'What kind do you like?'

She looked around. 'I don't know – wilder, I suppose. More natural, less contrived.'

He smiled. 'Like you.'

Silence hung between them, shy and shimmering.

'Let's go and find your parents,' he said.

She nodded and followed him, liking him instinctively.

She wasn't attracted to him as a man but felt drawn to his wit and infectious good humour. For a few minutes, she had felt like a normal girl. Not a girl with a huge sad secret.

With Niranjan, every minute was tinged with sadness because of the situation they were in. With this man, she had laughed. That was all, she told herself firmly. Hardly a reason to feel as if she had betrayed the man she loved.

They entered the living room, which was a babel of noise. Baila music played in the background, which she thought was nice. Nice to know that Anoja and Percy were not so rich and so sophisticated that they couldn't appreciate the lilting melodies and humour of Sri Lanka's own dance music.

'Stand here and don't move,' her new friend ordered.

She stood by a huge fern in a terracotta pot and watched. A woman in a beautiful crimson sari was surreptitiously digging her nose. A distinguished-looking man in national costume stood next to a woman who was obviously his wife, but his gaze was on a long-haired siren in a slinky evening dress. Behind the bar, a waiter glanced left and right and emptied a glass of whisky into his mouth. Priyanthi felt a little lost. The feeling vanished as the dark-haired stranger reappeared with a glass. 'Here.'

She took it gingerly. 'What is it?'

'Passion fruit juice. I didn't think you looked like much of a drinker.'

She laughed. 'I'm not.' She looked around and spotted her parents in a group. Suddenly she felt foolish, like a child at a grown-ups' party hanging on her mother's sari.

'Do you want to go back outside? I'll introduce you to some people there,' he said, watching the play of emotions on her face.

She shook her head in wonder. 'Are you a mind-reader?'

He bowed deeply. 'I fear you have found out my secret, princess.' He steered her through the door once more and out towards the group of people at the far end of the garden.

She hung back, shyly. She wasn't much good at social chit-chat.

'Relax,' he said softly. 'I know them. They're nice.'

Again, he seemed to have read her mind. This time, she didn't comment.

'This is Princess,' he announced to the group.

One of the men whistled. 'I'll be her Prince Charming any day,' he declared, to good-natured laughter.

Her companion slipped a friendly arm around her. 'For tonight, *I* will be her prince.' He looked at her. 'And I will be charming. I promise.'

The hand at her waist felt warm and comfortable.

Soon she was chatting with the other people, most of whom were around the same age as she was. Her prince, as she had dubbed him in her mind, stayed close, but not so close that she felt constricted. Niranjan would have enjoyed this, she thought wistfully.

'Your eyes dimmed. Why?'

She smiled at him. 'Just a sad thought.'

He studied her. 'Yes. There are many. You have known a lot of happiness and a lot of sadness.'

'Can you tell?' she asked.

He nodded. 'You aren't all that difficult to read.'

She suddenly wanted to change the subject. 'Speaking of reading, do you?'

'Read?'

She nodded.

'I learned how in the first grade and I've been practising ever since,' he said earnestly.

She laughed. 'You know what I meant.'

He laughed. 'Yes, I know what you meant, and yes, I read. A lot.'

She brightened up. 'I just knew you did! What kind of books?'

'Everything. But I have to admit I've got a special place in my heart for Shakespeare.'

'No!' she breathed.

He looked at her. 'Yes. Why?'

'I love Shakespeare! Especially the tragedies. I loved *King Lear*. I've read it a million times.'

'I like the comedies myself. There's a lot of pathos there. Take *A Midsummer Night's Dream* ...'

They spent the next hour listening to each other's views on Shakespeare, sometimes arguing, mostly laughing. Priyanthi had not had so much fun in a long time, and for a while Niranjan and her problems took a back seat. The other people in the group were nice too, some of them entering the discussion, some shouting to them to stop talking about dead people. When dinner was served, she remained where she was while her new friend went to get her a plate of food. The conversation continued through the delicious grilled prawns and basmati rice pilau. Some time later, she caught a glimpse of her watch and jumped to her feet. 'My God! It's almost midnight. My parents must be wondering what's happened to me.'

'Let's go and find them. We were going to a few hours ago, if I remember.'

She giggled. 'Shakespeare stopped us.'

They entered the living room and she saw her parents talking to Anoja and Percy Samaraweera. Probably plotting a marriage with their son, she thought sourly. But she was too happy for her ill humour to last more than a few seconds. 'Amma,' she said.

Enid turned. 'Priyanthi!' she exclaimed. 'There you are! We were wondering what had happened to you. You're such a naughty girl, disappearing like that!'

Anoja Samaraweera smiled warmly at them, her eyes moving speculatively from Priyanthi to her companion.

Priyanthi, busy with her mother, missed the look. 'Sorry, I met some people and didn't notice the time ...'

Her mother interrupted her semi-apologetic explanation. 'Oh, never mind. We weren't worried or anything. Anoja told us you were being looked after.' She turned to Priyanthi's companion, who was listening with interest. 'You bad boy! Didn't even come and say hello to Uncle Stanley and me.'

He smiled. 'Auntie Enid, I didn't realise this was your daughter. I apologise for kidnapping her like that.'

'Kidnapping? Naughty boy,' she said, wagging her finger at him.

Priyanthi was starting to feel a niggling suspicion. 'You know one another?'

Her mother laughed. 'Of course. I first saw this young man when he was still in his nappies.'

Now it was his turn to wince. Priyanthi stared at him. 'Who are you?'

'Romesh, child,' her mother answered for him.

'*You're* Romesh Samaraweera?'

He bowed. 'Guilty as charged. And you must be Priyanthi.'

She looked dismayed. 'You can't be.'

He looked curious. 'Why not?'

Obviously his mother wasn't as obvious as hers. 'Never mind,' she snapped. She turned to her parents. 'Can we go soon? I've got a headache.'

'I've been called a lot of things before, but never a headache,' Romesh murmured.

She didn't bother to dignify that with an answer. She was furious. With her parents. With his parents. With Niranjan for making her feel guilty about nothing. With Romesh for not telling her who he was, although that wouldn't change the fact that he was nice and fun. And obviously quite smitten with her. She was furious with herself for falling so easily into the net. Even if he really had no idea who she was. God, she felt like a fool. Again she looked at her parents, with more than a hint of desperation in her face. 'My head *really* hurts,' she said through gritted teeth. 'Please let's go.'

'Is it one of your migraines?' Enid asked solicitously.

How quickly she became all sweetness and light when she felt her daughter was about to make a big catch, Priyanthi thought cynically. 'Yes,' she said briefly, trying not to let her feelings show on her face.

'Migraines?' Anoja Samaraweera sounded concerned.

'Oh, it's just the pressure from all her school work. Nothing serious,' Enid said hastily.

Like examining a horse at an auction, Priyanthi thought. The buyer and the seller, one suspicious, the other reassuring.

Romesh looked at her. 'There are a few of us getting together here on Wednesday night. Nothing formal. We're just going to watch a movie and have dinner if my mother feels inclined to feed us. Would you like to come?'

'I have tuition on Wednesday,' Priyanthi said, looking longingly at the door.

'Nonsense!' her mother said robustly. 'Of course you can come. You study too hard.'

Priyanthi felt nauseous.

* * *

'So what was he like?'

She sighed. Niranjan sounded almost belligerent.

'He's nice,' she said carefully, not bothering to ask who he was talking about. The question had hung in the air for a full five minutes before he had voiced it.

'So when's the wedding?' His tone was mocking and her heart ached for him. Insecurity is such an awfully damaging emotion, she thought.

She smiled and tried to sound light. 'I don't know. You haven't proposed to me yet.'

He didn't even smile. 'Damn it, Priyanthi, you know what I mean.' His voice had risen slightly and a couple of sparrows who had been pecking at insects in the grass beside them flew away indignantly.

The park was almost empty today. It had been drizzling steadily since morning and even now, at almost four in the evening, the sky wore a dreary, weary look. The grass they sat on was slightly damp, but that was the least of Priyanthi's worries.

Niranjan had been spoiling for an argument ever since they had arrived at the park, wanting to know every minute detail of the evening. What she said, to whom she said it, whom she had met, what she ate, what she wore. She answered all his questions patiently, wondering why she was suddenly reminded of her grandmother. He saved Romesh Samaraweera for the last.

'Niranjan, I met Romesh. He's a very nice person. He's very handsome, very well read and very friendly.' Niranjan could feel his heart sinking with every word he heard. He forced himself to remain silent so she could continue. 'I also spent most of the evening thinking about you, wishing you were there. You would like him. He's nice,' she ended. Her voice was very calm, but her hand, which played idly with a lock of hair, shook uncontrollably.

Niranjan heard her. He also noticed her hand and was struck with remorse. Reaching out, he grasped it between both his and gazed at her. 'I'm so sorry, Priyanthi. I know I'm acting like a complete idiot but I can't seem to help it.' He pressed her hand to his cheek, closing his eyes briefly. 'I'm so sorry.'

She closed her eyes too. 'I don't know what to do, Niranjan.' Her voice was flat. 'I love you, I really do, but sometimes you make it so difficult. It's as if everything's a test of some kind.'

He looked guilty. 'It's so difficult.'

'I know. But do you have to make it even more so?' She stood up and dusted her skirt. 'I've got to go.'

'But we just got here,' he protested, and then fell silent under her hurt gaze. 'I'm so sorry. I really am,' he said.

'Wait a bit before you leave,' she said.

He nodded miserably. She walked away without looking back.

Her heart felt heavy as she walked off towards the park entrance. She felt tired of everything. The lies, the deception, the subterfuge. At times like these, she wanted to end it with Niranjan. Surely it would be better to be without him than to cope with the double strain of her mother's matchmaking and Niranjan's jealousy. But she loved him, and though life with him was so difficult, the thought of life without him was almost too much to bear.

So she ran between them all, calming them, reassuring them, allaying their fears, playing along with their plans and pretending to agree with their views when in reality all she wanted was the luxury of forgetting about all of them and simply concentrating on herself and her own feelings for a bit.

In spite of her problems, she had no sleepless nights – she was so exhausted that she slept the moment her head touched the pillow. She knew Niranjan loved her, and while she could appreciate the strain of what he was going through, she wished he would remember that just as much as her parents wouldn't approve of him, his wouldn't approve of her. The difference was that unlike Niranjan, who was angry at the world for what it was doing to them, she accepted their situation. She could see it from their parents' perspective and understood how hard it would be for them to accept this association. The race barriers had been up for far longer than their relationship. It just wasn't done. And the current political tension between the races didn't do anything to help.

Just recently, a Sinhalese girl had eloped with her Tamil boyfriend and had been forced to return home simply because no official would marry them. The boy had been badly beaten up by the girl's brothers, had sustained a neck injury and was now in a wheelchair. A week later, the boy's relatives retaliated by flinging acid on the girl's face. All because they were in love.

EIGHTEEN

❦

Priyanthi stared at the newspaper, the bold letters in the headline running together as tears welled up in her eyes. *Cyclone hits Bentota. Hundreds feared dead.* Swallowing the tide of panic rising inside her, she forced herself to read on. Apparently a violent cyclone, caused by a depression in the Bay of Bengal, had battered the southern coastline from Kalutara down to Balapitiya, but Bentota had sustained the most damage. It said the sea level had risen so high, it had washed right across the Galle Road, damaging houses, sweeping boats out to sea and uprooting trees.

It was this last line of the article that caused Priyanthi's heart to freeze in fear. Dear God, please don't let anything have happened to him, she muttered under her breath, not knowing to which God she was praying. Buddhism, after all, was a philosophy, and although some Buddhists paid homage to an array of Hindu gods, neither Enid nor Stanley believed in doing this. Niranjan's was the only religion she knew anything about, because he had related his seminary experiences to her. He was also the only one she knew who believed in a higher being.

Her father and mother, who were also at the table having breakfast, didn't notice Priyanthi's absorption with the news, her untouched plate or the sudden trembling in her hands and mouth. Surely the toddy tapper was safe. Surely he wouldn't have gone up into his coconut kingdom knowing a bad storm was brewing. But he had before, said a tiny, taunting voice in her head. Forgetting everything, she grabbed the paper and flew next door to find the only person who could put her mind at rest.

Stanley looked askance at Enid, who just shook her head in despair. He returned to his glum contemplation of the plastic packet of Astra margarine which sat in front of him. No butter these days. Too much cholesterol, the doctor said. Stanley, who loved butter and hated margarine with a vengeance, wondered which was preferable – to die of a heart attack or to live and have to eat terrible food.

Enid waited for him to make some comment on Priyanthi's erratic behaviour, but he apparently didn't think anything of it. Enid wondered what to do about their daughter. The child was going from bad to worse. Her lips thinned and her brow became creased with worry lines. Lately, this seemed to be the expression Enid wore most often. Her quick smile and sparkling eyes weren't seen so often any more. Although she didn't notice their gradual disappearance from her countenance, others did, and missed them.

Priyanthi hurried along the few yards that separated Niranjan's house from her own, the newspaper clutched to her chest. Luckily it was Saturday, so Niranjan would be home.

In the last two years, Niranjan had done well and was now a junior accountant at Ceylon Foods. When the job was first advertised, Stanley had told him about it, got him an interview and put in a good word for him.

The British boss was impressed with Niranjan's quiet manners and excellent school records and hired him on the spot. Violet was thrilled. 'We'll be able to make a nice match for him when the time comes,' she confided to Enid. 'Good jobs always help.'

Enid smiled and nodded and wondered how she was going to find a wife for Hemantha when the time came.

Niranjan was earning one thousand five hundred rupees a month and was well liked by the staff in the accounts department. His easy-going attitude and his home-cooked lunches made him popular among his colleagues. Even though he was almost six feet tall, he was thin and Violet still worried about him, as she had done since he was a little boy.

She woke up before dawn to begin cooking, and by half past ten, two lunches were neatly served on enamel plates (to prevent breakage), covered with another enamel plate, tied up in a snowy napkin, tagged with name and office address and ready for the lunch boy. The lunches were placed in the wooden box on the back of his bicycle, and off he went to pick up more lunches for more people. When he finished his rounds, he joined the hundreds of other lunch boys at their rendezvous point near Thurston Road, where the lunches were separated according to office locations, loaded into the wooden boxes once more and delivered. It was amazing how they managed never to mix up the lunches, considering their informal *modus operandi*.

Every day precisely at noon, when Niranjan's lunch was delivered to his desk, the other people in accounts came to peer into his plate and exclaim with envy over its contents. Rice, beef or fish curry, deliciously prepared vegetables and sambols, and often a banana for dessert. When Niranjan came home and told Violet about how everyone had commented on what wonderful lunches he always had, she beamed with pride and tried to outdo herself the next day. Bala had an identical plate delivered to St Mark's and received the same reaction.

* * *

Priyanthi pounded on Niranjan's front door. There was no response and she wondered if anyone was home. Then she heard Violet's voice out in the garden, calling out to whoever it was to wait a moment. 'Auntie Violet! Auntie Violet!'

Violet appeared, dragging a hosepipe behind her. 'Priyanthi. There's no one in the house. What did you want Niranjan for?'

Priyanthi's face fell and her racing pulse slowed down somewhat. 'Where's he gone?'

'Oh, just up the road to the shop. He'll be back in a few minutes if you want to wait.' Violet aimed a spray of water at some rather tired-looking orchids, which drooped even more under the onslaught. 'What is the matter with these plants? Oh, I'll have to ask your mother to come and look at them. She's so wonderful with plants ... real green thumb.' Violet sounded wistful.

Priyanthi didn't much feel like getting into a discussion with Violet about how wonderful her mother was, so she sat on the step and waited, although she didn't really want to be alone with her thoughts either. They were too terrifying.

She remembered that rainy day in Bentota all those years ago when she had felt this same fear for their friend. So much had happened since, she thought. She remembered the toddy tapper's words: *As long as you are together, you will remember.* Had he known what would happen? Had he guessed? Had he seen something all those years ago that they hadn't? Had he known about the heartache before it had even begun?

The last couple of years had been hard on Priyanthi and Niranjan, but the restrictions and difficulties seemed only to have fuelled the intensity of their feelings. Sometimes Priyanthi wondered if they would have felt the same way if things had been different. If both their families had been overjoyed at their association. Would the easiness of the whole thing have led to boredom? Would the possibility of it all have driven them apart? Was it the impossibility of it that kept them together?

So their meetings had continued, the deceptions had deepened, the love had grown, the commitment had solidified and the frustration had mounted. Sometimes it didn't seem worthwhile. Sometimes it seemed like the only thing in the world worth believing in.

'Pri?'

She looked up. Niranjan stood there, a look of concern on his face. 'What are you doing here? Why are you crying?'

She ran her fingers over her cheeks and found them wet. Funny, she thought, I can't remember crying. I don't remember wanting to.

'Priyanthi?'

With an effort, she pulled herself together. 'Have you seen the newspapers?' Her voice sounded husky.

'No. Why?' Niranjan laid down the thin plastic bag full of onions and potatoes and sat down next to her.

'There's been a cyclone.'

He looked a little confused. 'So? It rained so hard last night, I'm not surprised.'

'Bentota was the worst hit. They're saying hundreds have died.' Her voice broke and she rested her head on her knees. Her curved back looked like a resting bird, long and exposed and vulnerable. It shuddered gently as she breathed.

'Oh God.' Niranjan leaned back against the closed front door and stared up at the sky, which was a bright, happy blue this morning. He looked down at Priyanthi, longing to rest his chin on her down-bent head, to place his cheek against the nape of her neck which her long hair had parted to reveal. 'He will be okay Pri. He's strong and smart.' The words sounded weak to his own ears.

She shot him a look. 'Please. Please don't try to make me feel better by mouthing banalities,' she said harshly. 'I am worried and I know you are too. I also know you can't do anything to make this whole thing disappear. But be honest. I am not some child who needs false reassurances.'

Violet wandered over, looking faintly worried. 'Are you children okay? I thought I heard raised voices.'

Priyanthi forced a smile. 'I'm sorry, Auntie Violet,' she said. 'I just came across to ask Niranjan for some help. I have an essay that I have to turn in pretty soon and I'm stuck.'

Violet beamed. Young Priyanthi was so keen on her education. She had started at the Colombo campus last year and was apparently doing very well with her degree studies. 'Oh that's okay then,' she said. 'If Niranjan can't help, wait until Uncle Bala comes home. He'll be happy to.'

'Thanks,' Priyanthi said guiltily.

When Violet had gone back to her plants, Priyanthi turned to look at Niranjan. 'I'm sorry I lost my temper, Niranjan,' she said softly. 'I am just so worried about him.'

'I know,' Niranjan said suddenly. 'We'll go and see him and you'll see for yourself that he's fine.' The moment the words were out, he regretted them, but there was no going back now.

Her brown eyes had brightened instantly, the faith she had in him shining clearly, luminously.

'Oh Niranjan,' she cried. 'Thank you. Thank you. I was hoping you'd say that. When? When can we go?'

'I don't know,' he said cautiously, trying to ignore the uneasiness he was feeling. 'We'll first have to figure out how.'

'But we'll have to go soon otherwise there will be no point,' she said stubbornly. 'We can go tomorrow. It's Sunday so you don't have to work, and I don't have classes.'

'But what are you going to tell them?'

She thought for a moment. 'I'll tell them I have to go to Mala's place.' Mala was a friend whom her parents knew and liked, but they didn't know her well enough to know where she lived. It was perfect. 'We can leave early morning and be back by evening.'

'I don't know what time the trains leave,' Niranjan said a little desperately, because this was suddenly going too fast for him.

Priyanthi refused to share his concerns. 'We'll take the bus,' she said. 'There are private buses that go there directly, so we'll be there in no time at all.'

'But what if something happens? What if they find out or we get stuck there?'

Her face set in that mutinous way he had come to know and dread. 'I don't care. It's my problem anyway, not yours.'

He was angry too. 'It will be my problem if they find out you went with me. Your father will kill me.'

She looked coldly at him. 'I remember you saying you would die for me.'

He rose to his feet and picked up the bag of groceries. 'I'll check the bus and train times and let you know later tonight,' he said, and walked round to the back garden, leaving her sitting there.

She jumped up and ran home. She felt bad about manipulating him like that, but she had to see the toddy tapper and know for herself that he was all right.

* * *

She could barely contain herself all day. By evening, she was in a fever of impatience, but there was no word from Niranjan. She kept going out to the garden, hoping that he would come out and tell her what time to meet him, but his front door remained shut.

And although she was impatient, she knew he would find a way to let her know that he would take her. That was the thing she most loved about him. His deep sense of honour, his honesty, his goodness.

Since she had finished her Advanced Levels and begun university, they managed to meet more often, even attending a few parties together. Enid and Stanley had become a little more lenient with her lately, although she still had to be home before ten when she went out in the evenings.

She looked at the clock again. Almost seven. She squirmed in her chair.

Enid, who was sitting and sewing as she usually did at this time, looked impatiently at her. 'For goodness' sake! What on earth is the matter with you? You've been making all these noises and fidgeting all evening. Go and read a book or something.'

Priyanthi didn't bother to answer, but that didn't deter Enid. 'Why don't you phone that nice boy Romesh and ask him what they are doing tomorrow? They keep inviting you and you never go anywhere. One of these days, they'll stop asking,' she said.

'And I'll stop living,' Priyanthi muttered.

Enid put her sewing down. 'What did you say?' she demanded.

'Nothing,' Priyanthi said in a louder voice.

'What?'

'Nothing,' Priyanthi shouted.

Enid pursed her mouth and her eyes chilled. 'After all I do for you, the least I can expect from you is some politeness.'

Priyanthi rose from her chair. 'Amma, if you'd only stop

trying to pair me off with every man you meet, perhaps we might avoid these discussions. They're stupid and senseless.'

'What's wrong with pairing you off with a man? Every girl needs someone to look after them,' Enid said.

'I don't need a man!' her daughter exclaimed in exasperation, wishing she could tell her mother that she *did* have a man and that she was perfectly happy with him. She looked at the clock on the wall. 'I'm going for a walk.'

Enid looked suspicious. 'Where are you going?'

'Just up the road. I need some fresh air.'

'What's that supposed to mean?'

'It's supposed to mean exactly that,' Priyanthi said with a sigh, and left quickly before the argument flared up again.

Enid watched her leave and threw her sewing down. Her only daughter was becoming a stranger in front of her very eyes, and she seemed to be able to do nothing about it. She remembered with a pang how when Priyanthi was a little girl she'd come home from school, her eyes alight with mischief, and tell about how she'd seen Hemantha 'making eyes' at Radhika Paul. The times when Priyanthi used to proudly invite her mother to 'lunch', to eat the odd assortment of leaves and fruit and stones she solemnly served on her play plates. That cheerful, laughing child bore no resemblance to this moody teenager. Was I the same when I was a teenager? Enid wondered.

The mild impatience with which she had previously viewed Priyanthi had now blossomed into full-scale anger. Especially after Percy Samaraweera's party. As Enid had hoped, Anoja had invited herself over to tea and taken the opportunity of finding out every detail about Priyanthi: what her hobbies were, how her performance was at school, what kind of friends she had, what her life's ambitions were – questions that Enid had answered joyfully, albeit with some modifications to the truth.

When Stanley came home that night, she breathlessly told him what had transpired and was disappointed by his reaction. 'Not a bad chap, but a bit of a philanderer from what Percy tells me,' he said.

Enid was not deterred. 'Oh, who cares about that! Boys will be boys, you know. And anyway, all these things stop once a man marries.'

'Well, I want to make sure, because in this case, the man will be marrying my only daughter,' Stanley said.

'Don't go and say anything,' Enid pleaded. 'Let's wait and see what happens.'

What happened was that two weeks later, the family was invited once again to the Samaraweeras' home for dinner. This time, it was just Priyanthi and her parents (Hemantha had been left home for fear of jeopardising Priyanthi's chances of becoming a Samaraweera) and Romesh and his parents.

The two young people talked stiltedly and seldom, intensely aware of the nature of the occasion, although Romesh tried to make light of the whole thing, winking at Priyanthi and kicking her under the table every time his mother asked her another probing question.

After dinner, they went to the living room to have dessert and coffee. Anoja smilingly suggested that Romesh show Priyanthi the garden, which made Enid beam with delight.

Priyanthi thought she would vomit if she saw another arch smile. The mothers made cautious enquiries about each other's extended families, homes, children and housekeeping techniques.

'So what did you say Stanley's father was?' Anoja asked.

Enid preened. 'Oh, a Grama Sevaka. Down south, you know.' A Grama Sevaka was a sort of village headman and a prestigious title to hold.

'And you're from Kandy? My goodness, that's unusual.'

'Yes, but you know with his education and job and all, my parents didn't mind.'

'Is his family – you know, well off?' Anoja enquired delicately.

'Well, his father is dead now, but Stanley inherited the walauwwa and half the money. The fields went to his brother,' Enid said, conveniently neglecting to say that half the money was a few thousand rupees, most of which had been spent on death duties.

Anoja nodded. 'Yes, well, when Romesh gets married, he will automatically get a lump sum from his inheritance from his grandfather, and of course, he'll get everything we have.'

Enid nodded slowly, trying to guess what 'everything' was. The evening was going perfectly. Even Priyanthi was behaving reasonably well, although her monosyllabic answers at the dinner table had got on Enid's nerves.

The fathers decided to celebrate the union of their children prematurely and proceeded to get blind drunk on Percy's imported Chivas Regal. 'Have another, have another!' Percy urged.

'How to? This imported whisky must have cost a bomb,' Stanley said, already extending his glass for a refill.

'No problem! All in the family, old chap!' Percy said, slapping Stanley on the back.

Stanley frowned, his powers of comprehension seriously diminished by the alcohol. Enid, however, heard the comment and smiled broadly from across the room.

Out in the garden, Priyanthi told Romesh she was in love with someone else and although she liked him immensely, she could never marry him. She begged him to help her end this matchmaking before it got too late and the friendship their families enjoyed ended on a sour note. Romesh was disappointed but not overly so. While he quite enjoyed the idea of this shy yet spunky girl becoming his wife, he was not sure he was ready for marriage. He understood the situation she was in and liked her enough to promise his assistance.

A few weeks later, he informed his mother that although Priyanthi was a very sweet girl, he had no romantic inclinations towards her. Furthermore, he continued, he had seen Dicky Jayasekera's youngest daughter Irangani and had found her far more attractive. Anoja sighed. This wasn't the first time her beloved son had done this. Then she brightened up. Dicky was not only an old friend of theirs, he was also extremely wealthy and apparently devoted to his daughters.

She telephoned Enid and told her that Romesh had declared himself not yet ready for marriage, and that she, Anoja, personally thought a lovely girl like Priyanthi would be wasted on her useless son anyway. 'You'll find someone nice, dear,' she told Enid, who managed to answer casually enough, although she was devastated at the news.

Then Anoja telephoned Dicky's wife and invited their family over to dinner the following day.

Enid couldn't accept the excuse and blamed Priyanthi for the way her matchmaking efforts had ended. 'You'll end up an old maid. You see. Then you'll wish you had been a little more accommodating when I tried to find you a husband.'

Priyanthi rolled her eyes and made a mental note to telephone Romesh and thank him.

NINETEEN

The bus ride seemed endless. Niranjan shifted his thigh and wondered why every obese person in Colombo seemed to end up sitting next to him. It's probably because I am so thin, he thought. The bus crawled on, inexplicably so because it was early Saturday evening and the streets were visibly empty of traffic. The rush would start later on, when the Saturday-night crowds emerged from their homes, grimly determined to make the most of the weekend.

The woman sitting next to him sighed loudly and shifted on the narrow seat. Her breath smelled of onions and betel nut, a pungent, unpleasant combination. Her bare arm pressed against his, sticky with sweat.

Priyanthi would be worried. As always when he thought of her, a clutch of desperation gripped him. A what-are-we-going-to-do-with-the-rest-of-our-lives sort of desperation.

The Wellawatte vegetable market passed slowly outside his window. He looked at his watch. It was just approaching seven. She must be frantic. Or angry. But it couldn't be helped. He had had to go to his friend Joe's house to borrow some money for the journey tomorrow. Luckily Joe had been able to lend him the required hundred rupees. Niranjan promised to pay it back on Monday when the banks opened.

It wasn't that Niranjan didn't have any money. In fact, he had over ten thousand rupees in a savings account at the People's Bank. Since he had started working, he had been diligently putting away one thousand rupees every month. He gave his mother three hundred rupees a month, his share towards the household expenses. The other two hundred was spent on bus fares and cool drinks under hot umbrellas.

Niranjan was saving to get married.

Somehow the action of depositing that money every month made his dreams seem a little more real, made a life with Priyanthi seem a little more possible.

The bus passed the Dehiwala junction. Niranjan stood up and tried to squeeze past the fat lady, who refused to move her legs. Eventually, he climbed over them.

He pulled down on the bell and waited for the bus to stop.

It was quiet outside and the twilight calm was soothing. A few birds straggled home tiredly across the indigo sky.

Priyanthi opened the gate and walked outside. The road was empty and Niranjan's front door was shut. Through the transparent net curtains, she could see the lights were on.

She walked slowly until she reached the bokku, which was alive with the sounds of the creatures that lived in its murky depths and beneath the fan-like leaves of the swamp plants that fringed it. She picked up a small stone and tossed it into the undergrowth, watching with amusement as a mud-brown frog leapt away indignantly. A cloud of mosquitoes rose into the air and then vanished. Something, perhaps a water snake, disturbed the surface of the water, leaving a trail of tiny ripples in its wake. The water itself was murky and brown because it was mostly made up of waste from the houses down the road. The bokku was supposed to carry it off somewhere, but as with most of the drains in the city, it didn't. It became a dumping ground for rubbish and during the monsoon it overflowed into the road. When the rains stopped and the water receded, the bokku left its treasure of sodden sanitary napkins and rotting banana peel for people to step around and cars to drive over.

'Priyanthi!'

She jumped and swung round to see Niranjan standing there. 'Niranjan! God! Don't scare me like that,' she exclaimed.

He was angry. 'What are you doing here at this hour? You're asking for trouble, dressed like that!'

She looked down at herself, realising that because she had left the house in such a hurry she had forgotten to change her shorts or wear a bra. Embarrassment made her defensive. 'What's wrong with what I'm wearing? Anyway, there's no one here.'

He looked at her. The cotton shorts had once been red but were now faded to an indistinct pink. Beneath it, her legs seemed endless. The white T-shirt she wore was probably Hemantha's it was so big, but the wind blew it against her body, outlining dips and curves. Her hair hadn't been combed and tumbled down her back in an unruly mass. She looked beautiful.

His voice softened. 'Pri, don't get mad at me. I just don't want some lout to come and bother you. You know what these guys can be like.'

She listened quietly and realised that as well as being protective of her, he was also jealous. 'You're right. But actually, I was looking for you. What about tomorrow?'

'We're going,' he said. 'There's a train just after nine in the morning which leaves from the Dehiwala station. We can take that.'

Her face lit up in a smile. 'Thank you. Oh, thank you, Niranjan. You don't know how much this means to me.'

He stepped along the side of the bokku where the wall of the last house shielded him from the other houses down the road. The shadows concealed him. He beckoned to her. 'Come here.' He was smiling and his teeth shone whitely in the dark.

She looked around. 'No, Niranjan. Someone might see us.'

'No one will see us here. It's too dark. Come, please,' he insisted.

'No,' she said again, but her resolve was weakening.

He heard it in her voice. 'Please,' he repeated.

She glanced around again and leapt lightly to the other side of the bokku. He clasped her in his arms, she rested her head against his chest, listening to the rhythmic thud of his heart. They stood there oblivious of the mosquitoes that came to feast on their arms and legs.

She opened her eyes and saw someone walking towards the bokku. As she watched, frozen with fear, the person paused and lit a cigarette. He stood there smoking, then took a step towards the bokku. Priyanthi held her breath. For some reason, the cicadas, frogs and buzzing mosquitoes had gone absolutely silent and her gasp sounded loud and frantic in the stillness.

The person stopped and peered into the darkness. 'Who's there?'

She began to shake uncontrollably. It was Hemantha's voice, sounding belligerent as usual. He stood there for a few more seconds, staring right at them it seemed, and then continued down the road.

'Don't go now. He might be waiting,' Niranjan whispered in Priyanthi's ear.

She couldn't have moved if she had wanted to. A lethargy had washed over her entire body, making her feel as weak as a newborn. Somewhere deep inside her, she was angry too. With Niranjan, for insisting on that embrace. With herself, for standing here terrified in the midst of the stagnant water, mosquitoes and rotting garbage.

Finally, Niranjan moved. He made his way carefully along the edge of the bokku and peeped around the wall. The street was empty.

'You run home,' he whispered. 'I'll follow in a while. Hemantha may be watching. If he is, tell him you were at Radhika's house.'

She nodded and stepped around him.

'Nine o'clock sharp at the Dehiwala station,' Niranjan reminded her.

She nodded again and ran lightly down the road. There was no one waiting at the gate. The door was shut. She pushed it open and went in cautiously.

'Where were you?'

She jumped. Hemantha stood at the windows, half-hidden by the curtains, which billowed in the evening breeze. She felt her heart start to pound and willed herself to calm down.

'At Radhika's,' she said. Her voice sounded high and reedy.

Hemantha's eyes narrowed. 'I didn't see you,' he said.

'I was inside,' she replied, turning away to walk into her room.

'Are you sure?' Hemantha asked. He sounded more than suspicious. 'I heard someone at the bokku just now.'

Priyanthi felt the anger flood through her again, hotly and gloriously. 'Yes. That was me. I was taking a moonlight swim with the frogs and the mosquitoes,' she snapped.

Hemantha glared at her. 'You watch your mouth,' he shouted.

'You watch yours,' she shouted back. 'Go and find some other woman to harass and leave me alone.'

Enid came running out of the kitchen. 'What on earth is going on?' she demanded.

'Ask her,' Hemantha screamed. 'She's up to something, Amma. I know she is.'

Enid was bewildered. 'Up to something? What do you mean?'

Priyanthi shrugged, her fear quite gone. 'Mad,' she said.

Enid turned to stare at her son. 'Hemantha?'

Hemantha glared at her. 'You're so stupid. You all are. You think she's such a princess. You wait and see.'

Enid sighed. 'Wait and see what? What are you going on about?'

'She's got a boyfriend,' Hemantha spat out. 'Little Miss Innocent here is not so innocent after all. She was down at the bokku just now.'

'Did you see her?' Enid felt weak with fear. Dear God, she thought, Stanley's going to kill me this time.

'No, but I heard her.' Hemantha sounded a little calmer now that he had his mother's attention. 'God knows what she was doing.'

Priyanthi stood quietly through the exchange, wondering if the moment was finally upon her, the moment of discovery. She wasn't afraid. In fact, it would be a relief to have it all out in the open. At least she and Niranjan wouldn't be reduced to hugging beside stinking bokkus.

Enid looked at Hemantha in outrage. 'A boyfriend?' she said, her voice rising now. 'A boyfriend? Your sister doesn't go anywhere, she hardly has any friends, I am worried she'll end up an old maid and you think she has a boyfriend? That she's meeting him down at the bokku? You should be ashamed of yourself. She's right. You have a filthy mind.'

Priyanthi's mind was reeling. Good grief! Was she such an unlikely candidate for a boyfriend that even her mother found the idea completely unthinkable?

Hemantha looked stunned. Then his mouth twisted into its habitual sneer. 'Oh, I see. You can't bear to even think of it. Fine. Live in your little dream, but remember what I told you. She's not the innocent she appears to be.'

'Hemantha, go to your room,' Enid said in a tone that held more implacability than it had for a long time.

'One day she'll turn up pregnant and then you'll believe me.' He spat out the words.

Priyanthi gasped, her face crimsoning.

'Go to your room,' Enid said. Her voice was still quiet, but there was anger in it now.

Hemantha gave them both a mock-salute and sauntered off.

They watched as the door slammed behind him. Then Enid turned to face her daughter. 'Well?'

'Well what?' Priyanthi said.

'Where were you?'

'At Radhika's.'

'Priyanthi, there's nothing wrong with having a boyfriend. But we'd like to know.'

Priyanthi sighed. 'Amma, you said it yourself. Where on earth would I have the time or the opportunity to meet anyone?'

Enid gave her a long look. 'Oh, I think you could find both if you wanted to. Remember what I said. There's nothing wrong with having a boyfriend, but I'll have no daughter of mine meeting men by bokkus.' She went back into the kitchen, where her dhal curry had almost dried up on the stove.

She mechanically added more coconut milk and stirred the

curry, but her mind was far away. Could it be possible, she wondered, that Priyanthi actually was meeting someone? It would explain so much – her lack of interest in boys, her indifference to someone as charming and handsome as Romesh Samaraweera – but who? And why would she want to keep it such a secret? Despite her rudeness and insolence, Priyanthi was honest, one of the qualities that Enid particularly liked in her and wished Hemantha had too. The only reason she *would* keep something like that secret was because the boy in question was unsuitable. Which could mean anything.

An older man. A younger man. A married man. Or worse still, a Tamil man. Enid shuddered. She would have to watch Priyanthi carefully. No sense crying over spilt milk, she told herself. She looked down and saw that the dhal curry was almost dry again. She flung it into the sink, pot and all.

* * *

Priyanthi lay on her bed and tried to chase away the feeling of uneasiness which enveloped her. Her head felt leaden and light at the same time.

So close. They had come so close to being discovered. She tried to imagine what would happen when the parents finally found out, but even her colourful imagination couldn't conjure up the images. Which was probably just as well, she told herself.

She wondered if it was wise to go ahead with their plans for the next day, especially in light of everything that had happened this evening. Her common sense told her to cancel the trip, at least postpone it until it was safer. Until the cloud of suspicion which obviously hung over her lifted. Her heart impetuously demanded that they go.

It was suddenly imperative that she see the toddy tapper again. She hoped he was not hurt, that Sepalika, the children and the little mud hut were safe. Somehow, Niranjan's and her future seemed to be entwined with the toddy tapper and his family. They too had fought so hard for love and triumphed. Their two children, their tiny hut and their poverty seemed like proud battle scars. Priyanthi felt inspired. If they could do it, then we can too.

A knock on the door roused her from her reverie. Enid's head came around the door. 'Come and eat,' she said.

She started to say she wasn't hungry, but the beady look in her mother's eyes made her change her mind. 'Coming, Amma. I'm starving!'

She mechanically ate the food her mother set before her. Hemantha slouched in his chair and shovelled food into his mouth without a word, occasionally shooting her menacing looks, which she ignored.

He already had a double chin, she noted with distaste.

Stanley liked to concentrate on his food while he ate, which left only Enid to make an occasional comment and slant suspicious looks at her two children. Priyanthi felt hysterical laughter bubbling up within her, and coughed loudly to cover it, almost choking on her food in the process. Finally dinner was over and she escaped to her room. She was tired from the tension, but sleep eluded her, dancing mockingly away like a mischievous wraith every time she tried to hold on to it.

After hours of tossing and turning, she accepted that sleep would take its time coming. She let her fingers drift down the spines of the books in the shelf next to her bed and pulled one out. *Wuthering Heights.* How fitting.

When she had first fallen in love with Niranjan, she had given no thought to the consequences of such a love. Once the trembling excitement of those first few months had settled, the bleak clouds of despair which had been hovering above the relationship gently drifted downward to rest on it.

There were only two choices to be made. Break it up and go their own ways, which would be almost unbearable given that they were neighbours; there would be no respite, no time to heal. In its irony, fate would make sure they saw each other every day, opening up the wound every time they did. It would be an impossible situation.

The other alternative was to tell their parents and hope that some glimmer of understanding would penetrate the bigotry that clouded the issue of mixed marriages. It was pathetic, she thought, that the issue of religion was only secondary. In fact, she didn't think her parents would object too strenuously to her marrying a Christian as long as he was a Sinhalese. The problem was with Tamils.

In happier times, she and Niranjan had discussed children and how to raise them. Niranjan had wanted to baptise them and bring them up as Christians, which she didn't really mind. After all, Buddhism was a doctrine, not a religion, and she didn't really practise it anyway. In fact, none of her family did. Niranjan, ex-seminarian, still felt strongly about his religion and God.

She heard the front door shut. Her parents were going out for a walk as they sometimes did after dinner.

They walked to the end of the road and turned. Enid glanced towards the bokku and quickly averted her eyes. As if not looking would make it all go away. 'Stanley,' she said, 'do you think it's time we started looking for someone for Priyanthi?'

Stanley looked surprised. 'Isn't she still a bit too young? No need to rush these things.'

'Yes, I agree. But it's never too early to start looking. I was hoping she would take a liking to Romesh Samaraweera, but she didn't seem interested.'

'Good thing,' Stanley grunted. 'Nice boy and all, but from what I hear, he's got an eye for the ladies. Always gadding about with some society girl or another. Running around with Dicky's daughter these days apparently.'

Enid tried again. 'You know, it's better to find someone and get her settled down before something happens.'

'Like what?'

'You know these young people, what they get up to these days,' Enid said.

'I don't know about young people, but I know my daughter,' Stanley said shortly.

'Well, at least think about it,' Enid insisted, trying not to lose her temper.

'What's to think? I can't think of one man I'd like my daughter to marry. Except maybe for young Niranjan. Fine boy.' Stanley scissored his hands in front of him as he walked. He said it helped his circulation.

'Yes, but he's a Tamil,' Enid said dismissively. 'I'm talking about someone suitable.'

'When you find someone, let me know and then we'll talk about it,' Stanley said.

The conversation was over.

Enid wisely let it be, but something bothered her. Something Stanley had said. She just couldn't put her finger on it.

Twenty

༄༄

When Priyanthi awoke, it was to the sound of rain pattering on the window pane. She snuggled down under the covers and then suddenly remembered that they were going today. She washed quickly and put on blue jeans and a cotton shirt. She slipped into a pair of sturdy sneakers, brushed her hair, pulled it into a hasty ponytail and stepped out of the room, mentally bracing herself.

Enid looked up from frying eggs. 'Where are you going in this rain? And so early?' The question was to be expected, the tone was casual, but there was something new there that Priyanthi identified as suspicion.

'I'm going to Mala's. We were planning to go through our essays together.' She kept her voice light.

'What time will you be back?' Enid's back was turned to her.

'I don't know. About six,' she answered carelessly. 'Why?'

'Why?' Enid sounded indignant. 'I'm your mother. I have the right to know.'

'Oh. Okay. Now you know.' She leaned over and kissed her mother's cheek. 'Don't worry, Amma. You'll start to get more wrinkles on that smooth forehead.' She sauntered to the door. 'I'll see you later.' Then she stopped. 'Oh, I almost forgot. I need some bus fare.' She thought for a moment. 'About five rupees. Mala lives near Buller's Road.'

Enid's brow cleared. 'Ask your father. He's awake. And take care on those buses. Plenty of perverts around.'

She grinned. 'I never seem to get lucky.' She left, laughing at the expression on her mother's face.

She walked up the road, boarded a bus bound for Buller's Road in case someone was watching, got off at the next stop and walked quickly down to the train station. The clouds had parted to let a few watery rays of sunlight through and there was a brisk salt-scented breeze blowing in from the ocean.

She came down this road often. When she and Niranjan wanted to meet and didn't have the time to take the bus to Bambalapitiya beach or the park, they came here and hid away under their umbrella. There were a few big houses down this road but most of them were dilapidated. They had a look of haunted melancholia that made most people give them a wide berth. A few shanties had sprung up here and there.

It was a depressing road and walking down it usually gave her a vague feeling of hopelessness, but not today. She was busy thinking of other things. Niranjan. Hemantha. Her mother. The toddy tapper.

She chewed fiercely on her bottom lip as she strode along. Her mother was suspicious. There was no doubt. It had been relatively easy up to now because her mother had never had any reason to doubt her. In fact, she had been happy that Priyanthi was going to her friends' houses, going to the cinema, going to parties.

Now that the suspicion had taken hold, all that would change. Priyanthi could feel it.

Niranjan was looking at his watch when she rushed into the station, smoothing back her windblown hair. 'What took you so long?' he demanded.

She had no chance to answer because the train came in right then, drowning all but its own wheezing voice.

Niranjan pulled her through the turnstile, which was a wooden pole. The ticket man glanced cursorily at their tickets and waved them through.

They walked almost the entire length of the second-class carriages until they found an empty one, and barely had time to sink into seats before the train took off with a lurch, like some unsteady drunk.

'What happened?' Niranjan asked again.

'Hemantha saw me last night.' Niranjan turned pale and Priyanthi hastily continued. 'Not you, just me, and he's not even really sure it was me. He just saw me coming home and put two and two together.'

'And?'

'He made a stink. Called Amma in and told her all kinds of things about me. That I was going to show up pregnant one of these days.'

Niranjan's jaw tightened and his fists clenched.

Priyanthi saw. 'Oh for God's sake, don't start wanting to fight now. Just be grateful nothing else happened. I had to answer questions today before I left. That's why I was late,' she said, her mouth twisting.

'Maybe we shouldn't have gone today,' Niranjan said.

Priyanthi's mouth hardened. 'No one was going to stop me. This is too important to me. To us.'

Niranjan reached out and took her hand. 'There you go getting all angry with me when it's really other people you're angry with.'

She relaxed and smiled. 'I know. Why do you put up with me?'

He smiled back. 'Because you're going to be my wife some day and then I'll get even with you.'

Her smile fled. She leaned her head on his shoulder and closed her eyes.

* * *

Little had changed on the coastline since they had last been this way. A few more hotels peeped discreetly through the fringe of coconut trees but the inclement weather had kept most of the tourists away from the beaches. The boats were pulled high and tied securely to trees.

Past Panadura they started to see uprooted coconut trees and debris floating in the water and washed up on shore.

Kalutara was worse, with fisher people standing on the beach looking blankly around at the pieces of their houses. Children frantically scrabbling in the sand for their own toys or other people's treasures.

They silently watched the scenes of devastation unfold in front of their open window, their hands gripping each other.

As they entered Bentota, Priyanthi gasped. The sea level was high, with waves almost lapping at the railway lines. Most of the huge black rocks which ringed the shore were submerged. Planks, tyres, sheets of tin roofing, plastic utensils and coconut fronds covered the restless surface of the grey water.

Priyanthi rushed over to the opposite window, the one on the land side. People stood around surrounded by whatever they had managed to salvage from the storm. They all looked faintly puzzled. As if their brains were unable to take in this complete devastation of their lives. As if it had shut down in defeat.

More terrifying was the mud further inland. It lay like a suffocating sheet over trees and people and homes and schools and cars and fields and antique shops which advertised *Brand New Antiques* in an effort to lure tourists in.

It was as if God had wreaked a revenge that was absolute in that it was inescapable. From one side, death by water. From the other, death by mud.

Niranjan came and stood beside her in the rocking train as she tried to swallow the lump in her throat.

They got off the train at Bentota, a Bentota that looked like nothing they remembered. The wind was still strong and the seas were still high. The air smelled of damp earth and death. They made their way through the town, which was deserted except for a few open shops. The main road was awash with at least six inches of water and they had to jump to the side of the road every time a vehicle passed. Even so, the bottoms of their jeans were soaked up to mid-calf and their shoes made squishing sounds with each step.

There were no indecently dressed tourists in sight. Most of them had headed back to the safety of Colombo and taken early flights home. The few that braved the storm were huddled in their hotel rooms drinking hot coffee and cold beer and making long-distance calls to family in far-off places to tell them what had happened.

'*There was no warning!*'

'*No sun for days! We should have gone to Marbella!*'

'*Blew the beach umbrellas away. And a few of those quaint little houses on the beach too.*'

'*Imagine, the pool flooded over!*'

Disgruntled and peevish from being cheated out of their tourist-brochure tans, they were even more demanding, wanting discounts on their hotel bills, and insisting that they be given room service although the manager apologetically told them that because many of the staff were locals, they had not come in to work. 'They've got to stay with their families, you know,' he said smiling humbly. 'Some of their homes have been washed away or buried in mud. I know it's a nuisance, but this is what happens when we hire locals. I hope you understand.'

The tourists didn't understand. They came from countries where there was social security, insurance, housing regulations and sophisticated disaster task-forces. The enormity of this calamity was lost on them; it was completely incomprehensible simply because they had not ventured out to look at the scene after the storm. The little fruit stalls they had clucked over and called cute, the tourist shops where they had eagerly bought batik beach wraps and devil masks, delighted at how cheap they were, the wayside cafés where they had stopped for cold king coconut water and English sandwiches, the beach clubs where they had danced the night away in their new white cotton dresses which showed off their newly acquired tans, all these places that had enchanted them had ceased to exist. Most of them were piles of rubble. Some of them had been blown away by the storm.

Theoretically, Sri Lanka had the means to deal with such disasters. There were hospitals, ambulances, police forces and the army, which apparently was trained to react quickly and efficiently in situations like this.

The reality was not quite the same. The first thing the storm blew down was the phone lines. Not that it made much of a difference, because only about five per cent of the residents had telephones and that five per cent lived in big beautiful houses with views of the sea but well out of the reach of its fury. There was no risk of their homes being blown away. Some of them exclaimed with annoyance over the coconut trees which had fallen over their flower beds, someone else's car was dented by a falling tree, but other than small incidents like these, the telephone people were safe.

By the time the first villager raced up one of the rich people's driveways, pounded on the door, woke up the servants, who then had to be persuaded to wake the master, who then had to rub the sleep out of his eyes and listen before comprehending what the frantic villager was saying, by the time he reached for the telephone, found it dead, tried unsuccessfully to get it working again, by the time he got dressed, got into his car and drove slowly and carefully down to the police station, which itself was in a shambles with its own phone line down, by the time the sergeant got into the car and they drove to the next town where the local police were able to send an urgent message to Colombo, it was too late.

By the time help came, thousands of homes had been washed away or buried under the deluge of mud. Hundreds of people were dead.

To be honest, it wouldn't really have made much of a difference had the telephones in Bentota been working. Help would still have arrived too late. The storm struck suddenly and violently. The mud took minutes to loosen.

The burgeoning troubles in the north of the island didn't help. What had started as a few bank robberies and a few sporadic assassinations had escalated into something entirely different. No one wanted to be the first to name it, but it was obvious that if it wasn't already a war, then it would soon grow into one.

The enemy was called various names – terrorists, separatist rebels, liberation fighters. At one time, most of them had been part of the political process. They had belonged to parties, contested elections, won some and lost some. Eventually, the parties became divided. They fell into two loose categories – the pacifists, who still trusted the political system and hoped for fair elections, and the activists, who got bored with the talking and the ballot boxes and took matters into their own hands, along with home-made mortars and a few Russian-made T-56s. They had had another more powerful weapon – anger. This gave them the momentum to carry out small-scale but daring raids on police stations and post offices and arbitrary executions on politicians and the few farmers who remained in the area.

Despite the rigorous training the new army recruits underwent, they were no match for cleverly positioned land mines and hidden gunners in their carefully camouflaged camps. As more mothers wept at the funerals of their still-teenage children, patriotism palled. Although the war had barely begun, there was already a distinct feeling of desperation.

In other words, the army was far too busy trying to *stay* alive to save lives. Especially from anything as relatively innocuous as a natural disaster.

* * *

Priyanthi and Niranjan crossed the road in the same spot as they had the last time they had visited the toddy tapper. The little toddy stand that Sepalika ran was not there. They didn't know if the storm had blown it away, or if it had simply ceased to exist.

The road down to his house looked like a muddy river and was just as treacherous. Priyanthi clung to Niranjan's arm to keep from slipping or tripping over fallen trees and submerged stones.

At the spot where the little lane turned, they stopped, almost afraid to look. When they did, they saw it just as it had always been. A small coconut leaf-and-mud house with no door.

'Hello?' Priyanthi cried.

There was no answer, just the rustle of the wind blowing through the trees and the distant lowing of distressed cattle.

Niranjan put his head in the door opening. 'Hello? Anyone home?' he called, reluctant to go inside because his feet were caked with mud.

'Sepalika!' Priyanthi called on a rising note of fear.

They heard a cry somewhere behind them and turned to look. Two figures were hurrying towards them, through the empty field to the side of the house.

'Is it them?' Priyanthi demanded, shaking Niranjan's arm.

'I think so,' he said.

A voice drifted through the damp air. 'Who is it?'

The toddy tapper's voice. A little rougher than they remembered, but still his.

'It's us,' Niranjan yelled back. 'The friends from Colombo.' Next to him, Priyanthi was sobbing with relief.

A couple of minutes later, the toddy tapper and his wife stood in front of them, shaking their heads in disbelief. He turned to his wife. 'I told you. I told you they were coming.'

Sepalika smiled at their questioning looks. 'He dreamed of you the night of the storm. He said he heard you crying.'

Priyanthi smiled through her tears. 'I am. I did.'

He stood back. 'Look at you! All grown up. You took my advice. Stayed together.' He considered them. 'Still just friends?' Priyanthi blushed and he laughed. 'No matter. Time to talk later. But what are you doing here? This is so unexpected. I thought my dream was just the wishful thinking of an old man.'

'We read about the storm in the papers,' Priyanthi said. 'We were so worried. We had to come and see if you were okay.'

He smiled gently and took her face in his rough, callused hands. 'Dear Priyanthi,' he said.

Sepalika led the way inside. Thankfully, the little house was exactly as they remembered it, slightly dark and smelling comfortably of clay and leaves.

Niranjan looked around. 'Where are the children?'

He shook his head. 'We were lucky when the storm came, because the house is far enough from the sea and not close to any hills. But they said it could continue for several days so we sent them to my parents' home. I will bring them back once the rains stop.'

'So nothing happened to you?' Priyanthi asked incredulously. 'My God! We've just seen half the town in a shambles. You must truly be blessed.'

He smiled. 'I have always said I was. I have always been thankful for what we have. Now I have another reason. We lost the door, but Sepalika is weaving another.'

'Did your parents come to check—' Niranjan asked Sepalika.

Her smile went away. 'No, but they sent someone to see if we were okay.'

Her husband took her hand. 'At least they did that. They must care.'

She smiled a little scornfully and then went to see what she could cook for lunch.

'How long can you stay?'

'Oh, just a few hours. We have to be back before dark,' Niranjan said, a furrow of worry cutting through his forehead.

The toddy tapper eyed the two of them, sitting on the floor with their backs against the wall. He noted how close they sat, saw their loosely clasped hands through the darkness. 'So when did this happen?'

Priyanthi didn't feel any shyness or embarrassment discussing their relationship with the toddy tapper. 'It was waiting to happen. You saw it before we did, before we even knew such things *could* happen.'

He nodded. 'That's true. On the one hand, I was hoping you would see that fate had made your paths into one. On the other hand, I was hoping you wouldn't, because that path is long and hard. And dangerous,' he added.

Niranjan looked pensive. 'It hasn't been easy, but we won't let anything come between us.'

'Is it love?' the toddy tapper asked reflectively. 'Or just the lure of the forbidden fruit?'

Priyanthi sat forward indignantly. 'How can you even ask?' she demanded.

His calm expression remained. 'Because it is possible.'

'In the beginning maybe that was it. For both of us,' she said, looking challengingly at Niranjan. 'But all that changed.'

The toddy tapper nodded.

'What should we do?' Niranjan asked. 'You were so brave, but yours was just a rich-poor situation. It's so much harder for us. I'm afraid they won't even consider the idea.'

'They probably won't,' he agreed. 'But we already know that. The real question is, are you willing to walk through the fire to be together?'

'Yes,' they both said in unison.

He held up his hand. 'Brave words, but think hard. You are talking about something that is not just unacceptable in our small-minded society. It is completely, totally abhorrent. Not only will they not consider it, they will do everything in their power to prevent it. Remember, you won't only be battling two families, you will be taking on an entire country and a few centuries of prejudice. Can you do it? Are you strong enough? Is your love strong enough?'

The silence drifted across the room like a loud whisper.

'Yes,' Priyanthi said finally.

'Yes,' Niranjan said, but his voice was strained.

He looked at both of them. 'If I, a stupid, uneducated toddy tapper could win my bride, then you can win yours.' The words were meant for Niranjan but his compassion embraced both of them. He rose and went into the kitchen. They sat there in frightened silence, fingers clasping and unclasping.

Niranjan finally looked at Priyanthi. 'Are you sure?'

'I always have been,' she said simply.

Their friend came back with three cups of tea. 'You never told me how and when all this happened?' he said.

Niranjan took a deep breath. 'Well,' he began, and told him everything.

When Sepalika entered the room to announce that lunch was ready, they were still deep in conversation. Instead of interrupting, she sat quietly at her husband's feet and listened.

* * *

Enid was aware of a vague feeling of disquiet all morning. She went about her Sunday chores as usual, but Hemantha's words and mocking face came between her and her work. The rice was overcooked, the beef was tough and the white potato curry, which usually had a creamy gravy, was dry.

Hemantha had gone off to visit someone – these days Enid didn't even ask because she didn't really want to know – and so it was just her and Stanley who sat down to lunch.

'Where's Priyanthi?' Stanley asked.

'Gone to Mala's,' Enid replied.

'Mala?'

'Her friend from the university,' Enid said.

'Gone to spend the day?'

'Yes. I told her not to with the weather being so bad and all, but you know what she's like,' Enid said.

Stanley smiled affectionately. 'She's exactly like you were when you were that age.'

'Yes, but things are different these days. It's not like before. So many bad boys . . .'

'But our Priyanthi's a good girl, so what's there to worry about?'

Enid looked impatient, but said nothing more. Men could be so obtuse, she thought.

At around the same time that Priyanthi, Niranjan, Sepalika and her husband sat down to a reheated meal of rice, jak curry and dried fish, Enid entered Priyanthi's room. She pulled out Priyanthi's little address book and started flipping through it without a trace of remorse. Priyanthi was her daughter and she felt fully justified in doing whatever she had to do to protect her. She found Mala's telephone number and dialled it with slightly unsteady hands, wondering what she was going to say.

'Hello?'

'Can I speak to Mala, please?'

'This is Mala. Who's calling?'

'Is Priyanthi there?'

'Priyanthi?' The voice sounded puzzled, but also guarded.

'Priyanthi Silva.' Enid's hand was shaking so badly that the receiver was knocking against her gold earring, making little clacking sounds.

'Who is this?' The voice was insistent now.

Enid didn't have to continue the conversation any longer. She knew. Her hand was steady once more as she quietly replaced the receiver and sat down in the chair beside the telephone. The same chair that Priyanthi curled up in when she had those long, animated chats with her friends. She wondered whether to tell Stanley, but shuddered at the thought of what he might say. He'll lay the blame at my feet, she thought bitterly, just as he did with Hemantha. She wondered what had happened to the family she had once had, and laughed to herself when she thought of the children growing up and the little trivialities she had thought were problems.

Finally, she couldn't stand it any longer. She stood up and went out into the garden and to the wall. 'Violet! Violet?' she called, praying Violet was at home.

Violet popped her head out of the kitchen door. 'Hello! Sunday lunch already over?'

'Can you talk for a few minutes, child?' Enid said.

'Yes, of course,' Violet said, and walked over to the wall. When she was close enough to see, she saw that Enid's face was pale and that her lips were trembling. 'My goodness! What happened? Is Stanley okay?' They had all been worried about Stanley after his heart attack.

'Stanley is fine. It's Priyanthi.'

'Priyanthi? What's the matter with her?'

'She's been acting funny lately,' Enid said vaguely, not wanting to say too much, but also desperate to pour her heart out to someone.

Violet nodded. 'Yes, I also thought so when she came yesterday to find Niranjan. She looked very upset. As if she had been crying or something.'

The feeling of betrayal and disappointment Enid was feeling flowered into something more. Something more terrifying. 'She came here yesterday?'

'Yes. She said she wanted Niranjan's help with some essay.' Violet laughed. 'I thought they were fighting.'

Enid felt faint. 'Fighting?'

'Yes, child. I thought I heard them fighting and they were only discussing some essay. But what's the matter with her? Is it the pressure of university and all? You know, they really drive these children. I know someone whose daughter had a nervous breakdown because she was so worried she wouldn't pass.'

Enid murmured something appropriate. Her mind was crowded with thoughts, like scenes from a film, but they combined to make one huge empty space: Priyanthi at her sixteenth birthday, at Percy Samaraweera's party getting all angry because they had thought young Romesh was a nice match for her, arguing about arranged marriages, disappearing to her friends' homes supposedly to study, Hemantha's accusations last night, and then this morning – the casualness which had deceived her, Enid.

Her heart pounded unevenly. 'I don't feel too well, Violet,' she managed. 'I'd better go in and lie down. This sun is very hot.'

Violet looked concerned. 'Shall I bring you some thambili?'

'No, no. I'll just rest for a while and I'll feel better.'

Violet reached across and took her hand. 'Don't worry, Enid. Priyanthi's a good girl.'

Enid went back indoors, sank down on her couch and pressed her fingers against her throbbing temples. Her stomach heaved with nausea. A good girl, she thought savagely. The good girl is about to bring shame and disgrace on her family for good!

What was she going to do? she wondered despairingly.

* * *

The rain clouds had dispersed completely and the hot afternoon sun beat steadily down, the sea breezes making no difference to its ferocity. The two couples sat on an old mat outside the hut because it was too hot to stay indoors. 'Sometimes we sleep outside here when it gets too hot,' the toddy tapper said.

'Is it safe?' Priyanthi asked.

'Safe? What is safe?' he said, shrugging. 'These days, going to the market can be unsafe, going for a walk can be unsafe. Look what rain can do!'

Niranjan, who had been lying back with his arm across his eyes, stirred. 'Do you want to go down to the village?' he asked Priyanthi.

'For what?'

There was irony in the toddy tapper's laugh. 'To see the death and destruction, of course. It's real, unlike the cinema, and you don't have to buy tickets. It's free!'

Niranjan flushed. 'I didn't mean it like that.'

Sepalika looked a little shocked at her husband's mocking comments but she could see he was already ashamed of his words. 'I know, my friend. I know. It's just that I have already been out this morning to see if there were any shops still standing because we needed some things for the house. There are so many people just hanging around and watching that it makes me angry. And yet, there's not a lot they can do,' he ended reflectively.

'Was your father's house okay?' Priyanthi asked Sepalika.

She nodded. 'It's a proper house. Cement, stone, brick. A few tiles may have blown off but no real damage. But never mind that. Tell us what you are going to do.'

Their faces clouded. 'We don't know,' Priyanthi admitted. 'But it's becoming pretty obvious that we have to do *something*.'

'Get married,' the toddy tapper murmured.

They both stared at him. 'What?' Niranjan asked finally.

He smiled. 'You heard me. Get married. You intend to, don't you? Some day? So do it now. Then tell them. What are they going to do? Disown you? They can't do that, because once you're married, you belong to each other, not them. Then, when the babies come, everything will be okay.' He turned to smile at Priyanthi. 'Your mother will come rushing to be with

273

you. And his mother won't be able to deny herself her grandchild.' He sat back and closed his eyes.

'Oh God!' she moaned. 'Do you know what hell will break loose?'

His eyes remained closed, but a small smile played around his lips. 'But the hell will have to break loose some time. So what difference does it make when it happens? I think it will be a good thing for the two of you. It is obvious that you do love one another, but even the strongest love sometimes falters when it's one against many. But if the two of you are together, then you're invincible.'

Priyanthi shuddered. 'I can't bear to think about it! And anyway, we don't have enough money. We need to get a place to stay, I haven't finished school yet ... it's not that easy.'

'It's actually very easy. Most things in their purest form are. It is we who complicate them,' he said. 'You can get married right away, but hold off telling them until you have the money to go off and start your life together.'

'What good will that do?' Niranjan asked dispiritedly. 'I mean, what's the point?'

'The point, my friend, is that you will know, even if no one else does, that you are married. You will have made your promises to one another, legal and binding and all that, and that knowledge will give you strength, comfort you when you are apart, give you hope when you are together. Think about it.' He rolled to his feet in a single lithe movement, walked over to the door and paused to look back at the three of them. 'Anybody feel like a cup of tea?'

They sat there, all lost in their own thoughts.

Sepalika remembered her own marriage, the heartache and anger which had accompanied it, when all there should have been was joy and happiness. Her heart ached for the two people sitting before her, because she knew that they too would have to go through the same pain to be together. It was like some sort of Herculean rite of passage to love. Why did it have to be that way? her heart cried out bitterly but there was no satisfactory answer.

Priyanthi felt cold despite the heat of the afternoon. She absently rubbed her arms to get rid of the goose pimples that raised themselves along the length of them. What the toddy tapper said made sense, but how, she asked herself, could she keep up the charade? How could she sneak off to stolen kisses under an umbrella and then go home alone, knowing she was legally married? And what would happen when her parents were eventually told? Would it be better or worse? Did it make a difference?

It *did* make a difference, Niranjan told himself, a shaft of hope piercing the black fog of despair that seemed permanently to cloud his mind these days. He had been going over the toddy tapper's suggestion in his mind for the last few moments and it made sense. At least I won't be stewing in impotent jealousy every time her mother shoves some rich man in her face, he thought. But won't it be worse? a tiny voice whispered in his head. Won't it be worse knowing that your mother-in-law is trying to marry off your wife to the highest bidder? Niranjan sighed heavily and sank back on to the mat.

At No. 9 Araliya Gardens, Enid paced the living room and looked at the old grandfather clock for the umpteenth time. Half past four and still no sign of Priyanthi. *Brazen!* she thought angrily, quite forgetting that Priyanthi had said she would be home by six. It was not enough that she was sneaking off to meet that person, she was also taking her own sweet time!

In Enid's head, suddenly Niranjan, dear sweet Niranjan whom she had adored for his gentleness and respected for his devotion to his mother (unlike her Hemantha), had become an enemy. She preferred to think of him as *that person* rather than Niranjan whom she knew and had loved so well. The son of her best friend. It was easier to dissociate him from all he was connected to and hate an unnamed entity.

How he must have laughed at me! At all of us! Coming home all pious and quiet when in reality he was plotting this all along! As her anger gathered momentum, her imagination ran riot.

Wait until Hemantha and Stanley hear about this! But even

as she thought that, she knew she wouldn't tell them. The tight ball of anger in her head deflated rapidly, replaced by self-pity. *Why me? What have I done to deserve this? I only did what I thought was best for her, tried to find a match that was good for her. Who will want her now?* As that horrifying thought struck her, she sank down on the nearest chair, clutching her heart, which was pounding with agitation. *Who would want her now?* Not only would Priyanthi be considered soiled goods because she had had a boyfriend, but a *Tamil* boyfriend? No self-respecting Sinhalese boy would touch her with a barge pole!

Enid's eyes narrowed as she considered the limited options available to her. Let Priyanthi get married to that person and pretend she never existed? She shook her head violently. Over my dead body! Send her to Kandy to live with her grandparents? But she would probably carry on from there and bring shame to their Govigama name. Enid shuddered. No, Kandy was definitely out of the question. There was only one thing to do. Enid set her lips, squared her shoulders and picked up the telephone.

The red-orange ball of the sun was slipping beneath the horizon when Priyanthi and Niranjan took their leave of Sepalika, promising to visit again or at least write. Their friend was going to walk with them to the station and see them on the five-thirty train for Colombo.

It was much later than they had planned to leave, but neither of them had wanted to be the one to suggest they go. In the covert madness of their world, this day had been like a reprieve.

At the station, the toddy tapper gripped both their hands. 'Together you are invincible,' he repeated, and then gave them a gentle push. 'Go now.'

They went, turning back more than half a dozen times to look at him standing there, separated from their tumultuous world by a crooked wooden ticket barrier.

Twenty-one

After her illegal abortion, Hemantha's arrest and Stanley's heart attack, something inside Enid died. Something youthful and vital that had nothing to do with her forty-something years. It was a leftover from girlhood that had survived a lot but couldn't survive the trauma of those three events.

It was as if her sense of fun and her sense of humour had been lost somewhere in the cardiac ward of the General Hospital. Before, she woke up each morning with a feeling of anticipation, already going over the things she had to do that day in her head, a small preoccupied smile playing idly around her mouth. These days, waking up alone filled her with foreboding and she tiptoed through the day hoping there wouldn't be a fresh set of troubles lying in wait around the next corner. Her children, whom she had taken such a joy in, were now mere makers of trouble, bringers-on of headaches; she didn't see their wilfulness as cries for understanding, but as deliberate attempts to spoil her day.

She felt they had made it their sole business in life to give her grey hairs, to go against her wishes, to disregard her entreaties. Where before, she laid the table and sat with her family, looking at each of them and marvelling that they were hers, smiling inwardly at their disparaging remarks about her cooking because she knew they would want second helpings none the less, now, she didn't even sit down to eat with them, preferring to shuttle back and forth to the kitchen and fuss around the food even though it didn't need to be fussed around. This way, she felt justified in her self-pity. There was no time to sit down.

The demands were too many. She would get something in the kitchen later on.

Often Stanley would find her in the kitchen eating out of an old plate, lines of bitterness pulling at her mouth as she ate without any apparent enjoyment. Initially he had been concerned and asked her why she was eating alone. She asked what else she was supposed to do, with all of them constantly wanting second helpings and water and other things. It was a reasonable answer, but her tone was bitter. When she finished her tirade, he left the kitchen. A minute later she heard the front door shutting and wanted to let out a cry of triumph because she had been right: he didn't care. None of them did.

Stanley watched the happy woman he had married turn into a stranger and wondered if it had been his fault. He had been hard on her when Hemantha had been arrested, but justifiably so, he thought. She had been aware of what was going on and had kept things away from him, not out of concern for him, but for Hemantha. The result had been disastrous.

Sometimes he suggested going to the cinema, but she always had something else to do. 'And who's going to clean this house while I am watching a film?' When Stanley pointed out that it was Banda's job to clean the house, Enid replied that he had to be supervised.

It took about three more rejections before Stanley understood what was happening. And once he did, he had no idea what to do. He briefly thought about confiding in Bala and asking for his advice, but pride stopped him. He had tried to talk to Enid, but it was like talking to a wall. She was so deep into her anger and self-pity that it would take more than a gentle question to pull her out.

Even Enid's looks began to suffer. She no longer made her monthly visits to the beauty salon down Auburn Side, no longer bothered to have her greying hair colour-rinsed or her eyebrows arched. The frown lines on her forehead became permanently etched and she wore them proudly, like stigmata.

To the neighbours, she was still the same old Enid, gossiping and trading chicken curry and compliments. But the gossip had an edge that hadn't been there before. The compliments were tinged not with good-humoured envy, but with real jealousy.

Violet noticed and put it down to the stress of the family; *she* felt depressed sometimes.

Dierdre noticed and wondered when someone was going to do something, or say something before it was too late. Before Hemantha's scorn at Enid's repeated attempts to pacify him exploded into rage and he killed her. Or someone. Before Priyanthi upped and left home because she couldn't stand her mother's constant badgering. Before Stanley decided to find the companionship and love that he was denied at home some-where else.

Dierdre brought up the subject one day when Enid came over to her house with some recipe she had wanted. 'Enid, what's the matter with you these days, child? Is something worrying you? If you tell me, perhaps we can solve it together. That's what friends are for, after all.' She watched with a kind of horrified fascination as the shutters came slamming down over her friend's face. One after the other after the other after the other, sealing off an already closed expression. Rejecting the tentative offer. Resenting it.

'I don't know what you're talking about,' through lips so thin, they almost disappeared.

Dierdre sighed and gave up. She had tried. She only hoped it wouldn't take a tragedy for Enid to see the light.

* * *

When Priyanthi walked in the door at a few minutes after eight, she immediately felt the rage radiating from her mother in palpable waves. She tensed, smoothing her wind-blown hair as if that would somehow make a difference.

'Where have you been?' The question was hissed in a low tone so Stanley, who was in the next room, would not hear it, but Enid may as well have screamed it out, for the anger it held.

'To Mala's. I told you.' Priyanthi strove to keep her voice from trembling.

The phone rang. Priyanthi, who was closer to it, picked it up. 'Priyanthi?' It was Mala's voice, and immediately, Priyanthi knew something had happened.

'Yes,' she answered, keeping her voice neutral.

'Your mother called this afternoon. I didn't know what to say. You should have told me and I could have covered for you.' Mala sounded half-sympathetic, half-accusing.

'That's okay,' Priyanthi said carefully, 'I'll call you later,' and she replaced the receiver with a trembling hand.

Her arm was gripped hard. 'Answer me. Where have you been?' Enid sounded almost hysterical now.

'Out,' she replied quietly.

'Where? And with whom?' Enid's voice wobbled on the last word, and suddenly, Priyanthi was filled with remorse.

'I'm so sorry, Amma,' she said, her eyes filling with tears. 'I really am sorry. I hate lying to you.'

'So why do you do it then?' Enid retorted, the wobble now gone. 'Why do you lie to me and for how long have you been lying to me?'

Priyanthi stared at her mother, trying to formulate a response in her head when she realised that she didn't have to. Somehow, her mother had found out. She knew about Niranjan. Along with the fear came an easing around her heart. The show-down had finally come. Earlier than expected and with no warning, but at least now there wouldn't be any more deceit.

'For a while,' she said, casting her eyes away from the accusing stare.

'Come in here.' Enid led the way into Priyanthi's bedroom. She shut the door and turned to face her daughter. 'My God, child, what's wrong with you? Are you mad? Aren't there enough decent men in the world that you have to carry on with a Tamil?'

Priyanthi's back stiffened. 'What are you saying, Amma? That if someone's a Tamil, they're not decent? Don't you think that's an absurdly unfair statement to make?'

280

Something in Enid snapped. She raised her hand and slapped Priyanthi across her mouth. Hard.

Tears sprang into her daughter's eyes, but they remained unyielding. 'Thanks a lot, Mother. I didn't expect you to applaud but I did expect some measure of understanding. No wonder we're such a messed-up family. You should be glad that someone wants me, even a Tamil. No man in his right mind would want to marry into this.'

Enid's mouth fell open with shock. 'How dare you?' she shouted. 'How dare you say our family is messed up? Anyway, you needn't worry about someone to marry you because I've already spoken with your grandmother about arranging a marriage for you. Quickly. I had been hoping for a decent man with means, but now, thanks to your behaviour, we'll have to take what we can get.'

Priyanthi stared. 'A marriage? I'm not going to marry anyone but Niranjan. I love him.'

At the mention of the name, Enid reared back as if Priyanthi had struck her. 'Don't mention that name in this house,' she hissed. 'And if you refuse to go along with the match your grandmother finds, I'll tell your father and brother and let them deal with you.'

Priyanthi stormed to the door and flung it open. 'Tell them,' she challenged. 'You think I care?'

'Keep your voice down,' Enid ordered. 'You may not have any compunctions about giving your father another heart attack, but I do.'

Priyanthi looked at her mother and wondered where the laughing, humorous person she had once been had gone. 'Amma, I'm telling you this once. I am not marrying anyone else. So don't bother hatching any stupid schemes.'

Enid went to the door. 'We'll see about that.'

Enid's mother had been grimly triumphant when Enid called her to tell her what she had discovered. 'You see? I warned you, but would you listen? Oh no! My God, the shame! I knew mixing around with those people would lead to this. Even that I tried to tell you. Inviting them for Avurudhu and constantly going to one another's houses. God only knows if the boy's parents planned this.'

Enid sighed. 'Amma, I'm sure they will be just as horrified when they find out. They're nice people. It's him. The son. Shameless!'

'There's only one thing to do. Marry her off quickly before people find out. No big wedding and all, just a quiet thing, but not too quiet otherwise people will wonder if she's in the family way.'

Enid finished the phone call wanting to weep.

For the next few days, Enid watched Priyanthi like a hawk, but she only went to the university and back. She made no attempts to meet Niranjan, who was worried and hung around his gate hoping for a quick word.

One evening, he saw Enid outside and called across to her. 'Hi, Auntie Enid! Watering your plants again?'

She turned around, gave him a long, cold stare and turned back to her plants. She knows, he thought. He too felt relief and he didn't mind her coldness and silence. After all, Priyanthi was her daughter and she had had such high hopes about her marrying a doctor or lawyer.

Niranjan felt the generosity that winners feel towards losers.

One evening, he spotted Enid going to Dierdre's house and rushed in to telephone Priyanthi. They didn't speak often on the telephone, but Niranjan called whenever he had a chance. If someone other than Priyanthi answered, he hung up. Luckily for him, Hemantha was out and Stanley was chatting with Bala by the gate. Priyanthi answered.

'Where have you been?' Niranjan demanded. 'I've been out of my mind with worry.'

'Well, you should be. My mother found out about us.'

'I thought so. I saw her the other day and she completely ignored me.'

'She's talking about getting me married off to someone my grandmother is going to find.'

'No! I won't let that happen.' Niranjan could feel his heart start to pound. 'I swear I won't let it happen.'

'How are you going to stop it? How am *I* going to stop it?' She sounded weary.

'We'll get married.'

'What?'

'We spoke about it when we were down in Bentota. There's no point waiting. Do you still want me?'

She closed her eyes in relief. 'Yes, of course I want you.'

'Fine. I'll make some enquiries and see what I can come up with. But I've got to see you this week. I can't stand not being able to see you.'

'I'll find a way,' she promised, a smile in her voice.

She heard the front door open. 'I've got to go,' she whispered and replaced the receiver quietly.

Enid walked in and looked at her. 'Why are you looking so pleased with yourself?' She looked at the phone. 'Have you been on the phone?'

Priyanthi nodded, praying this wouldn't lead into another of their arguments. 'Sonali called me,' she said.

Enid frowned. 'Are you sure?'

'Yes, Amma.'

Enid gave her a long look and went to the kitchen.

I will not get into an argument with her. I will not get into an argument with her. Priyanthi repeated the words in her head as if they were some sort of mantra.

She managed to stay out of her mother's way for the rest of the week, simply by staying in her room and venturing out at mealtimes. The excuse she gave her father was that she was studying for an exam.

Enid spent the better part of Friday evening on the phone with her mother. Priyanthi tried to listen to what was being said, but Enid deliberately lowered her voice.

Later, as she and Stanley sat out in the garden, she brought the subject up. 'My mother is coming tomorrow.'

Stanley sighed. He didn't relish his mother-in-law's visits. 'Okay.'

'She's bringing someone with her.'

Perhaps it was her tone that made Stanley sit up and start paying attention to what she was saying. 'Who's that?'

'Arjuna Perera.'

'Who's Arjuna Perera?' Stanley asked, trying to contain his annoyance. His wife had been acting strangely these last few days, throwing him accusing looks, hardly speaking to the children. Frankly, he was getting tired of it.

'He's Sam Perera's son. You know, the people who live up at Hantana? They have a tea estate there. Moneyed people.'

'So what's he coming here for?'

'He's coming to see Priyanthi.'

Stanley was puzzled. 'Does he know her?'

'No, this is a proposal. He's seen her photo at Amma's place and thinks she is beautiful.'

'I know she's beautiful, but that doesn't mean she's going to marry this catcher,' Stanley said irritably.

'She'd better marry someone soon otherwise no one will want her,' Enid said acidly.

'What rubbish are you talking now? What do you mean, no one will want her?'

Enid sat forward in her white cane chair. 'I'll tell you what rubbish I am talking about. She's carrying on with Niranjan!' She sat back with an expression that wavered between triumph and concern. She hadn't meant to tell him, but she could also see that he was getting ready for an argument.

Stanley sat quietly for several minutes, his mouth pursed in a soundless whistle, his eyes staring up into the night sky, which was dotted with tiny stars. Distant planets. Distant peoples perhaps.

'Say something,' Enid commanded, more out of worry than anything else.

'What's to say?' Stanley said quietly. 'He's a wonderful boy, but he's also—' He broke off, not wanting to put his prejudice into words.

Enid relaxed. She knew she had won the first round. Much as Stanley loved his friend and his friend's son, he loved his daughter more.

'What's he like, this Arjuna chap?' he said.

She smiled to herself in the darkness. 'My mother thinks he's very nice, but we'll have to find out for ourselves tomorrow.'

'Does Priyanthi know he's coming?'

'No. I don't want to give her time to plan something.'

Stanley nodded, his heart already heavy with the pain his daughter would feel tomorrow. The pain of parental betrayal. Unreasonably, he felt angry with Enid. He wanted to shout at her to remember what their love was like when they first met, how determined to be together they both had been, how happy they were when their parents had given their blessing. He knew she was trying to do the best she could under the circumstances, but it was best for the family.

Not necessarily for Priyanthi.

Imagine having Bala for my daughter's father-in-law, he thought. Violet as her mother-in-law, gentle, understanding Violet who already loved her as if she was their own daughter. And Niranjan, honest, educated and everything a son should be, could be, as her husband. Stanley knew Niranjan would take care of Priyanthi, knew that he would never have to worry about his daughter's happiness. But he also knew that Bala would never stand for it either, would never allow his son to marry a Sinhalese girl, even if it was his best friend's daughter. He was too proud of his Tamil heritage, too protective of it, too hurt by the prejudices of an unfair and judgemental society.

Stanley got up and went to bed, but when dawn lightened the sky, he was still awake.

Next to him, Enid slept the sleep of the relieved.

'Your grandmother is coming today.'

Alarm bells clamoured noisily in Priyanthi's head. 'Oh. Any special reason?'

'She's bringing someone with her.'

'Who?'

'Arjuna Perera, Sam Perera's son. You know they have the tea estate in Hantana.'

'What's he coming here for?' she asked, looking straight into her mother's eyes.

Enid looked away, unnerved by their demand for honesty. 'To see you.'

Priyanthi sighed. 'Amma, do we have to go through with this charade? I told you I am not marrying anyone but Niranjan.'

'Over my dead body,' Enid declared angrily. 'Now go and wash and dress. Wear a sari. One of those cotton ones that Violet gave you.' She stopped as she realised what she had said.

Priyanthi looked at her and shook her head. 'Amma, you are truly unbelievable.' She went off to find her father and came upon him in the garden. 'Did you know about this man?' she demanded.

He nodded and, like Enid, wouldn't meet her eyes.

'Why are you doing this?' she cried, 'How can you do this? I am your daughter, not a piece of meat to sell to the highest bidder!'

He finally met her eyes. His own were red-rimmed and tired. 'I know you are not going to believe this, but I am doing it for you. Now please, do as your mother says.'

She stared at him for a moment longer and silently went in to wash and change.

* * *

Arjuna Perera was quite handsome and quite old. According to her grandmother, he was 'only thirty-four'. He walked in and greeted her parents respectfully, his eyes darting around the house in a quick assessment. Enid's mother acted as if he was her son, as if she was personally responsible for his wealth and success and status.

Priyanthi came out of her room wearing a simple blue voile sari, her hair braided casually. She looked young, beautiful and extremely remote. Arjuna Perera reacted instantly. His eyes widened and his breath caught.

She placed her hand in his outstretched one and then

withdrew it quickly. He didn't seem to mind. His eyes were busy running the length of her body, pausing occasionally. He did it covertly, though, because he had already made up his mind. Marriage to this one would be like a long, softly played symphony, he thought.

Another of Arjuna Perera's many qualities that endeared him to Priyanthi's grandmother was his love for classical music. Being a lover of classical music, he thought in terms of it. Especially when it came to women. Some were Bachs. Some were Vivaldis. Some others were like Rimsky-Korsakovs, wild, passionate and full of fire. This one seemed to be a mixture, outwardly appearing to be like a beautifully gentle Handel but with a fiery Puccini inside. The thought of discovering it sent shivers down his spine.

She was saying something. 'Would you like some tea?'

He smiled suavely. 'I'd love some.'

They both knew he wasn't talking about the tea. Enid and her mother exchanged coy looks. Stanley resisted the urge to grab Arjuna Perera by the collar of his imported shirt and propel him through the front door and back to his Hantana tea estate.

Priyanthi forced herself not to think. She only let the polite hostess in her emerge, afraid that anything else would lead to disaster. She had spent many hours awake last night, thinking about everything, and had finally come to the sad conclusion that her parents *did* think they were doing the best thing for her. That being the case, she didn't really have the right to get angry with them, although she did have the right to feel a new sense of despair. She perched on the edge of a chair and forced herself to listen to their conversation.

'She's doing a degree,' her mother was saying proudly. The glance she shot her daughter's way was nothing like the recent looks Priyanthi had been getting. This one was filled with pride and love. 'We'd like her to be able to finish it. An education is so important.'

Arjuna Perera nodded approvingly, privately thinking that he would teach her all she needed to know. 'I think that's a good idea. We would be travelling a lot so she could even study a language if she wanted to.'

Enid beamed.

Priyanthi felt mild nausea. They were talking about her as if she wasn't even there. She lifted her head suddenly. 'I don't want to study a language. I already speak two and I think that's more than enough,' she said clearly.

There was a moment of silence and then her mother rushed in to fill it. 'Well, these are just details which you two can talk about later, once you get to know one another.'

You two. Priyanthi wanted to stand up and tell everyone that she was already a part of a you two, that the other part was just a few yards away planning their marriage. Instead, she looked down at her grandmother's pink-painted toenails. Pretty girlish pink paint on an old woman. She thought of Radhika's bedroom, wondered what everyone would say if she told them she wasn't interested in marrying Arjuna Perera but that her friend Radhika with the big bum and high hopes would be. Then she remembered that Radhika was a Tamil, therefore ineligible for the Sinhalese Mr Perera. She sighed.

Arjuna Perera left after an hour of desultory conversation during which he studied Priyanthi microscopically. She almost expected him to open her mouth and check her teeth.

He helped her grandmother into his shiny blue BMW, turned to look meaningfully at Priyanthi. She looked away, but he didn't seem put out. He waved to the two people he already saw as his father- and mother-in-law and drove off.

Enid fluttered her hand and tried to stop the little flutter in her heart. Stanley glowered and showed his teeth in what was more of a snarl than a smile. Priyanthi didn't even look.

'That chap is not coming within a mile of my daughter,' Stanley declared before the car had even driven away.

'Why not?' Enid demanded. 'My God, Stanley, if you're waiting for Prince Charming, let me tell you now that he's never coming. Arjuna is polite, nice-looking and obviously well-off.'

'So what if he has money? I'd rather see my daughter married to a decent pauper than a rich rotter!'

'How can you call him a rotter? There are lots of them around here, but he's not one of them!'

Priyanthi left them arguing at the front door and went off to her room. Her head was pounding.

The following day, she came out of the university gates and saw Niranjan standing there. Her heart speeded up as it always did when she saw him. Outwardly, her face was as serene as always. 'Niranjan. How did you get out of the office at this time?' she said.

'I got short leave,' he said. 'Can you come out for half an hour?'

She shook her head. 'I can't. My mother never takes her eyes off me these days. She checks what time I go home.'

'Please? Just for a bit?'

She was angry at him for pleading, because he knew very well what she was going through. 'No,' she said, and started walking in the direction of the bus stop.

'Why are you getting so angry? What did I do?' he said. She didn't answer, so he hurried to catch up with her. 'Stop, for goodness' sake!'

She finally stopped, looked at his face and sighed. 'Niranjan, you know what it's like at home. If I could go out with you, I would. You don't have to say please.'

'It's important,' he said.

They had reached the bus stop. She moved behind the shelter so they were hidden from prying eyes and passing buses. 'What?'

'We can do it on Friday,' he said.

Her heart stopped. 'Get married?'

He nodded and smiled.

She smiled too, slowly and with great relief. 'Where? What time?'

'At about twelve at the Grama Sevaka's. But not in Colombo.'

Her smile dimmed. 'Then where? I can't get away for very long.'

'We'll have to go to Malwana. It's about an hour and a half by bus. It's safer there. You'll have to cut classes.'

She thought rapidly and nodded. 'Okay. But what about witnesses? Don't we need any?'

'Joe will go with us,' Niranjan said. 'And we can get someone from the Grama Sevaka's office to be the second witness. You have to bring your birth certificate, though. Can you get it?'

She nodded. 'My father keeps it in his bedroom drawer.'

'Good. That's all we need.'

'And after? Then what?' she asked, her eyes slightly troubled.

'That's up to you,' he said gently. 'You know I want us to have a home and maybe a family, but I also know what you'll have to go through when we tell them.'

She knew too. 'Could we wait a bit? Just a few months maybe?' she said.

He nodded, secretly relieved. He didn't feel financially secure enough yet. After all, she would be his responsibility and he was determined to give her as good a life, if not better, as her father was currently giving her. 'What happened with the proposal? The guy your grandmother brought over?' he asked, although it didn't really bother him any more. Not now.

'Oh, he was a total bore. Very rich. Very pretentious. He should have married my grandmother.'

They both laughed.

Around them, people swirled back and forth, getting on and off buses, talking, laughing. Couples stood everywhere, after-university pairs who held hands and gazed at each other. One couple was having an argument and their voices kept rising and falling. Rising when they got heated and angry. Falling when people turned to look at them.

A police car cruised by, slowing down to a crawl as it passed the bus stand. As though a silent order had been given, the couples began to drift away – some got on to buses, others walked off to find other, couple-friendly meeting places.

TWENTY-TWO

❧

By the mid 1980s, security in Colombo was tight. The city was sewn up with barricades and checkpoints at its entrances and exits. The civil war was being fought up north, but the violence found its way to most parts of the island. Bombs arrived on buses down pot-holed roads. On bullock carts down little-travelled lanes. On boats down rivers and along the coastline. In innocuous-looking suitcases carried by innocent-looking travellers.

When the first bomb exploded in Colombo, people were aghast. Anti-separatist feelings became anti-Tamil feelings almost instantly. Uneducated people found it impossible to make the distinction between peaceful Tamils and separatist rebels – they were all Tamils, weren't they? Educated people tried to see the situation in a more objective light, but it was difficult with hundreds being killed and maimed.

The international community reacted immediately with strongly worded condemnations. International aid organisations which, contrary to their impartial philosophies, loved to dabble in local politics, take sides, allege atrocities and demand investigations became very quiet.

People in Colombo didn't know how to react. A few offices and schools closed, many people stayed home, prices rose and housewives started a (justified) spending and stocking-up spree. Bus travel was avoided as far as possible.

That was after the first bomb.

After the next five or so, bombs took their place among expensive accommodation, insane traffic jams and Grandpass prostitutes. A necessary Colombo evil.

Precautions were taken, of course. Army barricades increased. Spot checks were carried out by army personnel who did little more than intimidate men and leer at women from under their powerful hats and helmets. Access roads to government institutions and politicians' residences were blocked off in many cases.

The government was protecting itself against two enemies. The separatist rebels in the north and the insurgents in the south, who had declared war against the government and had launched a reign of terror in the southern cities. A spate of assassinations left people wondering if there would be any politicians to contest future elections. So the governement was busy.

It was like shooting in the dark. With no target in sight. With no night vision. With no bullets. With thumb and forefinger guns and *dush! dush!* noises from children's mouths.

No one knew who the enemy actually *was*.

Technically they did.

Un-technically, they knew nothing. Every time a tip-off was received, the intelligence units of the armed forces sprang into action, hounding and rounding up anyone and everyone. Trucks were searched from top to bottom (with mirrors for the undercarriages).

Despite all this, bombs were detonated as scheduled (usually by a suicide bomber), the target, evidence and bomber blown to bits. Or a popular MP would be shot dead in the head as scheduled. On an election rally platform in front of thousands of people.

The news was carefully censored so people were only told about army victories. Those who had short-wave radios or relatives in foreign countries, and so heard the real news, listened with growing horror and shared their information with their trusted friends or relatives.

Forty-two soldiers ambushed and killed in Mullaitivu, child! My Elmo heard it last night on BBC!

Can you imagine – three army trucks blown to bits by land

mines. Taking new recruits to Jaffna! And government is saying no casualties!

They're saying more than a hundred have died at Elephant Pass – and my son is saying he wants to join the army! Saying he wants to kill some terrorists. They'll kill him first!

They had to be careful when sharing information, though: people were not encouraged to stand in groups of more than two or three and chat. Although the whispers continued, no one dared comment or venture an opinion.

Political analysts argue about when exactly the real war began. Pre-1983 or post-1983. For the victims and their families, for the innocent Tamil businessmen herded from their homes and shot at point-blank range, and for the innocent Sinhalese farmers who were woken up by fusillades of rifle fire, it didn't matter.

* * *

On Friday morning, Priyanthi stood looking through her closet, trying to push away a feeling of depression. *My wedding day shouldn't be like this!* In an effort to feel better, she picked out a white cotton sari and put it on quickly. She stood in front of the mirror and looked at herself. *Is this what it has come down to? Is this what my parents wanted? For their only daughter to sneak off to nowhere to get married?* A tear trickled down her cheek and she angrily brushed it away. There was no time for this kind of self-pity.

She quickly combed her hair, picked up her bag and checked to see if her birth certificate was in there. Even that had been easy. She simply took it when her parents were outside walking after dinner.

'Bye.'

Enid looked up from laying the breakfast table. 'Aren't you going to eat something?'

'I have an early lecture today. I showed you the notice we got,' Priyanthi said woodenly.

Enid smiled sunnily back. 'Oh yes. I forgot. Don't get late, though – Arjuna is in Colombo today and he's coming for dinner.'

Priyanthi said nothing.

'Do you have anything nice to wear?' Enid persisted, refusing to be put off by her daughter's lack of interest.

'I don't know.'

'Well, you run along. I'll look for something,' Enid said, still smiling. She put her hands on Priyanthi's shoulders. 'Don't be angry with me. I am your mother and I only want what's best for you. One day you'll thank me for this. Arjuna is nice and rich and obviously quite taken with you. You're a lucky girl. Don't think about all that other nonsense.'

I'm marrying that other nonsense today, Mother! She said nothing, just nodded and walked out.

She met Niranjan and Joe outside the university gates as planned. They were in Joe's old Toyota, which hiccuped to a halt near where she stood. She got in hurriedly, not even looking to see if anyone had seen her, and they drove off.

Both Niranjan and she were quiet on the way to Malwana, which was approximately an hour's drive from Colombo. Joe tried to make conversation but eventually gave up, sensing that they wanted to be left to their own thoughts.

Niranjan sat in the front seat, clenching and unclenching his fists and jaw. He was nervous, not about getting married, but about possible complications. Priyanthi was nineteen, which was over the legal age for marriage, so she didn't need parental permission, but he still hoped the Grama Sevaka didn't get suspicious. After all, there were just three of them, hardly a festive wedding party. Joe had been reassuring. 'Don't worry, man. Everything will be fine. Just leave the talking to me.'

Priyanthi studied the back of Niranjan's head and wondered if he knew he had a small patch of hair that stuck straight out without curling like the rest. She was not sad any more, but she was afraid. Her heart was beating unevenly and picking up speed with each passing mile. She prayed she would be calm by the time they reached Malwana. *What if the Grama Sevaka suspects something?*

'Did you bring the birth certificate?' Niranjan asked without turning around.

'Yes.'

'Good.'

Joe grinned to himself. True, they were eloping, but he still didn't think there was any reason for them to be quite so nervous. Joe was a Tamil too, and he admired Niranjan and Priyanthi for the step they were about to take. He knew how dangerous it was, but after all, they were going back to their own homes after the ceremony. That was the part he didn't understand. 'What's the point then?' he asked Niranjan the night before.

'If she's married, they can't make her marry someone else,' Niranjan replied.

'So why don't you just tell them?'

Niranjan sighed. 'It's not that easy, Joe,' he said. 'Her father has already had one heart attack. And her brother is a real thug. When the time is right, we'll tell them.'

'I think it will be far worse then, but have it your way,' Joe said.

Malwana, a predominantly Muslim town, was known for its abundance of rambutans, a sweet, lychee-like fruit which grew everywhere. As they neared their destination, the green of the trees gave way to a red haze of ripe fruit. Ordinarily, Priyanthi, who loved rambutans, would have wanted to stop and buy some from the road-side vendors who held out bunches of fruit to passing motorists. As it was, she didn't even notice them.

They stopped to ask a farmer for directions. 'Go straight until you come to the brick factory, then turn towards the paddy field and look out for the stream. The Grama Sevaka's place is about three houses after.'

Joe sighed, rolled his eyes and continued down the road.

Incredibly, the man's directions were right, and soon they

were pulling up in front of a small house with a rickety sign that said *Grama Sevaka* in neat Sinhalese script.

They went up the broken steps and knocked on the open door.

An old man in a dirty national costume, a white sarong and long white tunic, came to the door and peered at them.

'Yes?' His voice was high and quavering. He was at least seventy years old.

'Are you the Grama Sevaka?' Joe asked, taking charge.

'Yes?' He sounded irritable.

'We want to get married,' Joe said. Priyanthi stifled a hysterical giggle that welled up in her throat.

'Yes?'

'Yes,' Joe said, starting to get irritated. 'That's part of your job, isn't it? To marry people?'

'Do you have birth certificates?' the old man asked.

'Yes. Can we come in?'

He didn't answer, but led the way inside the house and into a room which obviously served as his office. From the cobwebs and dust, it was obvious that the Grama Sevaka didn't work very often.

'Witnesses?'

'Me,' Joe said.

'You? But you're getting married. You can't be a witness at your own wedding!'

Joe tried to remain patient. 'I am not getting married. These two are.'

'Oh. Who is the other witness?'

'We thought you could ask someone to be the other witness. We don't have many friends.'

'Oh no. Can't do that. You have to bring your own. We can't provide witnesses for every couple,' the man said irritably.

Joe smoothly pulled out a fifty-rupee note from his pocket. 'Oh well, then we'll have to find another Grama Sevaka who can,' he said regretfully. He fanned himself with the crisp new note.

The old man's eyes gleamed. 'Wait a minute! Maybe my wife

can do it. She's very busy and all, but we must help one another, mustn't we?'

Joe smiled. 'Oh definitely,' he said.

'The happy couple can sit here,' the Grama Sevaka said, indicating two chairs that barely stood.

Again, Priyanthi felt her laughter beginning to bubble to the surface and bit her lip hard to stop it. *If I start laughing now, I may never stop!* She sat gingerly at the edge of the chair, which creaked anyway.

Niranjan sat on the other chair and didn't look at Priyanthi. He surreptitiously wiped his hands on his pants. Like her, he had made an effort to dress up and was wearing his good beige pants and a white long-sleeved shirt.

'One moment, please. I will bring the wife,' the Grama Sevaka said.

As he passed Joe on his way out of the room, the fifty-rupee note changed hands.

The silence hovered in the room, crept upwards and hung on the cobwebs, burrowed under the dust.

'So smile at least! This is a wedding, not a funeral!' Joe said heartily, a little unnerved by their nervousness.

They didn't even look at him.

'For God's sake! The man will suspect something if you two keep on like this!' he said finally. 'Make an effort to look normal!'

Priyanthi recognised the truth in his words, sat up straight and tried to look a little less nervous.

Niranjan did the same.

The Grama Sevaka came back with his wife, a large lady who wore a reddha and a lace blouse which showed a tattered black brassiere underneath. She held a small posy of marigolds in her hand which she shyly offered to Priyanthi.

'Isn't it amazing what fifty rupees can do?' Joe murmured to Niranjan.

'Okay then, we'll start, shall we?' the Grama Sevaka said.

'We shall,' Joe said solemnly.

The entire ceremony took less than three minutes.

Throughout, Priyanthi heard nothing but the knocking of her heart against her ribs. Like a bird begging release. Joe had to nudge her when it was time for her to make her responses. She didn't hear Niranjan speak but he must have done because soon, the Grama Sevaka was pushing the register for them to sign. Her signature was a shaky scrawl. Niranjan's was stronger, she noted from far away.

The Grama Sevaka and his wife beamed and congratulated them. They accepted Joe's hugs. Then they looked at each other.

Please don't let this have been a mistake.

Please God, help me to look after her.

They paid the required fee, declined the Grama Sevaka's wife's invitation to stay for lunch, got back in the car and started the journey back to Colombo.

The marriage certificate sat snugly in Niranjan's pocket.

* * *

Priyanthi walked into the house and found her mother running to and fro. 'Oh there you are! Hurry up and change! They'll be here any minute!'

Priyanthi looked bemused. 'Didn't you say they were coming for dinner?'

'Yes. Now hurry up!'

'But it's only just past three.'

'Oh.' Enid stopped. 'I thought it was later.' Her eyes narrowed. 'Aren't you early? Did you miss a lecture?'

Priyanthi sighed. 'If I'm late, you get suspicious. If I'm early, you get suspicious. Maybe I should just give up university and stay at home.'

'No, no, that's not what I meant,' Enid said hastily. 'Don't be silly, child. I don't want you to stop your education.'

'No, you wouldn't, would you? My value on the marriage market would plummet!' Priyanthi retorted. *Although I am no longer on the marriage market!*

Enid looked hurt. 'Why do you say these things? Why are

you trying to start an argument? You know I have so much to do! Arjuna's parents are coming with him tonight.'

Priyanthi paused on her way into her room. 'Parents? Why didn't you tell me?'

'Because I just found out myself. He called and asked if it was okay.' Her eyes got misty. 'What a nice boy.'

Priyanthi shook her head in exasperation and continued to her room.

'Lie down and rest a little! You look tired,' her mother called out after her.

Priyanthi took off her white sari, folded it lovingly and placed it in her drawer. *My wedding sari. I'm going to keep it to show my children and grandchildren.*

She lay on her bed and tried to recall the details of the morning, but it was as if a cloud had come over her mind, temporarily obscuring the entire event. The posy of marigolds had been tossed by the wayside. She hadn't dared bring it home and Niranjan hadn't wanted to take it home either. Joe had offered to keep it for her but she had declined. It wasn't as if it was going to stay fresh for ever. Some cow must have eaten it by now, she thought.

Mrs Priyanthi Balasingham.
Mrs Niranjan Balasingham.

She smiled and drifted off to sleep.

Enid opened the door an hour later and smiled at the sight of her daughter fast asleep in her blouse and underskirt, a smile playing around her lips. For a moment, she was filled with remorse. Am I doing the right thing? she wondered. Will she be happy, this unhappy child of mine? Then she thought of Niranjan and the remorse fled.

She shook Priyanthi's shoulder gently. 'It's time to get up.'

Priyanthi stirred and, still asleep, murmured, 'Niranjan?'

Enid drew back in horror. Then she reached over and shook Priyanthi's shoulder again, harder than was necessary.

Priyanthi jumped up. 'Amma! What are you doing? You're

hurting me!' For a brief moment she wondered if somehow her mother had found out.

'Get up then and stop saying that – that person's name!' Enid said coldly. 'You have to wash and I need help with the table.'

Priyanthi sat there after she had left the room, tears welling up in her eyes. The door opened again and Enid marched in and dumped a parcel on the bed. 'Your father brought this for you,' she said, and marched out again.

Priyanthi sighed and opened the tissue paper. Inside was a beautiful pale green and gold sari and a matching blouse. Obviously someone had taken one of her blouses to the tailor for size. The tears spilled over now. She had just got married to the man she loved wearing an old cotton sari and they bought her this beautiful sari to attract a man she didn't love. It made no sense. No sense at all.

* * *

At exactly seven, Arjuna Perera's blue BMW pulled up outside. Enid fluttered to the door and smiled and waved. Stanley sat in his armchair and pretended not to notice his daughter's steady gaze. For the last fifteen minutes, she had been sitting opposite him, her eyes fixed on him. Pleading.

'Come, Stanley! They'll think you're rude,' Enid said from the doorway, still smiling.

Stanley stood up. 'What do I care what they think?' he muttered.

Priyanthi heard. She jumped up and rushed to him. 'Please, please don't make me do this! He's old and he's awful and I know you think so too. Please, Thaththi.'

She used to call him Thaththi when she was a little girl. His heart broke, but it was too late to go back now. He took refuge in impatience. 'Don't be silly. He's not awful. Just different from us. You'll get used to him.' He joined his wife at the door.

Arjuna came in first carrying two huge bouquets of flowers. He presented the orchids to Enid, who blushed and said, 'Oh, they're beautiful but you shouldn't have.'

Then he turned his heavy-lidded gaze to Priyanthi and laid

the sheaf of pink roses in her arms. 'Roses for a rose,' he said softly.

She burst out laughing. She couldn't help it. Even Enid's shocked 'Priyanthi!' couldn't make her stop. She laughed until she developed a hiccup and even then continued to chuckle. Suddenly everything seemed funny, not hopeless. Suddenly she realised that she didn't have to worry about marrying this man, that she could *never* marry this man because she was already married. Which made him just a man. Not a threat. Which turned her parents back into her parents, not the enemy determined to ruin her life. Which made his parents two old people who had come to dinner, not potential parents-in-law and therefore to be dreaded.

Nothing mattered any more, she realised exultantly.

She was married.

They couldn't touch her.

Arjuna Perera could never touch her.

'I'm so sorry,' Enid was saying to Arjuna in between shooting venomous looks at her daughter, who was inelegantly wiping her eyes with her sari pota. 'I don't know what's got into this child. She's not usually like this.'

No, not usually. Just on my wedding day!

Arjuna's eyes had chilled slightly as he viewed the woman he already thought of as his. This one would need some taming, he thought, and I'll take so much pleasure doing it! He smiled widely. 'Not to worry! It's wonderful to see her laughing and I'm going to assume it's because she's very happy.'

His parents were nice people, very gracious and obviously delighted that their son had finally found someone he wanted to marry. They were nice to Priyanthi and she felt slightly guilty. But it wasn't her fault, she told herself firmly. It wasn't her fault that no one wanted to listen to her.

After dinner, Arjuna invited her to walk in the garden.

She politely declined.

Again his eyes narrowed.

His lips curled slightly. A slightly cruel curl.

She saw it and shivered.

He saw her shiver and he smiled.

It was important that they understood one another.

There was a tense moment just before they left, when Arjuna's mother opened her small jewelled handbag and pulled out a moth-eaten velvet box. 'For our new daughter,' she smiled, holding it out to Priyanthi.

She recoiled. 'No. Oh no, I couldn't possibly.'

The old lady looked confused, a little disappointed. 'But why not, child? After all, when you marry Arjuna, everything I have will be yours anyway. It's only a small diamond sari pin. Take it,' she said persuasively.

Priyanthi shook her head. 'No. It's not right. Not yet.' She saw her mother looking furious and added, 'Maybe after the wedding. Not now.'

Stanley came to her rescue. 'Don't be offended,' he said to Arjuna's mother. 'We have taught her never to accept gifts unless it's proper, and after all, they're not even engaged yet.'

The old lady smiled back. 'Oh, in that case, why not set a date for the engagement? No sense in waiting. I know my son is sure.'

Oh God! Priyanthi thought. This is going from bad to worse. She smiled with an effort. 'I have to finish university first.'

'Well, you can get married and still go to university,' Arjuna said gently. He reached out and took her hand. She tried to pull it away but he held it tightly. 'I think my mother is right. Let's set a date now.'

Again Stanley stepped in. 'Well, there's no real hurry, Arjuna,' he said firmly. 'Priyanthi is quite right. Better that she finishes university first. It's only two more years. I am sure you won't mind waiting. It's not like she's going to run away or something.'

Arjuna gave in gracefully. 'Let's see,' he said, smiling blandly. 'We can discuss it later.'

They took their leave, insisting that the Silvas come to Kandy to visit them soon. 'Come for the weekend. We have a big house,' Mrs Perera said.

Enid beamed.

After they left, Priyanthi went out into the garden. 'I need some fresh air,' she said by way of explanation. Enid's lips pursed but she didn't say anything.

She stood at the gate and breathed in the fragrant night air as if that would dispel the deception.

'Priyanthi.'

She started in fright and looked up to see Dierdre standing there looking worriedly at her. 'Oh, hi, Auntie Dierdre.'

'Are you okay, child?' Dierdre asked, peering in the darkness.

'Oh, much better now the Pereras have gone back to their big house,' she replied.

'Yes, I heard about all that. Is he nice?'

Priyanthi grimaced. 'What's nice? He's rich and apparently that's what counts.'

There was a pause as Dierdre absorbed both her words and her tone. 'But my dear, if that's how you feel about it, tell your mother. I'm sure she can find someone else for you.'

'But I have someone else, Auntie Dierdre! Can no one understand that? I have someone else and I found him all by myself!' She stopped, horrified by what she had said. How she had said it. 'Oh God, I'm so sorry. Please don't tell my mother I said that, Auntie Dierdre! Please, she'll kill me!'

Dierdre reached out and took Priyanthi's hand, wondering when she had become so thin, wondering what had happened to the happy child she had once been. 'I won't tell, child. I promise. Now what's this about having someone? Is it the same someone I think it is?'

Priyanthi's eyes were wide with fear, white in the dark. 'Who?'

Dierdre laughed without humour. 'Child, I know they all say I am a gossip, but I am just observant. I see things that other people miss.' She lowered her voice. 'I have known about you and Niranjan for a while now. I am just surprised that no one else knows.'

Priyanthi relaxed a little. She knew from Dierdre's voice that she wouldn't say anything. 'They know,' she said.

'What? How did they – did you tell them?'

Priyanthi laughed again. 'I wanted to, oh how I wanted to. But I was too afraid. No, my mother put two and two together and figured it out.'

'What happened?'

'Arjuna Perera happened,' Priyanthi said bleakly.

Dierdre looked compassionately at her. 'Does that mean you'll go along with this? Give him up?'

Priyanthi shook her head slowly. 'No, I won't. In fact, I can't.'

Dierdre stared at her. 'What do you mean?' Then, slowly, it dawned on her and her grip on Priyanthi's hand tightened. 'Does anyone else know?'

'No.'

Dierdre let go of Priyanthi's hand. 'Oh my goodness. Oh my goodness. This is a fine state of things.'

'Auntie Dierdre, please don't tell anyone.'

Dierdre shrugged. 'Tell anyone what? I have no idea what you're talking about, child,' she said. 'Now go inside and get some sleep. You look exhausted.' She lowered her voice again. 'I might be an old good-for-nothing woman, but if you need someone to talk to, remember your Auntie Dierdre.'

The tears, always so close, started up again. 'Thank you,' she choked.

The sliver of light shining through the slightly opened door widened as it was pushed open further. 'Priyanthi! Priyanthi! What are you doing out there in the dark?'

'I have to go,' Priyanthi said. 'My mother doesn't like being kept waiting these days.' She went inside.

'What do you have to say about your behaviour?' Enid demanded as soon as she walked in.

'Amma, let it be,' she said wearily.

'Let it be! Let it be!' Enid's voice rose. 'You behave like some – some uneducated idiot, laughing stupidly, then offending those people by refusing their gifts, and you want me to let it be! You'd better pray that you haven't driven this one away like you did Romesh Samaraweera!'

Priyanthi glared at her. 'No, Amma, *you* better pray, because I don't want this – you do.'

She went to her room.

'Well!' Enid huffed, looking to Stanley for support. 'Did you see that? Did you hear her? Why didn't you say something?'

Stanley stared at her. 'As a matter of fact, I didn't think it was right for them to be giving her jewellery. It was like a down-payment or something!'

Enid stared at him, outraged. 'A down-payment! My God, you're talking like her! Next you'll be telling me to let her marry that Tamil from next door!'

Stanley glared at her. 'You know, the more I see of that oily Arjuna, the more appealing the idea becomes!' He turned and stomped off to bed.

Enid was too angry to sleep. Too angry to stay indoors and listen to them sleep. She changed her silver slippers for the Bata ones she wore around the house and went outside to the garden.

As always, the fragrance of her orchids and roses calmed her. She walked around straightening pots and twitching branches.

'Enid? Enid?'

It was Violet's voice. She tensed and pressed back into the shadows near the wall.

'Enid? I know you're there. Come and talk to me.' Violet sounded tentative, hopeful, slightly hurt.

Enid stepped out. 'Hello, Violet,' she said, trying to make her voice normal. It came out sounding cold and formal.

Apparently Violet heard it too. 'Enid, what is the matter? These last few weeks I've hardly seen you. You never come to the wall to chat, and the few times I have seen you, you seem to be – I don't know – avoiding me?'

Enid was glad the dark prevented Violet from seeing her expression. She felt angry, guilty, ashamed. 'What nonsense,' she said. 'I have been busy, that's all. You know, with Priyanthi's marriage plans and everything.' This last on a vaguely triumphant note.

'Priyanthi getting married?' Violet sounded shocked. 'To whom? You never said anything!'

Now Enid went closer to the wall. 'To a wealthy young man from Kandy. Friends of my mother. It's all arranged. Just have to set a date now,' she said complacently.

'But you said you were going to wait until she was at least twenty-one,' Violet said, still sounding shocked.

'Yes, well something came up, and anyway, what's the use of waiting? It doesn't do good to delay these things. He might change his mind. Men, you know – impatient.'

'So what if he changes his mind?' Violet sounded slightly angry. 'Priyanthi is such a beautiful girl. You can find any number of handsome, educated men to marry her.'

Enid's mouth twisted. Although she would have liked to believe that Niranjan's entire family had known what was going on, it was obvious Violet was completely in the dark. I'm not going to give her the satisfaction of knowing, she thought. 'I know. But he is the best one and we have already decided.'

'And Priyanthi? What does she think?'

Enid laughed gaily. 'Oh, she's already half in love with him. Brought her roses and all tonight.'

Violet relaxed a little. 'That's good then. Will we be invited for the wedding?'

Enid stared at her. 'Why do you even ask?'

Violet stared back. 'You have been a little odd lately, Enid. Very distant. I thought maybe you didn't want to be friends any more.'

'Oh Violet, stop behaving like a schoolgirl!' Enid snapped. 'We're both adults and sometimes things come up that take precedence over other things. That's all.'

'If you say so,' Violet said quietly. 'Well, I'd better go before Bala sends a search party out for me. I'll see you tomorrow.'

Enid stayed outside for a while, struggling with her guilt. She *had* been distant, she *had* avoided Violet, but what else was she to do? Every time she saw Violet, it all came back. The deception, the gall, the impudence. Part of her longed to tell

Violet, to at least have someone to share the shock and the horror of it with, because she knew that although Violet's reaction probably wouldn't be as strong as hers had been, she would still be shocked and remorseful.

But another part of her remained stubbornly silent.

She went in to bed. Stanley was reading and he didn't even look up when she came in.

TWENTY-THREE

Priyanthi sat under the araliya tree and tried to concentrate on the book she was reading, but the story of a young girl forced into a marriage she didn't want was too similar to what was happening to her, and every so often she had to pause to reflect, to compare, to wish futilely that things were different.

It was peaceful in the garden. A light breeze rustled through the leaves and occasionally a magpie hopped over to stare and squawk at the still figure.

'Priyanthi? Priyanthi? Where's that child?' Enid sounded irritated, which wasn't surprising, since that was all she sounded like these days.

'I'm here,' Priyanthi called back. 'Reading in the garden.'

Enid popped her head through the door, scanned the garden with suspicious eyes and relaxed when she saw Priyanthi. 'Don't stay out for too long. You'll get sunburned.' She went inside, but left the front door open.

Priyanthi grimaced. The effort of this constant watchfulness was making her mother even more unbearable. These days she snapped at the slightest provocation and was always banging things. Doors, pots, dishes.

It hadn't escaped anyone's notice that Stanley had been spending more and more time out of the house. He had taken up golf again and spent most of his weekends at the golf club chatting with his cronies and drinking draught beer. During the week, he went to work, came home late and usually read until bedtime. The after-dinner walks that he and Enid used to take were a thing of the past. They hardly spoke any more, except when it was absolutely necessary.

Priyanthi sometimes wondered if her father had found someone else. If he had, she wouldn't blame him; he was a good man and deserved more than the shrew his wife had turned herself into. But somehow, she doubted it. He was far too honourable.

Even Hemantha stayed out of his mother's way and his constant taunts had tapered off into the occasional rude comment or aside.

As for Priyanthi, she hardly ever spoke to Enid. She felt that every innocent comment was misconstrued, every word carried a spark which could set alight the fuse of the time bomb her mother had become. These days, she was required to inform her parents of all her whereabouts and provide phone numbers if she went out to visit a friend. Eventually, she stopped going; it was far too embarrassing, at her age, to have a mother calling up every half-hour to check up on her. Now, she went to the university and back home. She resented her restricted life and resented her mother for being the one to have created it.

Enid had effectively alienated her entire family.

* * *

The past six months had been difficult for everybody.

Violet watched with bewilderment as her best friend became a remote stranger right before her eyes. When she talked to Bala about it and asked him if he thought she had done something to upset Enid, he told her not to worry.

'Everyone has their problems,' he said glumly. 'Even us.'

She became quiet. They did have problems. Although she still rejected the idea of them leaving Sri Lanka, there was no doubt that the situation was becoming tense.

There was still fighting up in the north, and lives were being lost on both sides. It was true that in comparison to some of the wars being fought in other parts of the world, Sri Lanka's civil conflict was small. But then, Sri Lanka was a small country. The armed raids on police stations and checkpoints usually meant a few people on either side getting killed and weapons stolen. Some of them made the newspapers. Some didn't. Although other countries were by now watching carefully to see where it would all lead, the few attacks hardly even made the foreign presses.

Soon, that would all change.

Soon, people would become afraid to board buses to go to work. Army checkpoints would increase. Anonymous tip-offs would bring businesses to a standstill and the army would charge in and employees would charge out, treading on each other and leaving handbags and shoes behind. Soon, bombs would be as commonplace as beggars on the street and unattended bags would be blown up by the newly formed Bomb Disposal Squad. Children would be told not to pick up matchboxes for fear they might be cunningly concealed explosives.

But all this was not yet. Soon, but not yet.

Violet was worried.

Bala's dissatisfaction with what he saw to be the deterioration of normal life increased daily. He desperately wanted to emigrate but Violet always became teary-eyed when the subject was brought up. In her simple, unworldly way, she was convinced it was just a phase the country was going through that it would emerge from soon, tired but triumphant. Bala admired her optimism, even envied her for it, but he was too much of a realist to accept her idealism.

They received letters from their relatives abroad, begging them to pack up and come. Violet, who didn't go to work and was therefore at home when the postman came, usually destroyed the letters before Bala arrived. Then, when he was at work, she would reply, politely declining the invitations, insisting that everything was fine.

Deep inside she worried about everything.

Niranjan had been promoted to accountant and his salary was increased by one thousand rupees, but other than Joe, he had no friends. No girlfriends. He went to work, went to Joe's house occasionally, but that was all. Violet worried about him.

It wasn't healthy. He was a handsome boy with a good job and a nice personality. He was a little shy, but that was considered a good trait in these days of brashness and big mouths. Once, she had casually asked him about Kamini and got a blank stare in return.

'You know, Kamini, that pretty girl Hemantha went and harassed,' she persisted.

'I'm not interested in Kamini,' he said firmly.

Then who *are* you interested in? she wanted to ask, but she didn't dare. Her maternal instincts told her there *was* a girl, but why didn't he talk about her unless she was unsuitable in some way? What if she was a Muslim girl? Or a Buddhist?

At least Nirmala was still the same. Happy, loud and constantly getting into trouble at school. It was only her extremely high scores that kept them from asking Violet to find her another school. The tension which had the rest of the family in its grip seemed happily to have bypassed her. If she noticed their preoccupation and worry, she gave no sign.

Violet was worried about Enid, who never came to the wall these days. She asked Dierdre if she knew what the matter was and Dierdre looked strangely at her. Almost pityingly. 'I don't know, child. Must be the change.' Violet felt a rare spurt of anger at her friends. It was almost as if there was a secret everyone knew but her.

Stanley still popped over for a quick chat, usually on his way home from work, but it had been a while since the two couples had had one of their get-togethers.

Violet moped and lost weight and Dierdre looked envious.

* * *

'Ed,' Dierdre said, 'why don't we invite Bala, Violet, Enid and Stanley over for dinner tomorrow?'

Ed grunted.

'Ed!' Dierdre said loudly. 'I'm talking to you.'

Ed reluctantly laid down his book. 'What?'

'Let's invite the neighbours for dinner tomorrow.'

'Why?'

'Oh, I don't know,' Dierdre said vaguely. 'It's been a while since we've all been together. It might be a nice change for everyone.'

'Nice change?' Ed said doubtfully. 'They haven't been very close these past months.'

'But that's exactly why!' Dierdre said. 'I think it's time to put a stop to this nonsense. High time.'

Ed looked blank. 'What nonsense?'

She threw him an exasperated look and marched out of the room.

Ed sighed and picked up his book again.

'Enid! Enid!' Dierdre rattled the gate loudly.

Enid peeped through the open window. 'Dierdre! You gave me a fright! What's the matter?'

'You're coming for dinner tomorrow!' Dierdre said.

'We are? Hold on, let me come to the gate.'

'No, that's okay. Just show up at eight,' Dierdre said, and sailed off like a battleship in pink polyester.

Enid dropped the curtains, feeling her spirits soar tentatively. It had been a long time. She made a mental note to tell Stanley to come home early. At the thought of him, her mouth drooped and the brief excitement slid out of her eyes.

'Violet! Violet! Is anyone home?' Dierdre called.

Violet appeared at the door, drying her hands on her skirt. 'Dierdre! What's the matter? Is there a problem?'

Dierdre grinned. 'Only if you don't come for dinner tomorrow night.'

'Dinner? Is it a special occasion?'

'Does it have to be? No special occasion. Just friends. Be sure to tell Bala.'

The next evening, as Enid and Stanley latched their gate shut, they saw Bala and Violet coming out.

'Oh, hello!' Stanley said jovially. 'Going somewhere?'

'Only to Dierdre's.' Violet beamed, happy to see Stanley in such good spirits.

Stanley's smile slipped a bit. 'Now there's a coincidence! So are we!'

They walked the few yards to Dierdre's.

'So how's everything?' Violet asked Enid.

'Fine. Fine,' Enid said.

'How's Priyanthi's young man?'

'Oh, very well,' Enid said effusively. 'He comes to Colombo at least once a month to see her. I think we'll have the engagement by August this year.'

Violet smiled. 'That's wonderful. When will the wedding be?'

'Maybe about six months after,' Enid said vaguely, not wanting to be reminded of the quarrels she and Priyanthi had every time the subject of a wedding date was brought up.

Behind them, Bala and Stanley lit up cigarettes. 'Long time no see, Stan,' Bala said.

Stanley sighed. 'I know. Been a bit busy.'

Bala slipped an affectionate arm around his friend's shoulders. 'Mustn't let work come in the way of friendships.'

Stanley sighed. 'Yes, I know. Things keep coming up.'

Bala looked at him. 'Is everything all right, old friend?'

Stanley looked miserable. 'Yes, well, sort of.'

'If you need a sympathetic ear, remember you have one next door,' Bala said.

At Dierdre's, the men drifted off to a corner with a bottle of whisky and the women sat down to chat. Although conversation was slightly stilted, it was still like old times, and Dierdre felt a glow of accomplishment. Now if they could just come to their senses and let those two lovely young people be together, she thought.

When she went off into the kitchen to check the dinner, Violet and Enid giggled and whispered about her atrocious cooking. When she came back and demanded to know what they were laughing about, they both looked innocently at her and said, 'Oh, just.'

Violet felt better than she had in a long time. Enid was still a little distant, but tonight was a vast improvement on the way things had been. She decided to invite them for a thosa dinner the next day. Dierdre too.

* * *

At home, Priyanthi was whispering into the telephone. Niranjan could hardly hear her, but it was better to hear her indistinct whispers than not to hear her at all.

They hardly ever met these days. About once a month, Priyanthi missed a lecture and hurried off to some remote spot to meet him for a few minutes. They hugged and kissed and wept and swore undying love for each other and then went to their respective homes feeling even more miserable than before.

The fact that they were legally man and wife provided cold comfort.

'What did you say?' Niranjan asked.

'I said I can get away for a few minutes on Thursday,' Priyanthi whispered.

'I'll come and meet you outside the campus.'

'No, don't!' she said urgently. 'I'll meet you near Flower Road. Someone might be watching.'

'Can you call me tomorrow?'

'You know I can't. They check the phone bills. They'll see the number and there will be another row.'

Previously, with their parents so friendly, Bala's phone number appeared constantly on Stanley's bill. But these days, they hardly spoke. Priyanthi couldn't remember the last time she had seen her mother talking to Violet. She thought back to the days when she would laughingly call out to her mother to 'Stop gossiping with Auntie Violet and come home.' She felt a pang of guilt that she and Niranjan had been responsible for the widening rift between the two families who had been so close before.

She heard the gate open, quickly whispered goodbye and flew into her room and into bed. Enid peeped in and tiptoed out.

Priyanthi opened her eyes and stared up at the ceiling. When

314

she was a little girl, she had loved to gaze at the sky and find shapes in the clouds. As a surprise, Stanley had painted the ceiling in her room blue and put in white scuddy clouds all over it. She had squealed with joy and flung her arms around her father, declaring him to be the best father in the world. Enid had pouted and said, 'What about me?' and she had run over to her mother and hugged her.

Two tears trickled out of her wide-open eyes and slid down into her hairline.

Arjuna was coming tomorrow. She shuddered at the thought. He was becoming more and more possessive, even touching her when no one was looking, daring her to say something. He knew she was being forced into this marriage and, rather than making him feel uncomfortable, it made him feel powerful.

He had avoided marriage so far, preferring to play the field. He currently had a burgher mistress installed in a small house in Peradeniya. He visited her whenever he felt like it and the arrangement suited him well.

When Priyanthi's grandmother had broached the subject of marriage, his initial reaction had been one of boredom, but when he saw a photograph of the young girl with the sensual mouth, he became interested. Now she was a challenge and he vowed to tame her.

Priyanthi closed her eyes but she couldn't sleep.

A car cruised by.

It stopped at the gate.

Priyanthi sat up, twitched back her bedroom curtain an inch or so and looked out. She saw Hemantha staggering out, shouting a raucous good night to whoever was in the car, and she winced. Another row. As if there weren't enough of them already.

She waited for him to enter the house and go into his room, but all she heard was fumbling and cursing. She sprang out of bed and ran to open the front door before he woke everyone up. As she got to it, her father emerged from their room looking furious.

'It's okay,' she whispered. 'Go back to bed.'

He shook his head and came to the door.

Hemantha almost fell into the house. His shirt was filthy and torn and he had lost a shoe. He stank of alcohol. 'Ah! Hello, sister! Married your rich man yet?' he slurred.

'Go to bed,' she said firmly, shutting the door behind him.

'No. Don't want to go to bed. I want to talk to my sister. Is that a crime?' he demanded belligerently.

'We'll talk in the morning,' she murmured, looking fearfully at her father. He had been warned by his doctor to avoid any kind of stress. 'Now go to bed.'

'This family doesn't want me,' Hemantha shouted drunkenly. 'No one gives a damn about me!'

She finally lost her temper. 'Can you blame anyone? Look at your state! You look like one of those junction hooligans you love so much. You should be ashamed of yourself.'

Hemantha's face twisted into a scowl of rage. He moved surprisingly fast so she didn't have time to avoid his fist. She fell back against the wall with a cry of pain just as her father leapt forward and dragged Hemantha away.

'Thaththi!' she screamed. 'Be careful!'

Enid came running, still rubbing the sleep out of her eyes. 'What's going on here?' She took in the scene in a second – Priyanthi's already swelling face, Stanley's rage and Hemantha's drunkenness. 'Hemantha! Come with me.' Her voice was quiet but compelling. 'Come to bed, now. You need to sleep.' Hemantha, made suddenly afraid by his father's anger and by what he had done, went meekly with Enid.

Stanley led Priyanthi into the kitchen, where he put some ice cubes into a towel and held it gently against her cheek. She still sobbed quietly, unable to take in what had just happened.

Stanley looked down at his daughter's lowered head, at the vulnerable curve of her nape, and the grimness in his eyes increased. Something would have to be done. Something drastic and permanent. 'Don't worry, darling,' he told her softly. 'Don't worry. Your father will put an end to all this insanity. I promise.'

She didn't lift her head. 'What insanity?'

'Everything,' he said. 'Everything.'

A shaft of hope pushed through her pain. 'Everything?'

He nodded decisively. 'Go to bed now. If your cheek is bad, we'll go to the doctor in the morning. Although God only knows what he'll say.'

Priyanthi kissed her father gently on his cheek. 'You go to bed too, Thaththi.'

He looked tired. 'I will.'

Enid was still trying to get Hemantha to sleep. Stanley poured himself a large arrack and went outside. He sat on the small bench outside the kitchen door and took great gulps of the scented, slightly moist night air. The events of the last few years drifted in and out of his troubled mind and his mouth twisted with self-recrimination.

How could I have let this happen? he wondered. How could I have let my family fall apart like this? Why didn't I see it happening? Why didn't I do something? Where was I?

The answer hurt tremendously. I was right here.

He thought of the ugly bruise already beginning to appear on Priyanthi's jaw and he set his glass down and buried his head in his hands. What was I thinking about when I agreed to let her marry Arjuna? How could I have been so selfish? For months now, I have been watching my daughter turn into a pale, silent stranger before my eyes and I have done nothing to help her. I have watched my son lose his way and done nothing to guide him. I have sat here and left it to Enid, who has acted with efficiency, but not necessarily with love. And Enid herself – the love and the laughter left her eyes and I didn't even think to ask why.

He ran his hand across his moist eyes and went inside. The house was quiet once more and Enid was sitting up in bed, chewing on her fingernail. She looked at him apprehensively.

He smiled. 'Is he finally asleep?'

She nodded, her eyes widening slightly. She had not expected this gentleness.

'That's good,' he said. 'Now you get some sleep too. Tomorrow, we will talk and sort everything out.'

She sat up higher. 'What? Talk about what?'

He got into bed and laid a hand on her forehead. 'Everything,' he said, and closed his eyes.

Far from reassuring her and making her feel hopeful, his words filled her with dread. He was such an idealist, her husband. Only thinking about the children's immediate happiness, not about their long-term welfare like she did.

If Priyanthi didn't marry Arjuna, she would remain an old maid. Enid shuddered. What a shame! People would look pityingly at her. People would whisper about why no man had wanted her. Then someone, somewhere would say, 'Isn't she the one who was carrying on with that Tamil?' And their looks would become tinged with malice. Tinted with scorn. Pity would turn into disgust. People would avoid speaking to them, cross the street when they saw them.

Enid shut her eyes and prayed to the devas to save her daughter from this fate, which to her, was one far worse than death.

At least there was dignity in death.

TWENTY-FOUR

❧

The repercussions of that night were traumatic for Enid.

Hemantha was informed by his father that he had one month to reform his ways, after which, if there was no change for the better, he would no longer be considered part of the family. He would have to leave and find a place to stay and make his own way in life.

Enid listened with ill-concealed rage. His own way in life! He was their son! He was *their* life. But she said nothing. Stanley had been adamant about all of this, and this new determination was something she was still trying to get used to.

He had even taken a day off work to speak to her and the children.

Hemantha listened and looked suitably repentant, although inside he seethed with impotent rage. He couldn't defy his father because he had nowhere to go, no money, no real qualifications to get a job. His hands were tied. But not for long! he vowed to himself. One day I'll leave and to hell with all of them.

Stanley was encouraged by Hemantha's apparent docility, and although he knew it came from a lack of options and not from any real repentance, it was still a start.

Priyanthi was a different story.

Earlier, and in private, Stanley held Enid's hands and gently told her he could not and would not allow their daughter to marry Arjuna Perera. Enid's worst fears had been confirmed. She dashed away the tears that welled up in her eyes and demanded to know why not.

'She doesn't love him,' Stanley told her. 'In fact, she doesn't even like him. Anyone can see that. That's no basis for a marriage, Enid.'

'She'll grow to love him,' Enid said desperately. 'It happens all the time. She's just doing this to make us change our minds.'

'In that case, she must be really afraid. Doesn't that give you cause for concern?'

Enid sat up. 'I'll tell you what gives me cause for concern. That our daughter will spend the rest of her life alone. An old maid.' She spat the last two words out and they fell like stones into a still pool.

'Just because she doesn't marry Arjuna, it doesn't mean she's going to be an old maid,' Stanley said reasonably.

Enid's face contorted with scorn. 'Who else will want her?'

Stanley tried to hold on to his temper. 'Someone will. And she will want them. She has to at least *like* the man she marries! She obviously hates Arjuna and he doesn't seem at all upset by it, which is unnatural. It makes me think he's a little – twisted.'

Enid laughed shrilly. 'Listen to you – twisted! Stanley, I'm warning you – if you break up this match, you'll be sentencing your daughter to a life of ridicule.'

'Don't talk bloody nonsense!' Stanley bellowed. 'My God, have you so little love for her? Have you forgotten what love is? Don't you remember how happy we used to be? Don't you want the same for your child?'

Only one sentence penetrated Enid's fury. *How happy we used to be.* Past tense. Her anger left her in an exhausting gust and she slumped into her chair. 'Do whatever you want.'

He stood up. 'I'm doing what's right,' he said, his voice gentle once more. He felt pity for his wife. Somewhere between marriage and motherhood, she had lost an important quality. Compassion.

He phoned Arjuna at his office. 'Arjuna,' he said formally, 'I am very sorry, but something has come up and we have been forced to make some decisions about our daughter.'

The formality registered immediately and Arjuna became wary. 'Really, Uncle? I hope there is no problem.'

'Actually there is. We have decided to wait for a while before arranging anything for Priyanthi.'

Arjuna laughed lightly. 'Well, that's fine with me. I am willing to wait, although I had hoped we could get married this year.'

Stanley paused. Obviously diplomacy wasn't working or Arjuna was deliberately being obtuse. 'You don't understand, Arjuna. We have decided that this is not a good match for Priyanthi.'

There was a long silence. When Arjuna finally spoke, his voice was distant. 'Could I speak with Auntie Enid, please?' he said coldly.

Stanley stared at the phone, unable to believe what he was hearing. 'Why would you want to do that?'

There was a light laugh. 'Because I don't think she'll agree to this.'

'I am the head of this family, and I make the decisions for my children. There will be no marriage and that's that.' Stanley banged down the receiver and turned to see his wife standing there, her eyes spitting fury.

'I am the head of this family,' she mimicked scornfully. 'Did you have to be so rude? He is a close friend of my mother!'

'Yes, well perhaps your mother should choose her friends more carefully,' he said. 'That man is a cocky son of a bitch and the only way he'll be marrying my daughter is over my dead body!'

Priyanthi, who had been listening at her bedroom door, flew back into bed and lay there, her heart thumping. She couldn't believe what had just transpired; it was like a last-minute reprieve from a death sentence!

She was not so naive to believe that everything would be miraculously okay now. That they would immediately accept Niranjan. But at least she didn't have to put up with Arjuna's suggestive looks and sneaky hands.

She wished she could call Niranjan and tell him what had happened; he had been so worried, so angry at her parents for forcing her into an alliance with Arjuna Perera. And even though she reminded him that they couldn't marry her off to anyone because she was already married, it didn't make him feel any better about it. 'I feel like a eunuch!' he had said angrily.

She had held his hands and implored him to be patient. Her love flowed through to him like a strong, steady river which could not be dammed or diverted, and after a while he had relaxed, leaning his head against her shoulder. She smiled now and turned her face into the pillow, wincing as her cheek began to throb. It was angry and red and her father had declared that it was a miracle that her jaw had not been broken. She had overheard the conversation he had with Hemantha and sighed. Hemantha was not going to change. It was too late for tears or threats. She grimaced, wondering what Hemantha would do when he finally found out about Niranjan and her. But even that thought couldn't depress her for long.

Things were looking better than they had done for a long time.

It was as if the sun had finally started to shine after a long spell of rain.

Just before she fell asleep, she reminded herself to write to the toddy tapper and let him know the good news. She wrote regularly and he never replied because he didn't know how to write, but she knew he was thinking about them, wishing them well.

* * *

Bala sipped his tea and opened the newspaper. The headlines were the same almost daily: *Army foils rebel plan to capture police station.*

Bala laughed. 'Violet! Come and see this. They're getting more and more creative every day!'

Violet came, although not too enthusiastically. The way he referred to the army as 'they' always worried her. As if they were on a different side. She didn't approve of the separatist rebels and their cause. 'There's room for all of us, without all this hatred and killing,' she would say, and Bala would sigh and shake his head in disbelief. 'You're so sweet,' he would reply fondly, and she would feel mild irritation at his tone. What was 'sweet' about not wanting to fight?

She peered over his shoulder and read the news item he was pointing to. 'What's so creative about that?' she asked.

'Lies! All lies!' Bala said. 'I listened to BBC radio last night and they said that not only did they capture the police station, they killed three cops as well. You can't even believe the newspapers any more!'

Violet sat down. 'Bala, why are you getting so passionate about them? It's not wise, you know. Just let's go about our business and let them be.'

He stared at her. 'Them? They are *our* people, Violet.'

She stared back at him, an unusual hardness in her eyes. 'They are *not* our people. They are thugs who are killing people when there's no need to.'

He threw down the newspaper in anger and stood up. 'I'm going to work. Where's Nirmala? Is she ready?'

Nirmala skipped out after her father, her school bag dragging behind her. Violet didn't make the usual attempts to mollify Bala. For once, her patience had run out.

Bala dropped Nirmala at school and drove through the crowded Colombo streets, his anger temporarily put on hold while he navigated the rush-hour traffic. He weaved in and out of the lines of cars and swore at some of them, like everybody did. At a pedestrian crossing, he waited for a bevy of giggling schoolgirls to cross the road and thought momentarily of Nirmala. A grin replaced the frown on his face. Last week, her teacher complained that she was speaking French instead of Tamil. When Bala questioned her, she burst out laughing and said she was only speaking 'P' language, a language invented and spoken by children when they didn't want to be understood by adults. Almost every English-speaking child in Colombo knew it. Nirmala spent a hilarious five minutes telling her father about how confused the teacher had become, and although Bala tried to reprimand her, he couldn't help laughing.

Violet looked bemused. 'What is "P" language?'

Nirmala grinned. 'I can't teach you because then you'll know what I'm saying.'

Her mother shook her head in despair and lamented that she had two sons. 'Although even Niranjan wasn't this naughty when he was your age!'

Nirmala stuck her tongue out at her brother. 'That's because he was trying to be a priest! They've got to be holy, you know!'

Niranjan smiled absent-mindedly, ruffled Nirmala's hair and went to his room.

Bala frowned. Niranjan had become quite distant lately. He wasn't rude – just removed. Bala tried to talk to him, to find out if there was a problem at his office or even one involving a young lady. After all, Bala had been young once. But all his efforts were met by a blank wall and mutters that everything was fine. Bala respected the boy's privacy but he was troubled. He wanted to ask Stanley's advice, but he didn't like to bother his friend.

The car in front of him stopped suddenly and Bala jammed his foot on the brake, swearing fluently. The car behind him stopped too, the driver leaning viciously on his horn. A sweaty man pulling a cart alongside them thought the man was honking at him and let out a stream of bad language that Bala had to smile at.

He finally parked his car outside the school and went into the staff room. He greeted everyone pleasantly and noted with cynicism that only some replied. There were a few Sinhalese teachers known for their hard-line stance on the rebels and they were suspicious of anyone Tamil. They were not unfriendly, just guarded. As if I send daily communiqués to the rebel lines, Bala thought wryly, and went into his class.

That evening when he was driving home, the traffic was stopped as a line of ambulances drove into town from the Ratmalana military airport. Their sirens were silent, but that didn't necessarily mean they were bringing in fatalities. Sirens drew attention to the army casualties and the government probably didn't like that.

Bala counted twelve ambulances in all.

* * *

Priyanthi managed to meet Niranjan that Wednesday.

She had already told her mother she had a late lecture and slipped out before her class was over.

'What happened to your face?' he asked, shocked at the livid bruise.

Her smile dimmed when she remembered that night. 'A combination of alcohol and Hemantha.'

His face darkened and she sighed. 'It's all over now, so stop looking like that.'

'I can't help it,' he said apologetically. 'I can't stand the thought of anyone hurting you.'

'I can't stay long,' she said, turning away from a bus that passed by.

'How come you always say that? How about "Hello, husband, long time no see"?'

She laughed. 'You know, I find that so hard to believe. That you're really my husband.'

He laughed too. 'Want the evidence?' He pulled out their marriage certificate from his folder with a flourish.

She stared at it. 'Niranjan! What are you doing carrying that around with you?'

He smiled a little shyly. 'I keep it with me sometimes. When I get lonely or when I feel sad, I pull it out and look at it.'

Her eyes filled with tears. 'That's so sweet,' she said, touching his cheek. 'Can I keep it for a while?'

He gave it to her solemnly. 'Look after it. That's our warranty for the future.'

She folded it carefully and slipped it into a book. Then she brightened. 'You won't believe what happened! I don't have to marry Arjuna any more!'

Niranjan scowled. 'You can't marry Arjuna. You're married to me!'

She clucked impatiently. 'Let me continue. After the row with Hemantha the other night, my father got all strange and sat outside for ages by himself, and the next morning he spoke to Amma and told her that he couldn't allow me to marry Arjuna!'

'Why not? They were so thrilled about the whole thing.'

She frowned. 'You know, I don't think my father was ever happy about it. I think he went along with it because of Amma. Anyway, thank God he changed his mind. He called up Arjuna and told him.' She mimicked her father's voice. 'There will be no marriage and that's that!'

Niranjan burst out laughing. 'I would have loved to see his face!'

Another bus stopped and Priyanthi pressed herself against the concrete wall of the bus stop. 'I'd better go. Someone might see us.'

He reached out and took her hand. 'Please stay! Just for a few minutes more.'

She snatched her hand back. 'Are you crazy? Don't do that! What if someone we know is on that bus?'

He looked hurt. 'Don't be so paranoid! You treat me as if I were a leper or something.'

She was too upset to care. 'Niranjan, it's far too dangerous. If they know we're still meeting, they'll stop me coming to university. Then there'll be no way for us to meet.'

He knew she was right, but something about the whole situation made him reckless. 'I don't care. I want to tell them. Now. Today.'

She stared at him aghast. 'No! Please, let's wait until next week. Give it some time. Give *me* some time.' Her voice broke. 'I don't think I can take any more right now.'

He finally agreed to wait until next week and they parted.

She thought about his surprising insistence, and although she was filled with trepidation, she was glad that he was so determined.

We will be happy, she vowed to herself.

In a window seat on the 104 Borella bus, Hemantha leaned back and smiled to himself. There was no doubt. He had seen them with his own eyes, holding hands and looking all lovey-dovey.

They thought they were fooling everyone, but not him. His rage was laced with triumph. He felt vindicated. He clenched and unclenched his massive fists, and the old man sitting next to him inched away. Hemantha closed his eyes and tried to think what to do next. Show them up for the liars they were? Inform Arjuna and let him deal with it? No, that wouldn't work. He had heard his father getting all protective about his beloved daughter – shame really, because he had liked Arjuna. Underneath the fine clothes and polished accent, there was something raw about him that Hemantha related to.

He longed to find Niranjan and beat him senseless, but he was afraid of the repercussions. The Kamini incident had earned him a police record. Another assault and he would find himself in jail with a lot of far more dangerous individuals than himself. He decided to watch and wait. Use the information when the time was right.

* * *

Dierdre was out walking, looking for someone to gossip with, when she heard a muffled sobbing coming from Enid's garden. She heaved an angry sigh. Were they never going to give that girl any peace?

She pushed open the gate and marched in and then stopped at the sight of Enid sitting in Priyanthi's favourite spot under the araliya tree. Her face was buried in her hands and she was crying as though her heart would break.

'My goodness, child! What's the matter? What happened?' she demanded, hurrying over, pulling out one of her precious cologne-scented tissues from its imported sachet. She sat ponderously next to Enid, wincing as the rough gravel and stones buried themselves in her ample behind. 'Now stop crying and tell me.'

Enid tried to stop crying but she couldn't, although she was furious at herself for allowing Dierdre of all people to see her in this state. The whole street will know by tomorrow morning, she thought despairingly, wondering if she ought to ask Dierdre to keep this to herself.

'Don't worry, I won't tell anyone,' Dierdre said with surprising perception. 'We all have our problems. So what is this all about?'

Enid sniffed and wiped her face with the tissue. 'Nothing.'

Dierdre snorted. 'So you just felt like coming out here and crying for nothing!' She looked around. 'Where is everybody?'

'Gone. To work, to university, to goodness only knows where!' Enid began to cry again.

Dierdre nodded. 'I thought so. Son of yours giving you trouble again? You're not the only one, child. My two are getting up to all kinds of mischief in England. I get complaints from all the relatives saying they're going to clubs and getting involved with undesirable women and all, but what to do? That's the way with boys.'

Enid scowled. 'If it was just Hemantha, I could take it.'

'Priyanthi?' Dierdre looked surprised. 'But I thought everything was fine. Getting married and all.'

Enid's tears flowed afresh at the mention of the aborted marriage. 'Her father went and stopped the whole thing,' she said through her tears, no longer caring if Dierdre told the whole world. 'Telephoned that nice boy and told him that he didn't want his daughter marrying him. Now even my mother isn't talking to me. So ashamed!'

Dierdre sat back. 'Phew! What a mess! But good for Stanley. I don't think Priyanthi really wanted to get married.'

Enid looked up suspiciously. 'Why? Did she say something?'

'Oh no!' Dierdre said hastily. 'It's just that she's such a free spirit, you know.'

Enid's tears dried in an instant. 'Free spirit! The free spirit is going to be an old maid for the rest of her days. When people pass her on the street and whisper and laugh, then she'll wish she had taken my advice.'

Dierdre stood up with difficulty and hoisted Enid to her feet. 'Come, child, let's go to my place and have a cup of tea. Best thing for low morale.'

As they walked out, Violet came to her gate. 'Where are you two going?'

'To hell,' Enid muttered savagely, but not loud enough for Violet to hear.

'Just to show Enid something,' Dierdre said. Then she turned to Enid. 'Why are you like that with her? You act as if this is all her fault. She is a nice woman and your friend. You shouldn't be like that.'

Enid was taken aback. Dierdre was right, but she didn't know the whole story. 'I have my own problems,' she said sulkily.

'Yes, but they're your problems. Taking them out on someone sweet like Violet won't make them go away.'

Enid felt ashamed. 'You're right,' she sighed. 'It's just more complicated than you think.'

'Everything is as complicated as we make it,' Dierdre said wisely, hoping Enid would open up a little more and tell her the whole story. It might help her to get it out of her system. But apparently Enid had decided she had said enough.

They sat and drank tea and talked about the soaring prices of things, about young people and their problems and about the situation up north. If Dierdre thought Enid's reaction to this last was a little more heated than necessary, she gave no indication.

Violet went inside, feeling hurt again. Enid was so different these days. Last night she had seen Enid pruning her roses and leaned over the wall to chat. Enid pretended not to see her and went inside. Violet had been so upset, she mentioned the incident to Niranjan and Nirmala.

'Old people behave weirdly sometimes,' Nirmala declared with authority. 'You should see the teachers at school!'

Niranjan's reaction was different. He went red, muttered something and went out.

Violet stared after him. Something niggled in the back of her mind but she couldn't put her finger on it. She sighed. Oh well, if it's important, it'll come to me, she thought. She frowned.

There was enough to worry about. Mrs Paul popped in for a chat and told her that things were heating up in the north. 'If Mr Paul was still alive, I'd take Radhika and leave this place, but how to go with him in Kanaththa?' Kanaththa was the main cemetery in Colombo, a huge, sprawling area full of beautiful trees, gravestones and elaborate edifices to the dead. Every month, on the anniversary of her husband's death, Mrs Paul went to his grave, cleaned it lovingly, laid a bunch of flowers and lit a candle. As if he could still see and smell. 'They're saying people are being killed and all.'

Violet looked doubtful. 'Must be an accident. People wouldn't do those things deliberately,' she said.

Mrs Paul looked pityingly at her. 'Who knows?'

* * *

Priyanthi lay in bed with the lights out. She slipped her hand under her pillow, touched the still-crisp paper and smiled in the dark. Niranjan was right. It did help to allay the fears. It did dispel the loneliness. *My marriage certificate.*

She remembered the soulless ceremony in Malwana and her pathetic bunch of marigolds. Now she wished she had kept them. Now everything looked a little more possible. The front door banged. She jumped out of bed, praying Hemantha wasn't drunk again.

He was walking steadily enough, but as he caught sight of her standing by her door, he stopped. 'Hello, sister,' he said.

The tiny hairs at the back of her neck prickled with alarm. There was something in his tone that wasn't right. 'Better be quiet. They're sleeping,' she said softly.

He laughed. 'You know all about being quiet, don't you, little angel?'

Her heart began to thump unevenly. 'Are you drunk again?' She fought to keep her voice steady.

He shook his head solemnly. 'Oh no. Don't need to drink. I've found something far more entertaining to do these days.' He scratched his unshaven chin and regarded her with a malevolent smile.

He's playing with me! She turned. 'I'm going to bed.'

'Enjoy your sweet dreams while they last, little sister,' he said mockingly.

She locked the door behind her, suddenly afraid. Did he know? *How* did he know? Could he have seen them? Could someone else have seen them? She had to warn Niranjan, although she didn't really think Hemantha would do anything. He was too afraid of the police. Too afraid of being kicked out of the house. She pulled the marriage certificate out from under the pillow, slipped it into her little jewellery box and shoved the box under some clothes in her drawer.

* * *

A week later, just after Stanley came back from work, he heard Bala calling to him. 'Stan! Stan, are you there?' He sounded worried.

Stanley went out to the gate, pulling off his tie. 'What's up? Come and have a drink.'

Bala finished work early at the school, so he was already washed and changed. 'Don't mind if I do. Have you heard what happened? About the soldiers?'

'No,' Stanley said, getting their drinks. 'I didn't have time to even read the newspaper.'

'I just heard it on the radio,' Bala said. 'Sure to be trouble.'

They sat in the garden. Enid watched from the kitchen window, half glad to see Stanley with his friend, half worried. Maybe Niranjan had told his father everything and Bala was here to ask for Priyanthi's hand for his son. Better an old maid than the wife of a Tamil, she thought furiously.

'So what happened?'

'Land mine up north.'

Stanley frowned. 'Bad?'

'Apparently twelve soldiers and an officer were blown to bits.'

'Oh-ho!' Stanley said, leaning back in his chair. He looked at Bala. 'So you think there'll be trouble?'

Bala frowned. 'I don't know. Sure to be some repercussions. You know – tit for tat.'

Stanley nodded. 'This situation is really upsetting you, isn't it, Bala?'

Bala looked a little wary. Stanley and he had been friends for a long time and they discussed politics frequently, but the situation was changing these days. 'Yes, yes, I suppose,' he said. 'Damn difficult to see people of the same nationality killing each other.'

'You think this Eelam thing can work?' Stanley asked.

Bala lit a cigarette. 'I don't know,' he finally said. 'It's hard to say. Everything sounds wonderful in theory, but the reality is different. Look at what happened after independence. Got rid of the white men and we haven't been able to agree on anything ever since.' He looked shrewdly at Stanley. 'What do you think? Do you think it can work?'

Stanley sighed. 'As you say, in theory, everything works. Personally, if giving them a small part of the island will solve the problem, I'd say go ahead. It's just that the country is so bloody small to start with and who knows what they'll want next? Have you ever known anyone to be satisfied with what they have?'

Bala noted the 'them' and the 'they' and smiled to himself. He nodded. 'You're probably right. But what's the alternative?'

'I don't know. I'd say just go into Jaffna and blow the whole place to bits, but there are innocent people too. Violet's family is still there?'

'Yes,' Bala said. 'I told them to come and live with us but they are refusing to leave. They seem to think there's no immediate danger.'

'And you?'

Bala took a gulp of his drink. 'I think it's only a matter of time before someone wipes the place flat. But Violet's whole family live in a fool's paradise.'

Stanley looked sympathetic. 'Women are emotional.'

'Emotional is one thing. Foolhardy is another,' Bala retorted impatiently. 'I told her many times that the best thing is for us to leave. Go to Canada or England, but she refuses to even consider it.'

Stanley looked depressed. 'I know what you're saying, but we'll miss you if you do leave.'

Bala nodded. 'It will be hard for Niranjan and Nirmala too, but it would be the best thing in the long run.'

Stanley looked at him, wondering if this was the moment to bring up the subject of Niranjan and Priyanthi. Perhaps they could discuss it sensibly. But then, he spotted Enid anxiously listening from the kitchen door.

Bala was speaking. 'They're thinking of bringing those bodies to Colombo for a state funeral.'

'What?' Stanley looked shocked. 'Why would they do a damnfool thing like that? Don't they usually just send the bodies home to the families?'

Bala nodded. 'The only reason I can think of is that they're trying to drum up some sympathy so more of these young idiots enlist. God knows what will happen.'

'When is the funeral?'

'It's supposed to be the day after tomorrow. The twenty third. Bloody mad buggers.'

They stayed out talking until their wives called them in for dinner.

Twenty-five

◦✿◦

Bala wasn't too far away from the truth. Although the full motive for bringing those thirteen bodies back to Colombo may never be known, it was widely thought to be twofold: to garner some sympathy and to spark some outrage. Both would ensure another batch of idealistic young people, eager to defend their country and avenge the deaths of their countrymen, would enlist.

It was a devious plan, but harmless in its purpose.

But there were other elements within and outside the political arena who saw an opportunity far bigger than a new batch of cadets. They had their own plans and agendas, but these would have terrifying repercussions which would cause this month to go down in history books as Black July.

July the twenty-third began like any other day.

In Enid's home, Stanley woke up, got dressed and went off to his office.

Before Priyanthi left for the university, she tucked the marriage certificate in the pocket of her skirt. She had woken up this morning with an odd feeling of disquiet and decided she needed the reassurance it gave her.

Hemantha woke up late as usual and left the house without a word to his mother. That was not unusual either, and Enid was secretly glad because the anger and tension he brought in with him left with him.

She started her chores and gave Banda a shelling because he had not washed the grinding stone the previous night. 'Why can't you ever do as you're told?' Enid demanded.

'You tell me so many things, I forget,' he retorted cheekily, and Enid sighed.

In Violet's house, Bala and Nirmala left at seven a.m. as usual.
Niranjan went to work.
When they had all left, Violet laid a few jasmines at the feet of her plaster-of-Paris Virgin and then went off to clean the house.

Dierdre stood at the gate and waved to Ed as he drove off to work. She went inside and started a letter to the boys.

* * *

In the Borella area, a bunch of thugs casually walked into a Tamil shop and started smashing things. They broke windows and shouted insults. Then, when they were finished, they tossed in a small home-made petrol bomb and ran off before anyone called the police. Perhaps someone did, perhaps they didn't. In any event, the police never came.
In the Thimbirigasyaya area, a similar incident occurred.
In the Pettah bazaar, a small string of shops were ablaze.

'Violet! Violet! Are you there? Violet!'
Violet came running out. Enid sounded frantic. 'What happened? What's the matter? My God, it isn't Stanley, is it?'
Enid rushed inside the house. 'Can I use your phone? Ours is not working!'
Violet gestured towards the telephone. 'But what happened?'
Enid waved her quiet and started dialling. 'Hello? Hello? Is that the Colombo campus? I am the mother of a student there and I was wondering if everything is okay.' She listened. 'No, we heard about some incidents and I was a bit worried . . . Oh, thank you very much.' She hung up the phone and turned to Violet. 'Better go and pick up Nirmala from school. They're saying that if parents want to, they can take their children home early. I better wait for Stanley. May be he'll pick Priyanthi up.'
Violet still looked confused. 'Why? What's happening?'
'Dierdre just came and told me Ed phoned from his office to

335

say that there had been some problems in Borella and Nugegoda. Tamil shops burning and so on. I didn't get the full details, but today is that funeral, you know.'

Violet went pale. She reached for the phone with a trembling hand and dialled Bala's number at the school. After a while, she replaced the receiver. 'No one is answering,' she said. 'What should I do? If I go and pick Nirmala up from school and can't get word to Bala, he'll go to pick her up as usual and get frantic when he doesn't find her there.'

'Doesn't matter,' Enid said decisively. 'Better for him to be worried than for anything to happen to that child. I'll stay here in case the phone rings. Now go. Don't waste time trying to get buses. Take a three-wheeler.'

Violet grabbed her purse and ran out, twisting her hair into a knot. Her lips moved as fast as her feet. *Please, Mother Mary, don't let anything happen to my daughter. Or my son. Or my husband! Please bring them home safely, I beg you!*

A three-wheeler Bajaj scooter taxi was just pulling away from the pavement and she waved frantically. The driver poked his head out. 'Where to?'

'St Mary's,' she said. 'And then back to Araliya Gardens.'

He assessed her. He had heard the news of the incidents in town. Obviously this lady was trying to pick a child up from the school. 'Hundred rupees,' he said. Double the usual amount.

She just nodded and got inside.

The ride was nightmarishly fast. The driver saw opportunity and was determined to make the most of it. More fares, more money. He wove in and out of the traffic and ordinarily Violet would have been fainting with fear. As it was, she wished he would go faster.

She scanned the streets but everything looked normal enough. The daily bazaars at the junctions were in full swing and nobody looked worried or afraid. There were a few people talking together in groups, but that was all.

They finally arrived at the school. There were cars arriving, children leaving. Almost before the three-wheeler stopped, she jumped out and rushed in. She spotted Nirmala almost immediately. 'Come, come on! We have to hurry!'

Nirmala hung back. 'But Appa called and said he was coming to pick me up. We better wait for him.'

Violet stopped. 'When did he call?'

'Two minutes ago maybe.'

Just then, a teacher came hurrying over to them. 'Mrs Balasingham! Good thing I caught you before you left. Your husband is on the phone.'

Violet followed the teacher into the staff room and picked up the phone, sending up silent prayers of thanks. 'Bala?'

'Violet!' Bala sounded annoyed. 'What are you doing there?'

'I came to take Nirmala home. Bala, what are they saying? What's happening?'

'I don't know yet. There is trouble but only in some areas. Violet, I wish you had stayed at home. It is dangerous to be out.' Bala sounded harassed.

'I'll go home now. When are you coming home?'

'I don't know. Look, I have to go. I'll try to get home as soon as I can, but if I get delayed, don't worry.'

'Bala, please hurry,' she pleaded.

'I'll try. Now go home.'

Violet took Nirmala and hurried out to where the three-wheeler driver was waiting. 'Lady, I have other fares! Hurry up.'

Nirmala stared indignantly at him, but Violet stopped her with a frown. They set off for home.

'So you're Tamils, no?' the driver said, looking at them through the rear-view mirror.

'Colombo Chetties,' Violet said, squeezing Nirmala's hand.

Colombo Chetties weren't Jaffna Tamils.

The driver snorted. 'Same thing. Better be careful. Trouble for you people today. What can you expect after killing our boys.'

Nirmala opened her mouth, but before she could speak, Violet squeezed her hand again. Nirmala glared at her mother, but kept quiet.

'Burning and looting everywhere,' the driver continued, looking maliciously at them.

Violet finally spoke. 'I don't see any burning or looting.'

'That's because it is happening towards Borella and Nugegoda areas. It will come here, though,' he said, turning into Araliya Gardens so sharply that the three-wheeler rocked frighteningly.

They stopped outside Violet's house. 'Hundred and fifty rupees,' the driver said.

Violet stared at him. 'You said hundred!'

'You took your own time,' he retorted, holding out his hand. He leaned out and looked at the house. 'Nice house. You better look after it.'

Violet wordlessly handed over one hundred and fifty rupees and pushed Nirmala inside the gate.

Enid sprang up from her chair. 'What look so long? I was getting frantic, but at least you got her.'

Violet sank into a chair, exhausted. 'Yes, thank God,' she said. 'Bala telephoned the school just as we were leaving and he said he'll be coming home soon.'

Enid picked up the phone again. 'I don't know what has happened to Stanley. I tried to call but no one is picking up.'

Violet took the phone. 'Let me try and call the accounts department. Niranjan must be there and they have another line.' She dialled but no one answered there either.

They sat down to wait.

Ceylon Foods was located in Kollupitiya on the corner of a small cul-de-sac and the main Galle Road. Half of its windows overlooked the Galle Road. The other half looked down on expensive residences which had expensive cars parked in their driveways.

The accounts department of Ceylon Foods was on the cul-de-sac side of the building. Stanley sat in another part of the office. Being Chief Accountant, he had his office in what was called the 'executive area'.

By eleven in the morning, work at Ceylon Foods had come to a virtual halt. The phones were constantly busy; people calling in to check on relatives working there, and people who worked there calling out. Every time Niranjan tried to use the phone, someone else would beat him to it. He went looking for Stanley but couldn't find him.

At the same time, Stanley was entering the accounts department looking for Niranjan. Enid had finally managed to get through and Violet had entreated him to find her son and bring him home. Stanley asked a few people if they had seen Niranjan.

'I saw him going out,' said one.

'I think he left,' said another.

He looked for Joe, whom he knew to be Niranjan's friend, but was told he hadn't come in to work that day. Stanley went back to his own room and dialled the accounts department again. The line was busy.

Outside his window, the Galle Road was in complete chaos. In the space of an hour, the rioting had spread.

The small Tamil restaurant next door where Stanley sometimes ate was in a shambles. Hooting men lobbed vadais and idlis out into the street and threw out stainless-steel plates and cups, which made clanging noises when they hit the street. There was no sign of the people who worked there and Stanley wondered if they had got out safely.

Knowing it was not safe to linger any longer, he grabbed his briefcase and left. On his way out, he stopped by the accounts department again, but there was still no sign of Niranjan. Stanley scrawled a quick note for him and left it on his desk. *Gone home. Leave immediately. S.S.*

Outside, Senarath, who also lived in Dehiwala, was getting into his car. He hailed Stanley. 'Come on! I'll give you a lift home.'

'No, that's okay. I have to go to Colombo campus and get my daughter,' Stanley said.

'No problem. We'll go on Flower Road. It's only a small detour.'

'Thanks, Senarath,' Stanley said gratefully.

Priyanthi stood in a hallway of the campus and listened anxiously to the students talking.

'It's like a mad house! Everything's burning!'

'I called my mother and asked her to come and get me.'

'They're saying the Wellawatte area is in flames!' Wellawatte was the town immediately before Dehiwala where they lived.

She slipped away and went to the office, but the phones were dead.

'Someone must have pulled the lines down,' someone said.

Priyanthi went outside and watched the students leave, one by one, driven off by friends and relatives. Each arriving car had a fresh horror story to tell. Eventually, she stopped listening.

She was sick with fear that something would happen to Niranjan. She hoped her father would come and get her. Niranjan was probably with him.

'Here! Girl!'

She turned to see the watchman approaching. 'Better go home now. Trouble everywhere.'

'I'm waiting for my father,' she said.

'Can't wait here. Not safe. Go inside and wait. I'm going home now.'

Priyanthi stared at him. 'But what about the gates? You're not going to lock them, are you?'

'No. How to, with people still here?'

Priyanthi went inside. The huge building was already beginning to look deserted. She went into an empty lecture room and sat down.

Just before the watchman left, the Assistant Dean of the campus told him to lock the gates after all. 'Get the students out. They can wait on the road. It's not safe to keep them open. God knows what havoc they'll wreak in here,' he said.

So the watchman herded the rest of the students out on to the road and locked the gates. He remembered the girl who had gone inside and shrugged. She was not his problem.

Less than a mile away, on Galle Road, hundreds of cars crawled through traffic, swinging this way and that to avoid other cars, bicycles and people.

The petrol stations were like circuses. Car queues went from the pumps to the main road, snarling already chaotic traffic. Most petrol stations had hastily hand-lettered signs that said SORRY NO PETROL.

Bala pulled out from the queue he was in and swung his car towards home. He sensed that it was unwise to delay. He was worried about Niranjan but he was a sensible boy. Hopefully he was already on his way home. There was no way Bala could have driven to Niranjan's office to get him. Traffic had come to a virtual standstill. Cars crawled over pavements, down little-used side streets, through people's driveways. Gangs of men moved across the road, but for now, they were still laughing raucously and shouting obscenities.

Every half-mile or so there was a building in flames, but Bala didn't even look. He had only one thought in his mind: to get home to his family.

The Dehiwala junction finally came into sight. A mob of people were walking purposefully towards the city, swinging crowbars and cudgels, laughing and shouting to one another.

Compared to the insanity on the main street, Araliya Gardens looked uninhabited. Doors were shut and curtains were drawn. There were no cars in driveways or parked on the road outside. They had been hidden behind houses.

Senarath and Stanley stared at the locked gates of the campus. 'Bloody fine how-do-you-do,' Senarath muttered. 'Now what?'

Stanley got out and ran to the gates. He shook them hard. 'Hello? Anyone inside?' he yelled. 'Priyanthi? Priyanthi Silva!'

But there was no answer. Stanley looked around. A few students still waited outside. 'Anybody know Priyanthi Silva? Tall girl, long hair?'

They shook their heads. There were hundreds of students and many of them were tall and long-haired.

Stanley came back to the car. 'She must have gone home

already,' he said, hoping fervently that he was right. 'Must have got a lift.'

Senarath was gunning the engine. 'In that case, let's be off. Not safe to stick around these campus areas.'

Priyanthi was walking through the building when she heard the car pulling away. She ran outside, but it was already gone. Then she realised that the grounds were empty and the gate was locked. She stared at it disbelievingly and then rattled it hard. The chains clashed against the iron gates, but the locks were huge and sturdy.

The students on the other side looked at each other. 'Are you Priyanthi?' one of them asked.

She nodded, trying to hold back her tears.

'Someone just came looking for you. Not even a minute ago. They shouted and all and then left.'

'Were there two of them?' she asked, her heart lifting.

They nodded. 'Better try and climb over.'

She threw her bag over and started scaling the gate. An iron spike on the very top bit painfully into the palm of her hand, but she didn't care. Niranjan was safe! That was all that mattered.

'How will you go home now?' someone asked.

She jumped down, wincing as her knees jarred on the hard surface of the road. 'I don't know.'

'Where's Priyanthi?' Enid asked frantically.

'Isn't she here already? I went to the campus and couldn't find her. She must have left already.'

'Oh my God!' Enid moaned. 'Stanley, what if something's happened to her?'

Stanley tried to quell his own rising panic. 'No, don't be silly. Someone must have given her a lift. She'll be here soon.'

Just then, Bala's car turned into the cul-de-sac. Violet rushed to the car before it could stop. 'Where's Niranjan?'

Bala looked at Stanley. 'Didn't he come home with you?'

Stanley frowned. 'I thought he had come home. I looked everywhere for him, but someone said he had left.'

Violet was wringing her hands. 'Bala, what if something has happened to him?'

'Nonsense!' Bala said robustly. 'He's a man, isn't he? He can take care of himself. He's probably trying to get a bus home.' He looked around. 'Priyanthi? Hemantha?'

'God knows,' Stanley muttered, running his hands through his hair. 'I went to the campus and she wasn't there. I'm hoping she's on the way home.'

Enid was tugging at his arm. 'Stanley, what about Hemantha?'

'He'll be okay,' Stanley said impatiently.

Enid's mouth was trembling. 'But Stanley, there are mobs on the road! What if they do something to him?'

'Save your concern for Priyanthi,' Stanley snapped. 'She's a girl. Hemantha can take care of himself. He's probably on the road with the mobs.' He muttered the last bit, but Enid heard him and her eyes darkened with anger.

Bala heard too and wondered if Stanley was right. He hoped not.

Niranjan sat by the accounts department window and watched the cars pull out from the Ceylon Foods parking lot. He had asked one person he knew for a lift home and the man had looked shifty and muttered something about going in the other direction. It took Niranjan a minute to understand that the man was afraid to give him a lift because he was a Tamil. He hoped Stanley had taken Priyanthi home.

The phone was finally free. He called home.

Violet answered on the first ring. 'Niranjan! Where are you?'

'I'm still in the office, Amma,' he said, 'I was trying to find Uncle Stanley, but he must have left.'

'He said he was looking for you!' Violet said, unable to stop herself from darting a semi-accusing look at Stanley. 'Anyway, come home immediately. There's trouble everywhere.'

'What's happening? I can't see anything from where I am.'

Bala snatched the phone from Violet. 'Son, come home. Walk if you have to, but take the side streets. Avoid the Galle Road. But you'd better get out of there quickly. They're burning places down.'

'Okay, Appa. I'll leave now.' Niranjan sounded young and afraid.

'God be with you, my son.' Bala replaced the receiver and went to stand at the window. Violet was crying.

Dierdre rushed in. 'Ed has just come back,' she gasped. 'It seems they are now going down streets into Tamil houses, killing people and burning cars! He saw a mob going down Kawdana Road!' Kawdana Road was right opposite Araliya Gardens.

'What shall we do?' Violet sobbed.

Ed ran in. 'Get your valuables!' he said tersely. 'Just jewellery. Put it in a bag, get Violet and Nirmala and come!'

Bala rushed into their bedroom to do as Ed asked.

Violet hugged Nirmala and cried harder. 'Come where? Where are we going?'

Ed put his arm around her. 'Just to our house. It's not safe for you to be here.'

Stanley stepped forward. 'Let them come to our house,' he said. 'You take the Pauls.'

Bala came out carrying a pillowcase tied at the top. 'Come on,' he said quietly to his wife and daughter.'

But Violet hung back. 'Niranjan isn't home yet,' she said tearfully. 'We can't leave until he comes.'

Bala pushed her gently towards the door. 'He's a big boy, Violet. He'll look after himself. Anyway, when he comes and finds us not home, he'll know we're at Stan's.'

She went reluctantly, but left the door slightly ajar behind her.

Ed ran to get the Pauls and found Radhika already packing their jewellery. 'Thanks, Uncle Ed,' she said. 'I can manage. Get my mother – she's in a state.'

Ed found Mrs Paul standing in front of a portrait of her dead husband. 'What can we do?' she was asking it.

Ed took her arm gently and led her out of the house. 'Come, dear. Dierdre is waiting for the two of you.'

Radhika followed, looking strained and worried. 'Do you think our house will be okay?' she asked Ed.

'I'm sure it will be,' he replied, hurrying them along.

The sky was dark with smoke.

* * *

Later it was said that the initial looting and arson had been carefully engineered with a specific purpose in mind: to frighten the Tamils who lived in Colombo into going back to Jaffna 'where they belong'. Or to India. Nobody cared where particularly, as long as they left Colombo.

The few arsonists were supposedly instructed to set fire to some shops, intimidate a few people and create a mood of indignant outrage for the funeral of the thirteen soldiers.

Not in their wildest dreams could anyone have foreseen how quickly and completely the common man – the firewoodman, the fisherman, the laundryman, the newspaperman – would be infected with the insanity. But even that could be explained away. Sort of. These were poor, frustrated people and their vicious acts of brutalism could have been a venting of their general dissatisfaction with life.

But how did one explain away the others? The clerks, the managers, the shop assistants, the factory workers? The little old ladies who scrabbled among the fallen glass and broken beams in search of the spoils of war?

By noon, there were thousands of people on the streets. A few were workers trying to find their way home.

The others were men intent on murder and mayhem. They carried sticks, knives, axes, lengths of cable, and containers – plastic cans, tins, bottles – of petrol. Most didn't even know what they were doing there but were swept on by the hugeness of the whole thing.

They prowled the streets in packs of fifty and more.

Priyanthi hoisted her bag to her shoulder and set off towards the Galle Road.

Here, down these quietly expensive Colombo 7 streets, everything was normal enough. The stream of madness which was relentlessly wending its way down Galle Road hadn't yet flowed down these streets.

Priyanthi was out of breath from walking so fast and sweating by the time she got to the Galle Road. There, she stopped and looked about her with complete incomprehension.

The scene resembled a movie set. A film about group violence and disorganised crime. She half expected someone to shout 'Cut!' A director in a baseball cap and sunglasses. A canvas chair with *Director* written on it.

The road was full of cars, but the boundaries between cars going this way and cars going that way had long since disappeared. So had traffic lanes, which were hard to decipher even on ordinary days. Cars squeezed past one another, longing to go home to their garages, and in the process blocked what little manœuvring space there was left.

On the pavements, people walked automatically, shock making their eyes blank. They stepped carefully over burning beams and hissing power cables.

In between the cars, the mobs roamed, their collective snarl of fury audible for miles, their dragging knives making sparks fly on the tarred road.

Someone jostled her and she snapped out of her shock.

She had to get home. To Niranjan.

She squared her shoulders and began walking. The heat from the burning building next to her was almost overpowering. The smell was nauseating.

She coughed to clear her aching throat.

A burning wooden beam fell suddenly in front of her, sending a shower of sparks in all directions. She stepped to the side, lifted her skirt and continued. Her head was lowered so she didn't see the group of men approaching. 'Who is this? A lonely Tamil girl?' The voice was taunting.

She lifted her head and stared into the bearded face leering at her. 'No,' she said clearly. Behind the man were about a hundred others, peering over each other's shoulders.

'No?'

'I am Sinhalese,' she said, her head swimming from shame.

'Say "baaldiya",' he commanded her roughly.

She looked at him, wondering if this was some kind of a joke. Baaldiya? Bucket?

'Baaldiya,' she enunciated clearly.

The man relaxed and grinned. 'Tamils can't say the "b" in baaldiya,' he explained. 'They say "vaaldiya". Anyway, what arc you doing walking on the street by yourself?'

'I am trying to go home,' she said.

'You can go home with me!' someone shouted from the back, and the others burst into loud laughter. Priyanthi flushed.

'Okay, go,' the man who had first spoken to her said, and stood aside. She walked past them, her heart pounding, her knees as unsteady as a newborn calf's. Their lewd suggestions and wolf whistles followed her. She crossed the road, picking her way through the stalled cars.

The other side of the Galle Road was no different. Shops burned everywhere and a scream welled up in her throat when she saw a human shape on fire inside a window. Against her will, she moved closer and then realised it was a mannequin. Then she saw the dark red stain at the doorway which seeped out slowly and dripped down the two shallow steps and on to the road. She ran.

Somewhere before Bambalapitiya junction, she wasn't sure exactly where, an army truck stopped near her. The first she had seen. It was an open truck full of soldiers, standing with their legs apart, holding on to rifles and bayonets. 'Are you mad?' a young soldier shouted down to her. 'What are you doing walking by yourself?'

She started to cry. 'I'm trying to go home.'

'Where's home?' he asked, his expression softening.

'Dehiwala.'

'Want a ride? We're only going as far as Wellawatte, but it will be faster than walking.'

She nodded and they hauled her into the back of the truck. She stood uncomfortably among them and tried to acknowledge their friendly smiles. They smelled of youth and perspiration and fear. Another soldier spoke. 'Going home from work?'

'From campus,' she said.

He looked impressed. 'Smart girl, huh? Maybe you can tell us why these Tamil dogs deserve to live.'

Her fear fled. 'Only if you tell me why they deserve to die,' she snapped back.

He looked taken aback. 'Whose side are you on anyway?' he demanded.

'The right side,' she answered sweetly. 'Although obviously you're not.'

'Why not?' He didn't sound angry. Just curious.

'You are the army. Look at all your guns. Why don't you stop this madness?'

'No orders,' he said laconically. 'We have orders to only observe for now.'

'So you're just going to watch?' she said disbelievingly.

He finally began to look irritated. 'Lady, I just do what I am told to do. Anything else will get us into trouble. And for what? For these bastards who blow up our boys?'

She didn't say anything more. It had been foolish to get into a conversation in the first place. Just before the Wellawatte junction, they stopped and let her out. 'Go carefully!' the soldier shouted after her. She nodded.

Here it was even worse.

Wellawatte was a predominantly Tamil area. People called it Little Jaffna. Most of the roads had Tamil names. Ramakrishna Road. Vivekananda Road. The shops had names that weren't necessarily Tamil – Cheap Side, Colombo Traders, Daniel's Bookshop – but everyone knew who owned them.

The two sides of the Galle Road looked like solid walls of flame. Almost every shop had been set ablaze. Those that had escaped the arsonists hadn't been able to escape the heat. The pavements were littered with glass and wood from doors and shelves. A cash register lay on its side, its drawer open. Empty. Dead.

The streets were littered with empty cars, their fuel caps opened. They had been drained with hosepipes and greedy, sucking mouths. Ammunition for the anger. In the distance, she heard a muted roar. Her steps quickened, as did her heartbeat.

Just past the junction she stopped, afraid to go any further. About a hundred people crowded around something, screaming and cheering. Some laughing slightly hysterically.

Something – vulgar curiosity perhaps – propelled her into the crowd. The wall of sweat-stained, soot-blackened backs parted slightly to give her a glimpse of the man on his knees, who screamed for mercy, who called out to many unhearing gods to save him. She saw the wild fear in his rolling eyes, smelled the coppery odour of blood, which lay around him in a small but growing pool. He had deep slashes on his arms, his head, his torso, his back.

For a moment, his face blurred and reshaped to form Niranjan's face. She gasped and closed her eyes. When she opened them again, the vision was gone. This was not Niranjan. This was someone else's husband.

A man stood over him with a long curved fish knife. It was raised above his head, and the man, like an executioner, seemed to be waiting for some kind of signal.

She turned around and pushed her way out. She lowered her head and walked rapidly, her fingers childishly stuck in her ears. That was what she did when she watched scary films. The visuals didn't seem so frightening when they were stripped of groans or moans or screams or snarls.

Despite her blocked ears, she heard the roar of the crowd.

She saw death's many faces during that long walk home.

A father and son abandoned their car and ran into a small

church in search of sanctuary. But God was busy elsewhere. The mob followed them in, dragged them out again, pushed them back in their car, locked it and casually set fire to it.

Priyanthi saw the fists beating ineffectively against the hot glass. Their eyes met, hers and theirs. Theirs screamed out that they didn't want to die. Hers said nothing. There was nothing to say.

A few hundred feet away, she saw her first 'necklace'. Tyres piled one on top of the other like giant doughnuts. In the middle, in the doughnut hole, a man, unable to move, unable to do anything but die. They set fire to the tyres from the bottom up, making ribald jokes about which body parts would burn first. The fire caught on quickly, moving up from tyre to tyre like a leaping beast.

She saw a dead man lying alone, of no further use to anyone. She knew it was a man because he wore trousers and a shirt. Someone had taken away his head.

More necklaces.
More summary executions.
More car burnings.
The more she saw, the less everything mattered.

In Dehiwala, she saw the old woman. She was about seventy, a nice old woman who was someone's grandmother. She should have been at home, worrying about her children and grand-children. Instead, she was inside what remained of Sunrise Grocery, on her hands and knees, scrabbling among the broken glass and shattered shelves.

Priyanthi stopped and watched.

The old woman snatched up something and rocked back on her heels to examine it.

It was a string of yellow shampoo sachets. Sunsilk with Egg and Protein. Almost five rupees each. She smiled a denture smile and stood up, not bothering to dust the soot from her pretty cotton sari with the old-lady chintz print. As she started to leave, she spotted something else. She scrabbled once more, unmindful of the tiny cuts on her hands, and this time emerged with a small box of Rinso.

Blue Rinso.

To make her clothes whiter, brighter.

Priyanthi vomited.

After an eternity, she saw Araliya Gardens and began running.

She ran straight into a burly man who brandished a sword. Like a medieval knight who had lost his horse. And his senses. 'Ho! Not so fast.' The huge meaty hands held her arms.

She struggled to get free, everything she had seen suddenly rewinding and replaying in her head. 'Let me go! I'm not Tamil,' she screamed. As she uttered the words, she was filled with self-loathing. How quickly one adapted. How strong the instinct for survival was.

'What are you then?' he demanded in coarse street Sinhalese.

'I am Sinhalese,' she sobbed.

'Oho. Upper-class. Okay, go, sister.' He pushed her and she stumbled.

She kept running. On the way down Araliya Gardens, she passed another mob in front of a house. She tried to remember who lived there but her brain wouldn't work.

The gate was locked. She climbed over it just as the front door opened a crack.

Enid came running out when she saw who it was. 'Priyanthi!' she cried, enfolding her daughter in a crushing embrace. 'Oh thank goodness you are okay. I was out of my mind with worry!'

They hurried inside. It was dark. The curtains were drawn, no lights were on. Stanley was pacing the living room. When he saw Priyanthi, he rushed over and hugged her wordlessly. Over his shoulder, she saw her bedroom door open, saw Violet peeping out. She broke free of her father's embrace and ran to her. 'Is Niranjan home? Did Niranjan come home yet?'

Violet shook her head, her eyes filling with tears. Mother and wife searched each other's eyes for hope. 'He'll come soon,' Priyanthi said. 'I can feel it.'

'Hemantha isn't home either,' Enid whispered.

No one said anything.

Priyanthi wasn't wrong.

Niranjan had taken his father's advice and kept to the back streets. In Bambalapitiya, he went down to the rail tracks and walked alongside them. They would take him home. Trains passed, full of people. Inside and outside. They clung like panic-stricken limpets on to the roof and the sides. The exterior of the trains could hardly be seen. They looked like giant worms covered with ants.

The beaches and the fisher huts were empty. Their occupants were elsewhere. The next day, the huts would have televisions and VCRs and other expensive electrical gadgets that would run on car batteries. Their children would gleefully ride around on fancy bicycles and their women would wear dead people's clothes and jewellery.

Niranjan kept walking.

Finally, he saw the end of the road next to Araliya Gardens and turned into it. He saw a mob of about forty men approaching and casually went into someone's garden and hid against the high boundary wall until they passed. Then he continued. He reached the bokku and crossed it carefully. Just before he emerged on the other side, he heard another mob and pressed himself back into the bushes.

There was a pounding on the gate.

Stanley stood up. 'Stay here and don't come out.' He went to Priyanthi's bedroom. 'Lock the door from the inside and don't open it until I say so.' He waited until he heard the click of the lock and then went to the front door. He opened it and stepped out.

About fifty men stood there armed with sticks and knives and jagged-edged bottles. 'Any Tamils here?' one of them demanded.

'No,' Stanley answered steadily.' We are Sinhalese.'

'Where are the next-door people?'

'Gone. They went this morning.'

'Where is their car?'

Stanley shrugged. 'I don't know. Maybe they went in it.'

'We want to come in to see if they are here.' The man started rattling the locked gate. Another began sharpening his knife against the wall. Others waited, tapping their weapons against their palms.

Enid appeared behind Stanley. The men paused to take in the new person. 'This is my home,' she said clearly. 'Please leave. We are not Tamils, nor do we have Tamils in this house. So please go.'

They went. Stanley watched as they turned the corner and disappeared up the street. They went back inside. Enid was shaking uncontrollably.

* * *

Niranjan watched them go, and when they were out of sight, he slipped out again and ran to his house. Both the gate and the door were open. He ran inside, calling, 'Amma! Amma?' in a soft voice. Only silence answered him. For a moment, panic gripped him and then he forced himself to think. They must have gone next door or to Dierdre's house. He decided to stay where he was, rather than risk going out again. He went to his bedroom and lay down on his bed, praying that Priyanthi was okay.

God, let us get through this.

Exhaustion tightened its grip on him and he fell into a deep sleep.

At the top of Araliya Gardens, Hemantha and his friends stood, wondering what to do next. They passed around a few bottles of arrack looted from a liquor store and laughed about how loudly the Tamil man had screamed when they began beating him up.

Suddenly Hemantha remembered. 'Come on!' he shouted

drunkenly, and they willingly followed him down the quiet street.

He pushed open Bala's front door, looked around and cursed loudly. 'Bastards got away.'

They split up to see what could be taken from the house, and one of them came running back to Hemantha. 'Come and see Sleeping Beauty!' he chortled.

Niranjan awoke with a start and saw ten faces looking down at him. Ten faces with one message. Niranjan didn't move, nor did he speak.

'This,' said Hemantha grandly, 'is the man who dares to touch my sister ...' he paused for effect, 'yes, my sister, with his filthy Tamil hands.'

There were gasps from the others.

Hemantha laughed drunkenly. 'Oh yes. But now we must show him the price he has to pay, don't we?'

They took their time.

When they finished, both Niranjan's legs were broken, his wrist and hand were smashed and his face was a bloody mess. The back of his head was soft with blood and brains.

They stood back and admired their handiwork, then they left in search of more arrack.

Next door, Bala, Stanley and Nirmala huddled together and listened to the sounds of breaking glass and shattering furniture. Violet sobbed for the home she had so carefully and lovingly put together. Bala held her hands and ground his teeth in impotent rage. Nirmala's teeth were chattering.

Someone shook the gate.

Stanley pushed the curtains aside and saw Dierdre. 'Open up, Stanley! Open up!' she screamed frantically. 'For God's sake, open the bloody gate!'

Stanley rushed outside and opened the gate. 'They came to your house? Did they see the Pauls? Where's Ed?'

Dierdre was sobbing hysterically.

'What is it?' Stanley demanded urgently. 'What happened?'

'Niranjan,' she sobbed. 'Hemantha.' Wordlessly, she pointed to Bala's house.

'Niranjan isn't home yet,' Stanley said, but his heart started to pound.

Dierdre nodded. 'He came. I saw him. Then Hemantha went in and—'

Stanley left her and ran next door. His eyes took in the mess. The words *Die Tamil Dogs* scrawled across the white walls. In blood red. He rushed into the bedroom and stopped stricken with shock. Niranjan lay where they left him. That he was dead was painfully obvious. Stanley fell to his knees weeping and screaming. 'Oh my God! Oh my God! Bala! Bala!'

Behind him, someone else entered the room and stood there, taking it all in.

Priyanthi went to her husband, gently gathered his broken body in her arms and held him. She heard wails and moans and screams as the others came running in. Violet collapsed on the floor next to her and she gently gave half of Niranjan to his mother to hold. 'He's killed my husband,' she murmured.

Enid stopped sobbing. 'What?'

Priyanthi groped in her pocket and pulled out their marriage certificate. She held it aloft and her eyes and her voice were clear. 'Your son killed my husband,' she said.

Enid took the paper and read it. 'My God.' She staggered back and Stanley ran to catch her before she fell.

Priyanthi laughed quietly and bitterly. 'And you were afraid I was going to end up an old maid! Widows are far more difficult to marry off. And Sinhalese widows of Tamil men . . .' She shook her head pityingly. 'Completely impossible.' Her eyes were quite dry as they scanned her family and his. They came to rest on Violet. 'Let him rest. He's very tired,' she said gently, and walked out of the house.

Despair does not sit comfortably on the smooth countenance of youth. Its weary fingers claw restlessly at the dewy skin that stretches tautly over loss, and struggle to enter the white whites and opaque blacks of unseeing eyes.

People glance frequently at the figure sitting stiffly in the jolting bus, trying to penetrate the solitude that lies over it like a shroud. A child makes its unsteady way over to where she sits and stares directly into her expressionless face. Her stillness unnerves him and he giggles and points and says, 'Pissu gaani.'

Mad woman.

Other people smile nervously, glad that the quietness has been disturbed. In a place where garrulousness is a way of life and secrets are only for spoilsports, her mysteriousness upsets them. Makes them want to unfold her. Reveal her. Gaze at the core of pain in her. Then, they will nod their heads with satisfaction and resume their idle chatter. Return to their soggy sweets and tepid tea.

Even her hands are quiet, and that offends them. Someone so obviously troubled should twist their fingers. At the very least. Any sign of turmoil will appease them. Will satiate their curiosity. Will vindicate their voyeurism.

The bus lurches in and out of a huge pot-hole. It rained the previous night and the hole is full of water. It splashes the spittle-stained sides of the bus and sends a fine brown spray in through the open windows.

There is a distinct thud as her unanchored head hits the aluminium side of the bus. Gazes swivel voraciously, but she is as she was. A bump will appear on her temple, but that will come later.

The journey has been long. Tentative overtures have ripened into animated discussion. Now, personal family dramas and tragedies are being shared. It is a typical bus ride.

Only she spoils it for them.

She and her spoilsport silence.

She and the pain she wears like a mask.

She sees the towns come and go but her gaze fixed on far-away never wavers. The bus stops in Bentota. She makes her way stiffly to the front of the bus. Then she turns around and looks at them. 'I have just lost my husband,' she says.

Then she gets out and waits for the bus to pull away so she can cross the road.